ARCANE

compiled by

STACEY JAINE MCINTOSH

IRON FAERIE
PUBLISHING

Cover designed by
Lafae Cover Designs
www.facebook.com/lafaecoverdesigns

Iron Faerie Publishing
www.ironfaeriepublishing.com

ISBN: 9798727509661

Printed in the United States of America

First Printing March 2021

arcane
(adj.)
sccrct, mysterious,
understood only by a few.

CONTENTS

A NECROMANCER'S REGRET by David Green..........................5

    IT CAN ONLY END ONE WAY 6

    A SOUL THAT FESTERS...........................23

    THE BATTLE OF BADON HILL 46

    RETRIBUTION 78

PROTECTOR OF THE PATH by Diana Brown..........................94

    TIME AND TIDE...................................95

    THE LIBRARIAN...................................116

    FRAGMENTS FROM ARAM 140

    THE WEAVER IN THE WINDOW 160

THE SOUND OF SILENCE by Lyndsey Ellis-Holloway............187

    BEWARE THE SILENCE 188

    THE BROKEN CLOCK 214

    DEATH AT THE THEATRE 244

    THE MONSTERS WITHIN 272

A DREAM OF DRAGONS by Vonnie Winslow Crist 303

    VEIL 304

    BAYOU 324

    DRAGON RAIN 345

    MAGIC 364

ABOUT THE AUTHORS 384

ABOUT THE PUBLISHER......................................387

A NECROMANCER'S REGRET

Someone who claims to communicate with the dead in order to discover what is going to happen in the future, or who is involved in black magic. Magic that is often used for a corrupt purpose. These four stories are such tales.

DAVID GREEN

IT CAN ONLY END ONE WAY

I remember the words as if it were yesterday. The day that set me on this dark path. The moment that love sealed my fate.

"I'll love you for eternity," I whispered, staring into Aileth's deep eyes. Caressing her face, I drank in the details of her beauty. Counting each freckle on her milk white skin, the way her raven hair fell below her shoulders.

We met ten years earlier and lived a life of solitude—our respective races would oppose our union. Faint age lines adorned her face now, though they added to her allure. She grew old, as all humans do.

As one of the Elven kin, my appearance hadn't changed. The gift of immortality. My love for Aileth its curse.

"Galan," she muttered, dimples appearing on her cheeks as she smiled at me, though she held sadness in her eyes. "That's impossible, and you know it. I'll die, and you'll live forever and love again. You must. I refuse to watch you from the afterlife, moping around for eternity!"

Aileth laughed at her own joke as I gazed out across the meadow. We ate our meals outside our cottage most nights to watch the sunset beyond the rolling hills. Aileth prepared us baked bread, and a perfumed wine for the evening, its bold scent filled my nostrils as I listened to bluebirds singing from the surrounding trees.

Happiness filled my heart, but at her words, the beginnings of a dark obsession bloomed.

"My love," I said, taking her hand in mine, "I'll find a way we can be together for all time. I swear it."

She laughed once more.

"Enough of this talk," she cried, bouncing to her feet and dragging me up with her. "Dance with me."

And we did; our music the chirping of the birds in the sky, and the rustle of wind in the leaves.

***

Over the following years, I witnessed age ravage Aileth. Her strength waxed and waned as sickness assailed her, and time turned her hair white. Her spirit never dimmed, nor her mind, though my obsession troubled her—my quest to grant a human eternal life.

I delved into arts known to my kind, the benign magic of nature, but my frustration grew when I found no solution to my dilemma. Despite this, my skills in healing illness anxtending life improved, I dare say I knew more than any other being—though my knowledge proved futile.

One winter, a wasting disease plagued Aileth. I worked on potions and poultices as she warmed herself by the fire. Wrapped in fur and reclining on a litter, my love complained of a cold in her bones she couldn't shake.

"Galan," she called, her voice weak and creaking.

"Hmm?" I replied, my attention fixed on my work.

"Come to me, you haven't talked to me in too long."

"Nonsense," I replied with a wave of my hand, "I brought you medicine two hours ago."

Aileth sighed and fell silent as the fire crackled and popped.

"That's what I mean," she said, "all you speak to me about is my sickness. Asking me to drink this, smell that, chew on another thing. Will you just *talk* to me?"

I fought back a spike of annoyance—couldn't she see what I did for her?—as I realized the truth in her words.

Laying down my tools, I crossed the room and kneeled in front of her. I hadn't studied her in ages, instead recalling her face in my memory too often. Through my care, Aileth had reached one-hundred-and-thirty-two-years. A blink of an Elf's eye.

Her liver spot-marked skin had turned paper thin and her hair like the smattering of melted snow instead of the luscious locks of her youth. Those eyes though, they were the same—a stare filled with strength, beauty and wisdom.

"Look at you," she whispered, taking my hand in her gnarled

fingers. "Unchanged. As you'll always be. No wonder you never speak to me, you can't bear to see what I've become."

"That's not true," I said with passion. "My work consumes me. I'm close! I know it. The key factor escapes me, but I'll discover it. I won't let you down."

A tear ran down her cheek, and I reached out with my finger, wiping it away.

"Galan, why won't you let me die? It's well past my time."

"I promised you, Aileth. I won't let that happen."

"Pah," she said, rolling her eyes. It delighted me to see the fire within her burning bright. "Might as well move the mountains. Some things are inevitable, my love. Would you finish your work for tonight and hold me? The cold bites."

I nodded and leaned in to kiss her lips. Adding more wood to the flames, I joined Aileth under the furs, holding her in my arms until she drifted into sleep. As I stared into the fire, I refused to accept her words. I would find a way.

***

Four years later, I lost Aileth.

My love's body had failed long before then, and my arts kept her spirit shackled to it. Aileth spent most of her time looking up at the ceiling, drifting into waking dreams and bouts of lucidity. She never berated me, but I could see the pain in her eyes when I'd bring more poultices and potions, the shame when I would clean her.

As her speech failed her and she faded further, my head told me to end her suffering but my heart wouldn't allow it. I spent sleepless nights experimenting; searching for some final boon to restore her.

The inevitable, as Aileth said, soon arrived. She hadn't opened her eyes for a week, the shallow movement of her chest and the faint rattle of breath were her only signs of life.

Despair took me. My failure almost at hand.

I sat by her side and waited for her to pass, speaking to her of our shared memories and of a fake future we would still have, only leaving her side to prepare fresh medicine to funnel between her lips.

At some point I dozed, the sleep deprivation and warm fire lulling me into an unwanted slumber.

"Galan."

The weak whisper woke me. Aileth stared up from her litter, her eyes fierce and determined—their virility at odds from her time-ravaged face.

"It can only end one way," she said, biting out each word. "Live for me."

I wept as life left her and continued to hold her hand long into the next day; hoping against hope that she'd return from death.

On the hill we'd watch the sun set behind, I buried her. Grief caused me to descend into a madness I'm uncertain I'll ever recover from, though the immediate years are missing from my memory.

As I returned to myself, an idea formed. Something forbidden, but a solution. A way Aileth could return to me. My soul forever tarnished, pieces of me lost.

Necromancy.

***

A Necromancer. To speak with the dead—and master death. I couldn't extend Aileth's life, but I *could* see her again. With her last words, I knew her spirit remained strong.

In the last decades of Aileth's life, travel had proved impossible, but now I could seek arcane knowledge far and wide.

For Aileth, I submerged myself in the Dark Arts.

At times, I wished for my time again—to change my actions and perform in a different way. A useless sentiment, I thought, but still a staff I used to beat my spirit with. With each morsel of Necromancy, my soul fractured. The magic is evil, I know that. To affect that which is no longer living is an affront to the universe, but we make rules for breaking and I would not let petty morality stand in my way.

I scoured the universities of Elven-kind and plundered aeons-old ruins for hints of the Dark Arts. I studied our histories, searching for hints of Necromancers of the past. Such discoveries were hard-earned, my kindred burying the sins of such spell weavers. Elves would hunt them down; destroying them, their creations and writings without mercy.

Still, I discovered the edges of a puzzle, and over the years I pieced together what I desired. My craft increased. I performed experiments on animals and creatures—killing them, then returning their spirits to their bodies.

It took years to perform it without fail on a mere rat.

I persevered, moving my Necromancy to the fallen Elves in their forgotten crypts and battlefields. My race is immortal, but not unkillable. Before the humans arrived into the world, our kind fought one another, each family seeking dominion over the other. Foolish, but it left me with ample opportunities to learn. I would walk the scenes of battles lost and won, hearing the whispers of spirits surrounding me. Though their bodies were long destroyed, I conversed with them. A word or two at first, before I grew powerful enough to pull their shades from the afterlife.

They would screech with torment each time, and I would squash my regret until it no longer existed.

If the Elf's body remained, I could draw the spirit into it, reanimating them to some resemblance of life. It wasn't enough, something of themselves remained missing. I practiced again and again, but a key aspect eluded me.

I discovered more fragments of knowledge, truths in how the universe worked. Through extreme measures, manipulation of time appeared possible. I uncovered abandoned work into how each decision we make causes time to branch off into a separate timeline. I realized that somewhere, in a different plane of existence, I could have succeeded and Aileth would be alive. The thought made me sick with envy, my blackened soul twisting further.

Humans, I discounted; their magic basic, concerned more with conjuring cheap tricks than the mysteries of life. I almost paid the price for my arrogance.

My Necromancy affected animals and my kind, but I soon discovered it didn't extend to the humans. Centuries wasted! Then, I realized why. Humans were the children of the new God, governed by different rules than the older beings of the world.

Much to my delight, I came upon humans as obsessed with mastering death as I—their limited years lending impetus to discard the notions of right and wrong. Cults devoted to Necromancy sprang up in their cities and townships, ones which I exploited for my own gains.

With the humans' help, my knowledge increased tenfold, and I soon learned the hole in my knowledge.

There is an innate balance to nature. To restore a life, you must take one—sacrifice.

***

I returned to the cottage I'd shared with Aileth after centuries away. Its condition elicited an emotion I'd forgotten—regret. Walking through its rooms felt like stepping into some half-forgotten memory. I kneeled by the fireplace and attempted to picture Aileth, but my mind couldn't do it.

"How long since I sat here with you, my love?" I said aloud.

The answer came to me. Five hundred years I'd spent honing my craft, losing myself to Necromancy.

I threw myself into repairing our home. Aileth would have expected it of me, and I delighted in the simple effort.

Satisfied with my work, I returned to the Aileth's grave. Closing my eyes, I reached out with my senses, calling her name into the aether.

"Galan?"

My body trembled at her voice. Weak, but present!

"Aileth, my love. Do not fear, I've come for you."

"No Galan, please. Don't…"

I closed my mind to her. Spirits always protested, but my obsession assured me Aileth would forgive me.

"Why are you doing this?" a voice sobbed, the cries startling me. I'd forgotten they were there. The sacrifice.

Above Aileth's grave, a human hung tied to a stake. A cult member I'd gained along the way.

"You understand Folsteth," I muttered, "better than most. Your death is necessary, and I won't forget it."

I stood and gagged the man again to silence his screams, pulling a sack over his head for good measure. I didn't want him watching as I bent to the task I dreaded—exhuming Aileth's body.

With tears in my eyes, I gazed upon her corpse. I knew what to expect, but witnessing her devoured corpse I couldn't have prepared myself for. I focused my energies, pulling magic from all the living things surrounding us—save Folsteth, his use would come later—and weaved flesh back to her now mended bones. Sweat poured from my brow, into my eyes, and made my palms slick as I worked. I'd performed flesh-weaving many times, but I wanted Aileth to be perfect. The surrounding grass turned brown as I sucked on its life source, trees withered and died as the birds we used to dance to fell from the sky.

At last, I sank back, my work complete. I couldn't turn back time and restore her to youth, but there she lay; the Aileth of her later years.

"Now, dear Folsteth, your moment arrives."

Chanting the arcane words, I reached for my dagger and ran it across his neck. Crimson blood rushed out of the wound and cascading upon Aileth. Feeling his spirit departing to the afterlife, I clung to it and sent my senses searching for Aileth's.

Tendrils of green mist rose from the grave, silent lightning danced in the sky above us as nature protested my actions.

After minutes of calling, I had her. I pulled her spirit into the world, forcing Folsteth's shade in its place. With care, I willed it into her body and waited.

Aileth's chest rose, and she coughed, her eyes fluttering open. I smiled down at her, tears flooding down my face as her lungs filled with breath.

"What have you done?" she asked, then screamed, her cries echoing around the dead hillside.

***

Aileth's madness lasted for months. I expected it. The longer the spirit remains from the body, the harder it is to adapt to the flesh.

I nursed her during this time, like I did in her last faltering years alive, and I felt some damage done to my soul repair. Now she'd returned, I could give up parts of my Necromancy—using it only when I needed to repair Aileth's body and to keep her spirit tethered to it.

With my help, movement returned to her limbs. Stiff at first, but progress. Her screaming fits lessened, and she understood my words. Aileth couldn't speak, but she'd look at me with her deep, fierce eyes when I would encourage her to eat, drink, walk and sleep. It would only be a matter of time until speech returned, and our love would rekindle.

"I told you I'd find a way, Aileth," I would say, keeping a steady flow of speech. Narrating every task, I performed, like how you'd teach a babe to talk. "We'll be together forever, as I said we would, my love."

"So, you say, but if you loved me, you wouldn't have done this."

I fell to my knees. At last! Aileth had spoken. The madness lingered, but that would lift. I raised my hands to her face, but she pulled away.

"Aileth, why do you flinch?" I asked, startled by the hatred in her eyes.

"The Galan I loved is no longer there, vanished well before I died. I don't know who you are."

I wrung my hands, not understanding why she meant to hurt me, after everything I'd done for her.

"Aileth, please. I did the only thing I could."

She laughed, a harsh croaking sound that grew in strength and fury.

"All you've done is cause me pain," she shouted. "You kept me alive well beyond my time. I had to watch my body fail and wither, while you were as strong and as beautiful as the day we met! Suffering with illness and pain for decades, not to mention the shame of having you clean the drool, piss and shit from me each day."

I shook my head, cowed by the passion in her words.

"I did it for love."

"You did it for yourself," she snarled. "You were too afraid to experience my death. I begged you to let me die, I pleaded for you to live. And look what's become of you. You've destroyed yourself and locked me in a failing body—destined to be old until the end of time."

Aileth panted, her fury simmering but her energy spent. We stayed like that, Aileth sat in her chair and I kneeling at her feet long into the night.

***

Her words rang true.

As Aileth's strength returned, she took to spending her time outside the cottage, watching the hilltop. I didn't know if she peered at the sky, or longed for her grave—she wouldn't say.

We became strangers. I grew to understand that my actions were unforgivable, even those from before my descent into Necromancy.

One day, I joined Aileth as she gazed into the surrounding fields.

"You killed everything here," she said after a spell. Birds hadn't returned since my ritual to recall Aileth, and the trees and grass remained dead. "Was it worth it?"

I bowed my head in shame. Darkness still swirled in my soul, but I distanced myself from it—though I knew the damage my Necromancy had caused would never leave my spirit.

"I wish for my time again," I whispered, giving words to the thoughts that plagued me on my descent into Necromancy. "My actions would be different."

"Desiring things you can't change. The real Galan *is* in there somewhere." Aileth said, pity in her voice.

A thought struck me. The knowledge I'd uncovered about time and its nature exploding in my mind.

"You're right," I said, getting to my feet. "I can't change things for us. My actions have sealed our fate... but for another version of us? I could save them."

Aileth turned, the first time she'd faced me for months.

"What are you talking about?"

I explained it to her then. How I could revisit our past and create a different future for ourselves—one free of the mistakes I'd made.

"It requires an enormous price, Aileth."

She nodded, drinking in the information.

"Tell me."

I hesitated. The cost would be everything I'd worked to avoid.

"A sacrifice. That who you love the most—their soul would tear a portal through time, but it would wipe their essence from this world forever."

Aileth took my hand, her skin rough, fingers gnarled. She hadn't touched me since she returned. I looked at her, and she smiled back at me.

"Do it. Please. Let's give ourselves a chance of peace. In this life and another."

***

We stood on the dead hilltop, Aileth knee deep in her grave. Our last sunset.

"Ready?" I asked.

Aileth nodded in response, then tilted her head backwards exposing her wrinkled throat. The first stage of my penance would be to kill her, freeing her spirit for the ritual.

I considered when would be the perfect moment to travel back to, and one conversation stood out.

"I'll love you for eternity," I whispered, staring into Aileth's deep

eyes.

"Galan," she muttered, dimples appearing on her cheeks as she smiled at me, though she held sadness in her eyes. "That's impossible, and you know it. I'll die, and you'll live forever and love again. You must. I refuse to watch you from the afterlife, moping around for eternity!"

"My love," I said, taking her hand in mine, "I'll find a way we can be together for all time. I swear it."

The hours before that would be when I'd arrive. My past self would be out on the hunt. Aileth would be who I sought.

Unsheathing my knife, I held it to her throat.

"I'm sorry, Aileth." I said, steeling myself for what came next.

Breathing in, I held my breath. I'd killed so many times since learning the Dark Arts, but this wasn't the same. My resolve faltered.

"Galan," Aileth whispered, smiling with my knife against her neck. "I forgive you."

She grabbed my wrist and dragged it through her flesh, her blood released like a flood. I helped her body fall into the grave and reached out with my senses. Drawing her spirit into my embrace I held it tight and focused on the point I needed to travel to.

Frost covered the dead grass on the hilltop as a green fog oozed from Aileth's grave. I muttered the incantation, thinking of the point in time I desired. Realizing her spirit, it shimmered in blues and greens above her grave. I plunged the knife into it; the air around the knife solidified, and I wrenched my arm sideways.

A portal tore across the hilltop. Through it, I viewed a clear sky, fresh grass and heard the singing of birds. I stepped into the past.

***

Behind me, the portal back to my world shimmered. It would remain until I returned—I couldn't stay here. Doing so would upset the natural balance and order of time; I had to act with haste and hope my actions would set this Galan and Aileth on a distinct path.

Smoke rose from the cottage's chimney. I lingered outside for a spell and caught my reflection in the window. My golden hair had lost its lustre, my eyes stared back at me from black pits above hollow cheeks. Necromancy hadn't just changed me on the inside, my image carried its cost. The smell of baking bread filled my nostrils and brought me to tears. I plucked up my courage and entered.

Aileth had her back to me, but hearing the door, she spun and took my breath away. Her youthfulness stopped me in my tracks, my hand on the door handle.

"You're not my Galan," she said, wariness in the way she held her shoulders.

"No."

"Who are you?"

"May I enter?" I asked, holding my hands up. They shook.

"Yes, come sit by the fire."

I did as she told me. We sat opposite each other, as we had countless times in a different life, with the flames crackling beside us. I had to remind myself that this wasn't my Aileth, and never could be.

"I am Galan," I began, "but one who has lost his way, one who's done terrible things, telling myself I did it for love—but fear drove me."

To her credit, Aileth didn't even blink.

"What scared you, Galan?"

"An eternity without you. I came to realize too late, that it can only end one way. You've always known that, haven't you?"

A tear slid down her cheek.

"Yes."

"Then why did you fall in love with me?"

Aileth looked up at me with pity. I wanted to reach out to her, to hold her one last time. To kiss those lips—but this wasn't my Aileth.

"Because one lifetime with you is enough for eternity, Galan." I let out a ragged breath and stared into the flames. I felt her hand on my cheek as she drew my face back in her direction. "Why did you come here? I can see it cost you an impressive deal."

I laughed, tears catching on my lips.

"Because there's a way you and your Galan can avoid my fate. Convince him to let you go. To allow you to die when your time arrives. To grieve and to live again."

Aileth nodded. I could see her pondering my words, their ramifications. The way things may have gone for me and my Aileth. She took my hand and squeezed it.

"How should I say it?"

"Make him promise you. I could never break one to you, but you have to act fast. Today. As soon as he arrives home from the hunt."

I stood and walked towards the door.

"Galan, wait!"

I looked behind me and drank her in, Aileth in the prime of human life. To see her this way, one last time—a gift I never knew I'd receive.

"Thank you," she said. "I won't let you down."

"You never did."

I left, striding to the hilltop without a backward glance.

Necromancy had left its stain on me, a marked soul I'll never clean. As I passed through the portal and back into my time, I knew I could never atone for the grief and pain I'd caused. I looked into the star-filled sky before bending to fill Aileth's grave, and thought of the different future I'd created—and believed they'd avoid my mistakes.

A SOUL THAT FESTERS

"Please," she said, tears sliding down her face. A bolt of lightning lanced across the sky, illuminating my laboratory. "This is madness. Can't you see what you've become?"

"Yes," I whispered as I took a step toward her. I still see those wide, frightened brown eyes. The moment she saw the full extent of the evil within me. "It's too late."

Lightning flashed. Avelene screamed, and thunder swallowed her cries.

So many lost years, passed like dust on the wind. Let me tell you how my experiments brought me closer to my goal. How I loved again and almost repented; the lies I told myself, convinced that fate decided my path. The story of how Galan of the Elves abandoned the light, and the world's beauty. How I embraced my blackened soul and added Necromancer to my name.

***

Part of my tale, you already know. How I, an Elf, fell in love with a mortal woman. *Aileth*. We lived in solitude, a secret from our distinct races. As she grew old, I exhausted my arts in preserving her and extended her life beyond any reasonable expectation. For love, I told myself. I searched for a way to save her from death, but I failed. The only option I hadn't explored called to me as she perished.

Necromancy.

Obsessed, even after her passing, I ranged far and wide for a way to bring her back. The world had changed much since I met Aileth. Elves shrank from the world, their power-hungry ways causing mutual destruction and distrust, and humankind filled the void. Cities grew like rancid blisters on the green earth, though I came to appreciate humanities inventiveness. We shared similar goals; a way to defeat death chief among them.

I'd long delved into the outlawed Dark Arts of the Elves and exhausted that knowledge without finding the key to unlock true Necromancy. I could conjure petty spells and cheap tricks; converse with spirits, and sense where death had taken place. My innate magic corrupted as I used it to kill and experiment, though this black sorcery worked on nature and Elves alone, which would not do. Humankind's workings escaped me, and so I turned my observation on them.

I heard whispers of human cults searching to overcome death and endeavored to locate them. My search led me to Portcastle, a burgeoning city built on a coastline and an abandoned Elven castle overlooking it. I took up residence in the citadel and planned my experiments.

***

The isolated Castle Vorn did nothing to lessen the evil that withered my spirit. Elves had died there, their shades lingering as Elven spirits do. They haunted the castle with memories of aeons passed. Whispering to me, gnawing at my soul. Legions of rooms remained empty as I slept, ate and worked in my laboratory in the tallest tower. Two balconies hung from the spire, one overlooking the ocean and the other affording views of Portcastle. The sea would writhe and grow violent when I watched it; inky clouds gathered above me. They unleashed driving rain as though my rotten presence spoiled the surrounding elements.

The proximity of my putrid soul affected Portcastle, too. At first, I would visit it at nighttime's, hooded and cloaked to hide my Elven features, casting a glamour to further conceal them. My kind kept to themselves, and I wished to observe and acclimatize to the human city and their ways. The place appeared peaceful and prosperous, though a sinister undercurrent rose to the surface as I extended my stay.

Still, those first years among the humans of Portcastle gave me pause. Their vibrant, curious natures—the same characteristics I admired and loved about my dearest Aileth—drew me to them, and a part of me wished to repent and abandon my wicked learnings.

I'd return to Castle Vorn, determined to change. To throw off the shackles of the past and embrace life. My obsession would twist and clutch my heart, driving me further into self-destruction.

***

For my visits to Portcastle, I infiltrated the humans with ease. I adopted the fashions of the time; top hats and canes, flowing cloaks and shirts adorned with frills and velvets. I wore coloured eyeglasses to hide my Elven eyes and dyed my hair raven black, though streaks of my natural white emerged. It helped age me, as did the glamour, and I couldn't help think of my Aileth as I inspected my image that first time. I'd watched her grow old for more than a hundred years, while I remained the same; to her, a constant reminder of her truncated life.

Walking the cobblestoned streets, I scoured the city for whispers of cults. And I heard them. An inn of ill-repute, *The Sorry Sailor,* garnered a reputation for meeting the needs of those searching for items hard to attain or the taboo. I frequented there and became familiar with the innkeeper and his staff. I made note of several patrons who disappeared into the inn's cellars on frequent occasions.

What more, I tasted the shadow of death in the air. These sorry souls had suffered.

One late afternoon, I took my usual seat in a booth that afforded a comfortable view of the inn's entrance, bar and door to the cellar, and waited. A nervous fellow with hungry eyes had caught my attention on previous visits, and I decided that I'd press my case for information that night.

"The usual, Old Gentleman?" The innkeeper called as he saw me sitting in the booth. I smoked from my pipe, a habit I'd gained from the humans, and smiled at the name he'd used; the workers of *The Sorry Sailor* didn't know me as Galan.

"Please innkeeper," I replied, making my voice gruff and hoarse and living up to the Old Gentleman moniker.

I gazed around as I waited for my red wine. My regular presence affected the inn, in a way the cult did not. *The Sorry Sailor* held host to vibrant, raucous music, good natured banter and the occasional brawl; not the worst place despite its reputation. Now, the musicians stayed away. The innkeeper's face had grown drawn and pinched, while his patrons nursed their drinks with sour looks on their faces. Frequent brawls resulted in spilt blood and death. This told me the cult counted no Necromancer or magi within their ranks, otherwise I'd have discovered the inn in this condition. It didn't dismay me. I felt sure I'd discover the knowledge I sought without a teacher, and a cult had other uses. Driven devotees, with their fractured souls, weren't for turning away.

"Anything else, Old Gentlemen?" The innkeeper asked, placing my red wine before me. He'd cleaned the mug, something that had fallen out of practice at *The Sorry Sailor*. I repressed a sigh, and told myself that the disease I spread was an evil I had to endure, if I were to see my Aileth again.

"Leave the bottle," I replied, pointing to the wine in his hand. "I will stay awhile tonight. A quiet evening, by all appearances."

The innkeeper made to spit and caught himself. "Aye," he replied with a scowl, "folk are staying away. Portcastle ain't as safe as it used to be. They say a creature watches from that castle yonder, sending us nightmares and dark thoughts."

"Nonsense," I replied, keeping my voice smooth. "No-one's lived there for—"

"Two hundred years. We see its light, in the tallest tower. Mark my words, Portcastle's changed and not for the better." He gazed out of the window. Rising above the city, my castle stood stark against the fading sky behind it. "We ought to chase whatever's up there away."

As he spoke, the inn's doors opened, and my nervous fellow stalked in. I stared at his eyes and saw a fire in them. This man craved knowledge, an obsession smoldered within him. Like me. He passed my booth and disappeared into the cellar.

"Tell me," I said, changing the subject away from my home. A problem for the future, I told myself. "That fellow. I've seen him for a few nights now. Does he work here?"

"Never you mind, Old Gentleman." The innkeeper replied, staring at the cellar door. "More of his friends will arrive soon, best you keep your eyes averted. Portcastle ain't safe for an old fella like you, asking questions. Enjoy the wine."

I drank and watched as more humans arrived and disappeared into the cellar. One caught my eye and stole my breath. The woman appeared as the image of my Aileth. She wore her raven hair in a tight bun, and her deep brown eyes stood out against her porcelain, freckled skin. Her plain, low-necked dress flowed to the floor, and she stared at me as she made her way to the cellar. I looked away and blinked away tears that stung my eyes.

A relative? No. My love hailed from different parts; but the likeness unnerved me. A sign I trod the correct path, I told myself.

I glanced once more, but Aileth's double had disappeared. The rest of the evening blurred as dusk became night, and I lost myself in memories of Aileth. Before midnight, I paid my tab and left *The Sorry*

Sailor.

Fog had fallen on Portcastle, and shadows invaded the cobblestoned streets. I wrapped my black coat around my shoulders and became one with the darkness. And waited.

***

Soon after, my quarry appeared. The nervous fellow, the man with such desire inside him, left *The Sorry Sailor* and walked alone through the silent Portcastle streets. I followed, one with the shadows. Oil burned inside the streetlights, but the clouds in the night sky and the carpet of mist hovering above the cobblestones conspired to smother their illumination. The man wandered towards the waterfront and paused by the sleeping docks. He stared up at Castle Vorn, perched up high on the cliff-face overlooking the city.

"An impressive site," I murmured, moving beside him.

The man spun and jumped, a hand clutching his chest. He resembled a rodent; a filthy animal I'd experimented on and others kicked on the street. His hungry eyes darted around my body, taking in the details of my appearance. I surmised he possessed a quick mind, but some tragedy unbalanced him, and drove him to answer the questions I sought.

"I've seen you," he accused and took a step back, "at *The Sorry Sailor*. You following me, old man?"

"Galan," I said, "and few know my name. Yes, I've watched you. I know what you desire and have the answers you seek."

I let the sentence hang in the air and studied his reaction. His eyes bulged and his breath quickened. I'd laid the bait, and the rodent

29

sniffed at it; tempted to take a bite.

"I ain't searching for nothing," the man muttered, though he didn't look away. He required assurances. Proof of my assertions.

"Death hangs over you, yes?" I asked, watching his reaction. "You've lost someone and heard the whispers in the dark corners of the city. Who? A parent? Lover? Perhaps a child?"

The man bowed his head and choked out a soft cry. Cupping his chin, I tilted his head upwards. I saw it then, the grief. I'd guessed him older from the lines on his face and the grey at his temples, but a callow man stood before me. A novice parent racked with the pain of losing a child.

"My daughter," he gasped. "My entire purpose. Gone."

"I understand." I replied, and I did. Too well. "You and your friends in *The Sorry Sailor* seek to conquer death. Necromancy. I can show you."

A rat scurried by us, and I held up my palm, muttering words of incantation. The rodent froze as I drained away its life. It squealed then flopped to the floor, dead. I waited a moment, then pointed at the corpse. The spirit I drained flowed back into it. The rat screamed as it shot to its feet and darted away. A cheap trick, but one I'd mastered years before.

"Why?" He replied, staring up at me with hope in his eyes.

"I, too, have lost someone. And I wish to understand more. Come."

I pointed to Castle Vorn, and he gaped at me.

"You? The rumours…"

"What I practice, the answers we seek, are not wholesome. We pay a price, and it's taken from our souls. Necromancy is a taint, but a necessary one if you wish to see your daughter again."

I walked away and smiled as I heard him rush to follow me.

"Iain," he said, "that's my name."

The streets of Portcastle didn't earn their dreadful reputation that night as I strode through the city. The evil festering in the shadows sensed the intent in my blackened soul and fled from my path. We cut through the fog and passed through the moors unmolested and silent until we reached the castle. I turned to Iain on the threshold and opened my senses. I felt his determination, the strength of his spirit.

"There is no turning back after tonight," I warned, holding up a finger. Over the years, I learned the best way to strengthen a human's resolve is to dangle a carrot before them, and threaten to take it away. "If you leave now, I won't follow you again."

"Show me," he said, his eyes shining with eagerness. "Teach me your secrets."

I pushed the double-doors and held them open. Iain climbed the last few steps and moved beyond me, into the castle.

"Death holds more answers than life," I said, removing a curved dagger from my belt. From behind, I gripped his shoulder and drew the blade across his neck.

Iain turned, a confused look on his face as his life source gushed down his chest. He held his hands to his ruined throat, gurgled, then dropped to his knees. I kicked him onto his back and watched the hunger fade from his eyes as the midnight bells rang from the city.

***

31

Iain. The first human life I took. As I chanted the incantation, the spell I knew would anchor his spirit to me until I dismissed it, my soul splintered and the festering evil within me spread. The cost of Necromancy. Each act carries a cost.

His green hued shade hovered before me, its image trapped in the eternal throes of anguish. I studied it in a detached manner; noticing the differences between a fresh spirit and those ancient ones that roamed my castle and the graveyards I'd searched.

"Answer me, and I'll set you free." I said, addressing Iain's specter. As I'd told him, answers lay in death. I exerted complete control over his spirit, and wished to discover more of the cult meeting in the bowels of *The Sorry Sailor,* and had no time for mistruths. Iain's murder allowed me to further my studies, his an essential death to deepen my knowledge.

The shade howled at me; rage mixed with grief. The dead who haunted my castle answered in kind, and I waited for them to subside.

"Your group," I asked, "what is your aim?"

The spirit snarled. I held my fist before me and squeezed. Iain's ghost writhed as it screamed.

"You know it, Necromancer!" It cried. "To do what God won't and banish death."

"Who is your leader?"

"A woman, Avelene. She's driven, more than I. She says she's close."

"Avelene," I murmured. "Who is she?"

"A scholar," the shade wailed, causing the surrounding torches to flicker. Mist drifted through the open door; Iain cast his green hue onto it. "Said she'd studied Elven magic and says the key lies between their world and ours."

"Yes," I said, reflecting on my research. "For complete mastery, one would learn of the Elven ways and the human deity. To conquer death is to become God."

"Release me," the shade wailed. I looked at it again, having forgotten its presence as I dwelled on my thoughts.

"Perhaps," I replied.

I called on my black magic and thrust the shade back into Iain's body. Blood still gushed from the wound in his neck. Kneeling, I peered at his dead stare. For a fleeting moment, I believed I witnessed a flicker of life in his orbs. I reached out with my senses and felt the fabric of reality tear, a slither of space and time open as Iain's spirit passed through.

Smiling, I got to my feet and dragged the body with me. I had learned much.

***

An urge quickened within me; the desire to explore human death. My experiments moved beyond potions, spells and animals as I delved into the limits of humanity.

Iain's throat had presented a problem. If I'd returned his spirit, the wound would cause him to die again. Would repairing such an injury avoid the problem, and would death of another kind present its own problems?

I studied and dissected Iain's corpse, repairing it and delving into it again. I worked long into the nights, and would hear laughter and tears echoing around my laboratory and castle. When I realized the noises were my own, I feared madness had sunk its claws into me. Now I see it had, but years before when my obsession began as my Aileth faded.

I spent more time at *The Sorry Sailor,* watching the cults comings and goings. When Avelene would pass, I'd maintain eye-contact. Sometimes I'd nod and smile. She'd regard me with stony silence, though she wouldn't look away. She always dressed in black, and when I slept, her face merged with Aileth's.

In the evenings, I would stalk the streets.

Rumour spoke of a devil, preying on the innocent of Portcastle. I doubt they all were, but virtue or guilt didn't matter to me. I required specimens, more humans to carry out my work. Some were from the cult; I'd approach them as I did Iain and tempt them back to my lair. Some even agreed to my experiments, believing together we'd conquer death.

My proficiency in killing grew, as did my control of the human spirit, though the key to returning one to life eluded me. The length of time between death seemed not to matter, which bolstered my morale, though the condition of the body did. A human killed by poisoning would allow its spirit to linger for a spell, whereas one with an obvious wound rejected it outright.

The piercing of reality dumbfounded me. For Elves, death worked in a different way. We are immortal beings, but not unkillable; our spirits wander the earth until they're destroyed. Not so the humans. It occurred to me that their souls journeyed to another place.

But where one goes, one can return.

The constant death affected me. At times, I forgot my Aileth, and lost sight of what drove me to such depravity. I took pleasure in the kill, in the experiments. Portcastle grew worse; ominous clouds gathered over it, the streets overflowed with litter, the dead and dying; the surrounding waters proved toxic to the fish that swam there. The people starved, turned wicked and sour. I cared not. I looked at them as rodents, like Iain. A species beneath me, designed to further my studies.

Castle Vorn grew cold, no matter the number of fires that burned. I felt the ancient Elven shade's crowd around me as I worked, as I roamed the abandoned corridors. Shadows thickened to greet me, and I embraced their touch.

Then Avelene spoke to me, and the fester in my soul receded.

***

"They call you the Old Gentleman," she said. I looked up, startled. Deep in thought, I'd lost track of time and forgot to take my leave. Avelene peered down at me. Her voice crystal chimes, and like her face, the match of my Aileth's. I felt guilty as she flinched when I met her eyes. "They should call you the sad one, sitting her alone night after night."

"My lady," I replied, forgetting to mask the youthfulness of my voice. Her eyebrows raised on hearing me speak, and she peered at me closer. "Aye, lonely I am. It festers inside and drives me. I sense the same need in you."

"Is that why you stare at me with overwhelming sadness in your eyes?" She asked, tilting her chin.

"You are so much like her," I whispered, "I can't help myself."

"When I look at you," Avelene replied, ignoring my words, "I see you're not so old. Why do you disguise yourself?"

I glanced around. The innkeeper glared at me, as he now did to everyone in *The Sorry Sailor*. More patron deaths had occurred there, and he held the responsibility for several.

"Not here my lady," I answered, getting to my feet. To her credit, she didn't back away. She possessed a powerful spirit. "Allow me to accompany you. The streets aren't safe."

"And I would be from you?" She asked, meeting my eyes again.

"Yes," I whispered.

We left the inn and strode into the now ever-present mist that clung to Portcastle. The fog seemed to ooze from the cracks in the ground, making the stones slick underfoot. Avelene shivered, my presence lending a bite to the chill. I swept my cloak from my shoulders and draped it over her.

"But the cold," she said, laying her gloveless hand on my bare forearm. She gasped. "You're like ice!"

"It doesn't affect me anymore," I said, fighting the urge to kiss her lips, and she gazed up at me. If I closed my eyes, I could pretend Aileth had returned to me.

"Who are you?" She asked, coming to a halt. We stood by the waterfront, the same spot I'd disclosed my secrets to Iain. I gazed up at Castle Vorn, an evil presence looming over the city. It stood silhouetted against the moon, which had appeared from behind a cloud bank.

"A traveler," I replied, removing my top hat and dispelling my glamour. Her eyes widened. "Someone who has, and is, lost. As you have. My name is Galan."

"An Elf," Avelene breathed. "You live up there, don't you? In the castle."

I looked out toward the water. The full-moon reflected on its surface. It shimmered as the gentle waves rolled.

"Something drew me there. A powerful Elven mage once dwelled within its walls. Now it's filled with haunted memories and half-forgotten dreams. And pain."

Avelene opened her mouth to answer, but I held up my hand. My skin prickled, the sense of being watched strong. I turned and gazed around, though the inky shadows that I left in my wake revealed nothing. Leaning closer to her, I whispered with urgency.

"I know what you seek, so I extend this offer once. Come with me, help me, and we'll conquer death. Together. We can take back what your God took from us. But leave with me now, tonight."

I held out my hand, palm upwards. I must confess, a part of me hoped she'd decline and flee into the fog. She took it.

"Avelene," she said. I closed my eyes, and Aileth's face swam to the front of my mind.

"Come," I replied. The moon passed behind the clouds, and the evening plunged into darkness.

***

Avelene stayed with me, and for a while, the eroding of my soul came to a halt. Ashamed of my experiments, and the state of my laboratory, I locked it and forbade her to approach. She took rooms on the opposite wing of the castle, and the corridors bloomed with life again. We studied together and drew close.

She'd lost her parents and brothers in a fire some years before and used her inheritance to fund her research. Long enchanted by the Elves, she'd heard stories of their immortality, magic and, in some cases, Dark Arts. Avelene peppered me with questions regarding my kind, and I sought answers on human theology and their new God. My Necromancy, I kept hidden from her. It ashamed me, even though I knew it a necessary evil. In truthfulness, I enjoyed how Avelene helped me colour the darkness of my soul with light. Even though she'd explored a cult devoted to death, I sense she wouldn't kill. She possessed a curious mind and sought information only for her purpose.

We settled into life at Castle Vorn and seldom ventured into the city. I taught her the art of potion making and the history of the Elves; she instructed me in the ways of the new God. The storms that racked the coast abated somewhat and my heart remembered to love again, though I kept this emotion to myself, though I harbored hope.

"Tell me about her," Avelene said one night, as we studied in the library. The area had remained abandoned apart from dust until her arrival. Now, we spent most nights there, a roaring fire and blankets for her to fight against the chill. "The one you lost."

I closed my book and stared at her. We sat across from each other, the fireplace in between us. Just as Aileth and I used to in our cottage.

"We created a world together, just for us. A human and an Elf. I told her I'd love her for eternity, and my desperation drove me to seek a way to do that. I didn't think I could love again—"

Coughing, I broke off and stared into the flames.

"Galan." Avelene called. She looked at me, eyes like stone. "You can't recreate something you had with her. I'm not Aileth."

"But you're so like her," I protested. "I thought—"

"That we'd live up here, our own world? I see how you look at me; you're confused. You love me, but your obsession with her still drives you. The things you've done... The Devil of Portcastle. A strange coincidence that the streets have grown safe since I arrived here. I'm not a fool."

I didn't answer. Instead, I gazed into Aileth's face—no, Avelene's. Avelene. I looked away, ashamed.

"Your obsession has festered in your soul, and no matter how much you repent, it doesn't change what you've done. What would Aileth say?"

"My actions are necessary. She'd—"

"What's locked away in your laboratory?"

I felt battered, bewildered. Avelene's porcelain skin appeared pinched, and black shadows hung under her eyes. Blinking, I understood. Every time I glanced at her, I desired Aileth. I hadn't noticed what living near me had done to her. My soul wasn't the only that festered. I gazed around the library. The fire crackled but birthed no heat. Dust lay thick in the gloomy room, and I detected the Elven shades in the corner of my vision. Watching. Whispering.

I'd created an illusion for myself. A reality for Avelene and I to drift in. One that didn't exist.

"Leave me," I muttered, getting to my feet and turning my back on her. "Go. There are no answers for you here. Return to the city."

"Galan—"

"Run!" I snarled, hurling my book into the wall. A cloud of dust exploded from it, and it dropped to the floor with a thud. Seconds later, I heard Avelene's footsteps as she fled.

***

The madness and evil I thought I'd held at bay returned, but in reality, it had never disappeared. I spent days wailing and gnashing my teeth, howling at the heavens and night sky. Aileth's death returned to me anew. The castle's shades gathered around me; whispering, tempting me to plunge deeper into evil.

I desired new specimens for my experiments and took the plunge.

My time with Avelene taught me much. The humans believed in an afterlife, and my senses agreed; I felt when their spirits departed. Avelene spoke of sacrifices drawing the spirit world closer to ours, of the terrible power such an incantation held. Emboldened, I reckoned my Elven Dark Arts mixed with the new ways of the humans would yield results.

As I departed Castle Vorn for the city at its doorstep, I felt eyes upon me, though I told myself that my madness taunted me. I thought of Avelene and hoped she'd recovered a little of herself since I'd chased her away.

Portcastle remained as I remembered it. Dirty, wicked and festering with evil. Like my soul. The shadows and dark corners embraced me once more, and I welcomed them. The ever-present mist conspired to hide me, as I stalked the streets for two 'volunteers.'

I didn't need to search far. I found two leaving an inn close to the moors leading to Castle Vorn; drunk and unsuspecting. They stood arguing, holding lanterns that offered little illumination against the oppressive gloom, and soon came to blows. One fellow struck the other, driving him to the ground. The attacker raised his lantern above his head, ready to bring it down on his fallen friend.

"Wait!" I cried, emerging from the fog. My appearance startled the drunkard, and he scrambled back. I stooped and examined the unconscious man. "He's dead."

A lie, and a convincing one for an inebriated simpleton.

"Dead?" The drunk cried, falling to his knees. "Have mercy on my soul. I didn't mean to."

"That doesn't matter, the city watch will never believe you. But I saw. Come with me, I'll help you hide the body."

We pulled the man up between us and slung his arms across our shoulders. I steered my 'friends' to Castle Vorn, and I must confess I don't believe the drunkard knew where his journey ended. He muttered and pleaded beneath his breath as he staggered towards my home.

We entered the castle, and I led the way to my laboratory.

"This way," I breathed, "I can hide him here."

I pushed through the heavy doors and pointed to the middle of the room. Two beds lay there, between them a small table with medical apparatus. The balconies were open; through one, I saw Portcastle. The city lights appeared brighter than I'd seen them for some time. Bells rang in the distance.

"On the bed," I said, "there's a marvellous fellow."

As my helper heaved his friend, I retrieved a syringe from the table. I stepped towards him, thrusting the needle into the side of his neck and injected the fluid within. The man sagged, and I caught him, pulling him towards the other bed.

***

I strapped the pair to their beds and prepared myself. One, I would kill first but leave the body intact. In fact, I'd done it with poison. I knew the spirit would reject the body until the organs had time to heal, or repaired through other means, but that discovery could wait. For now, I had to test the theory.

I felt the poisoned man die and sensed his spirit passing beyond our reality. Focusing on it, I muttered an incantation. Marking it so I could find it again.

Lightning illuminated my laboratory, and thunder followed. A storm formed over Portcastle. On the wind, I thought I heard voices but paid it no mind. I often heard whispers in Castle Vorn. Why would that night differ? The bells continued to sound.

I approached the unconscious man, the fellow we'd dragged from Portcastle. Unsheathing my curved knife, I held it high. Lightning flashed again and reflected on the blade.

"For you Aileth," I whispered.

"Galan."

I staggered and almost dropped the knife. Avelene stood behind me, a torch burning in her hand. Looking at her face, I noticed the many differences from my Aileth; they shared passing similarities that my grief and obsession had magnified. I heard voices echo from the corridor beyond her, and more shouts drifting from outside in between peals of thunder.

"Why are you here?" I asked, glancing at the bodies I stood between.

"They've come for you, Galan," she said, "the city folk know what you've done. They watched you, saw you take these men. I came with the mob to warn you. Run."

I staggered to the balcony overlooking Portcastle. A river of flames ran below me; townsfolk holding torches high, hefted straws and carts to the castle's foundations and setting them alight.

"No," I growled, "I must complete my work."

Lightning flashed, and thunder rang behind it. Smoke rose through the windows, and I saw flames in the corridor. The wooden beams above us groaned.

"Please," she said, tears sliding down her face. A bolt of lightning lanced across the outside sky, illuminating my laboratory. "This is madness. Can't you see what you've become?"

"Yes," I whispered as I took a step toward her. I still see those wide, frightened brown eyes. The moment she saw the full extent of the evil inside me. "It's too late."

Lightning flashed. Avelene screamed, and thunder swallowed her cries.

The beam above her broke as the bolt struck the tower. I watched in slow motion. The broken timber fell, crushing her. Avelene died, my second love and another I couldn't save. Her torch fell from her hands and caught the draping tapestries.

"Fools!" I cried, running to the balcony. My grief hot with anger. "Don't you see what I'm about to achieve? How dare you try to stop my work?"

I crossed the room, knife in my hand and arm across my mouth. Choking on the smoke that filled my lungs. The storm increased, matching my fury at the insects and rodents seeking to tear me down. Another beam snapped, bringing down a shower of stone.

I had to act. Lifting the blade, I drove it through the unconscious man's throat. His eyes shot open, and he gargled on blood. I stabbed again, and willed the life from his body. As his spirit rose, the tear in time and space appeared and I focused on the spirit of the poisoned man, the one I'd marked.

I felt it and laughed. My cries echoed above the cracking flames, the rolling thunder and the jeers from the mob.

"Return to me," I cried between laughs. I wept as the spirit re-entered our world. As I directed it towards its former body, a bolt of lightning struck the tower.

The explosion blew the weakened roof apart. I stared, opened mouthed as the wind ripped at me. A shower of debris fell, and I dived to the side to avoid my end.

As the dust cleared, I climbed to my feet. The bodies from my experiment lay buried under rock and beam. Avelene, too. I fell to my knees as the spirit turned and drifted from this world, back to its eternal afterlife.

Smoke and flames built around me, as I kneeled and stared at the knife in my hands.

"I could end it now Aileth," I sobbed, "but I'll never see you again. And I promised that I'd love you for eternity."

The floor beneath me shuddered. I climbed to my feet and staggered towards the other balcony, the one overlooking the sea and placed my trust in fate.

I jumped and plunged headfirst into the black waters beneath as Castle Vorn crumbed above me.

***

Sometime later, I drifted to a beach. Alive.

My experiment worked. I'd brought a life back. A trade. A sacrifice. I paid the price with my festered soul.

My research and findings were lost, but I, Galan, had achieved Necromancy and would continue my quest.

For Aileth.

THE BATTLE OF BADON HILL

"You placed me on the path to unite the clan's druid," Huel grated, thrusting a finger towards the hooded man sitting across the fire, "but the Saxons push us further west by the day. *Wealas* they call us, as if Britannia doesn't belong to the Britons. Now you tell me to draw my forces to Badon Hill and wait for an attack? Madness."

"I warned you," the druid whispered. "You came to me, begged for my knowledge. I gave it. You didn't ask how to keep the throne."

"Enough riddles, druid," Huel growled, fighting the temptation to reach across the flames and throttle the seer. "How do I win?"

"I have seen the future, Huel. The Saxons destroy our way of life. Britannia walks a distinct path after the Battle of Badon Hill, our beliefs forgotten. They succeed. Oh, you may win the battle, but it only delays the inevitable. They push the Britons into Wealas and many more flee across the sea to Celta. Already, we've lost much. Britannia forgets, and the histories won't remember us… If you ignore my advice."

The flames warmed Huel against the chill of the druid's words. The man sat unmoving, face lost in the shadows of his hood, a dead rat laying on the ground before him. He'd met the man once before, when the prophet told him how to unite the Britons. Huel didn't enjoy hearing his words, but he believed them.

"That can't happen," he whispered, staring into embers.

"No. We can change our future, but you must follow my instructions to the letter. You and I must crush the invaders, now."

"We can defeat them?" Huel asked as hope bloomed in his chest.

"Aye," the druid replied. "I've lived many lifetimes and viewed all the possible futures. The ways of the Saxon's don't appeal to me. Their victory means invasion for centuries. Destruction. Persecution of our people. The Romans took much from the Britons. The Saxons will wipe us away. I wouldn't see us lost to the fogs of time."

Huel clapped his hands together, his booming laughter echoing around the empty plains.

"What do you need? I don't even know your name."

The oracle hesitated.

"Draw the Saxons to Badon Hill, that place is where we turn the tide. My instructions may enrage you, but listen and obey. This is the only way," he said, pointing at the dead rat. Its limbs twitched before the rodent let out a shrill scream that pierced the silent night. The rat scampered to its feet and hurried away from the fire. Huel's gaped after it, then turned to the hooded man. "My name is Galan. Now your cousin Morgan. Let us speak of him..."

***

The Saxons' scouts rode hard on Morgan's heels.

"The Gods spit in their eyes," he snarled, glancing over his shoulder, aching limbs protesting. He hadn't slept for days.

Three of the heathens pursued him. Morgan got sloppy on his return from spying on the Saxon army's movements and allowed the invaders to detect his presence. They'd chased him for hours and closed the gap. He narrowed his eyes as he scanned the horizon. *Badon Hill is too far away. The Saxon scum will reach me before long,* he thought with a grimace. *Looks like I'm fighting.*

Morgan loosed the clasp of the sheath holding the sword in place on his hip, not wanting to fumble with it in the moment's heat. Holding the reins in one hand, he reached for the bow slung across his chest. He let his horse have its head and guided the beast with his knees as he nocked an arrow. Morgan glanced over his shoulder and picked a target, a Saxon who rode fifty paces behind him in a direct line. He swiveled and let the arrow fly. The shaft struck the rider between his eyes; its impact unseating him.

Riderless, the horse panicked at its sudden freedom and stumbled into the path of another pursuer. The Saxon's steed collapsed in a mass of limbs and dirt as Morgan, baring his teeth in a feral grin, threw the bow over his shoulder and yanked the reins, turning in a tight circle. He aimed his horse at the last standing rider and drew his sword.

Morgan felt a thrill at the sound it made as the blade tore through the air. He bore down on the Saxon, his pursuer hesitating from the confusion and speed of Morgan's attack. He reached for his weapon too late.

Morgan closed the gap and swung his sword in a wide arc. The Saxon screamed as fiery blood splashed across Morgan's face, his blade tearing a gash from the invader's throat to forehead. He spun his horse and thrust his sword through the Saxon's chest. The man fell, dead before he hit the ground. Heart thumping, Morgan glanced around. His pursuers dead, he slammed his blade into its sheath and resumed his journey.

***

Morgan pushed his horse, maintaining its gallop. It sweated and trembled beneath him, and Morgan felt a pang of sympathy for the beast, but his need to reach Badon Hill outstripped the animal's comfort. The Saxon armies marched, and the Briton's had much to prepare.

"Faster, my friend." Morgan breathed, leaning across his horses' neck. The stallion whinnied in response and picked up speed.

The Saxon scourge had his people on the run. His cousin and war leader, Huel, picked Badon Hill as their last stand. A hill fort that commanded views of the surrounding countryside, and one they could defend until reinforcements arrived. Morgan reckoned his cousin's choice for the battle a sound one; the Saxon's *had* to meet and deal with them. *They could skirt Badon, but it's not wise to leave an army at your back*, he thought, enjoying the rushing wind on his face.

A nagging thought troubled him. Huel had left the preparations to others, behaviour most unlike him as the war-chief enjoyed throwing himself into any situation. Instead, he spent most of his waking hours with the druid, Galan. The war-chief would confer with the hooded newcomer before deciding on issues. Morgan felt uneasy when he watched the druid; the darkness inside his cowl stretched, blacker than pitch. *Who knows what manner of creature this Galan is?* He thought with a grimace. *Though Huel trusts him, and his word is law.*

His bloodlust from his skirmish had faded, and his tired limbs reminded him of his weariness. Morgan studied the horizon as his destination appeared through the summer haze. Green fields led to Badon Hill. The sound of horns drifted towards him and dug his heels into the horse's flanks. Huel would be in another meeting, and Morgan's news couldn't wait.

***

Morgan rode his horse straight through Badon's gates to the meeting hall. The fort buzzed with activity as soldiers readied for the coming battle. He tugged the reins, bringing the animal to a halt. Morgan hopped down and threw the reins to a waiting stable-boy.

"See he's well cared for," he said, patting the steed's foam-covered neck, "he's carried me far."

"Yes, master," the stable-hand replied. He led the horse away, whispering to it as he did.

Morgan glanced around. He craved ale and a bucket of steaming water to wash away the dirt and Saxon blood. It would have to wait. He marched into the wooden meeting hall with its straw covered floors and vaulted roof. Clan-chiefs sat around a long table that ran the hall's length, talking and, to Morgan's relief, drinking. At its head sat Huel with Galan, hooded and cloaked, beside him. Morgan raised a hand to his cousin, who nodded in response. He made his way to Huel, nodding and clasping forearms with comrades and acquaintances as he passed through the hall.

"Cousin," Huel said, rising and wrapping Morgan in a bear-hug. Though blood, the two men couldn't appear more different; the war-chief, massive, red-haired and hale, his younger cousin lithe and black of hair and eye. Morgan loved Huel like a brother, and they were the only family each other had. Huel pulled away and studied his face, noticing the dried blood and grime. "What news from the east? You saw battle?"

"Aye, Saxons scouts. Dead. Huel, thousands of the bastards assemble in the countryside. I make them two days ride away." He felt Galan's eyes upon them. "Cousin, I reckon they outnumber us five-to-one."

"More for the slaughter," Galan whispered. "You bring splendid news."

Morgan eyed the druid with a frown. "Death is a necessity, priest. We shouldn't revel in it."

"As you say," Galan replied.

"Huel—"

"Peace, Morgan. Sit. Rest. We'll talk later."

"Alone, I hope." Morgan said, glancing at the druid. The shadows inside his hood appeared to swirl.

"Britons!" Huel called, holding his arms wide. Silence settled on the gathering as Morgan found a seat beside his friend, Kai. The men embraced each other, and Kai pushed over a full jug of ale. Morgan filled a mug, drank his fill and smacked his lips before pouring more. "The Saxon's approach. My scouts say they're but two-days ride from here. Let them come! Our swords, axes and arrows will meet them!"

The clan-chiefs battered the table and answered with battle cries. Morgan joined in despite his misgivings. He's seen the approaching horde, but the exultation of his fellow Britons set his blood aflame.

"A battle at last," Kai whispered, "better than all this running scared and hiding."

"My fellow Britons, we fight for our survival. We've owned these lands since the Old Ones lived among us. The Romans came, but we remained. Defiant in the face of their legions! We battle for our fallen ancestors, and the generations to come."

The hall erupted into cries and the rattle of weapons and jugs on the table. Morgan felt himself swept along in the euphoria. The hall's floor vibrated, the ceiling shook.

"The Saxon scourge has pushed us west. Wealas, they call us. But we are Britons. This is our land. Our kin who cling to the coast, and those who've fled to Celta shall return. Once we drive the Saxons into the sea, we'll call Britannia home once more." Huel paused, arms stretched wide as he gazed at the clan-chiefs. His stare swept the room, lingered on Morgan for a moment before he glanced at Galan. "I ask you to trust in my words. We must prepare ourselves to sacrifice for the greater good."

Morgan felt a chill kiss his skin. He watched Galan and felt his stare returned.

"Go now, Britons. The Saxons approach. Let them come. They'll break on Badon's walls and die on our swords. Britannia!"

"Britannia!" The clan-chiefs screamed. Huel fell into his chair, and turned at once to Galan, their heads close as they conversed.

"You seem troubled," Kai said, nudging Morgan with his elbow.

"Just weary from the road," he replied, hiding his face with his tankard.

"I know you better than that, liar," Kai laughed. "Your troubles will melt away with more ale, and a Saxon on your blade."

"What word on the reinforcements?" Morgan snapped, slamming his ale down. He glanced around as the clan-chiefs moved towards the exit and lowered his voice. He felt Galan's regard on him once more. "Huel made no mention of them. I've *seen* the horde. There's no way we can stand against them alone."

"Huel has a plan," Kai said, shaking his head. "He's kept us alive this long—"

"And what of that bastard Galan?" Morgan hissed, months of frustration bubbling to the surface. Before the druid arrived, Huel used hit-and-run tactics and diversions, never allowing the horde to settle. Now, the Saxon's turned the screw and pushed the Briton's back. For Morgan, it appeared clear his people fought a losing battle, and he blamed Galan. "The charlatan has poisoned the war-chief's mind. He accepts counsel from no other. I don't trust him. He leads us to ruin."

"Careful," Kai said, glancing towards the head of the table. Huel watched them. "You speak of treason. Galan is the war-chief's man. That's enough for me."

"Kai—"

"Peace, Morgan." His friend said, draining the ale in front of him as he climbed to his feet. "I don't wish to argue with you."

Kai slapped him on the shoulder and departed. The crowd dwindled, leaving Morgan alone with his cousin and Galan.

"Morgan," Huel called, "I have a task for you."

"Cousin," he said, approaching the war-chief. "I must speak. We don't have enough men. I fear this charlatan has steered you wrong."

"Enough," Huel snapped, rising to his feet. He glowered down at his cousin. "You know not of what you speak. Our aim isn't survival, it's reclaiming our home and to build for our children and theirs. This is the only way to restore Britannia."

"Forgive me, Huel," Morgan said, bowing his head. "What is your task?"

"Reinforcements," Huel answered. Morgan looked up in surprise to see his cousin grinning. "Artur and his men wait for our word. When the Saxons attack, they're to drive into the rear and smash them against our barricades."

Morgan nodded. "A sound plan. Yes, it'll work."

"I know," Huel answered with a wry smile. "I need you to escort Galan to them. He has instructions to relay. I'd send you alone, but he insists he must meet with Artur, and you're to accompany him."

Morgan opened his mouth, then closed it again. Galan rose from his chair, his hands hidden in the folds of his robes.

"I'll have horses waiting," he said, nodding to Huel before leaving.

"Wonderful." Morgan replied, frowning after him. "Cousin, why do you place such stock in him? How can you trust a creature who hides in the shadows?"

"Because I have reason to," Huel said, gripping Morgan's shoulders. "Do this for Britannia. Obey Galan's words as if I spoke them. Go."

Huel stooped, and the men touched their foreheads together. Morgan spun and strode after the druid, his heart heavy with doubt.

"Cousin," Huel called. Morgan paused and glanced over his shoulder. "If a time comes where you're tempted to act against Galan, remember me and these words: He's our future. Please."

Morgan pushed through the doors into the daylight without answering.

***

Even though the balmy afternoon sun hung in the air, Morgan felt cold as he led a fresh horse through the hillfort. He glanced up at Galan, who sat atop his steed, a black stain against the blue sky. The druid's presence rattled him, even though he rode in silence. He appeared to exist despite the light, unaffected by its warmth and glow.

"I mean no harm to Huel or your people," Galan murmured, as if he read Morgan's thoughts. "I know my appearance gives you misgivings. My studies and... talents have left their mark on me."

"What do you mean?" Morgan asked, peering up. He thought he could see the angular shape of Galan's jaw inside the shadows of his hood.

"The arts I practice came at a substantial cost. I've only dabbled with them over the last millennia when I've had to. I learned the folly of such ways too late. My magic isn't a trifling matter the body, or the soul, recovers from. Despite my best efforts."

Morgan closed his mouth with a snap.

"Millennia?"

"Mount your horse," Galan said, pointing ahead at the fort's gates. Morgan blinked at his long, black fingernails. "We must return before the morning. Speed is of the essence."

"How far is Artur's camp?" Morgan asked, swinging onto his animal's back.

"A three-hour ride."

"Plenty of time for some answers, druid," Morgan said, staring across into the inky pit that concealed Galan's face. "Lead on."

***

They rode in silence for a spell. Morgan eyed the skies and fancied ominous clouds hovered above them as they cut through the countryside. They kept their horses at a steady gait but didn't flog them; Galan's snapped at Morgan's steed if they ever moved too close together.

He pondered the druid's words. Morgan didn't trust him, far from it, but now the possibility that the man possessed an addled brain ranked high in his thoughts. *No druid has lived for a hundred years, let alone millennia,* Morgan thought.

"Are you going to ask me those questions that sting the tip of your tongue, or continue to frown at me until we reach Artur?"

"Fine," Morgan shouted above the clatter of horse's hooves on soil and stone. "I reckon you're mad."

"That's not a question." Galan said. He didn't raise his voice, but Morgan heard every word.

"Peace!" He cried, tossing his head. "Explain how you've lived for millennia."

Galan yanked on his reins. His horse reared, and the druid rode the wave until the beast settled. Morgan circled back and moved alongside him. The druid raised his hands to his hood and lowered it.

Morgan gasped. Galan's skin and hair appeared drained of all colour, whiter than snow. Not a single wrinkle or blemish marked a face of sharp bones and angles. Morgan made eye contact and looked away as a jolt of despair passed through him. Crimson orbs, filled with earth-shattering sadness and unknowable wisdom, sat below an unlined forehead.

Galan pushed his flowing hair behind his pointed ears, and Morgan drew his weapon in a smooth motion.

"Fae!" He cried. "Impossible."

Galan bared his ivory teeth, though the smile left his blood-red eyes unaffected. "Aye. I'm the last of my kind. I've walked these lands since times your histories don't recall. My kin ruled it; myths and legends, or Gods, you might call us. Before we destroyed ourselves, humanity ascended. You do your best to annihilate your kind too, but you haven't quite succeeded yet."

"I don't believe you," Morgan said, his horse reading its rider's emotions and backing away.

"Believe your eyes then," Galan said with a shrug. "I'd rather you took me at my word, but that will never work with you. It's of the utmost importance you trust me, so I won't mislead you."

"Why?" Morgan asked, his sword's point still aimed at the druid.

"Because in every future I've viewed, you kill me and the Britons fail. Except in one. That's the future we desire."

Morgan urged his horse forward and placed the point of his blade against Galan's neck. Tales told of the Fae; devious creatures who tricked honest humans. Stories for old wives to tell children who sat wide-eyed at their feet. Others said they were Gods, their ancient minds a mystery to men and women who crossed their paths.

Galan looked as if he'd been ripped from a nightmare, and the words he spoke made Morgan's instincts scream. They warned that evil sat before him.

"If I kill you, Fae, why bring me? To destroy me first?"

Galan laughed, and Morgan heard the whisper of madness in it.

"No. Britannia needs you alive. From what I've seen, if I don't journey with you, I'm dead and the Briton's lose. Morgan, what I achieve, you'll despise. Believe me, it's necessary. Now, time runs away from us. Are you going to relieve my head from its shoulders, or shall we ride?"

"If a time comes where you're tempted to act against Galan, remember me and these words: He's our future. Please."

Morgan recalled his cousin's words. With a snarl, he sheathed his weapon and spurred his horse on. Galan drew up alongside him, hood raised, and they resumed their journey in silence.

Artur's sentries found them at nightfall, as they passed through a ravine that led to a vast forest, a place where the Saxons wouldn't stumble upon them. Morgan recognized Hamma, a fighting man of the same age, and dismounted as he approached.

"Well met," the sentry cried, clasping forearms, "what news?"

Morgan glanced at Galan, who sat unmoved on his horse.

"Badon Hill prepares, the Saxons march. This is Huel's druid. We bring instructions for Artur."

"Druid," Hamma said with a solemn nod. "You're fortunate Morgan is with you. The sentries wanted to kill you both before they recognized him. Better safe than sorry, they say. Follow me, I'll bring you to Artur."

Morgan turned to lead his horse and saw Galan beckon him closer.

"I'll talk to Artur; you stay with your friend when we reach the camp."

"Hiding something from me, druid?" Morgan snapped, his mistrust spiking.

"Artur and I will argue, and your presence will make it worse—"

"You've witnessed all futures, and it's necessary. So, you've said. I'll keep my distance, but speak loudly. I'll listen to what you say. Gods believe me, I will."

"As you wish," Galan said, and eased his horse forward. Morgan led his animal, scowling after the druid.

Artur's camp appeared well organized and structured. It didn't surprise Morgan. A Briton and born leader, Artur trained with the

Romans and led an uprising as the legion's grip on Britannia slackened. He used many of their tactics and kept their standards. Morgan had to concede Artur's methods worked; to a man, the Briton's respected him and his unit.

Singing drifted Morgan's way from the surrounding campfires as the warriors ate and drank, though the activities weren't boisterous. Artur's men were well-drilled and, if he made the call, would mobilize for battle within minutes.

Hamma led them to a tent in the camp's center, a little larger than the others but simple.

"Wait here," he said, ducking inside. Morgan peered through the flaps and saw Artur sitting behind a wooden table, studying parchments. He looked up as Hamma approached and smiled. He had a boyish face framed by golden hair that fell to his broad shoulders. They exchanged brief words, and Hamma returned.

"Artur will see you," he said, nodding at Galan, who disappeared inside. Hamma looked at Morgan. "Not going in?"

"Quiet," he replied, holding up his hand. He saw Artur's smile slip as he peered up at Galan's hooded face, but couldn't hear the words. "Come on."

"Where are you going?" Hamma asked, grabbing Morgan's forearm as he walked away.

"To the rear of the tent," he replied.

"Eavesdropping? I'm not doing that to Artur," Hamma said, tightening his grip. Morgan grabbed Hamma's wrist and twisted it.

"I'm not interested in what Artur says," he snapped as Hamma let go of him with a sharp intake of breath. "I don't trust Galan."

The men stared at each other. Morgan sized him up, and reckoned he'd take Hamma in a fight, though the noise would alert too many.

"Fine," Hamma breathed, "I don't like the look of him either."

Morgan ducked and crept along the side of the tent, the voices growing louder inside.

"... Huel told me himself, Galan. Follow the Saxons at a safe distance, attack from the rear when they charge. Has that changed?"

"Yes. Delay the charge. He wants the Saxons engaged and committed before you attack."

Morgan heard a hand slam against wood.

"Do you realize how many they number?" Artur grated. "The delay will cost thousands of Briton lives."

"Saxon, too." Galan replied. Morgan's stomach churned. He'd fought his entire life and knew death to be a part of life. His blood sang when he engaged in battle, but he prayed to the Gods before and after. Morgan understood what it meant to take a life. To Galan, death seemed to hold no meaning.

"I won't stand by and watch—"

"It's necessary, Artur. Huel doesn't mean to win a simple battle. He aims to purge Britannia of the Saxon scourge, and this is the only way. The Gods revealed it to him, and I witnessed it. Do you defy them?"

"No." Artur whispered.

"Good. Stay camped here through the night, then move to Badon Hill at midday. When the Saxons attack, wait until we engage them at the walls. Then charge."

"As my war-chief commands."

"If all comes to pass, we'll meet again, Artur. I wish you well."

Morgan hurried to the front of the tent and reached it as Galan exited. Hamma nodded.

"I'll escort you to your horses."

Morgan grabbed Galan's arm and let the sentry move ahead.

"Delay the charge?" He seethed. "Get fucked, druid."

"Huel's orders," Galan said with calm authority. "It's—"

"If you tell me it's the only way one more fucking time, I *will* kill you." Morgan said, allowing Galan to pull out of his grip.

"I hope not," the druid replied, following Hamma's path.

Morgan watched him, his fingers finding their way to the pommel of his sword.

"Gods damn you, the Saxons and all the fucking futures," he growled before stomping after Galan.

***

Dawn broke across the horizon, turning the black night grey.

"Do you require rest?" Galan asked. Morgan swayed in his seat as the horses moved at a steady canter. His body urged him to sleep, but hunger gnawed at him too. And the ever present uncertainty concerning the druid. Questions plagued him: what did Galan, a Fae, seek? What made it important for such a creature that the Britons succeeded? The nagging queries spiked his temper, and even glancing at the druid, sitting in silence on his mount, caused his blood to boil.

"How many times do I say yes?" Morgan grumbled. They'd taken a different route on their return, wary of Saxon outriders, and Badon Hill lay some two hours away still. To his surprise, Galan laughed.

"I don't view the future beat for beat. Just the important moments. Time is like a stream; throw a pebble in it, and the flow of water is unaltered. Throw a boulder, that's a different matter. The current will take another path. These are the diverging moments I see." He held up a hand and brought his horse to a halt. "I sense death. Recent and nearby."

Morgan blinked as he gazed around, his mind slow and unresponsive. Galan turned his horse and shot off into a gallop. Morgan followed.

A hundred paces to the right, he saw Galan dismount in the gloom, and he remembered. This had been the place Morgan fought off his pursuers the previous morning. The druid moved between the dead Saxons, shaking his head at the sight of the one with the sliced opened face and throat. He took one glance at the scout with the arrow protruding from his forehead and walked to the tangle of horses. Galan stooped and dragged a corpse from the pile.

"This one will do, I suppose," he said, pulling his hood back.

"For what?" Morgan asked, peering down at the body. If it wasn't for his limbs pointing in odd directions, the Saxon appeared asleep.

"We need numbers and locations of the Saxons," Galan murmured, his crimson eyes glowing in the gloom.

"I told you, they outnumber us five to one."

"That army, yes. I need to understand more, as do you." He lowered his voice, almost as if he spoke to himself. "How many I'll need."

"So, you can talk to dead Saxons now?" Morgan asked with a scowl.

"Not just Saxons," Galan replied, closing his eyes. "If the deceased souls are still close. Otherwise, it gets tricky."

Morgan leaped back and unsheathed his sword as Galan removed a curved dagger from his cloak. The druid ignored him, instead approaching his horse with a hand outstretched. The animal nuzzled his palm with a whinny.

"I'm sorry," Galan whispered, and ran the dagger across its throat.

The horse collapsed with a screech, flailing its limbs.

"You *are* mad," Morgan muttered as he gripped his sword in both hands. He glanced down with a cry. Green mist swirled around his feet, like it oozed from beneath the soil. Morgan shivered, his bladder on the verge of loosening.

Galan approached the dead Saxon, muttering words that caused sweat to bead on Morgan's face despite the chill.

A scream erupted from the Saxon, a curdling cry. Morgan dropped his sword with a clang and fell to his knees. He wanted to look away as the corpse opened its eyes, its mouth wide as it cried out in death, but he couldn't tear his gaze away.

"Answer me," Galan said, his voice solid as stone and full of command. Morgan's brain screamed for him to talk, even though the druid aimed the directive elsewhere.

"I shall," the corpse screamed in anguish, "ask your questions, then free me. I beg you."

"The army marching on Badon Hill. How many?"

"Ten thousand," the Saxon snarled.

"And further to the east?"

"The same number, with more set to sail across the sea after Wintertide."

Galan glanced at Morgan, his blood red stare penetrating his soul. "Twenty-thousand Saxons in Britannia, with more to follow. You see what stands in our way?"

"Release me!" The corpse cried.

It wailed, and Morgan jammed his eyes shut and covered his ears as the sound drove daggers into his brain. He opened his mouth to add his own agony to the scream, but the sound cut off. Morgan looked around. The mist had vanished. Galan stood with his back turned, gazing off towards the east. Morgan climbed to his feet, retrieved his sword and approached. Murder in his eyes.

"Ah," Galan whispered. "The time comes."

The druid half-turned as Morgan struck him on the side of his head with the pommel of his sword. Galan collapsed onto his back; red eyes filled with pain as he stared up at Morgan. The dead Saxon lay next to him, unmoving.

"What black magic is this, Fae?" Morgan bit out, spinning the sword in his hands and pointing the end at Galan. "Does Huel know?"

"Necromancy," Galan replied with a wince. "And yes, he does. Your cousin understands the stakes."

"Liar." Morgan screamed. His voice echoed across the grey hills.

"I've only ever told you the truth, Morgan."

"Why do you care what happens to the Britons? Why not flee to

Celta? Fuck the rest of us."

Galan laughed. He touched the back of his head. Black blood smeared his fingers.

"I'm not a druid. They are capable of limited magic, skills that pale to those I possess. Though more than the Saxons. If the invaders succeed, magic leaves this world. Forever. Your folk are the last of the humans that walked alongside my kin, and the druids preserve it in a way. Without the Britons, I'll fade and wither. I'm the last of my kind, but I intend on surviving, and I'll see magic reborn in these lands."

Morgan glared at Galan. He wanted to shout liar, but his words rang true. He'd thought the Fae mad, and perhaps that remained the case, but he'd witnessed his Necromancy. Galan had his own goals, but the Britons would benefit.

Morgan glanced at the dead Saxon. No matter what Galan said, no matter the Britons' benefit, the Necromancer drew on pure evil. *What becomes of us if we use such black arts to defeat the Saxons?*

Morgan hefted his sword and tightened its grip.

"So why not kill me? If it's so important you succeed, why not remove me as a threat?"

"I've seen futures where I have." Galan said, his brutal honesty shocking Morgan. "At various stages, too. It always ends in disaster. Sometimes I die before this point, other times during the battle of Badon Hill and more times still in what comes after. Many of the futures diverge here. My future, and the path of the Britons, hangs on your choice. I cannot defend myself, or attack. You must decide."

Morgan stared down at him. Tales of the Fae flooded his mind;

untrustworthy and filled with malice, stories he remembered from childhood of them leading humans astray to suit their own designs. The screams of the dead Saxon, reanimated, rang in his ears; the anguish in those cries shook his spine and caused his stomach to cramp. Morgan studied Galan; his colourless hair and skin, the skeleton beneath almost tearing through. Those crimson eyes.

And yet…

"If a time comes where you're tempted to act against Galan, remember me and these words: He's our future. Please."

Huel. He knew. He reckoned it necessary.

If Galan told the truth.

Morgan gripped the handle of his sword in two hands, and raised it above his head, blade pointing downwards. With a cry, filled with frustration and impotent rage, he thrust with all his might.

The point drove through the dead Saxon's chest.

Galan blinked up at him, the whisper of a smile on his face.

"Get on my horse. We ride together. Don't speak to me for the rest of our journey." Morgan breathed.

The Necromancer climbed to his feet. He stared at Morgan and opened his mouth then thought better of it and moved away, pulling up his hood.

Morgan dropped to his knees and beat the ground with his fists. Spent, he fell forwards and glanced at his sword, pinning the Saxon to the floor. The blade vibrated. Morgan grew still and listened. He felt the earth vibrate as the faint sounds of horns and the rattle of metal reached him.

The Saxons approached from the east and marched on Badon Hill.

***

Galan told the truth. As they raced into the hillfort, the gates slammed shut behind them, Morgan tracked down Huel and revealed the druid's Necromancy.

"I know," Huel sighed, his craggy face showing signs of weariness and regret, "it's necessary."

"Fuck Galan, fuck you and fuck necessity," Morgan growled. He stalked away as the Necromancer watched, in search of boiling water, ale and food.

The Saxons would arrive before nightfall and, if their usual habits played out, would attack under the moonlight. His stomach full and skin clean, Morgan rested and fell into a fitful sleep. He dreamed of the shoreline; the sea filled with Saxon longboats as far as his eye could see. Galan stood alongside him and they watched Briton villages burnt, their men slaughtered, the women and children in chains. Trees withered and the green grass turned black.

"This is what we fight to avoid," the Necromancer whispered.

Morgan woke, the words fresh in his mind, the images vivid. Saxon horns blared and Briton alarms answered. He dressed with speed, pulling his padded tunic over the chain mail protecting his body. A helmet followed before Morgan grabbed his sword and shield and left for the ramparts.

***

"Well met Morgan," Kai said, staring over Badon Hill's wooden battlements. His breath fogged the chill air as Saxons poured over the distant hills, the torches they carried illuminating the plains better than the pale moonlight. Archers stood a few paces back, facing the invaders.

"Aye," Morgan said, and spat over the wall. His heart rate increased at the sight of the heathen invaders. *Gods damn them,* he thought, *they won't rest while a single Briton draws breath.*

"Cousin!"

Morgan glanced to his side. Further along the battlements, flanked by Galan and his herald, stood Huel. The war-chief, dressed in similar attire to Morgan and held twin hand axes.

"Huel," Morgan replied, nodding across to him. He ignored Galan, though felt his eyes on him from the depths of his hood.

"A fine night to kill Saxons," the war-chief replied with a laugh. He pointed with an axe toward the approaching army. "They appear eager for it."

Morgan studied the invaders. Their ragged front lines came to a halt around four hundred paces from Badon Hills' walls. They faced a gentle incline, but that gave the Britons an advantage—fighting downwards trumped battling upwards any day. The Saxons mustered at the foot of the hill, their ranks swelling as more joined them. Chants drifted towards Badon, along with the clang of swords and armour.

"Ever witnessed ten thousand men in one place?" Kai asked, leaning on his spear.

Morgan gazed out. Saxons filled his vision. He could smell their eagerness and stale sweat.

"No," Morgan replied. "How are we to withstand this?"

"Through me."

Morgan spun to find Galan stood at his side. The Necromancer placed a hand on Morgan's forearm, black fingernails digging into his skin.

"Don't touch me, Fae," Morgan snarled, but kept his voice low.

"Stay within sight of me when the fighting begins," Galan said, his voice filled with command again. "For Britannia."

Morgan pulled his arm away as Huel's herald blew two short blasts on his horn. The archers stepped forwards. Morgan and Kai retreated, to give the bowmen room to work.

"Any moment now," Kai muttered. He gripped Morgan's shoulder. "Gods favour you."

"You too," he replied, mimicking the gesture. Morgan raised a hand to Huel, who returned the salute. Soldiers flooded onto the walls, bolstering their numbers against Saxon ladders that would seek purchase against them. More Britons waited behind the gates, barricading them further but ready to push into the fray and break the Saxon press. Two thousand Britons, ready to defend Badon Hill to the bitter end.

Ten thousand voices roared at the bottom of the hill. The Saxons screamed at the heavens, and urged their fellow fighters on, steeling their nerves before the imminent charge. The Britons answered in kind. Morgan's blood ran hot; he wished he could charge them alone, lay the Saxons to waste. Battle fury often took him, and he could feel the desire to fight building in him.

Horns erupted above the din, and the Saxons charged, screaming as they raced uphill. At three hundred paces, Huel's herald blew a short blast.

The archers nocked arrows and raised their bows.

The Saxons reached two hundred paces. Morgan bared his teeth.

At one hundred paces, the herald signalled for the archers to attack. Bowstrings twanged as they fired into the charging mass of bodies. The Saxon frontline collapsed, the invaders behind stumbling over their fallen comrades. The Britons fired again and more joined them; screams of agony joined the battle cries. Morgan's head swam as blood, shit and piss filled the air. In the corner of his eye, he saw Galan sway and remembered his words from earlier that day.

"I sense death."

An archer fell into Morgan, and more dropped around him. He threw the already dead body off him and crouched under his shield. Arrows filled the skies as the Saxons replied to the Britons volley.

"Return fire, damn you!" Morgan cried as missiles thudded into his shield as a ladder slammed against the wall. Kai scrambled to his feet and flung his shoulder against the battlement, shoving the ladder backwards.

Morgan yelled as Kai's head jolted. His friend turned, a lazy grin on his face and an arrow protruding from his eye, a crimson tear trailing down his cheek and into his blonde beard. A fluke shot that caught him through his eye guard. Kai toppled, dead, as the Briton archers fired back. Morgan crawled to his friend and took his hand.

"Vengeance on the Saxons, this I swear."

Screams of men in their death throes filled the night. Morgan glanced over towards Huel. He stood with a shield over his head, surveying the scenes beyond the walls. Galan sat with his head in his hands, slumped against the battlement. Morgan climbed to his feet and stared out as the Briton archers attacked. Saxons climbed over scores of dead but still surged forwards as they lifted ladders from the floors under a hail of arrows. Corpses piled against the base of Badon Hill's fort as the Briton archers leaned over the walls and fired downwards.

The moon watched from above as death filled the air.

The ramparts rattled as ladders slammed into them, quicker than the defenders could push them away. Morgan unsheathed his sword and leaped forward as a Saxon head cleared the battlement. He swung with a snarl, decapitating the invader and kicking the ladder away.

"Let them come!" He roared, the blood from his blade running over his fist. Morgan felt Galan watching him once more and snarled, throwing himself at another ladder.

As more Saxons crested the walls, Huel's herald blew three quick blasts on his horn. The archers swiveled and fired towards the Saxons milling at the gates. The fighters waiting behind them flung them open and charged out, a sudden surge of violence that caught the attackers unaware.

Morgan laughed as he plunged his blade into a Saxon who almost left his ladder, swinging again and severing his arms. The man toppled and collided with the attackers behind him, sending them back into the masses below. He heard the clang of iron and looked to see Huel engaged with two Saxons. The massive war-chief danced between them, faster than his size should allow. Blood spilled in his wake as he dispatched the men.

Another horn blast, and the archers fired into the crowd again as the Britons at the gates disengaged with the Saxons, retreating behind the walls to safety.

Morgan gazed out at the throng milling below him, listened to the injured and dying screaming their last cries. The battle had raged for less than an hour, and he reckoned over a thousand Saxons lay dead at the doors of Badon Hill.

***

Morgan's sword hung heavy in his blood slicked hand. Gore crusted his forearms and his heart thundered in his ears. The Britons stayed resolute, but still the Saxons came. Twice the defenders had pushed through the gates to relieve the press, but now the pile of corpses pressed them in. Morgan tripped as he stepped back. Dead littered the ramparts walls; Kai and other defenders buried beneath the Saxons.

"Huel!" He cried. "We can't hold for much longer. We need Artur."

As the war-chief looked his way, a Saxon cleared the wall. He ran at Huel, who threw up an axe too late. The Saxon's sword slid down his forearm and bit into his shoulder. Huel snarled and attacked with his spare axe, the metal tearing the Saxon's throat open. Another invader cleared the wall, spear in hand, and charged. Morgan raced towards them, helpless as the Saxon thrust his weapon into Huel's side.

The war-chief dropped to his knees and grabbed the shaft, pulling it further into himself and his killer within reach. He hacked with his axe, chopping the Saxon's leg at the knee. The invader collapsed to the ground, and Huel hacked again, finishing the job.

"Cousin," Morgan cried, kneeling before him. He gripped the back of his neck and touched his forehead against Huel's.

"Listen," the dying war-chief breathed, "the earth groans."

Cries of confusion echoed from beyond the hill fort's walls. The ground shook as a thousand horses charged across the rolling hills. Morgan glanced at Galan, who peered over the walls, arms stretched wide.

Artur and his men raced to join the fray.

"We're saved!" Morgan said, turning back to Huel. Dead eyes looked back. Tears streaming down his face, Morgan laid his cousin to the ground. "Fuck the Saxons. Heathen scum! They'll pay. They'll fucking pay!"

A resounding crunch tore through the night. Galloping horses collided into flesh and bone as hooves trampled Saxons into the blood-soaked grass. Morgan crawled to the walls and pulled himself up. Artur's cavalry cut a swathe through the Saxons as Badon Hill's gate flung open, Britons pouring out to engage the attackers. Morgan's spirit urged him to join them, to spend his fury and grief on every Saxon he could.

"The anvil and the hammer," Galan called, not looking his way. "Yes, I believe the hour approaches."

"Why did you ask me to stay within sight of you?" Morgan asked. In the corner of his eye, he thought he saw a familiar green mist creep across the battlefield.

"I shall reveal all," Galan said, turning to him. A sudden wind swirled and pushed the Necromancer's hood back. His crimson eyes glowed in the dark. "You seek revenge on the Saxons?"

"Yes."

"Good. You shall have it."

It wasn't his imagination. Green mist swirled among the corpses. Galan threw his head back and shouted incantations that set Morgan's teeth on edge.

"No," he cried, too late. He understood what the Necromancer attempted.

Morgan took a step forward and raised his sword.

Pain exploded in his chest. Morgan clutched at his breast, his sword dropping with a clatter. He couldn't breathe. The agony doubled, and he fell to his knees, gasping for breath.

Morgan's vision dimmed, and time slowed.

"What—" He croaked, but Galan's voice echoed through his mind.

"I've stopped your heart but don't worry, I promised you revenge. You're needed, after all. I often pondered why you, the one who could have stopped this, had to remain alive. Then I realized. Your lust for battle, the grief of your fallen friends and kin. Your hatred of the Saxons. Of me. These emotions will drive your new army forwards. A plague of death upon the Saxons, here and overseas. You'll make me proud."

Morgan sagged forwards. A massive weight pressed against his back and chest. Around him, the dead climbed to their feet. Huel, Kai, Britons and Saxons. As Morgan died, his army raised their weapons and welcomed their new leader with screams that thundered through Badon Hill.

***

The undead army screamed at the heavens, unleashing their grief and reliving the pain of their deaths. Fury coloured their cries; a deep rage drove them. Anger at the Saxon hordes that stood in their way. A seething animosity from being pulled back from the sweet oblivion of the afterlife.

At their head stood the undead named Morgan, a vessel for their purpose.

The Saxons melted against the undead's charge. Some dropped their weapons, unmanned, and wept as their former comrades and enemies began their violent frenzy. Others gathered what remained of their courage and fought back.

The Saxons fell, and Galan watched. As they died, they joined the undead army, and Morgan drove them on. They wouldn't rest while a single Saxon breathed on Britannia's green lands.

***

Galan moved through the battlefield. Apart from the dead horses and blood-soaked ground, it appeared peaceful enough. The mist cleared, and so had the undead army. It charged the Saxons, devouring any living heathen in its path, the fallen joining its ranks.

After living for so long, Galan had moved past pride but felt a whisper of satisfaction at this feat. He'd tied the undead army to his will, which he'd fused inside Morgan, tying it with the Britons lust for revenge and hatred of the Saxons. They would chase the invaders from these shores and use their boats to chase them overseas to their homelands. When the last Saxon died, the undead army would crumble into dust.

The Saxons would die, and Galan's magic, the essential element that kept him alive, would survive. The Necromancer knew death and wasn't ready to join it yet. If ever. *What would your Aileth think of this?* A voice whispered in his mind, but he dismissed it. He knew his old love wouldn't approve.

Galan scanned the horizon and saw his quarry. The blonde-haired man in the bloodied armour saw him and waited.

"Artur. I said we'd meet again," Galan said.

"Druid," Artur replied with a wary nod. "The dead rising. Fighting with us against the Saxons. Your doing? It is evil."

Galan inclined his head. "Good, evil? We're above such petty morals. The Gods will demand it Artur, I acted as a vessel. They look to you now, as do the Britons. With Huel dead and all his kin."

Artur glanced around. "There are other clan-chiefs."

"Aye," Galan replied, "but our new Britannia deserves a King."

RETRIBUTION

I try to count the years since my birth, but fail.

How the world has changed. My memory fogs when I think of the centuries before Aileth, when the Elves ruled and the humans crept from the dark corners of the earth. I cannot recall her face, but the moments I spent with her live in my heart, and the actions I performed to keep her love have left their mark on my soul.

Twelve-hundred years have elapsed since Badon Hill, my last genuine act of Necromancy. With the Saxons defeated, and Artur crowned King of the Britons, my influence faded and I returned to solitude, safe in the knowledge magic would remain in the world. But I had no purpose. I had become God, granted life and stole it. Uncovered the secrets of death but I, Galan, the omega of my kind, wasted away. Fated to occupy an eternal, empty existence.

I renounced my Necromancy, it's what Aileth would have wanted. And so, I watched the years pass and the Britons prosper. Generations lived and died while I blinked. Wars waged and battles won while I slept.

I live alone in a grand mansion atop a hillside, overlooking the sweeping, barren moors. I built it myself, and savor its solitude. In truth, I designed it too large; most of the rooms are empty save for dust and regret. The location reminds me of Badon, or my castle that overlooked Portcastle, the place where I sank into the depths of true Necromancy, and of the hill where I resurrected Aileth, then returned her to the afterlife. All those centuries ago. Perhaps I'm drawn to such places because of her. I seldom leave, and when I do, I disguise myself with an Elven glamour. My kind, the Fae as the humans would say, have faded into the myths of time, and I prefer it that way. A town lies close to my home, Swansea they call it, and the people there whisper of my abode, and curse it as haunted.

They're correct. For I, Galan, drift alone through its long corridors and dusty rooms. Gazing at its barren walls by candlelight. I'm a specter of an era forgotten, and a love lost.

***

What, you might ask, does an immortal Elf, a powerful Necromancer, do? Write, read, and paint. I record my memories before they fade to dust, and I devour works from the humans; I've grown fond of them. Their inventiveness amuses me. They remind me of Elven children; tempestuous and arrogant, but full of wonder. Where we Elves temper these characteristics with age, the mortals don't—no doubt their short spans light a fire in their souls.

Painting, yes. That is my passion. I touch paint to the canvas and lose myself in the craft. Days will trundle by before I emerge from my fugue state, amazed at the images my memories have conjured: forests, mountains and cities of my past. Faces I have trouble putting a name to. This gave me an idea.

Aileth.

Her face escapes me, though I reckon some five-thousand years have blown by since I last saw it. My love for her engraves itself in my bones. I talk aloud at strange times, always to my Aileth. I wonder if I'm mad, but dismiss the notion. Madness assailed me when I began my journey to Necromancy, and it never left.

Tonight, like every night, she shall be my muse. In front of my easel, I'll lose myself in my art. Her memories will flood my mind, and I'll pour them onto the canvas.

Aileth, I'll see your face once more. I promise.

***

Are you in there, my love? In my soul? You inhabit my thoughts. Your kiss haunts my lips, and the memory of your touch lingers on my skin. How I wish for a mortal life, like yours. To die and live with you ever-after.

How I regret my actions.

Do you watch me from beyond and look aside in disgust at what I've become? Or is it pity? Save it. I don't deserve your sympathy.

***

Where do I begin? I sit with my brush against the canvas and hesitate. I'm thinking too much. My art comes easy when the colours and the pictures locked in mind flow through me, but now I force it. Try to wield my memories and order them on to the canvas.

I lower the brush and breathe. Closing my eyes, I picture our cottage. How faded, its beauty washed out at the edges. But it's there. I see myself; bright and untarnished from my blackened soul, sitting and watching the sunrise over the hill on the horizon. I smell lavender. Turning, my breath catches in my throat.

Aileth.

She looks down at me, a smile on her freckled face. Wide brown eyes shine with devotion. Aileth sits beside me and lays her head on my shoulder.

I love you; she murmurs.

Forever, I whisper.

The easel is blank, but the memory is strong. Vivid. I dip my brush and start my work, frowning as I still detect lavender on the air, but dismiss it as a figment of my imagination.

I'm aware of my painting, but it's as if I'm not creating it. More like the brush is stripping away the canvas' blankness and Aileth's face is underneath. It's always lived there, waiting for me to uncover it.

I see her emerge in exquisite detail. The Aileth of her youth, when we first fell in love. Her eyes bore into mine as I paint around them, and tears stream down my cheeks, wetting my tongue. It's her. How could I have forgotten such beauty?

As the oil dries, I fall to my knees before her.

"I'm sorry," I whisper, gripping the sides of the canvas in my hands. "For what I've done. I'm not the man you loved, but I wish I were."

She's before me, and I gaze up at her image as the hours trickle by, overcome with weariness. Fatigue I haven't felt since I performed powerful Necromancy.

"I love you, my Aileth," I murmur, and press my lips against hers. They taste of lavender and salty tears.

I shift the easel and point it towards my bed. Climbing in it, I watch her face until slumber welcomes me.

***

"Galan."

The voice whispers to me as I sleep. I often hear words murmured in mind, ghosts of the past torment me in my rest. My eyes remain closed, but my skin is chilled. The flames crackle and pop in the fireplace, though its warmth is muted. I smell lavender on the air, and understanding hits me.

"Aileth?" I say, my throat hoarse. Propping myself up on my elbows, I look towards her portrait. My love stands beside it, as if ripped from the image and made whole. She appears more alive than anything else in the room; vibrant and almost too palpable. "Am I dreaming?"

I swing my legs onto the floor, hoping the touch of my toes against the wooden boards will ground me. Aileth watches, her face stern but beautiful. My cheeks are wet, and I raise my fingers to them and feel

82

fresh tears.

"You're asleep, though this is real," Aileth says. She glides closer to me, and I see her feet hovering. "As much as you attempt to hide from your magic, Necromancy runs through your veins."

Her mouth twists as she says the word, and shame threatens to devour me.

"I used it to create your portrait?" I ask. My thoughts come slowly, as if a fog settles on my senses. "Yes. It's no ordinary painting."

Aileth kneels and stares into my eyes. I gaze back, longing to discover some sign of her old love for me. It's there, deep inside.

There's a ghost of a smile on her lips. "Galan, nothing you do is ordinary."

"I summoned you," I say. My eyes widen. "That means—"

Aileth raises a hand to my cheek. It doesn't, can't, touch me, but I turn my head into it.

"I've always remained close," she whispers, and my black heart soars. "Watching you. I've witnessed your struggle, and the terrible acts you've inflicted on the world. Tell me, why did you act at Badon Hill? Why not let the future proceed and allow magic to fail?"

"In those first years, I told myself I did it to preserve something beautiful. Using my corrupt soul for the greater good." I close my eyes, there's no point lying to her. "But I did it for self-preservation. I didn't want to fade away, and I hoped that I'd discover a way to reunite with you. If the magic died, I feared I'd lose that chance."

She nods, already knowing the truth. "Why did you stop searching?"

"Because I don't deserve a happy fate. I read the stories the humans write. Every tale has a hero. A savior who achieves their heart's desire. I'm a villain, Aileth; killed too many to recall, fractured my soul beyond repair. I don't deserve you, my love."

"I still remember you as you were," she murmurs, "in the world's youth. Open your spirit, Galan. Think of all those you've hurt. Honour them as you have with me. This is your task."

Aileth fads away. I reach out for her, my fingers clutch as her form, but it's like catching smoke.

The warmth of the fire returns to the room as I curl into a ball and weep until morning's light creeps through the curtains.

***

Aileth's portrait watches me from above the fireplace. I hung it there after she visited me. I've slept three times following that night and she hasn't appeared, though I feel a pregnant expectation in the air.

Her words intrigue me and frighten me in equal measure. *Think of all those you've hurt. Honour them as you have with me. This is your task.* Have I not tortured myself over my deeds? Do my thoughts not dwell on the souls I've used for my perverse magic? Ah, but there is a difference. Reverence. Atonement. I smile at Aileth's image, as perfect as life itself, and it gazes back.

I understand what I must do.

***

"There's a cart outside, shopkeeper," I say, my glamour intact. The local artisan's jaw droops as he reads the parchment with my order. I

84

glance around as he considers the list. I can't help but smile, as I catch my appearance in a mirror. I'm dressed in the human's current fashion; a black suit, tie and cloak with a top hat and cane. They amuse me with their changing ways, and I must admit to missing living amongst them. Closing my eyes, I listen for the cries and bustle of Swansea's streets; the scents of cooked meat and ale in the air from the nearby taverns.

"You'll empty my shop!" The man, Rodri, squeals. Blinking, I suppress a chuckle. Sweat runs down the mousey looking fellow's forehead and I can't decide if it's his impending workload that bothers him, or the sheer strangeness of my request.

"Money isn't an issue," I say with a smile.

"I don't mean offence, Sir," Rodri replies, hands on hips. "It's just that, what will I have to sell if you buy everything?"

I laugh and wrap an arm around his shoulders, steering him towards his workshop. "My friend, you won't *need* to work for quite some time after today! Do we have a deal?"

Rodri glances at the parchment again. "This is enough material to create your own gallery. Why do you require so much?"

I scan the artisan's workshop. It's full of canvas', oils, brushes and easels. Everything I desire.

"Rodri, you've answered your own question," I say, turning to him and extending my hand. "Art is my passion, and I aim to produce a collection that speaks to the soul."

He shakes my hand with a sullen expression. "I'll load the cart."

"Cheer up, my good man," I say, pulling a heavy coin pouch from my cloak, "you've earned yourself a small fortune."

***

Aileth's portrait had to come first. My obsession for her led me down the path of Necromancy, and all my sins emerge from that black pit. Next, I paint Morgan, the Briton. Another face almost forgotten, a different soul I corrupted. A steadfast man, I used him to create my undead army that swept the Saxons from the face of the earth. I let my mind drift to the moment where the futures converged, when the warrior stood over me, sword above his head. The point he made his choice and created a new fate for us all. The hatred in his eyes haunts my memories, and I recreate his animosity on the canvas.

Then, there's Avelene, the woman who almost turned me from my evil path. A soul I thought I loved, as I did Aileth, only to realize my abuse of her too late. I'd transferred my obsession on to her and let it blind me. When I looked at Avelene, my mind revealed Aileth, and my eyes ignored the effect my festering core had on her. She didn't deserve her fate. I create her image as it should be, and not the one I projected.

More follow. The unfortunate humans of Portcastle I performed experiments on. Artur, King of the Britons, who suffered betrayal from his own kin and died alone. Faces appear with no names attached to them, but I delve into my memories and remember their souls. I lose myself in the act. Brushes drop from my blistered hands as I paint and I leave them there, discarded, and reach for fresh ones. I do not eat or sleep, the work only pauses when I refill my oils or lift a new canvas to the easel.

A frenzy grips me. The images flow from inside, and I realize my Necromancy is its source. I refuse to open myself to it, but it controls the illustrations and I understand why. Each time I performed my foul magic, my soul fractured, the corrupt presence inside me leaching into the essence of those I sacrificed. They've existed within me for centuries, trapped. When I spread their faces across the canvas, I'm releasing them. Expunging them from my withered soul.

Even though I go without nourishment or rest, I feel stronger than I have in aeons. My work heals me, but I don't want to ponder that. My soul doesn't deserve to mend.

Still, I work and create. My study fills with portraits, and soon I line the corridors with them. Through it all, Aileth watches from above the fireplace.

***

I touch my brush to the canvas with a trembling hand. Closing my eyes, I wait for the images to assail my thoughts. Nothing comes. I'm empty at last.

Getting to my feet, I gaze around my study. Eyes stare back. Everywhere, from every angle. Colours of blue, black, brown and green filled with anger, hatred, pity and regret.

"What now?" I ask Aileth's portrait. She doesn't answer. My limbs shake, and hunger gnaws at my stomach. I feel stretched, and the room spins as I wretch, but there's nothing inside me to vomit. Turning, I flee from the study. I don't know where I'm heading to, but I stagger past the faces haunting the corridors. There's a double-hinged window ahead of me, looking out onto the moors beyond. I lurch towards it, the daylight beckons me, the sunlight kisses my pale skin. It's too far. My strength flees me and I drop to my knees and crawl. Fingernails dig into the dust-bitten carpets as I inch closer to my goal, but I succumb and flop to the floor. Darkness takes me.

***

"Galan, wake up my love."

"Aileth, I'm spent." My voice is dry, cracking parchment, and my throat prickles as if I've drunk shards of glass.

"Nonsense," she replies. "Galan never finishes until the task's done. Isn't that what set you on this path?"

I crane my neck. Aileth stands with her hands-on hips like she did when she'd find me distracted with an experiment or a fresh potion designed to extend her lifespan, instead of skinning a deer all those years ago.

"Perhaps I've learned the error of my ways," I reply with a grimace as I roll onto my back. Night has replaced day.

"I think you may have," she replies. "Though this time, you must complete your task. Galan heed my words. Necromancy is evil, but the act of creation is healing you. It doesn't wash away what you've done. Opening yourself to it once more doesn't mean you must use it, either. Do you understand?"

I nod. "I'm afraid."

"We all are by the end." Aileth replies as she fades.

"I love you," I say.

"I know," she whispers. "Eat. Rest. You need your strength for what comes next."

Aileth disappears into the gloom. Lavender fills my nostrils.

***

After eating, I fell into a sleep filled with nightmares, though I knew each scenario well. No demons chase me, and I don't plummet from the skies towards a waiting death. I experience all the moments I interacted with the faces I painted; re-live their deaths, understand my victim's fear and helplessness. I awake before dawn, drape a blanket around my thin shoulders and depart my home for the moors. The crisp air feels satisfying in my lungs. Sitting by a lone tree that I planted when I first discovered this place, I watch the sunrise, and feel its warmth caress my skin and chase away the chill. Its beauty strikes me as it used to, back when Aileth and I would stay awake all night just to see the first morning light together. I smile at the naïve romance of it and revel in my memories as the horizon merges with the orange glow of the sunrise.

Before leaving, I retrieve an item buried amongst the roots of the oak. A small case that contains such pain and sorrow. I don't open the box, but I sense the putridness inside speak to me. My dagger, etched with evil runes of a language long-forgotten, yearns for use. Necromancy is an insatiable energy, and the blade hasn't tasted blood in centuries.

Carrying it into the house, I leave it on a stand in the centre of my study and prepare for my next task. I arrange all the portraits so they standalone; some I hang, others I position on chairs and tables or prop them against the walls. They fill my study and line the corridors to the entry hall where I now wait for nightfall. Darkness suits my business

89

better than the light.

I've dressed in my finest clothes after washing and combing my lengthy, unruly hair. The shadows that surrounded the black pits of my eyes retreated as my painting soothed my soul, and I gazed long at my reflection. At the Galan, I used to be.

My hour approaches. I could run. Leave this place and start somewhere new. Immerse myself in an unusual city and a fresh life. Bury my dagger again, or turn it on myself and join the damned Elven spirits trapped in between existence and the human afterlife. I'd thought about it often, but could never bring myself to do it.

I can't flee. My crimes mount higher than the tallest mountain and have gone unanswered. I desire peace, and for that, I must remain and see this task through. Did some part of me know where my path would lead when my painting began? I like to think that's the case, and this isn't happy fortune. I want to believe I sought retribution.

"Galan," I say, my voice bouncing around the entry hall, "you can do this. Be brave."

I suck in a breath that fills my lungs to bursting and ease it out. As I do, I close my eyes and draw my senses inwards. Years ago, I cut myself off from my Necromancy, but it never disappeared. It can't. What's learned stays remembered, and this foul magic is unshakeable. Instead, I erected mental barriers and tended to them with vigilance.

Now, I destroy them.

As they crumble, black tendrils ooze from the dark corners of my brain and whisper with seduction. I feel life surrounding me; rats in the walls, mice scurrying underfoot, owls swooping for prey amongst the trees for miles around. An oily stain flows from my soul, and bile rises in my throat. My head spins as Necromancy flows through my veins once more. I don't embrace it, nor do I force it under control. Instead, I let it be. I exist with it and open my eyes.

The dead watch me.

In front of each painting stands the spirit the image belongs to. I walk forward, and they don't react. They peer at me, and I meet their eyes. As I move beyond them, they follow. I journey through the corridors of my home and the green-hued specters, all those I've killed and whose faces and souls I carried with me, trail in silence.

My pace is slow as I approach my study. An icy cold nips at me, and my breath fogs the air. Inside, more ghosts await me. Standing either side of the stand that holds my dagger is Morgan and Avelene, as it should be. The Briton warrior's eyes burn with a frigid hate, and pity fills my former lovers. Shame burns my cheeks and I stare beyond them, towards Aileth's portrait.

"She doesn't come?" I ask, halting before the dagger.

"Do you seek justice, Necromancer?" Morgan barks, his voice like chains dragged across coal.

"Yes," I whisper.

"Do you repent?" Avelene asks, her voice soft and somber.

"Yes," I reply.

"Kneel," Morgan commands.

I hesitate. "I thought it would be her."

"Kneel," Avelene intones.

Dropping to my knees, I keep my head bowed, and a tear falls from my eye. As it trickles down my cheek, lavender fills the air.

"Open the box, Galan," my eternal love says. She *is* here!

Aileth stands before me, smiling at me as she used to. Kneeling, I shuffle forwards and reveal my dagger. Its blade shines, the black magic that flows within it keeping it sharp. My love grips the handle and holds it to my throat. I feel the keen edge bite into my Adam's apple.

"I'm ready," I whisper.

Aileth nods. As she draws the knife across my skin, energy swells around me. The dead rush forwards as one and enter the blade. All save Aileth. Blood gushes on to my chest and I struggle for breath, but still the power builds.

I collapse on my side, life seeping from my wound, and my eyes bulge at the site beyond Aileth. A portal opens. It shouldn't happen. My kind don't travel there, doomed as we are to haunt the earth for eternity.

The afterlife is for the humans, but the specters call it for me.

As vision fades, the last breath rattles in my chest and I whisper: "I'm sorry."

My body dies, those final words on its lips, but my spirit lifts from the corpse. Aileth takes my hand and stares into my eyes.

"Galan, you have wronged so many. You come with me for judgement, from the one humans answer to. I don't know what will happen to you. I'm giving you the chance; stay here, if you will. Or journey with me, and trust in absolution."

I tear my gaze from Aileth, and glance at my dead body. At Galan,

Elf and Necromancer, last of his kind. I turn to the portal. White light shines through it. I take Aileth's other hand.

"Lead on, my love," I say, and kiss her cheek. "My time has come."

We step into the brightness, and though it blinds me, I feel at peace. I head into the unknown, and I welcome my fate. As long as it is with my beloved, but I understand that choice is neither mine, nor hers. I have sinned and spread darkness upon the world I now leave behind, but I seek my penance with open arms. My fingers tighten around Aileth's as the light consumes me.

My name is Galan, and my story is at an end. How would you judge me?

PROTECTOR OF THE PATH

Water, while essential, can be treacherous and yet it has always captured the imagination. The stories of spirits inhabiting the water exist throughout many cultures. They exist as cautionary tales by parents to keep their children safe from harm. These four stories are such tales.

DIANA BROWN

TIME AND TIDE

The marbled ray was following her again.

Meralah had all but memorized the pattern of spots on its back; it was definitely the same one. She trailed a delicate blue fingertip along the crystal wall as she walked; the groundfish adjusted its position so that the edge of its fin trailed along at the same spot on the other side of the barrier.

As if it wants to hold my hand.

She stopped walking and turned to look directly at her companion. The ray's body drifted away a little, pivoting to face her. Meralah stepped closer, her palm flat against the transparent wall, and studied the fish's eye-bulbs as though staring hard enough would make it possible for her to hear its thoughts.

It held her gaze for a brief eternity, then plunged gracefully into the meadow of Neptune grass that surrounded the Palace. Meralah stood alone, the Neptune grass rippling gently with the tides.

***

A thousand years earlier, she had been a Weaver, crafting patterned cloth and ornate rugs from the fibers of plants and animals. She had created new dyes and patterns, experimenting with her art to craft patterns different from anything else in the entire Crystal Palace of the Aegean, repeatedly earning discipline from the Palace Craftmaster.

"Do you think what you have done is new, or unique?" the Craftmaster had asked. "Endless generations have preceded you, created and eliminated possibilities until we found the pinnacle." There had followed a long lecture on why the shade of green already used, the pattern already in place was superior to any other, making any deviation from the established artisanship inferior and undesirable. Meralah had stood quietly, pretending to listen, then looked carefully through the entire Palace for a less stifling vocation, a Master with a bit less pride and a bit more curiosity.

What she found dismayed her more than the Craftmaster's lecture. Her people, she came to realize, were stagnant. The Crystal Palace bore few decorations; its "arts" were all practical. Metalsmiths crafted utensils and tools. Woodcrafters carved furniture and fittings. Craftsmen created the same things, in the same ways, as had been done for thousands of years, convinced that their art was at its zenith, and that any deviation was a deficit.

Once she realized it, she began to see it everywhere. The

complacency.

Immortality meant there were few children born. When nobody dies, there is no need to replenish the population. This, in turn, meant there was little importance placed on family structures. Without the need to care for families, there was little drive to maintain intimate relationships. Cocooned in their Crystal Place beneath the sea, threats were few and transitory.

In that safe, sheltered environment, her people had lost their heart.

Convinced of their own superiority, they had little interest in the people that populated the world outside their crystal walls. While they operated as a community for sustenance and defense, they had few emotional ties as individuals. Over time, their passions had become as muted as their art.

Meralah wondered if this was how nations and peoples faded into extinction. Then she wondered why she didn't know. The Halls of History contained what must be the history of the entire world. Emissaries regularly traded with sailors for books to add to the Great Library. The knowledge was there to find, if only she would seek it.

One hundred twenty-three years and four days after the Craftmaster's stern lecture, Meralah changed her vocation to Scholar.

She read voraciously. Never content to just absorb the information that was there, she compared endlessly, looking for the patterns that spanned all cultures. Three centuries of reading the world's history convinced her that The Complacency was a malaise. Two more centuries of study left her concerned that it might be a fatal one.

A decade later, she began to plot the populations of water-people on a great map of the world, exploring the decline of the river nymphs, merfolk, sirens, the rat-like Fir Darrig, alven, kappa, adaro, rusalka, and the Longhuang—all extinct or nearly so. The Curator thought it an excellent line of research, to understand the Lesser People of the Seas.

But why, Meralah wondered, *are they considered "lesser"?* She added the Crystal Palaces to the map.

"Ah!" the Curator exclaimed mildly when he noticed. "You've added…Oh, I see! Always looking for the larger pattern, aren't you, Meralah? A few more millennia, and you'll make an excellent Scholar—perhaps even a Curator!"

"Wise One…" Meralah opened cautiously. "I regret that this effort may be flawed."

"Flawed? In what way?"

"I am aware that other Palaces exist, but in the course of my study, I have located little information beyond their locations. In examining the flow around each Palace, I am starting from an unknown base. After all, such widely separated peoples may develop very differently."

"Nonsense." The Curator smiled indulgently. "They are nixies, just like us."

Meralah resisted the urge to roll her eyes. To point out that societies do evolve—well, perhaps not their own, but *elsewhere*. That the Crystal Palaces had operated as insular city-states for millennia, and perhaps not *every* nixie stronghold was as ossified as the Aegeans.

She took a deep breath, which she *hoped* sounded contemplative, and asked, "How do we know?"

"Come with me." The Curator walked out of the room without waiting for her acknowledgement.

She caught up with him at the base of the ramp to the Rotunda of Wisdom, the cloistered portion of the research library accessible only to senior Scholars.

"You've demonstrated competence and perspective, Meralah. I think you're ready to expand your studies."

The Curator spoke placidly, of course, but Meralah's pulse raced with intrigue. She followed so closely on his heels that she had to take care not to step on them.

The Rotunda of Wisdom, she was astonished to discover, had very few books. Two shelves stretched from floor to ceiling against the back wall. The rest of the room was occupied with furniture and gadgets.

No, she corrected herself. *Not gadgets. Artifacts.*

She pointed and stared and asked questions, but the Curator dismissed them with a placid gesture.

"They have all been studied. They are all documented. You may read about them as you wish."

He brought her to stand before a massive Looking Glass.

"This," he announced, "is the Great Mirror. It shows us fleeting glimpses of every Palace."

Meralah stared at the flickering images—nixies going about their business dressed exactly as she was, walking on carpets of the same colors and pattern.

"I—don't understand," she said at last. "We don't correspond or trade with them, but we…spy on them?"

"Leaping limpets, of course we don't *spy* on them," the Curator chuckled. "But the Mirror shows us that they are carrying on as normal, just as it shows them that we are in no distress. If we should see something odd in the Mirror, we would know that our cousins are in need of aid. It's a sort of…warning system. It allows us to support one another without interfering in anyone's serenity and solitude. And that, clever one, is how we know that they are still there, still nixies, just like us."

Meralah smiled, though her heart sank. The other Palaces she had glimpsed in the Mirror *were* just like this one. She couldn't help but wonder whether *any* of them would stir themselves from their routine to help a cousin in need. She took to watching the Mirror for hours at a time, but the view was always familiar.

***

The first few days, the ray had been a curiosity. Meralah had been entertained by the sight of it trailing her down the corridor, swimming along the other side of the crystal wall as she strode toward the Halls of History. Then she had begun to experiment. She stood in the side hall and watched as it ignored other passersby, drifting to the windowed wall only when Meralah appeared. Three times, she had tested it. Three times, it had ignored everyone else, appearing only for her. She began to wonder if it were some sort of sign.

Nixies are not religious by nature; immortality tends to negate belief in gods. But when you have eternity to study the world, you learn that everything has patterns: science, history, people. When something unusual happens, a nixie studies it to see where it fits. Especially *this* nixie. Meralah was a scholar; understanding the world's patterns was her vocation.

A day or two of research turned up multiple, competing sets of information. But across most of the sources, a few commonalities emerged. A ray, it seemed, was a symbol of readiness.

"Everything is now in place," read one source. "You are capable of moving forward," read two others. "Have faith in your abilities." "Trust your inner guidance." "Stay on course." "Move forward." "Don't' be distracted by foolishness." A ray, one source noted, was a Protector of the Path.

***

On the eleventh day, when Meralah arrived in the Rotunda, she found someone already watching the silent figures waver across the glass.

"I didn't mean to take your seat," Xenna said without taking her eyes off the mirror.

If she hadn't meant to take the seat, she wouldn't be sitting in it. This must be a polite way of offering to give it up.

"It's fine. There's another bench here just behind." Meralah settled herself on a cushioned bench, settling her notepad on its wide, flat arm.

"If my calculations are correct," Xenna stated in a tone that clearly conveyed that it wasn't a matter to be questioned, "the Tide should begin within the next hour."

What an odd thing to say. The tides run continuously. Meralah thought to herself.

"The Tide?" she asked aloud.

"The Tide of Time."

"The Tide…of time…"

"You mean you haven't heard of it? I thought that's why you were staring at the mirror all week."

"I was just watching the other Palaces," Meralah explained. "What's the Tide of Time?"

"When Jupiter is Trine Uranus and Neptune is Opposite Mars…" Xenna launched into a complicated recounting of stellar alignments.

Meralah had not yet begun to study the stars. Xenna's long list of conjunctions and relationships was gibberish. She waited patiently for it to end.

"…so, on a cycle of between 2,300 and 4,700 years, there is a period of hours or days in which the Great Mirrors are able to show events from the past or the future. If the field is strong enough, they say that sometimes small objects can even fall through to another time."

"Fall through? You're not going to try to…time travel or something?"

Xenna's looked startled, then amused, then thoughtful.

"I don't think so. Only small objects have ever been recorded to come or go. But it would be interesting if someone were to drop into our library and tell us the future."

"If they did, we could record everything, then watch to see if it came true. A real test of time travel."

"Interesting…"

Xenna went silent, relaxing into the chair with her notepad on her knee. Meralah settled into the corner of her cushioned bench. The two women watched the mirror with the patience of immortals.

When the image of a Crystal Palace was briefly replaced with a great, shimmering hall of stone, Xenna's stylus flew across the page. Everything else in the room was still. Meralah's foot began to itch, and when she reached down to scratch it, she found a corner of paper jutting from between the cushions. She scratched her foot idly, then retrieved the small scroll.

It was very fine paper—no, parchment. Made from plant fibers, not wood. And at the top, someone had drawn the image of a ray. She stared at it for a long moment, then flattened the scroll and began to scratch at it with her stylus. A few minutes later, the ray had been joined by a nixie, swimming along beside it, her fingertips grazing the edge of the fish's fin. Beneath it, added a caption.

Protector of the Path

She admired her work for a moment, then let the scroll roll back up, returning her attention to the mirror. Meralah watched inattentively, her mind on the picture of the ray. When she opened the scroll to look at it again, she was astonished to find words written beneath her own!

A moment's review confirmed that the language was ancient Greek.

Nikostratos

A name. An object…across time?

Was he not able to read what I wrote? Clever of him to write back in a language he could expect us both to know. A scholar, then.

Meralah

She wrote her name, then stared at the page, but nothing appeared. Perhaps because she was still holding it? She had let the scroll curl itself back into a cylinder before, and left it sitting on the bench. She set the scroll aside, and turned to stare at the Great Mirror, counting slowly until she reached ten, then unrolled the scroll again.

Hello, Meralah. Do I know you? One of the court mages, perhaps?

Her heart skipped a beat.

Hello, Nikostratos. I am a scholar, not a mage. And I am certain we are not acquainted. I am in the Palace but there is no "Court" here.

She let the scroll curl closed, and this time she waited only a second.

Please, call me Nikos. If you are not a mage, then how...?

She tucked the scroll in her pocket and flitted down the ramp to the primary archive to retrieve a slim volume from a disused shelf. She consulted it, then replaced it, and wrote her reply: a brief explanation of the Tide of Time, and the observation that, since no Nikostratos appeared in the Palace's ledger of occupants, he must be in her future.

She closed the scroll, then reopened it. Nothing. Nothing? She closed the scroll and set it on the shelf, then retrieved it. Still nothing. The Tide centered, somehow, on the Mirror. She must be too far away. She sped up the ramp and settled back on the bench. Xenna shot her an annoyed look, then settled back in to watching the Mirror.

Remarkable! Who knew when I left my home, I would end up travelling across time as well as space?

Is the Palace not your home, then?

It was not until recently. My home is the Isle in the Center, which presently suffers the wrath of Poseidon. The mountain coated us in a fine layer of ash. While none were harmed, a part of our home was buried. Soon thereafter, the earth began to shudder, and the waves climbed as tall as the trees. There can be no question that the mountain will soon burst its shell. We felt it safer to take refuge in the Palace until the event is over.

A wise choice. Are you, then, a wise man?

Meralah smiled to herself as the scroll rolled itself closed. An image of men dancing with bulls flickered across the Mirror.

Pamplona, Meralah guessed.

Wiser some days than others, I think. Certainly, wise enough to know that if I am in your future, you have questions that do not center on ash and earthquakes. What shall I tell you about instead?

Tell me about our people. Is life in the Palace the same?

To answer that, I would have to know what life in the Palace is like now—or, should I say "then"?

Meralah described the stagnant air of her people. She *tried* to stay objective—but could not help mentioning the sofa that had been placed over the corner of the rug when she had varied the blue dye and added a small shape to the pattern. How the rug seemed to reflect her own self—a blemish in the pattern, to be concealed and pointedly overlooked.

When she was done, the scroll contained a fair description of the Palace, and a clear description of her frustrations and concerns for her people.

I would not have recognized this as our people, Meralah. We have changed a great deal, it seems. We are a thassalocracy now—an empire built upon the sea. From the Palace, our people have spread across the Aegean and even along the coasts. Not inland, of course, except a space in the Galilee, but we maintain ports, and fortifications to defend them.

Our art is limited to a few tints and dyes, but it is colorful for all that, and its themes are rich and imaginative. In Gla, they even decorate tiles to place upon the rooftops! We have been in this place for thousands of years, and all of our rich history is represented by our artists. Even our structures are decorated, the stone carved in pleasing shapes and the walls adorned with murals that sometimes travel from wall to wall, surrounding those within on every side.

Walls of stone?

I saw an image in the Great Mirror—a hall of stone with its walls painted red, and murals in black and white and red. A seascape, with great cliffs at one side.

The cliffs are Tyrins, the city where Heracles undertook his great Labors. We have a port there. The room you saw was the Palace's civic hall, where citizens come to pursue affairs of governance.

It was beautiful. I saw it for only a moment.

106

We value beauty. There are over a thousand rooms in the Palace, each adorned with murals, or decorated with figurines of gold, alabaster, and ivory.

When Meralah reopened the scroll, a small object fell into her lap—a dolphin, carved of translucent stone with a fine gold chain threaded through a hole in its dorsal fin. She turned it in every direction, handling it delicately. When she had memorized it from every angle, she tucked it back into the scroll with a thank you message.

A thousand rooms! The place has grown twice its current size. Thank you for showing me the dolphin. It fills my heart, to know that our people will grow out of their malaise and find the love of beauty again.

When she opened the scroll, the dolphin was still there. She thought for a moment that her message had not travelled, but new words had indeed been added to the scroll.

Please, keep it. A gift—a promise from the future that you can carry with you.

Meralah wanted to weep with gratitude and hope. The scratching of Xenna's stylus reminded her that such an action would gain her unwanted attention. In the Mirror, the red mural appeared once more. Meralah was able to name it this time: The Civic Hall.

Thank you, Nikos. I will return your dolphin to you when my years catch up to yours. I give my word.

That is a noble sentiment, even if it is impossible. To grow from the place that you describe, to the rich and vibrant culture we have now will be the work of centuries.

How wonderful if it were to happen so quickly! Perhaps your dolphin will be the catalyst for that change. If you can tell me when you are, I will look for you when that time comes. Or perhaps we can even determine where you are now—my-now. If so, I will travel the world entire to bring your dolphin to you immediately.

When she opened the scroll again, she saw that Nikos had started, then scratched out his words, several times before writing

I am in my fourth decade, and surely have not yet been born ~~where~~ when you are. And you will certainly be long dead by the time my birth occurs. I think, my dear new friend, that this is the closest we will come to meeting one another.

Fourth decade? An infant! But why should I not live to see you once you have been born? Do you think I will swim out of the Palace and get eaten by a hungry shark? When I have caught up to your time, we will have all eternity to become acquainted, and to take joy in the beauty that our people will create.

Swim out of the Palace? Do you live beneath the waves?!

What an odd question. Of course, I—

I live in the Crystal Palace beneath the Aegean Sea. Do you live on the land?

I told you, my home is on the Island at the Center. Crystal Palace? You're...a nixie?

I am. We are –aren't we? You said you had left your island—an outpost of the realm—to return to the Palace. To come here, you must be a nixie.

His reply was lettered carefully, as though he had written slowly and with deliberation.

I did not travel to a Palace beneath the sea, Meralah, but to our Imperial capitol, the Palace we call Cnossos. I am not a nixie; I am a man.

Meralah froze in shock. The Great Mirror displayed an image of a ring of islands, covered in ash and shaken by earthquakes, but Meralah did not see. Her world had gone silent, her vision narrowed to the letters on the parchment.

Nikos was a human? They would never allow a human... No, <u>we</u> would never allow a human. The nixies had kept themselves secret from men for millennia, and yet when she had told him she lived in the Crystal Palace, he had known what she was.

His empire spread across the Aegean, and he knew the Crystal Palace. The nixies would never join a human empire, so they must be allies. And even if they weren't, she told herself firmly, Nikos was still someone she wished to know.

You have touched my life with beauty, and it is my honor to call you friend, even if you are only a man. If you will tell me something that will help me mark the year, I will come to find you when that year arrives.

It is the 7th year of the reign of the 14th king since Theras.

I do not know the name of Theras, but I will watch for it. For me, it is the 274th day of the 14th Cycle of the 1,348th Great Cycle.

It seems we need a common reference. Let's see... Near the great River Aur, on the desert plateau at the plain of Imentet, which is called The Chosen Place, does there stand the Father of Terror, a great statue of a man with a lion's body, resting at the base of pyramids?

We call the river "Nile" and the plain "Gizah." The sphinx is there, and the pyramids.

Good. Do you know how old the statue is?

Not exactly, but I can look it up.

Do. As I write, the statue is 1,000 years old.

"A thou-" Meralah bit the exclamation off as Xenna turned to glare gently.

"You're very restless today Meralah," Xenna observed impassively.

"The, uh, Tide is an impressive event."

Xenna gave her a skeptical look, then turned back to the Mirror. Meralah meandered thoughtfully down the ramp, the open parchment clutched in one hand. Behind her, the Great Mirror showed the ring of islands again, this time buffeted by massive waves.

In the archive, she sought out a history of Egypt, and noted the time given for the construction of the Great Sphinx. She moved on to the shelves of local history, rummaging unsuccessfully through shelf after shelf.

"Are you looking for something specific, Meralah?" The Curator's voice brought her frenzied activity to a standstill. She took a deep breath, attempting to sound serene as she responded.

"I am looking for a reference to Theras, Curator, but I cannot remember in which volume I saw it."

"Perhaps you have misremembered the name." The Curator smiled and indicated a thick book with a red spine, tucked away on the bottom shelf. "Try that one."

"Thank you, Curator."

Meralah snatched the book up and began to sift through the index. She did not find Theras, but she did find Thera. An island. A ring of islands that was constantly destroyed and rebuilt by the volcano at their center. Volcanos, plural. Four of them.

A thousand years after the unveiling of the Great Sphinx, after a minor eruption and two rounds of earthquakes, the largest volcanic eruption in the history of the planet had darkened the skies as far away as China, and brought about the end of the empire they called Atlantis.

Meralah scrawled a warning to Nikos and raced back up the ramp to deliver it. Xenna stared openly as Meralah rolled and unrolled the scroll, setting it down, picking it back up again. Each time, there was no change. No response. The Curator, who had followed Meralah up the ramp at a leisurely pace, stepped into the room just as the Tide swept over the Mirror once more.

A great wave—easily five times the height of the Crystal Palace—tumbled a mighty fleet of ships. Swept through the great harbor and over buildings of stone that gleamed red and white in the ash-tinted sunlight.

"Do you recognize the location, Curator?" Xenna's voice seemed to come from across the sea.

"The buildings look Minoan," he replied, turning his glance to Meralah.

Three thousand years in the *past*, a megatsunami radiated outward from Thera, washing over the Aegean. Its first stop—its first target, the one that would bear the brunt of its force—was the neighboring island of Crete.

"It is the palace at Knossos, Curator, the center of the Minoan empire. The most advanced civilization of antiquity."

"I thought as much, when you came looking for the book on Thera."

"How did you recognize it?" Xenna demanded. She held up her notepad. "There wasn't even enough to clearly identify it as Minoan until that last image."

For an instant, Meralah was tempted to remain silent. She did not want to share Nikos with these impassive, disinterested people. She tucked the scroll unobtrusively into her pocket, but the dolphin burned in her hand.

Nikos' dolphin. My chance to light the spark of beauty in my people's hearts again.

She looped the gold chain around her finger and let the luminous pendant dangle.

"You were right, about objects falling through time."

The Curator stared intently, and Meralah's heart leapt.

"Definitely Minoan," he observed. "See the way the hole has been carved in the fin?"

Xenna barely glanced at it. "I'm afraid I have not yet dedicated any time to studying primitive human adornments, Curator. I did, however, observe in the early images…"

The two began to discuss Xenna's notes on the scenes from the

112

Mirror. Meralah tucked the tiny dolphin into her pocket and walked morosely down the ramp.

***

She slept and woke and worked, and every day was like the last. The ray still accompanied her down the Great Passage, and she still trailed her fingertips languidly along the glass, but she no longer felt the wonder and curiosity that it had once invoked. In fact, she didn't feel much of anything. Perhaps she was becoming like those around her—impassive and aloof.

She sought out the works of Plato, and read all he had to say about the people of Atlantis. He painted them as epicurean and voracious, their downfall, a just punishment from the "gods." She read more broadly, and realized that the Athenians had been in thrall to the Minoans, sending sacrifices to the bull-god at the Labyrinthine Palace of Knossos. Plato clearly had an axe to grind.

But wrapped in his vengeance was a thought that Meralah couldn't ignore. He held the empire of Atlantis up as an example of his philosophy that all realities begin with ideas. That the world we live in is a reflection of those ideas, and while it can never quite rise to the quality of those ideas or the ideals they represent, we should nonetheless strive to get as close as we are able.

***

On the thirty-eighth day, she stopped once again to stare at the ray. Once again, it turned to face her. Once again, it disappeared into the Neptune grass and left her staring at the meadow rippling gently in the tide.

The tide. The Tide of Time. Time. Time and Tide. Inexorable and unchanging. And if she stayed here, staring at the rippling grass, she too would become inexorable and unchanging.

She fingered the waterproof cylinder that hung from her belt—the one that contained her precious scroll.

She watched as a feathered sea slug crawled across the surface of the Crystal Palace, and a white-spotted octopus dined on a spider crab.

She looked to the distance, where a reef shark, fin-tips dipped in black, patrolled for his breakfast.

She paused as she approached the egress. She wondered if she ought to speak to the Curator. And then she realized that it would not upset him if she did, or if she didn't. She nodded at the wardens and stepped into the chamber.

When the portal was secured behind her, she opened the outer gate. For a moment, she felt panicked. She had never been far from the Palace, and had never been wholly alone. But far above, she knew, dolphins frolicked in the whitecaps, and Nikos' descendants still sailed the Aegean. She would not be alone forever, if she were brave enough to rise.

Her blue skin and ocean-green eyes made her nearly invisible in the murky depths. The denizens of the deep ignored her, and she might have passed completely unnoticed were it not for the translucent flash of white at her throat.

Beneath her, the Neptune grass parted. The spotted ray propelled itself upward, 'til its fin tickled her feet. She ran her hand along his rubbery skin as has drew alongside her. He pirouetted in the water so she could stroke his belly, both of them careful to ensure she did not get shocked. When the great ray was oriented alongside her again, Meralah let her left hand dangle idly, swimming only with her right.

She ascended, the ray's fin tickling her fingertips as it escorted her.

THE LIBRARIAN

In a thousand years as a scholar, one thing I never learned was how quickly determination can become dread, and dread terror. Or perhaps that is my own folly, an excess of imagination born of excessive feeling.

It may be that the Craftmaster and the Chief Scholar were correct that real, deep emotions are a hazard. Or perhaps, after the unreality of being denied for millennia, they are merely wild in their release. Whatever the truth may be, I know only that since I set out from the Crystal Palace, my heart has not been at ease.

Vodich has remained at my side. The electric ray who first called to me from outside the crystalline walls of my former home has been a steadfast, if inscrutable companion. He is a mystery unto himself.

But the symbol of the sea-ray represents the need to trust in one's instincts, and whatever instinct drew him to me, mine have answered. We are bound by trust, which needs no reason.

When first I fled the home of my youth, I swam upward, toward the sun. The unexpected flutter of a fin at my fingertips changed my course. Vodich led me at a gentler slope, above and away from the Palace just far enough to feel the temperature rise, and to discern a change in the quality of the light. Then he levelled off, turning to lead me toward the center of the sea.

When we reached the place where the tides pull in every direction, and therefore in none, he settled lightly to the sand without digging himself in, and waited.

I hovered with him for a moment, waiting to see which direction he would turn.

He has brought me here, to a place with no direction. He is waiting for me to choose my path.

My heart fluttered wildly in my breast. When I abandoned my former home, I had considered only what I was leaving behind. I had given no thought to what might replace it. Or perhaps I had—but that thought was buried beneath a tsunami more than two thousand years ago.

Nikos.

The man with whom I had corresponded across time. I had understood too late that he was not in my future, but my past. My warning had not come in time to save him from the towering wave that had destroyed his homeland.

I had mourned the death of my only friendship, brief and tenuous though it may have been. But Nikostratos of Cnossos had taught me to look outside my own people for companionship and understanding, and in so doing he opened my mind to what awaited me outside the crystal confines of a home populated with immortals who whiled away each day not realizing that they no longer lived.

He spurred my courage to step away from all that I had known and embrace the ever-changing eternity. The moment I left my living tomb, Vodich had sped to my side, my companion and the symbol of my choice. He had hovered outside the palace for months waiting for me to make the decision, and when at last I departed the familiar sea of Neptune grass, he had chosen to be at my side.

And here he hovered once again, waiting for me to do what I ought already to have done: decide where I was running *to*.

My fingertips trailed absently to the small pendant that lay against my throat. Nikos' dolphin, the proof that our friendship had not been the work of my imagination. As though summoned by the contact, Nikos' words leapt into my mind.

Near the great River Aur, on the desert plateau at the plain of Imentet, which is called The Chosen Place

Very well. The Aur—the Nile—would be my Chosen Place. Not the river, but the delta, where Nikos' Aur meets my sea.

As I turned to swim in the direction of the southern tide, Vodich stirred up a puffy cloud of sand, then rose until he was an arm's length beneath me. The flood of relief made me realize I had been afraid he would not come.

Vodich accepts fishes from me when he is starving, but mostly we swam near the seabed, where he could skim for the shellfish that he prefers. For a while, my thoughts were empty as I stared at the ever-changing hues of the water and sand. But my mind was not born to idle, and eventually my thoughts turned to the few things I know about the Aur and its delta.

A great human city—Aliksomething-or-other—has stood there for many centuries. It was founded more than a millennium after the destruction of Nikos' Cnossos, but still in that era, when human empires had spanned the Agean. It was a center of human wisdom, home to their first dedicated place of advanced learning.

"The Library." I laughed joyfully. "Of *course,* the Library, Vodich. All answers are to be found in the Library. We are going to the Museion, the Temple of the Muses that is home to the greatest library of the surface world."

I did not know what I was seeking in this human Library—but the same instinct that had led me to Vodich called me there. Against all my upbringing, I was learning to trust that instinct, and I swam southward with confidence.

***

The water turned brackish and cloudy; we had arrived at the mouth of the Nile. The water was shallow, and intruding sunlight introduced new colors to the water, but the constant stirring of silt made it impossible to see beyond the length of my arm. I collided constantly with the small fishes of the delta, and though I knew them to be mostly harmless, the constant buffeting by unseen entities left me in a state of continual alert, twitching at each harmless touch.

I turned athwart the roiling river-tide and swam. I could see little, but trusted that Vodich was following, his electrical sense telling him my location. When the water cleared, he was there, as always. I swam toward him and reached out to touch his skin.

We swam that way—him below me, my hand resting on his back— until we could see the causeway. Definitely Man-built, not a feature of the sea. This was the spot.

I rose to the surface.

Behind us the silted islands of the delta were obscured by masses of reed plants, still silhouetted by the last rays of a sun that had already dropped below the horizon. Squat buildings lined the shoreline, and I saw none that struck me as different from the others.

I saw no sign of a lighthouse, much less one that should be towering above everything else in the area. The island and causeway rose high, however, and the Pharos was on the far side. It would be visible from the ocean side. I rejoined Vodich and, keeping the island at my right hand, swam around to find the Great Harbor guarded by a squat, unlit fortification. Had we come to the wrong place? No, the mouth of the Nile was unmistakable. We swam into the harbor, keeping low to the sandy floor.

The waters should have been clear, unobstructed. Instead, monumental shapes loomed ahead. Above, the sun that lit these shallows dropped from the sky, leaving the waters to their natural state and allowing my eyes, attuned to the depths, to see without interference.

Harbor reefs grew everywhere, clutching life-forms adhered to squared and unnatural silhouettes. The scattered shapes began to coalesce, and I finally understood them to be the remains of fallen structures. As we rounded one of the great blocks, a statue appeared, a Man holding a great urn and staring forward impassively. Nearby a land animal, four-legged and without fins, crouched in the sand, the head of a Man affixed to its shoulders.

Sphinx. I had found the Temple of Isis. The remains of the Great City sprawled half-buried through the harbor. The toppled blocks suggested a great disaster had come suddenly upon them.

I had known that the lives of Men were brief. That their eras came and went with the rapidity of the seasons. But it had never occurred to me that, in our insulated and leisurely home, news of the destruction of a single human city might not be significant enough to reach us. I had arrived, not at a thriving center of knowledge, but at a ruin, a monument to the brief and fragile lives of the lesser races, their lives bound inexorably by their mortality.

How many humans had died here? Did their ghosts still roam the shattered remains of their ancient city? I clutched my dolphin pendant tightly in one hand, beset with a wave of grief for the people of this city, who had perished in upheaval and disarray, victims of the violence of the earth. The harbor took on a sense of unreality, every shape a fragment of the bones of the dead metropolis.

From the corner of my eye, the statue of Isis moved.

I whipped around to see a hundred eyes staring back at me. A tiny school of tilapia swam past. I laughed at my prior state of alarm, and the Chief Scholar's voice echoed in my mind.

Emotion does not serve us. We must assess what we see based on intellect, observation.

Fine. It might have been right for *this* situation, but it was still no way to live. I turned away from the lifeless granite Isis to continue surveying my surroundings.

I kicked a foot, and found my movement arrested! For the briefest of moments, this was all I knew. I could feel nothing restraining me, yet none of my limbs obeyed my commands. A tingling spread across my skin. It reached my head, and my hair flowed out in unnatural directions.

The tingling rose to agony. My skin burned. No, not my skin but the nerves beneath it, searing my inner flesh. Throat paralyzed; I couldn't even scream. I was caught in some manner of magical trap, perhaps conceived to prevent thieves from entering the ancient temple.

A rounded shape sailed across the sand toward me.

No, Vodich! It's a trap!

I could not call out a warning to my friend. We would both be caught up in this ancient spell. Unable to drown, we would starve to death here together.

But as Vodich raced beneath me, my limbs were released! He had seen—or perhaps sensed—what I had not: a knifefish, concealed in the vegetation clinging to the stone block near my feet. I had disturbed its electrical field, and it had attacked and shocked me. Vodich's electrical assault had disrupted it, freeing me and leaving the great eel dazed and disoriented. I swam as fast as my still stunned limbs could carry me, following Vodich and beseeching the sea to care for him.

I found him unharmed, his electrical attack far more powerful than the one I had endured. I glided to his back, wrapping one elbow around the base of his tail and lying on his back. My body was still vibrating gently from head to toe with the aftereffects of the attack, and "with Vodich" was the safest place I knew to rest.

My dreams were beset with images of the colossal waves and tumbling earth that Nikos had called "the wrath of Poseidon."

***

I woke to the frenzied fanning of Vodich's fins. He was struggling to move as swiftly as he could with my weight encumbering him. Behind us an enormous pair of jaws, framed in massive spikes, inched ravenously closer.

I was facing the wrong way to help Vodich swim, and if I turned around my feet would be within range the predator's mouth. I reached for the knife at my belt and kicked off in the direction of looming death.

I reached for the fish's upper lip, to keep myself away from its teeth. The fish jerked its head and attempted to snatch me into its maw. We both failed.

We passed close enough for me to feel the churning of the water as it entered the beast's mouth. I snatched hold of one of the spiked teeth with my left hand and wrenched it as hard as my weakened arm could manage, bracing my feet beneath its mouth and plunging my knife into its left eye, uncertain whether this would frighten it or merely increase its determination.

The monster was infuriated. I should have made an easy dinner, and it had not been prepared for a fight. It turned leftward in circles, trying to reach me, but I still had a grip on the great fang. I clutched it with all my strength, repositioning myself by crab-crawling up the fish's side as the beast endeavored to shake me loose and into its maw.

I plunged my knife into its remaining eye, then pushed off upward, swimming away in the direction I thought it least likely to consider. As I gained distance, I could see the dark stripes on its side, and recognized it as a tiger fish, vicious carnivores that eat crocodiles and sometimes attack Men. As I floated above, it was joined by three others. Like most denizens of the sea, a tiger fish knows neither mercy nor compassion. They made their assessment based on observation and intellect: the moment they determined their companion was disabled; they began to eat it alive.

I fled, swimming frantically in Vodich's direction and hoping they would be too busy devouring their friend to notice one tiny Nixie. When I caught up with my companion, I hugged him as tightly as one can hug a broad, flat creature and babbled terrified thanks. I was losing count of the number of times he had saved my life.

He had settled near a grouping of upright blocks, the remains of some small chamber, half buried but still held together well enough to see the semblance of three walls and a tiny portion of roof. I scanned it carefully and found no threat. At last, a safe place to rest and recover. Vodich skimmed for shellfish. I curled up against the back wall and slept the sleep of the dead.

I awoke in a disoriented panic, my eyes flitting in every direction to find the threat. The sight of Vodich nestled into the sand at the entrance to our shelter calmed me, and as my mind cleared, I remembered where I was.

I ran my fingers over the great block of stone at my back, feeling the tiny pits and grooves quarried by centuries of water. The blocks had once been smooth and beautiful, but all things come to ruin. Its beauty had been fleeting, its destruction inevitable. I wondered whether my search for beauty, for liveliness, for hope was similarly doomed.

I had bristled at my peoples' stoicism and lack of interest in anything creative or innovative. But here before me was the proof that such things do not last, whereas the staid and defined culture of my former home endured. Had I been wrong to seek more than the life that was allotted to me?

I looked over to where Vodich rested on the seabed. I could not have been wrong to choose the life that brought me such a companion. I rose and stretched, and Vodich shuddered the sand from his back. I leaned my back against the cool stone and called to him.

"Good morning, Vodich! It doesn't appear that our answers are in this library after all. I was thinking we might go to Cnossos." I paused here, but he did not react to that news. Ah, well. At least that meant he had no objection. "But how about breakfast first?"

Vodic skimmed along the sand away from me. As he did, the stones behind me parted and I fell backward, accompanied by a tumbling current that drew Vodich back into the room. As he reached the spot where I had been standing, the stone doors closed, trapping us on opposite sides. I cried out to Vodich, but my shout was muted, even in my own ears. I knew he had not heard me.

***

The room was dark. Not the dismal murk of the delta, but true black. Stone on all sides, with no source of light. Even my eyes, designed to see in the ocean's depths, could find neither shape nor shadow. This time, I really *had* triggered some sort of trap, and it appeared likely to become my grave.

I hovered, terrified, then sank to the floor in despair. To have some so far and die in a long-forgotten thieves' catch… I thought back to the first day I had seen Vodich following me. We had been on opposite sides of a wall then, too, he swimming along outside the Crystal Palace as I walked its Outer Corridor.

So, we end as we began, I thought morosely.

Sound interrupted my self-pitying reverie. Not a specific noise, exactly, but rather a…*change* in the way that sound…sounded.

The room was slowly emptying itself of water.

I couldn't see it, of course, but I could *feel* it. Differences in the pressure and the quality of sound. I hadn't been speaking, but my heart had been pounding, and I had been weeping. And those sounds took on a different tone as the water around me changed.

The room drained slowly; it was more than a full minute from the time the top of my head was exposed until my chin was above the waterline. In all, I must have stood for a quarter of an hour listening to the water recede, and feeling my way around the room until I found the small drain holes in the corners.

When the room was empty, save for myself and a few small puddles on the floor, I pressed again on the outer doors, and called again to Vodich. My voice rang out loudly, and I hoped that he heard me, knew that I was still alive.

The wall behind me opened, and my prison was bathed in dim blue light, reminiscent of the harbor floor on a sunny day. After the pitch blackness of my prison, even this was a painful shock. I focused my dazzled eyes as best I could and stepped quickly through the door before I could be trapped again.

I found myself in an arced and gleaming corridor of ivory stone. I must have stepped *inside* some part of the ruins. Had it all looked like this once?

The walls were occupied primarily with shelves, carved directly into the stone. A few straight surfaces existed, but most were angled, creating cubbies like those used to store wine but filled with rolls of paper, papyrus, and vellum. The straight shelves held small artifacts drawn from many cultures, ranging from the practical to the artistic.

Below the level of my waist, the walls were solid and decorated with intricate carvings, mostly creatures of the land and sea. I fingered the dolphin at my throat and my terror turned to wonder. Nikos had been an amateur compared to these craftsmen. The delicacy and detail of their work brought the very stone to life!

A faint sound and a flash of motion from the far end of the corridor heralded the arrival of tiny cart which trundled toward me, steered by no hand that I could see.

I stepped backward in shock, and again in fear. Seeing that the cart stayed to the center of the path, I pressed myself against the shelves and fixed my eyes on one of the dolphins carved into the opposite wall as I waited for the ghostly vehicle to pass.

It rolled up to the end of the corridor, stopping at the doors which once again appeared to be a solid wall. The cart paused only a moment, then turned itself around and set out down the corridor once more. As it passed me for the second time, I noticed the parchment laid on its surface.

KALOS IRTHATE

Welcome.

Apparently, the ghosts were not opposed to company. My hands shook a tiny bit as I wondered whether this was a good thing. But I obviously wasn't going out the way I came, and the tiny automaton was headed in the only other direction available. So, I followed it.

I walked lightly, both admiring and apprehensive at this ghostly ruin come suddenly alive. I wondered vaguely whether I would know if I were hallucinating, but concluded that if I were, my fascination would long since have outstripped my fear. My pulse tapped in my ears as I followed the little cart around into a cavernous hall filled with shelves, and scattered with tables and benches.

The cart navigated around those obstacles, stopping at the center of the room. Behind a shelf at my right hand, I heard a scuttling. I drew my knife, ready to defend myself from some air-breathing scavenger, and stepped carefully to the side to gain a view of my foe.

A tall, thin man with white hair and tawny skin dropped a scroll delicately into its bin.

"Kallimara," he said to me.

Greek. A scholar.

"Good morning," I replied in the same language, returning my knife to its sheath but leaving my hand resting on its hilt.

"I am Im-Hotep. Welcome to the library."

I stood, dumbfounded, and finally stuttered my name.

"I believe you are the first of your people to visit the library, Meralah." He was the soul of hospitality, settling me on a cushioned bench, bringing food and drink, and tending to the deep scratches the tiger fish had left on my legs.

My soul poured out onto the marble tabletop. My frustration with my stagnant culture and my peoples' lack of curiosity. My friendship with Nikos and its tragic end. My companionship with Vodich, and our trip to seek the Library, only to find it destroyed at the bottom of the harbor.

"The buildings, yes. But the library is intact, as you can see."

And indeed, it was. The great room was the center of a star, shelf-lined corridors its rays, extending in every direction.

"And *you* are…" I began hesitantly. Im-Hotep smiled back at me.

"The Librarian."

"You come here every day, to keep a library that is believed to be destroyed?"

"Come here? No. I live here. The ruins you saw without are likely the result of the same event that trapped me here. I have long since ceased to keep the time, but it must be measured in centuries."

I understood then that he was mad. Men do not live for centuries.

"Do you think your own people the only immortals left in this world, Meralah of the Nixies? My people lived in this place for a millennium before the first village of Men was built on the shore. The earliest Men, the ones from this region, were our friends. We built the Great Corridor beneath the water to give them safe passage between the island and the shore. We sheltered them here, from storms both natural and Man-made. By the time Others came, our peoples had intermarried for several of their generations, and our appearance had grown sufficiently similar that the Others did not realize we were not Men. And when the wisest of them sought to create a palace of knowledge, we assisted them."

Elves. Elves in the Museion.

"The Library was my creation. For every scroll that was copied and stored above, one was stored here below. Though most Men knew nothing of our existence, a few trusted colleagues visited us here. In addition to their own writings, they found the collected knowledge of my people. It was one of those Men who built the doors through which you entered."

"Built? I thought…" I felt foolish, but continued nonetheless. "I thought they were magic."

"They seem so, do they not? The gentleman—Hero, he was called—was ingenious with science and machinery. He built the wandering cart that I sent to you, as well. By the wrapping of its strings, you can create a pre-ordained path for it to travel. The fountain there— He pointed toward a tiny fountain set upon a table in the center of the room, burbling away with no apparent source of water. "was his creation. A terribly clever human. One of the last to study with us."

"One of the last?"

"A century or two later, Poseidon sealed the doors. No one has visited since. But now you are here, and our library will be cheery again."

"I'm sorry, friend, but I cannot stay."

"Not stay? After risking death to come here?" He waved vaguely at the scratches on my legs. "You sought the library to feed your curiosity—and you have found it. Having found what your heart most desired, you may now indulge your curiosity for as long as you wish."

"But Vodich…"

"An ephemeral life. He will be gone in the blink of an eye. Besides, the door by which you entered is the only way in. And it's quite inaccessible from the inside."

I looked at the little cart, used its orientation to identify the corridor by which I had entered, and fled to the end of the hall. The wall was smooth and unfeatured. The slimmest line showed where the two blocks of stone met, but it was visible only because I was determined to see what I knew was there. No knob, lever, or mechanism presented itself. I pressed randomly at the carvings on the wall, pausing to gently stroke the dolphin, symbol of protection, resurrection, and joy. Of Nikos. But the little dolphin did not free me this time.

The Librarian was patient, soothing, and implacable. He had long since come to terms with his imprisonment, and was prepared to wait until I had come to terms with mine.

Frustration became despair, despair boredom, and boredom

curiosity. I began to prod idly at the bits of parchment, reading random scrolls in Greek or Latin, and setting aside others that I could not understand. The Librarian taught me Assyrian and Persian, and I read the works of scholars from lands of which I had never heard. He guided me always to the oldest texts—the least-copied, he explained, had the least errors of transcription or translation. I learned, whenever possible, from the original voices. From Hipparchus, I learned the astronomical studies I had neglected in earlier years. From Erasistratus and Herophilus I learned about Nikos' people and, surprisingly, about myself. Erasistratus' descriptions of the nerve systems of Men helped me to understand my reaction to the knifefish's jolt. Our bodies must be similar in that way.

I saw Nikos everywhere in the library, its ornate and detailed carvings directly related—in my mind, at least—to the tiny dolphin that hung at my throat. They had been made by men—and elves—from far away, not at all his people. But their beauty was Nikos' beauty. For me, each gleaming white image began and ended with the one that rested against my skin. The past, as represented in these works, was all the future that was left to me, and I spent my time seeking to understand it through the scrolls and the memories that the Librarian shared with me.

He spoke of the world of men, one in which cultures crashed into one another, then adopted one another's ways so that from one century to the next they were never same. He drew great canvases of chaos in my imagination, which he described as the Childhood of Man. The Library, he explained, had been the beginning of Man's adulthood, the time when they began to appreciate knowledge over conquest, stability over change. To appreciate that their rampant emotion was a forced to be managed and controlled rather than indulged. Plato had been right; the world could never live up to our ideas and ideals.

The Librarian's words were hypnotic, his wisdom expansive. When he described how the Gods of Man kept them forever in tumult, I forgot to laugh at the idea of deities, immortals who take an interest in managing mortals. I merely regretted the destruction of beauty and stability that those gods had wreaked on places like Alexandria and Cnossos.

At my mention of Cnossos, my mentor lit up, and drew me to a corridor where I found endless tales of the culture and history of Nikos' people, the Minoans. Unrolling one scroll, I found a sketch of the mural that had adorned the Civic Hall. On another, I found a sketch of a sea-ray and a dolphin, and a description of their symbolic meaning. That one I quietly rolled up and slipped into the case which still contained my correspondence with Nikos.

The image of the ray seemed to shake me out of a stupor. How long had I been idling in this place while Vodich searched for me? My thoughts were interrupted by the sound of the robot-cart trundling down the corridor, bearing lunch. The Librarian was thoughtful in ensuring that I remembered to eat.

Eat? I stared at the dish: nuts, herbs, and fish. Where was he getting fish?

The Librarian knows how to open the doors.

He lied to me. I have been his prisoner, not his guest or colleague.

As though a flood-gate had been opened, a door burst in my mind and my weeks—months?—spent with the Librarian flickered through my mind like images from the Great Mirror. I saw myself leaning further in to the Librarian, joining his way of thought, until I had begun to view my emotions, my passions, as a danger to be buried. Until I had begun to think like the people I had left behind.

I thought of Vodich, and briefly wondered whether elves had the power of mesmerism.

Well, if they did, then I must learn to resist it. If Im-Hotep could acquire fresh fish to eat, then there was a way to open the doors. And if he was willing to lie to me about it, then I must find the secret without his knowing that I am doing so. I realized that the robot cart never failed to find me—which meant the Librarian never failed to know where to send it. I would have to search cautiously. But where to begin?

The cart!

It had been built by the same man who designed the doors, the Librarian had said on the day I arrived. What was his name? Heron? No, that was a bird. Hero. And he was one of the last, so his scrolls would be among the more recent ones. The ones the Librarian had guided me away from.

How could I study the scrolls in that corridor without drawing his attention?

The corridor to the left of it was also recent—but the one to the right contained scrolls from the Elven library. I searched them, and found the language similar enough to my own that I was able to puzzle out their content. When the Librarian inquired, I told him I was researching what was known of my own people. I held my breath, eyes wide, waiting to discern whether he would believe me.

After a long moment, he strolled to a shelf on the opposite side of the corridor and retrieved one of the tiny artifacts from its shelf. A piece of mirror. A piece of a Great Mirror. Tiny images still flickered within, nixies going about their day. These, however looked nothing like nixies I had seen before. Their clothing, colors, patterns, lives were all different and vibrant. It must be an illusion. Elven magic.

"It is broken," the Librarian observed. "Perhaps it shows only the distant past. That piece came from Aram. Ten thousand years ago, a falling star destroyed the Crystal Palace there. The broken fragment may only able to show what was, before that time."

Something about this didn't sound quite right, but I wasn't sure why. There would be time to ponder it later. For now, I didn't need to know about my people. I just needed the Librarian to *think* I did.

At times, he came to assist me, pulling out rolled documents that he thought might interest me—the locations of other Crystal Palaces, or the names of Nixies who had left them and become known in the World of Men. At times, he left me alone to my studies, and I could creep into the neighboring corridor to search for Hero.

I came to understand his habits as he did mine. He fished in the mornings, returning to provide lunch, and appearing clean and dry in the afternoons to guide my studies. I used the mornings to review each of Hero's scrolls until I found the document describing the Magic Doors.

They were ingenious! A release lever that, when pressed, activated a series of counterweights that opened or closed the doors. A pump that could move water—combined with a pressure detector. If, after the doors closed, pressure rose above a certain threshold, the mechanism to drain the room was activated. If the pressure was below that threshold when the doors closed, the reverse mechanism was invoked. Once that cycle was complete, the opposite door opened.

But I had pressed every relief and every carving on the wall without effect. I tried to envision the opening of the original doors. I had leaned against the doors themselves, but that couldn't be it. I had pressed against them more than once, and leaned there for an extended period of time without triggering the mechanism. I tried to replay every movement I remembered. What had happened just before the doors opened?

Vodich.

The ray had skimmed across the entry arch, touching the stone floor. The *floor.*

I retrieved a few elven scrolls and settled in the central library. When my jailor returned, he would find me diligently studying the history of my people.

"You're smiling." He observed as he entered.

My heart fluttered, and I stared at the scrolls for a moment before responding.

"I think," I said slowly, "that I am beginning to remember who I am. And thanks to the guidance you have provided, I've learned things about my people that I never knew before. Their history is much more…colorful than their present."

"All races were young at some time. Though it seems that the Nixies…have matured. Set aside their 'colorful' ways in favor of wisdom and stability."

Is this why he had imprisoned me? To teach me that the stagnant ways of my people, and of this place, were preferable to the possession of a true and open heart? In my mind, I scoffed rebelliously—but he had almost succeeded. For a while, I had been content to believe him, to abandon my faithful friend and remain in this place. Yes, he had told me it was inescapable. But it was I who had been willing to take him at his word.

I had been electrocuted, and nearly eaten by a fish as large as myself. But really, both of these were minor predators. I had faced larger ones without fear, but always as a member of a hunting party. The first time I had to face them on my own I was ready to give up, crawl into a safe space, and pretend that reading scrolls somehow meant I was not simply stagnating in a dead library, in exchange for safety.

No, I had no right to scoff. But would never hide from life's dangers again.

The next morning, when the Librarian disappeared to fish, I tucked the broken bit of mirror into my pocket and returned to the corridor of my arrival. This time, I knew what I was looking for, and about how far from the door to look.

It was right where I expected to find it. An almost unnoticeable flaw in the pattern of the floor, placed so close to the wall the one would never step on it inadvertently. I pressed my foot down, and the end of the corridor opened. I raced across the gap, hurling myself into the room at such speed that I bruised a shoulder bouncing off the far wall.

When the doors closed, I greeted the darkness as a welcome shadow that must precede the dawn. The room filled faster than it emptied, and within minutes I was hovering near the ceiling, hands pressed against the outer doors so that I would feel their every motion. I did not wait for them to open fully, grabbing their edges and propelling myself through the moment the gap was wide enough. Eyes dazzled by the sunlit harbor waters; I saw only the outlines of the massive stones. I swam for the entry arch, seizing the edge of a block so that I could brace myself if the water began to rush back through the doors and try to carry me with it.

When my eyes adjusted, I scanned the bright waters of the harbor. Vodich was not immortal, and I had no idea how long I had been imprisoned. He might be dead. He might have returned to wherever he had come from. Wherever he was, he was not waiting in this ruined room.

If I am going to make friends of ephemerals, then I must learn to deal with losing them. Vodich would only be the first. I was adamant that he would not be the last. The Librarian had learned the ways of mortals well enough to walk among them. So, would I.

I would seek out new acquaintance, among those who valued passion and curiosity. Plato *had* said that the world will never rise to the quality of our ideas. But he had also said that we should never stop striving to get it as close as we can.

As I approached the mouth of the harbor, a familiar flutter tickled my foot. I stopped swimming, and when Vodich came alongside, I kissed him gently just behind his eyestalks. I wanted to thank him for waiting, for not giving up on me. To tell him how grateful I was not to be on this journey alone. But I had no words, and he would not have understood them, so I rested my cheek on the smooth, dappled skin of his back and after a long moment, I turned. With my hand resting on his back, we left the ruined Library behind and passed into the open sea.

FRAGMENTS FROM ARAM

The water was too salty.

Fleeing the harbor at Alexandria, Meralah had turned east, away from home.

Or could she even call it "home" now? In fleeing the Crystal Palace of the Aegean, she had turned her back on her people. Or had *they* rejected *her*? No, they had rejected the world. Innovation. Growth. Learning. They had chosen to be a stagnant people, and stagnant waters were rarely healthy. For immortals to choose stagnation was a form of death.

Meralah had chosen life. Or life, in the form of her companion, had chosen her. The great marbled ray had seemed to watch her, wait for her. And when she had left the Crystal Palace, he had appeared at her side, and remained there. When the mad Librarian had beguiled her mind and imprisoned her in the remains of the Great Library, Vodich had been helpless to free her—but he had waited. And when she escaped, he had returned to her side.

They had drifted for a few hours while Meralah pretended to herself that she was considering where to go. In the end, there had been only one logical choice. The ocean to the west, past the Pillars of Hercules, was too cold for Vodich. So, they had turned east, swimming along the Egyptian shore.

A series of Man-crafted canals and natural lakes had brought them at last to a tropical sea, warm and beautiful and dense with bright fishes. But the shores were too near, and the water too buoyant, the shipping lanes overrun with vessels great and small. Vodich skimmed the seabed, and Meralah kept one hand lightly on his back, lest a moment's inattention bring her too near the propellers of the surface craft.

It was a lovely place, but she would not find what she sought here. They continued eastward, toward open ocean. There was a Crystal Palace in the Erythraean Sea. Nixies. And, perhaps, a new home.

Her free hand unconsciously found the hard outlines of the fractured bit of glass tucked in her pocket—the remnant of a Great Mirror. The Mirrors connected her people, allowed them to see that life continued in the tiny enclaves strewn about the world's oceans. The Librarian had told her that this mirror had come from the Palace at Aram. The sea that once existed there had long since turned to desert, but the Mirror held remnants of its former magic, showing her glimpses of

Crystal Palaces in which creativity and beauty still flourished.

Somewhere her people still thrived, and truly lived.

At first, Meralah had twitched at every stray movement within the scope of her vision, expecting danger from all sides. But the sea was calm and harmonious here. After a week, the jolt had become a ripple. After two, her muscles were no longer tense. In the fourth week, she began to look around herself with curiosity rather than concern.

They swam for the Center, the place where the tide pulls in every direction and, therefore, in none. Her people would not build their home in the Stillness at the Center, but it would be nearby. So, they followed the currents toward the place where all tides are equal. When they arrived, they would swim a spiral that would eventually lead them to the Palace.

When they finally reached the Center, Meralah almost missed it.

The center of her sea had been an open, almost featureless place. The center of this ocean was wild with life. A colorful, teeming coral atoll stretched as far as the eye could see. The water could not be truly still with so much life moving through it, but the pull of the tides was muted, and if she couldn't find the exact center, she could identify it sufficiently for her purposes. The massive reefs would not allow for skimming the sand; they rose and swam their spiral from above.

It was Vodich that found the Palace. Meralah nearly swam past, but he turned spirals to draw her eyes in the right direction until at last she saw it nestled in the base of the coral, framed in brightly colored life. She didn't see movement within, but she didn't expect to. The magic was designed to protect its inhabitants from discovery.

She swam nearer, peering through the sea urchins and swaying grasses to locate the entrance. Chaffweed obscured the threshold, and monitpora grew on its surface like colorful shelf mushrooms on a fallen tree. This portal had been long since reclaimed by the sea.

She followed the translucent barrier upward, to its end. Tiny clown fishes darted through holes obscured by the reef. This was not a Palace but a decaying ruin, its magic fading as its essence was absorbed into the reef. She hovered for a timeless moment, one hand on the remains of the wall, the other wrapped around the gleaming dolphin pendant that hung at her throat. It felt like a moment, but perhaps it was a year. There was no sun to mark the hours here in the depths, so for Meralah, time simply paused. How long does it take to grieve an entire people? When the current of her grief began to ebb, she reached into her pocket and pulled out the fragment of mirror. Nixies still moved within it, smiling, laughing, dancing in brightly colored clothing. *This* community might be gone, but her people still existed within the world. She would, if she must, swim each ocean until she found them, swimming east until she reached the west again.

They travelled past the southern edges of the continent, until the land began to shatter into islands. Beyond was the Eastern Great Sea, which stretched from pole to pole. There would be no shallows there, and Meralah was uncertain how deep Vodich could safely swim. Rays are designed for bottom-skimming, with mouths below and eyes above. He would be vulnerable in the open sea, unable to see threats that rose from beneath. If the waters grew too cold, his electrical organ would stop functioning, rendering him defenseless.

She hesitated.

Vodich was ephemeral, his natural life extending not more than fifteen or twenty years. Meralah was immortal. She could wait to make the journey when it would not endanger her friend. In the interim, she would seek out another Library, and attempt to determine which of her people she was seeing in the mirror.

The thought of seeking out the palaces of Men filled her with terror. Men, she knew, imprisoned what they did not understand. As far back as her memories reached, she recalled tales of abduction and abuse.

And then she remembered Nikos.

The only Man she had ever spoken with had been kind and amusing. Her hand rose once again to the tiny dolphin pendant, carved by a Man who had appreciated beauty, and been generous enough to gift his artistry to someone whom he would never meet. The pendant had been sent to her across a tiny rift in time.

Her own people had discounted its beauty and its value—less kind, less generous than the Man. They had been so determined that they had achieved the pinnacle, they dared not credit foreign artistry.

Meralah had believed herself a revolutionary, to question the unchanging patterns of her peoples' clothing, and their lives. But in that moment, hovering in a foreign sea with the dolphin's stone dorsal fin digging into her thumb, she understood that those challenges had been shallow. She began to question not just the nixies' lives and patterns, but their core truths.

Were Men really a danger? Or had her people created fears where none were needed, to keep their worlds apart? What other truths had she learned that were untrue?

Meralah went still, frozen with the weight of the question, then shook herself. She released the pendant and pulled the shard of Mirror from her pocket once more. Within its chipped edges, people danced the dance of life. People like her—and unlike her. Nikos had shown her that men, too, were simply people like her—and unlike her.

She would seek out the Libraries of Man and use the knowledge to find the people who were most like her.

Having never been among Men, her first task was to observe. To learn enough of their interactions to navigate their world, sufficiently to locate a Library. She stayed close to landforms, looking for small communities to observe and perhaps, eventually, approach.

She prowled the ocean just beyond the surf, learning to recognize what she saw. Clothing, she learned quickly, indicated structure. Those in trousers gave commands, while those in draped wear followed them. Those in simple trousers were lower in the structure than those who layered wood or metal over their trousers. The latter often bore weapons, and Meralah assumed they were hunters or warriors. Some manner of hierarchy was necessary to govern such a large species, and it was logical that those who protected or provided food would be at the top of the structure.

On a sunny day when the waves were high, and the air was calm, Meralah crept ashore and commandeered a pair of trousers. She pulled them on beneath her tunic and walked at the edges of the settlement, listening and trying to remain unobserved. She overheard conversations in a rapid and musical language that she did not understand. She needed a scholar.

Her knife hanging at her side, she approached a Man in draped clothing—a female, she realized as she drew nearer. She greeted the woman politely, relying on her tone of voice to convey her intent. The woman turned, gazed with startled eyes into Meralah's blue-skinned face, and began to scream.

The scream drew hunters, and Meralah stood with her hands wide, advertising an absence of dangerous intent. The hunters drew weapons and charged at her. The nixie scowled, confused by their senseless response; she held a hand up flat and commanded, "Stop!" but they continued to advance.

Meralah ran with all her might, barely managing to stay ahead of her pursuers. Their longer legs reduced her lead with every step. The hunters spread out around her, herding her toward what they believed to be a dead end. When they had pushed her to land's end, she leapt from the clifftops into the sea.

In time, there would be the opportunity to consider how to distinguish Men like Nikos from Men like the ones she had just encountered. But such thoughtful consideration would have to wait. Meralah was *furious*. She might have breached hospitality by pilfering clothing, but surely that did not justify their threatening her very life! *Some* Men might be good, but *these* Men…

As if responding to her wounded sense of justice, a fleet of ships rose from the horizon and came to rest in the harbor of the barbaric and inhospitable settlement. Armed Men streamed forth from the ships, and Meralah would have been pressed to describe the chaos that followed. She had read of war, and thought this must be it, but the pandemonium before her was too much to capture and quantify at once. For a full day, the air was filled with the clashing of metal, the tromping of feet, and the cries of the defeated.

When the sun set, those from the land retreated to a poorly fortified stronghold, and the invaders returned to their ships. The seafarers seemed to have got the better of the day, and Meralah felt a certain satisfaction that a price had been exacted from those who had treated her with such hostility.

The sea rose and the pressure of the air descended. She and Vodich would depart for the depths to rest peacefully beneath the swirling storm that was surely preparing to roil the surface. Meralah untangled herself from the billowing trousers, spinning them into a tight roll which she tucked into her knife-belt.

From her place between the harbor and the sea, Meralah scanned the vessels. Men scurried in every direction, all intent on their tasks. A few looked toward the horizon; the Men in the ships were preparing to leave the protection of the bay.

A pallid man, his face covered in swirling hair, stood at the rail of one of the ships. Meralah's attention was drawn to his stillness. He watched, staying carefully out of the path of the rushing sailors. Meralah swam closer and called out to him.

The man turned, looking for the source of the sound.

"*Salve!*" she tried in Latin.

His forehead creased, and after a moment he called out to her.

"*Capisci l'italiano?*"

147

Italian?

"*Me katalavaíneis*?" she called in Greek. *Do you understand me?*

He smiled and called "hello" in Greek.

"A storm is coming. You should stay in the protection of the bay."

"Our ships may be run aground."

"Perhaps. But if you leave the harbor they will surely be destroyed."

Meralah didn't wait for his answer. She ducked beneath the waves, reached her hand out to Vodich, and lead him away to the safety of the depths.

While the storm raged above, they relaxed on the seabed. They ate, Vodich skimming the sand for shrimp as Meralah speared fish with her knife. She didn't know if the sailors had survived, but that was not her concern. She had warned them, which seemed a suitable thanks to the Men who had punished those who had sought to do her harm. Or so she told herself.

The Man with the hairy face had not feared her. Had not tried to attack. He had greeted her. Had listened to her. She hoped he had stayed safely in the harbor.

When the seas calmed, she returned to the little bay and was relieved to find the ships still there. One had, indeed, been forced aground, but it was intact. Most of the Men appeared to be on the shore. She scanned the brown faces on the shore, looking for the pale-skinned, bearded man.

"*Kallimara*!"

The voice came from over her left shoulder. When she turned, he was standing at the ship's rail.

"Good morning."

"To whom are you speaking, Marco?" Another white-skinned man approached the rail.

"To the water nymph that saved our lives, Uncle."

"Marr-ko?" Meralah tested the sound of the name on her tongue. "I am Meralah."

"Meralah!" the young man called her name like a celebration. "This is my uncle, Maffeo, whom you have made very wealthy."

"Wealthy?" Meralah knew she had probably saved his life but couldn't understand how that would make him wealthy.

"If you hadn't warned us, we would all be dead. Instead, we will soon return to Setsen Khan with the obeisance of the Japanese emperor."

Her face must have shown her lack of comprehension. Marco spent the better part of the next hour telling her about King Kublai, who ruled the world of Men from this island to the Black Sea, wrote poetry, and had built over twenty thousand schools.

Schools?

"Does he build libraries?"

"Libraries? Not as such…but he does gather scholars and wise men around him. Are you a scholar?"

"I'm…researching the history of my people."

Marco named many unfamiliar names of scholars gathered by his great and benevolent "khan". Haiyun, master of Buddhism. A scholar called Zhao Bi. Jamal ad-Din, an astronomer. Kidinnu, a mathematician.

"Kidinnu? The astronomer?"

"Yes!" Marco brightened at her recognition.

"Is he immortal?" Meralah had read the works of Kidinnu in the library at Alexandria.

"Immor... Oh! No! He is a Chaldean, from the same region as the famous Kidinnu."

From Aram.

"I would like to meet this Kidinnu."

The Chaldean, Marco explained, resided at the Khan's palace in Shangdu, a miraculous city of surpassing beauty and dignity in which the great King spent his summers. This idyllic retreat was located high in the mountains, and as Marco described the path, Meralah's hopes sank.

"So...to reach this place, I must leave the seas for an extended time?" Vodich could not make such a journey.

"Oh!" Marco looked surprised, then thoughtful. "Of course, you must stay in the sea..." He trailed off, his eyes on the horizon, then refocused. "The Great City has rivers and canals which are connected to an underground sea. From there, caves run for miles out to the ocean. Perhaps..."

He continued to speak until he had shared every detail that might be helpful to her. He was a keen observer, and his enthusiasm was contagious. By the time he was done speaking, she was confident she could find the way.

Her confidence had probably been misplaced.

After a month of following every channel and sea-cave that lead inland, she began to doubt she would ever find the City of Wonder that Marco had described to her. She briefly considered giving up, heading eastward to the open sea to find the Nixies of the Great Eastern Ocean. But faithful Vodich was still at her side, and she would never be beguiled into leaving him again. She continued to search each cave, less from the conviction of finding Shangdu than "because it was something that she could do without abandoning her friend."

That, of course, was when they found the path.

The tunnel was pitch black. Even Meralah's vision, tuned for the depths, gathered nothing. She placed her hand on Vodich's back and followed, trusting him to guide her. For three days they swam thus, until the confined tunnel opened out to a massive cavern. She couldn't see it, but she could feel the difference in the water. They had reached the underground sea.

She strained her eyes for any hint of light but found none. Vodich swam steadily, confidently, and she followed until he slowed, circled briefly, and led her into another tunnel.

They emerged in a saltwater pond that burbled up in a verdant valley. The air was light and lacking in oxygen; they must be far above the sea. The high-walled canyon was lush with life even in winter, and patterned with rivers, waterfalls, and ponds.

Patterned.

Water tumbled from above in towering falls, but the ponds and streams that they fed were hand-crafted, guided carefully to avoid crossing the saltwater canals. Foliage was thick at the canyon walls but sculpted in the valley. Animals roamed freely and trees were placed artfully, with open spaces between them. Where the valley widened, a massive wall rose up, separating this carefully fashioned Eden from the world beyond.

Behind her, a second wall cordoned off the furthest corner of the vale, protecting a gleaming marble structure which Meralah assumed was the summer palace. From somewhere within the inner wall, a geyser spurted periodically, calling out with a loud grunt as it sent a glistening fountain streaming skyward.

Meralah watched, and hid, and waited. There were no small shellfish or other creatures for Vodich to eat in the shallow pool, so in the gloaming she hunted. She was not skilled at stalking on land, but the animals were docile and easily approached. Neither she nor Vodich would go hungry. During the day Men occasionally walked the grounds. Although she did not understand the words they spoke, she listened carefully, nonetheless. Late one afternoon, she heard the word that she was listening for. "Kidinnu."

One of the two men that had just passed by was the Chaldean. She stared at their faces, memorizing each, and listened as they spoke, until she was certain she had matched the voices. Certain that she knew which of the men was the one she sought.

Each night for a week he passed by about that time, on his way to a broad circle of bricks from which he observed the stars, making constant notations and mumbling to himself. The other man—an assistant or servant of some sort—carried items to and fro, then left him alone, returning at some arranged hour to carry the items away. He seemed harmless enough, but after her reception in the settlement, Meralah preferred to approach cautiously. Once she was confident of the pattern, she waited near the brick circle, concealing herself behind a tree until the servant was out of sight.

"Kidinnu the astronomer." She addressed him in Aramaic.

"Blue fairy spirit." His face was impassive, but his eyes were alight with curiosity.

"Meralah of the Nixies."

His eyes widened just enough for her to perceive it.

Their conversation was cautious at first, as they danced around their mutual uncertainties. They introduced themselves more fully as they spoke.

Meralah learned that the Chaldean was the descendant of those who had built the Hanging Gardens at Babylon, and that residing within this crafted parkland afforded him the opportunity to compare research with great minds from across the known world. She found it odd that he volunteered so much of himself to her, while asking no questions, and eventually realized that he was doing so intentionally.

He watched her as he talked, studying her reactions. She thought that he was merely gauging interest, but as he spoke more of his culture, she understood that he was—not frightened of her, exactly, but cautious. She was a magical creature, and he was trying not to offend her—from fear that she would leave, or perhaps that she would be angered and harm him in some way. The thought made her chuckle to herself—but also convinced her that he was trying to be respectful. And that made her comfortable enough to talk.

She spoke of her people, and the more she told, the more he nodded. When he finally had enough information to make the connection, he spoke of the "ancient water spirits" that had once inhabited his homeland, in a sea which had become land so many generations ago that few remembered water had ever flowed there.

If the histories of Men were reliable, the nixies of Aram had departed when the sands claimed the area, dispersing through the oceans of the known world so that the loss of a single home could never threaten their future again.

She told him of the Great Mirror in the city that had once been her home, how it watched over the other nixies, allowing each Crystal Palace to see that their kindred were alive and well—or if they needed assistance. She handed him the shard that had once been part of the Great Mirror at Aram.

He took the glass with interest, studying the images that flitted by; small blue people like the woman before him, going about their lives wholly unaware that within sheltered Shangdu, a stranger was looking over their shoulders.

"Do you know," he asked, holding the mirror out for her to examine, "which of these images originate in your home, and which are from elsewhere?"

She didn't, but she took the shard and stared into it, anyway. The smiling nixies flashed before her view, one after the other, but this time she stared at what was beyond them. She clearly saw two separate Palaces, neither of which was her old home.

"There are two different Palaces here, but I do not know either of them."

He pointed at a design in the background of one of the images: a triangle with a swirling bottom, like a mountain perched atop an ocean wave.

"That symbol is used by island peoples in the Great Sea to the east. The other must be the enclave in the Great Sea to the west of the Roman Sea. To my knowledge, your people have left behind their other homes, and these are the only enclaves that remain."

He stared expectantly.

"Certainly, the Crystal Palace in the Erythraean is gone. I touched its ruins as I travelled here. But my people still live in the Aegean—what you called the Roman Sea. I don't know why they don't show in the mirror, or why these places didn't show in ours."

Could the mirrors have broken, their connection severed? No, then this mirror could not show both Palaces.

The shuffling footsteps of Kidinnu's servant interrupted her thoughts. She tucked the shard of mirror into her pocket and disappeared behind the tree.

"Come again tomorrow," Kidinnu murmured as he gathered his belongings and handed them to the servant.

The Men disappeared into the night, and Meralah returned to Vodich. When they were settled safely at the bottom of the pool, she took out the shard of mirror again and stared, unblinking. She tried to remember if she had ever seen images of home in the mirror, or if they had disappeared only recently. She fell asleep with one hand on Vodich, and the other clenched around the shard of glass.

When evening fell, Kidinnu and his servant came again. Meralah saw no signs of deception, but chose a different tree for concealment, nonetheless. When the servant departed, she stepped out from behind the astronomer, greeting him and taking a seat on the end of the bench where he sat. He showed no surprise at her greeting, merely reoriented himself and, plucking a scroll up from a tray, began to speak.

"The mirror does not show your home because it does not exist."

Meralah opened her mouth to argue. Was this…Man…calling her a liar?

"Be serene, my friend. I do not accuse. But I do wonder…Perhaps you would tell me a little more about your home?"

She could see that his curiosity was specific. He was gathering data, not prying. So, she answered. She spoke of the sameness of life, the determination to maintain their culture exactly as it was. And she spoke of the Tide of Time, the brief period in which their Great Mirror, instead of showing the other nixies, showed events from other places and times.

The astronomer's ears perked up.

"Are you educated in the science of the stars?" he asked.

She had read the Greek and Egyptian works on the subject, and a few works by the earlier Chaldean, whom she could not help but refer to as the "original" Kidinnu, which made him laugh.

"The stars do not foretell the fates of men, as the Egyptians might have you believe. Rather, they foretell the tides of history. See there," he pointed to a group of stars, drew out the shape of a great serpent. "The dragon once sat at the top of the sky, but the earth shifts. In a few more centuries, the wagon will stand at the top of the sky. And when that occurs, the Chinese dragon-empire will fall, in favor of an empire of trade."

He gathered up a different scroll and continued.

"Three thousand years ago, do you see the clash of Nergal and Ishtar?" The scroll was an ephemeris, a recording of the positions of the planets and stars at specific times. His fingertip indicated a conjunction of Venus and Mars.

She nodded.

"The god of destruction overcame the goddess of the seas. At that time, a great upheaval in the Roman Sea destroyed cities, and buried islands. A mountain beneath the sea exploded, spreading its ash through Egypt and even into my homeland. "

This time, it was Meralah's eyes that widened.

"The eruption of Thera." The event she had seen in the Great Mirror during the Tide of Time.

"Now look at the quadrant of the sky. This clash occurred in the constellation of the Great Twins."

He stared expectantly.

"In Gemini, yes....?" This was one of the few constellations their systems had in common, but clearly it had more meaning for him than for her.

"The Twins guard the entrance to the underworld, preventing the living from entering." He paused again, continuing only when it became clear that she did not see a connection. "Your people, neither living nor dead. Unable to enter the underworld, unable to continue their lives and to grow."

"Are you saying that my people died in the eruption? That I'm some kind of…. ghost? That's ridiculous!" She had leapt up from the bench and was glaring directly into the Man's eyes.

"Dead? No." He help a hand up, palm facing her. "Suspended. Pulled out of time by the collision between their own magic and the gods' quarrel."

Suspended in time, unable to move forward, physically or culturally. Not stagnating, but…imprisoned.

"No. If that were true, how could I be here?"

"That I do not understand. If my theory is correct, you should not have been able to just…leave. Not without a guide to show you the path."

Vodich. The ray, symbol of readiness, and Protector of the Path.

"Walk with me, Kidinnu. There is someone I want you to meet."

On the way back to the briny pond, she told Kidinnu about Vodich. How we had followed her from the other side of the transparent walls of her home. Because she could see him, it never occurred to her that he should not be able to see her through the protective magic of the walls. She told the Chaldean how Vodich had guided her away from her home—and how, when he had changed her course, the temperature of the water had changed with it.

When she stepped into the pool, Vodich came to her side and she laid her hand on his back, introducing Kidinnu and inviting him to stroke the ray's velvet skin. The Chaldean knelt at the pool's edge, his sleeve dragging in the brackish water, and petted the ray as though he were touching the cheek of a god.

"It would seem that your home is lost in time. But if you seek another, I know that Setsen Khan, the Wise King of this place, would allow you to remain. Or will you seek out one of the remaining domains of your people?"

She considered for a moment. The water here was not true seawater; Vodich could not live in it for long periods. She wondered briefly if the Chaldean could help her create a way to take him safely across the sea. But these were idle thoughts, and she rejected them as swiftly as they emerged.

"My people might be *lost* in time, but they need not be *trapped* there. Vodich showed me the path, and now I must show them." She placed her hand on the Man's bedraggled sleeve and looked into his eyes, then through them to his soul. "Thank you, Kidinnu of Chaldea. Your name will be recorded in the history of my people."

She laid her cheek on the ray's back.

"Vodich, let's go home."

THE WEAVER IN THE WINDOW

At the center of the Horologium, an old man adjusted a gear, tinkering until the assemblage around it moved at a speed that satisfied him. His metal tools chimed and jingled, echoing in the vast chamber as he balanced the mechanism to a standard that only he perceived.

A younger man, his dark hair tousled above blazing eyes, prowled a vast circle around the room's outer edge, glowering at the shimmering constellations that dotted the pavilion's dome. On each circuit, he slowed to glare thunderously at Hippou and Delphinos.

The horse, and the dolphin, the old man observed. *So, it's Poseidon who has angered him, then.*

A cheery whistle drifted in from the corridor. The young man's scowl deepened. The whistle was joined by the harmonious pad of footsteps just substantial enough to be heard by an attentive listener.

"Kairos!" The old man called in greeting.

"Grandfather!" The greeting burst into the room with no less force than the young man himself. He paused at the door for no more than a second, but in that time seemed to take in all that there was to see: not just his grandfather and brother but the entire sweep of the cosmos and each gear of the mechanism at its center.

"You have arrived just in time," the old man said with a smile.

"Of course I have." Kairos *almost* smothered a grin. "The question, as always, is what I am just in time *for*."

The old man returned a conspiratorial smile.

"I have adjusted the fine mechanism, but the Imerológio needs to be tuned."

Kairos steadied the massive gear while the old man adjusted it less than a millimeter.

"Good Day, brother!" Kairos called out from behind the gear.

Aion paused an extra half-second, glowered just a bit more intensely, and continued to pace the perimeter without a sound.

"Have you any idea…?" The old man asked, not bothering to lower his voice.

"Uncle Poseidon insulted him. Called him... superfluous, I think." Kairos imitated Poseidon's deep, gravelly voice. "The cycle of thousands of years is already known to the immortals, youngster, and the mortals never live long enough to see it."

Aion went still. Kairos saw his brother tense, then force himself to appear relaxed as he turned to address them.

"He offered mortals a *salt* spring—as if a river of undrinkable water were something they would value. How does *he* know what mortals do or don't see?"

Aion's eyes narrowed and his mouth stretched in a taut and satisfied smile. "Or *im*mortals, for that matter…"

"Whatever you have in mind, brother, is it really worth it? All you're going to do is prove to him that he got to you."

The petulant scowl was familiar, but the words were delivered in a tone of certainty and determination that unquestionably heralded something new.

"Do you think so? Well, then I'll show you, too."

As his older brother stalked out of the room, Kairos trailed behind, cheerily attempting to simultaneously broker peace, find out what Aion was planning, and laugh at Poseidon's ability to get his nephew worked up.

In the Horologium, Cronus, Master of Time, watched the gears turn and the constellations drift by, and waited to see what would happen next.

***

AION

I paced the Horologium for years, watching for the moment when the stars would align.

Immortals have no need to hurry.

I walked opposite the rotation of the zodiac, pausing almost imperceptibly each time I passed the symbols of the arrogant uncle who *would* learn to show me more respect. The Mechanism of Time

162

turned in its endless and unstoppable circles.

Circles. Cycles. Rotations. My *time. The endless and repeating cycles of the universe.*

And finally, on an unremarkable August day, my uncle became annoyed.

He lifted his trident as he had a thousand times before, and struck at the base of a mountain, causing the earth to quake. But on this day, I heard my brother's footsteps behind me and knew that it was time.

I reached out my finger and pulled a tiny cog out of place. The machine carried on without it.

On an island in the Aegean, the earth rumbled. A mountain exploded. A wave swept three islands clean of everything that was not held within walls and drowned much of the rest. And at the bottom of the sea, a tiny community of immortals, subjects of the sea god, fell out of time.

***

Roiling water, molten rock, and clouds of ashen confusion tumbled outside the crystal walls. Within, hands paused at their work, curious eyes exploring the whirls of ash and salt dancing amid plumes of displaced sediment. An entire people paused, without realizing that they were witnessing the end of Time.

When the tumult subsided, the sea looked much as it had before, save that the water was heavy with unsettled silt. In a large room on the southwest side of the Crystal Palace, the weavers returned to their looms, weaving the patterns that had been woven for millennia, unaware that nothing new would ever be created there again.

ARCANE

When the dust settled, the Neptune grass undulated outside the walls as it had always done. The nixies soon forgot the swirling storm and returned to their daily lives, as they had always done. In the Erythraean Sea, a scholar touched the frame of a Great Mirror, pausing its travels to focus on the Crystal Palace of the Aegean. She saw her cousins pause in their work; she looked beyond them to the pandemonium outside their walls.

When the chaos reached its peak, the mirror went dark.

The Erythraean nixies sent an envoy to check on their kin. He encountered devastation on the human islands, entire cities annihilated by the wrath of the sea-god. When he reached the place where his cousins had once lived, he found only a meadow of Neptune grass rippling gently in the clear waters of the Aegean.

In the Horologium, Aion pocketed the unmoored gear with a satisfied smile.

***

KAIROS

"WHERE ARE THEY?" The butt of the trident thudded against the marble floor. The entire building shuddered.

"Why ask me, uncle?" Aion's nostrils flared. "What could a *minor* incarnation like me do to *your* people?"

The Sea God's bushy eyebrows drew together. The white hair contrasted sharply with his increasingly ruddy skin. Uncle was *really* angry this time.

"WHAT HAVE YOU DONE?" *Thud. Shudder.* The butt of his trident struck the marble floor, which vibrated with the Sea God's

164

wrath.

"Perhaps you had best tell him, brother." I tried to fill my voice with confidence and cheer. Uncle glowered, but Aion turned uncertain eyes in my direction.

"He's only going to get angrier." I paused, then decided to appeal to his vanity. "Besides, we're all dying to know how you pulled it off."

Good call. Aion's uncertainty turned to swagger.

"They're exactly where you left them, Uncle. I wouldn't *dream* of interfering in *your* domain. I merely removed them from *mine*. "

Uncle's face contorted in rage. I was just...confused, and a little lost.

"WHAT HAVE YOU DONE TO THEM?" *THUD. Shudder.*

"I haven't done anything to them, Uncle. They are exactly as they were. Exactly as they will always be..."

My brother was fiddling with a tiny piece of metal, rolling it over and over in his fingertips, trying to look nonchalant.

"WHAT DO YOU HAVE THERE?"

Aion gripped the tiny gear between two fingertips and held it aloft.

"This? Just a bit of detritus from Grandfather's machine. It didn't appear to be doing anything, really. It looked..." He stared directly into his uncle's eyes. "...superfluous."

He snatched the cog into his palm, closed his fist, and strode out of the room with a gait too controlled to be genuinely casual.

Thud. Shudder.

The entire building seemed to join the sea god as he shuddered in impotent rage.

***

I squinted at a segment the Mechanism of Time, looking for the telltale scratches of a spindle that had once born a tiny cog. I could spend years at this and not examine the entire machine. After a few weeks, Grandfather took pity on me.

"There."

When I turned my head, I found his wrist inches from my face, pointing into the Mechanism. I followed his wizened finger to the tip of an empty spindle. The Mechanism chugged along effortlessly around it.

Moments like that, I'm reminded that Grandfather is a Titan. I'm a little in awe of him and his Mechanism. As complex and interdependent as everything was, Aion had removed one of its pieces and it all still ran flawlessly.

But that tiny cog had been a city full of intelligent lives.

"Can nothing be done, Grandfather?"

"Lives are measured in moments, Kairos, and over that I have some power, but I do not control the sweep of time. That belongs to Aion. If he has decided that the era of the nixies has come to an end, that era is his to mark."

"But to leave them suspended in time, not knowing, with no way to escape..."

"Perhaps," Cronos' eyes twinkled, "the god of Opportunity will show himself to the Lost People."

"Me? What can *I* do to help them?"

Grandfather smiled, lifted his eyebrows briefly, and turned back to his Mechanism.

***

God of Opportunity. Nice turn of phrase, Grandfather.

It's not precise, though. In the House of Time, my domain is the opportune *moment*, that critical juncture where circumstances align to create...*possibility*. But how could I create an *opportune moment* for a people who lived in a single moment, no longer experiencing the passing of time?

I stared at the empty spindle for days, hoping it would spark an idea. Mostly it just sparked Aion's attitude. I love my brother, but he can be a real jerk. He was proud of himself for locking intelligent beings into eternity, just to get back at our uncle for a ridiculous and minor insult. Not really his best characteristic.

When I got tired of my brother's infinite pacing and constant glare, I built myself a cozy spot on the mezzanine at the base of the Horologium's dome. Seeing the mechanism from above, surrounded by the stars of the night sky, I began to understand how a handful of individuals could become invisible in the great sweep of Time. My anger faded, though I still didn't like what he had done. I was determined to create an opportunity for the nixies, if there was any one among them prepared to see it and seize it.

Grandfather appeared one day with a pane of glass in his hand: A Window in Time, focused on the Crystal Palace that had once stood at the bottom of the Aegean. That, somewhen, still stood there. I stared into it for endless hours, both fascinated and appalled by the unchanging pallor within. And then, I found the Weaver.

167

She looked no different from the rest, but occasionally the patterns in her cloth varied. She added new colors to her palate—the colors of the sea at the end of Time. Traditional shapes sporadically gave way to the whorls of the chaotic eddy into which the Crystal Palace had disappeared.

Could she still see the end of Time? Did she remember?

No, of course not. They were all frozen in an artificial moment. None of them could possibly remember the destruction that had now never passed over them.

And yet, the Weaver wove the churning brine into the corners of her cloth.

I asked Grandfather to narrow the Window to focus on this tiny sea elf who could remember across Time.

The weavers wove the patterns they had always known. Except one. No matter how often she was scolded, the force of Ennui could not stifle her. Eventually, she tired of the artless artisans, seizing an opportunity to maneuver herself in amongst the researchers in the Great Library, where even among the old scrolls new thoughts must occasionally be permitted.

Good for you, little one.

I found myself beginning to like the little Weaver in the Window. If any of them could figure it out, she would be the one. The Fates, after all, are weavers, laying out the threads of the lives of men. Perhaps this little Weaver would craft a future for her people, if I could find a way to create the opportunity.

Fortunately, we were both immortal.

Time is on our side.

The steady pace of Aion's feet drifted up from below, still pausing briefly each time he reached the Horse and the Dolphin.

Or not.

***

It took me years to find the current; a tiny, simmering tendril of tide that snaked out from the caldera of the sleeping mountain and led to the juncture where past and present had parted. I ached to follow it, but the gateway was too small for a man to fit through and there was no telling what extra mischief might be triggered if a god were to attempt it. I would need to send an envoy. I searched the waters near the caldera for a sea-ray.

The ray, Protector of the Path, is a symbol of readiness for the journey ahead, being on the right path, the moment of readiness; this, of course, makes it my personal herald. I searched until I found exactly what I was looking for, a mature ray but one young enough to spend years on the task, if necessary. When I had conveyed my instructions, I placed one hand on the ray's back and swam with it, guiding it to the tendril of time. It found the Current almost immediately.

It swam a meandering path and then, with a ripple of light on its spotted back, it disappeared. I stared after it for a long moment, then returned to the Horologium, to watch for it in the Window.

***

Aion never noticed my messenger. It was merely one sea creature among many, a life too insignificant to register on the cycles of Eternity. The Weaver and the ray, however, found one another almost immediately. Of all the nixies in the Palace, all the creatures in the sea, these two seemed to recognize one another, and their mutual attention wove gentle Threads of Fate between them.

The Weaver and a few of the scholars seemed to understand that something was wrong with their time. When the Great Mirror in their library rippled and began to show them the world of men, they stared into it, observing and making notes. While others started at the mirror, the little Weaver was writing and then re-reading her notes. So it went, over and over. She would scribble a note, roll up her parchment, and then open it again to read what she'd just written.

I watched her carefully, trying to understand. She unrolled her parchment and a small white object fell out from it.

Clever Yfantis! You're not reading your own notes—you're reading someone else's!

She had found a tiny ripple in time and was passing notes through it to…whom? She showed the tiny artefact to her colleagues, who dismissed it. This seemed to signify the end of their observations; they scattered and returned to their various scrolls and studies. The Weaver tucked her tiny treasure into a pocket and walked away.

The next morning, she left the Crystal Palace, the tiny white stone hung from a chain at her neck.

***

AION

I didn't notice the fish at first. Why would I? It wasn't until I saw the water-elf swimming away with it that I realized it was one of my brother's pets. By then, it was too late. The miserable little beast could clearly feel the difference in the Current. He followed it straight out to the present.

"KAIROOOOS!!!! How DARE you?!"

Where is he? Too cowardly to face me? FINE. Let's see how he likes this.

I adjusted a wheel on the Mechanism, an infinitesimal change. Beneath the waters of the Aegean, the little elf and her companion turned toward Egypt.

***

THE LIBRARIAN

The Librarian did not *know* he was the last of his kind, but he suspected it. As a young man, he had studied the arts of alchemy and mysticism. He had designed and built massive pyramids to serve the Pharaohs in the afterlife, but he had no intention of joining them. He was immortal, and when he tired of the quarrels of men, he prayed the gods to allow him to stay here, within the Library, for eternity.

He had now lived enough centuries to regret the prayer.

A visitor. A visitor! How many centuries has it been since the last man entered the Library? Not a man! A woman! No—a water nymph of some sort. A nixie! Nixie? Immortal! At last, a companion to share in my research...

***

KAIROS

"From one Library to another. That's really clever, brother. Don't think I missed the irony of trapping her in a Library sealed by Poseidon."

171

Aion just smiled that smug, annoying smile.

"My little *yfantis* runs the threads of her own fate. She'll find a way out."

Aion *turned his back on me* and continued tromping around the Horologium. Jerk.

Let him be as smug as he wants. She'll find her Moment, and when she does, I'll be there.

I crafted a Moment, and was pleased to see the Weaver notice it, and seize it. As the Library's exit began to fill with water, I called out to my envoy, sending the little ray to wait. When they were reunited, the Weaver pressed a gentle kiss behind its eyestalks and laid her cheek on its skin. I sighed as though the embrace had been offered to me directly.

She looked to the West, a journey that would take her back through the Aegean and out to the Great Sea. Aion blew gently on the Mechanism, and she turned east instead, ensuring that, for a while at least, they would remain within the sphere of our influence.

***

AION

Good. She's headed for the Erythraean. For all the good it will do her.

I had quietly ensured that the Crystal Palace in the Erythraean met its end centuries ago. But gods hold sway only where their worshippers live, and I wasn't prepared to let her escape to the wider world.

I may not be able to do anything about the nixies in the two Great

Seas, but they're beyond Poseidon's reach too. Poseidon. Wonder why he hasn't interfered. Or is he the one who put my brother up to it? No matter. The little wanderer is the last Nixie who will ever speak Poseidon's name.

***

KAIROS

I had been so intent on the fate of the Weaver that it had never occurred to me to look beyond Egypt and Persia to see how the remaining Nixies fared. I wept with her when she discovered the loss of her kinsmen. When she squared her tiny shoulders and made to leave, I held my breath, waiting to see which direction she would choose.

East. Further east. Beyond the boundaries of our domain.

Aion gave me that smug look again, but something was bothering him. Fortunately, my brother can generally be relied upon to give up information when goaded.

"What are *you* so pleased about? In another few hours, you won't be able to influence her any more either."

"There aren't any other nixies for five thousand miles. She'll never find them in the open sea. And if she does, it's not as if they'll know any more than she does." Aion returned to his endless pacing.

Other nixies?! Outside our sphere, of course! He could only influence the ones that were subjects of Poseidon. Wait—"know any more than she does"? Know what? The only thing to know of course! There is *a way to free her people!*

I had long since forgiven my brother for using the nixies this way.

But it still made me feel better to know he hadn't actually trapped them with *no* way to escape. It made him feel like a better person, somehow.

So, there's a way to free them, but it's not across the sea. How to get her to turn back...?

I scanned Persia, then looked beyond to Cathay. I had followers there, a Viennese family that had always taken care to listen for my footsteps and make ready to greet me. They had prospered immensely by being always ready to seize opportunity. Perhaps I could spread those profits to the little Weaver now.

The father I found in Khanbaliq. Too far. But the brother and son were at a seaport in Korea. I opened a Window of Opportunity, and the sharp-eyed merchants saw it. Instead of returning to Khanbaliq, they set out with the navy to invade a neighboring island. I had no interest in the competition and conflict. I watched, instead, for Possibilities.

By the time the Window of Opportunity had closed the young man, Polo, had conquered the islands of Cipangu and brought the obeisance of their Emperor from Edo to his Khan. More importantly, he and the Weaver had crossed paths, and he had sent her on a quest.

***

THE ASTRONOMER

One sees all manner of wonders in the court of the *Setsen Khan*. I have ridden an elephant with a leopard laid across its back before me as a hunting hound, and slept in buildings roofed with gold, but I think that nothing will ever be as wondrous to me as the evening that a creature of magic stepped forth from the greenery of the Khan's summer palace in Xanadu, and called out my name as if she knew me.

She was unremarkable in her features, this "Meralah of the Nixies," save that she stood no taller than my breastbone, and her skin was tinged blue as the depths of the sea. She stood before me clad in a tunic adorned with what I later came to know as the patterns of her people and a pair of trousers she had clearly taken from some place nearer at hand. Her gaze was steady, eyes the hue of the ocean's green, and she spoke in a tone of gentle command, clearly confident that I would do as she instructed.

When I later inquired, she explained, with great sincerity, her observations of the customs of men: that those in trousers gave orders, and those in skirts and robes followed them. She had gathered the trousers to ensure she would be heard. My robes she apparently mistook for the garment of a serving-woman. I was tempted to laugh aloud, but I too was once a stranger in a foreign land. Her misimpressions could not be any less accurate than my own, when first I had arrived at the court of the Khan.

After many hours spent exchanging tales of our homes and our people, I was able to connect her word, "nixie" to a relative of the Jinn—formed not from fire but from water—or perhaps some manner of peri. The most ancient references say they lived near Babylon millennia ago, before the ocean turned to desert. But this was before the time of men, and little more is known. Each night after we parted, I stayed up several hours recording every detail; surely this will be one of my greatest contributions to scholarship.

It will also, unquestionably, be the most unusual consultation of my career, for this "nixie" had come to seek my advice. On the night of our acquaintance, she brought forth a remarkable bit of magic, a Glass ensorcelled to display images of her kin. It came, she claimed, from my own home nation, and its images had once included her relatives who lived there. The water elementals I had identified were known to her as the Nixies of Aram. After careful examination, I ascertained that the Glass showed only two enclaves—one in the Great Eastern Sea beyond Cipangu, and one to the West, beyond the pillars of Hercules. My new friend, however, insisted there was a third.

She faded into the darkness as my assistant approached, leaving me with more questions than answers. I slept little, born upright by curiosity and enthusiasm. I gathered the details that she had offered and consulted the stars—not the ones in the sky, but in our history. From the time we parted to the hour of our next meeting, I studied the great celestial patterns. By morning, every surface in my residence was laid over in charts and ephemerides. By noon, I had an answer almost as remarkable as the question.

Across the expanse of time, I saw Nergal the destructor burst forth from a mountain, overcoming the sea in which my new friend made her home. But the tumult she had witnessed from the windows of her palace was more than just the common wrath of gods. Some opportunistic deity had wrapped the event in the tendrils of eternity, pulling her kindred out of time itself. Or perhaps it had merely been the effect of their magical nature. Whatever the cause, the result was clear: the court of the nixies had been suspended in time and space, alive but not living, imprisoned and unable to cross either to the afterlife or to the world of their origin. How, then, could this one be here? How could she see and follow the currents of time? Was she god-touched?

When next I encountered her, I posed the question: how had she escaped? She bade me follow her, that she might make an introduction. She stepped into a salted pool and was immediately joined by a sea-ray of some unfamiliar sort, whom she affectionately addressed as "Vodich" and identified as her guide and companion.

Among the people who reside in what was once Subartu, "Vod" is water. But in what was once the realm of the Hittites, "Vodich" is a guide. I briefly wondered which was intended, then decided that perhaps it was both.

She laid her hand gently on its back, inviting me to do the same. I ran my fingertips over its skin, careful to avoid the protruding eye-buds. When I trailed my hands around the edges of its pectoral fins, she was quick to caution me; the beast was able to deliver a shock, the organs for which were located beneath. This, I deduced, must be the source of its ability to sense the Ethereal Current.

I tried to convince her to stay at Xanadu. Though my words were those of a host, acknowledging her lost home, I must be forthright and admit that my invitation was a selfish one. I would write of her, of course, but to be *accompanied* by such a magical creature would surely have been a mark of fame. Without question, the Khan would have rewarded me handsomely. I could sense her indecision and assumed she must be considering seeking out the remaining enclaves of her people. She surprised me once again.

"My people might be lost in time, but they need not be trapped there. Vodich showed me the path, and now I must show them."

She placed her hand on my bedraggled sleeve and stared into my eyes. In that moment, I felt her attention in a way that I have not experienced before or since. I saw within her eyes the immortal span of years that stretched behind and before her. When she spoke again, it was almost a ceremony, bestowing an honor unlike any other I have known.

"Thank you, Kidinnu of Chaldea. Your name will be recorded in the history of my people."

I was briefly overcome by the awareness that when my people have ceased to exist, when the very memory of them has been consumed by the abyss of time, Meralah of the Nixies will remember me. I stood mute, unable to produce a statement worthy of the occasion.

She looked away, whispering to her companion. When she was done, she stood upright and rested her hand on the creature's back. Two ripples briefly glinted in the starlight, then settled, leaving the water as still as glass. No Nixie was reflected therein—just the infinite stars reflected in the currents of the salted lake at Xanadu.

***

AION

"How could he even KNOW?! He's not even our subject!"

"Even we, Grandson, are merely part of a greater Whole. While he may not know us by name, the larger Pattern is Universal."

Grandfather's voice was patient. Grandfather's voice is *always* patient. It only made the moment more infuriating. Or maybe it was just my brother's infinitely cheerful smile that was galling me.

"You. Ruin. EVERYTHING!" Shouting at Kairos only makes me angrier. He never responds, just stands there smiling until you leave, or talk to him. Once, I asked the annoying little jerk why he does that. He told me he was just "waiting for the right Moment."

Sometimes, I really loathe that little brat.

Still, his stupid pet can't lead them *all* out. I WILL NOT let him ruin this!

***

APHRODITE

"I don't know what I'm going to do with them, 'Dite. Kairos doesn't hold a grudge, but Aion has become so volatile. I don't know why he feels the need to *fight* with everyone. He just can't seem to let go of his anger toward his uncle. I don't understand it!"

"Of course you don't brother." *Men never do.*

To Cronos' credit, though, he recognized my tone and finally shut up for a minute.

"You are a Titan, and the Master of Time. Keeper of the Past, Present, and Future. Kairos' work…intersects with yours. But Aion— his patterns overlap and interweave with yours. Everything he does depends on you, and you on him. "

Cronos looked at me like I was stupid. I mean, yes, I was stating the obvious, but was he really unable put those facts together?

"Kairos is independent. You may see Aion as a partner or complement—but you are a TITAN. He can never be your equal. And for a young man, to know he can never be equal means he is 'less than'. He's just trying to find some way to identify himself independently. And 'Sei didn't help any, tweaking his nose like that."

I could see the light finally beginning to dawn. My brother may be slow—or perhaps he just operates on a different *time* than the rest of us—but he isn't stupid. Once he starts to put the picture together, he has a terrific grasp of the intricacies. And he was smart enough to realize that anything he did was only going to make it worse. Setting himself up as Aion's adversary or his superior wasn't going to achieve anything positive.

"Why don't you leave this one to me, Cro? I promise I'll keep the boy from killing anyone."

"How do you propose to do that?"

"If there's one thing I know, brother, it's how to soothe men."

Cronos' face turned red, and he began to huff.

Idiot. They're my great-nephews for goodness' sake.

I flashed him my best "vixen" smile and sashayed out of the room before he could manage to form any words.

***

KAIROS

The Weaver returned to her home, but my brother had done his work well. Lost in time, her people had no desire to be found. Unable to remember the life they had lost, they were also unable to pursue it.

She had returned to her home but spent most of her time outside its walls with her companion. I was reminded briefly of one of Cousin Apollo's girlfriends, a priestess called Kassandra. Once she had been touched by the God of Truth, she no longer belonged among the fantasies men craft for themselves. My little Weaver seemed to be in the same position, knowing what her people did not wish to know, speaking truth to those who were happier with their illusion.

It was enough to make even me a bit melancholy. I presume that's why grandfather sent my Aunt to me, and I'm glad he did. It was she who found the answer. We might not be able to save the Weaver's people, but we can offer her a home and a future, nonetheless. Aunt Aphrodite even promised to square it with Aion.

***

AION

Aunt Aphrodite is right. Killing another god is more trouble than I'm prepared to deal with. While it might be really *satisfying* to throw my uncle *and* my little brother into a fiery pit, I don't want to end up like Prometheus, or worse.

Still, it's NOT RIGHT! The little brat nearly ruined my revenge, and gods know the arrogant old fart was due for a comeuppance.

I hate, hate, HATE that she's going to escape. But I have to hand it to Aunt Aphrodite, it is a good plan. And Aunt will turn her into a *mortal*. I may have to let her live for now, but in a few years—not even an eyelash in the Great Sweep of Time—she'll die out, just like her people. The immortal nixies will worship my uncle no longer, and my victory over him will be complete. And as for my brother, he'll have to watch his little pet elf fade away and die, and he won't even be able to blame me for it. Aunt has him convinced it's some kind of *reward*!

***

181

ARCANE

MERALAH

It felt like I had been swimming in circles for days. Probably because I had. Vodich and I had been circling the Palace for no reason except that I couldn't sit still and couldn't think of what else to do. Perhaps it was some effect of the magic that held them in time, but my people didn't *want* to know. I couldn't convince anyone to even try to leave with us.

"Well, Vodich. They aren't coming, and we can't spend the rest of eternity swimming in circles. I think it's time to go. I'm not entirely sure where, but...not here."

I wasn't even sure if we *could* escape again, but for some reason, with Vodich at my side, it just seemed...possible. A fin fluttered against my cheek and I tickled his tummy in return. We took one last circle around the Palace and when we reached the northeast, he turned out to sea. The current grew warmer, and then began to bubble and grow cloudy with silt. I kept one hand on his back and trusted to my guide. He had never led me wrong before.

We surfaced near an island in the dark of night, gliding slowly to the shallows. Hazy clouds obscured the stars. Vodich wasn't moving right, his fins rippled too slowly. Had the water been too warm for him?

He settled himself in the sand at the edge of the shore, the water barely deep enough to cover his eyestalks. Something was clearly wrong, but I couldn't tell what it was. I stroked his back, abruptly aware the tiny bumps and wrinkles that had not been on his skin when we first swam together.

We've been travelling together for years. Vodich is...old

"Vodich, my friend, have I run you too hard? I don't know what it is to get old, but I have read that it's fatiguing."

He ruffled his fins, a cheery gesture, and I scratched his back gently.

"You are my best friend, Vodich. My only friend. If there is something you need, only tell me so I can make it so."

Vodich skimmed to the side, maneuvering his body to rest on my arm. I could feel his tiny heart beating against the back of my hand. And then, a moment later...I couldn't. I stroked his fin, and there was no answering flutter. I wrapped my other arm around him, rested my cheek on his back and wept until the moon disappeared from the sky.

When the darkness began to fade, I dragged my friend's body away from the shallows and pushed it beneath the sea. One last time we swam as we so often had: Vodich beneath me, my hand resting on his back. I guided him to the bottom of the sea and nestled his body into the sand. Here, he would rejoin the Great Cycle, his body providing food to the shrimp and crabs that had once been his nourishment. And one day, another ray would come along and eat *them,* and the circle would continue unbroken.

Having returned my only friend to the sea, I made once more for shore. Vodich had brought me here; now it was time to find out where "here" might be.

I was prepared for land this time, having learned something of the customs and clothing of humans. I wore loose attire that made it easy to hide my hands and feet; I concealed my face with a heavy scarf laid over my head.

Daylight revealed that it had not been clouds that obscured the stars but smoke. Something was on fire on a nearby island. The island itself must be on fire to produce that much smoke.

I followed the milling schools of humans to a vast building, pushed through into its courtyard by the force of the throng. I maneuvered my way to the edge of the crowd and headed for the shallows. Small structures dotted the walls at the edges of the piazza. The spaces between them offered room to sit or stand out of the path of the mob.

The white walls were painted in bold colors, reds and blacks layered in intricate drawings portraying animals and people. The wall behind me was decorated with dolphins, and I fingered the tiny pendant that still hung around my neck, carved by a long-ago friend whom I had never met, but might have loved. I wandered through the courtyards until I reached one that offered room to breathe. From the conversations of the people around me, I gathered that this place housed city government, and its business would not start for a few hours. This left the space open enough to truly see its artwork.

Across from me, a vast mural depicted a seascape with towering cliffs. Something about it tickled my memory. Something from my conversation with Nikos? I reached into my tunic and retrieved the container that still held the notes we had written to one another.

Three thousand years ago, I had passed this parchment back and forth through time with a man doomed to die. His island home had been built atop a volcano. When it began to steam and spew ash, he had left home and gone to his peoples' capitol at Knossos to take shelter in the Palace there. But he had been outside—in the palace courtyard—when the volcano erupted, destroying his home, and sending towering waves to all the nearby islands.

A hall of stone with its walls painted red, and murals in black and white and red. A seascape, with great cliffs at one side.

The cliffs are Tyrins, the city where Heracles undertook his great Labors. We have a port there. The room you saw was the Palace's civic hall, where citizens come to pursue affairs of governance.

The Civic Hall?

I turned my eyes to the great clouds of smoke in the sky. Not smoke—ash!

"Vodich!! Dear, dear friend."

A passerby, thinking I was talking to myself, shook her head at me. Let her shake. Let her think me as mad as a Maenad. Vodich had brought me to Knossos, and somehow, he had brought me here in time to save Nikos! To get him off this island and to the mainland before the palace was destroyed.

I pushed my way back into the courtyard, shoving through the milling assembly until I found the mural of the man dancing with a bull. This was the place that Nikos had sat. Would sit. The gleaming bench just beneath the bull's hooves was empty, but the cloud of ash hung in the sky. He would come.

I studied each man that passed by the bench, tall and short, tiny and fat, cheerful and dour. A short man paced the plaza, his blue eyes surveyed everything around him, resting equally on the people, the structures, and the murals that adorned them. He examined the world as though he had never seen it before, and constantly rubbed his hands together as if he were cold. When he settled himself upon the bench, he dropped his hands between his knees but never ceased their motion.

I stepped through and around until I stood before him, little more than an arm's breadth separating us. He tilted his face up at me and smiled. When his gaze lit on the dolphin at my throat, his hands went still. He held his left hand palm-up, raising it so that I could see the small white pendant that lay within, surrounded by the sand he had been using to smooth its edges.

"Nikostratos Andreou of Akrotiri." I had intended to pose it as a question, but it emerged as a statement.

"I beg your pardon." He stared into the shadows of my headcloth, squinting into the sun as he attempted to ascertain my features. "I am a visitor to Knossos and only recently arrived, but I am certain that if I had heard such a beautiful voice, I would remember it."

I held out one cerulean palm, offering him the ivory tube that held our impossible correspondence.

"My name is Meralah, and I have so much to tell you."

THE SOUND OF SILENCE

Stories of the Tiktik, may have been inspired by real life events, despite how fantastical they seem. A theory holds that the hunting calls that the creature makes may be calls of nocturnal birds. These four stories are such tales.

LYNDSEY ELLIS-HOLLOWAY

BEWARE THE SILENCE

"We're going to get caught," Katie whispered, looking over her shoulder at the Train's security personnel, and glancing away as one of them caught her eye. "We're going to get caught and we're going to be in *so* much trouble."

"Oh, come on Katie-Kat, where's your sense of adventure?" Devon whispered back, grinning at the nervous girl as she shuffled into the centre of their group to avoid being seen. "We've all got our stories straight, and if they look it up, they will find coursework that matches it, so what's the issue?"

"The issue is that we're *lying*!" Katie scowled as she crossed her arms over her chest and huffed.

"Don't be such a 'fraidy Kat, we won't get caught," Devon winked, only to wince as someone elbowed him in the ribs.

"Shut up, brother dear, and shift, the line is moving," Casey sighed, rolling her eyes. She used her fingertips to push him forward "I get it, Kat, seriously I do, but we agreed to join them on this insane escapade because *they* agreed to take us shopping afterward, remember?"

Linking her arm with Katie's, Casey beamed, tucking a wayward strand of shocking red hair behind her ear. "Just think of all those vintage clothes we can bring back, we will be *the* talk of the school, and all of it paid for by the boys. Anyway, none of those ghost stories Devon reads ever come to anything, you know that best to just indulge his stupidity for five minutes." She glanced at her twin who stood chatting to the tall, dark, and handsome Adam. "Besides, this way we get to spend some time with the boys, shows we're better than those dingbats back at school."

Katie smiled, her bright blue eyes flickering to Devon for a moment as she squeezed Casey's arm and giggled. "Fair point."

Casey blushed, skirting around her best friend's last words, but not before shooting the blonde girl a disapproving look. "Just imagine her face when we have all these genuine vintage clothes, *brand new*, and she's got squat because her and the airhead brigade chose the 30th century for their class project rather than the 21st."

"God forbid she couldn't have her holophone or emotifilter on permanently," Sarah added, rolling her eyes and flicking her long blonde ringlets over her shoulder as she made a face.

The group laughed collectively as they stepped forward, smiling at the security officer manning the barrier.

"Hand over the scanner, where and when are you travelling to?" The man asked with a sigh, raising an eyebrow at the group of teenagers and weighing up whether or not he was about to have trouble to deal with.

"21st century, the year 2020, American town by the name of Providence," Adam said as he stepped forward, holding his tanned hand over the scanner. The group had mutually agreed that if anyone could be convincing it would be Adam—Devon was likely to giggle and give the game away, Tom could be read like a book, he screamed trouble just by looking at him. No, Adam was their ticket through, he *looked* sensible.

"Reason for travel?"

"School project, we have a group history presentation to do on a century of our choice."

"Why Providence, then?" The officer asked, eyes narrowing as he glanced over Adam's shoulder to the others.

"Random rolled American towns in that time period, and this is the one we landed on," Adam shrugged.

***

"Alright. I take it from your age that you've travelled by Time Line in the past with school?"

"That's right."

"So, you know the rules? I'm not going to stand here and repeat all of them and waste the next twenty minutes of my life, am I?"

"Oh no Sir, not at all Sir, we'll behave, Sir," Devon grinned, freckled face peering over Adam's shoulder, gasping for air as his friend elbowed him in the ribs in the same place he'd already been nudged. The officer scowled.

"No, Sir you don't, we know the rules—our teachers made us memorise them before they would authorise chips to allow us to buy tickets," Adam interjected before the officer could reprimand the group for Devon's insolence. "No interfering with the locals, act like tourists and leave a minimal footprint—we can bring back souvenirs but only stuff that we have bought in the shops and everything will be screened on our return."

"Amongst others, but you've got the major ones for what you're travelling for. Keep *him* and the others out of trouble. Go to your allocated car, find your seat, and put on the emergency signal band immediately. If you aren't wearing them when the Train goes through the scanner you won't be travelling, got it? Any trouble hit the button and Agents will arrive within ten minutes."

The officer let Adam through the barrier, glared at Devon as he scanned his wrist, and showed the rest through one at a time. As the group made their way down the platform, they could still feel his eyes boring into their backs, but they were through and, on their way, so it didn't matter anymore.

Casey cast a glance back at the officer and her eyes met with the woman with shocking red hair, who had been next in line. A shiver went down her spine and she scowled, why did the woman look so familiar? She stopped, barely aware of Katie jolting to a halt beside her as they were holding hands.

"Casey?" Katie whispered, squeezing Casey's hand as she

followed Casey's line of sight, eyes narrowing at the red-haired woman who was watching the group head down the platform with a pained look. "What's her problem?"

"Not sure. Come on," Casey muttered, shaking her head and picking up the pace to follow the others, glancing back at the woman until she was no longer in view.

Settling into their designated train car, the group breathed a sigh of relief. Casey leaned forward to punch Devon in the shoulder.

"Ow! What is with all the abuse today?!" he yelped.

"Could you just for *once* bite your tongue and not be a gigantic ass please?" she hissed, glaring at her twin. "I swear Devon, one of these days your jokes are going to land you in some serious hot water if not all of us."

"Alright, chill! Fucking hell Casey, these people expect a bit of teenage banter, don't they? Group of boys out with the girls? Showing off?"

"Casey isn't wrong Dev," Adam sighed as he leaned back in his seat and closed his eyes. "You're going to get us in deep shit one of these days."

"Buzzkills. All of you," Devon muttered, slouching in his seat

While Devon continued to sulk, the rest of the group fell into idle conversation. Sarah and Tom giggled and kissed at one end of their car, while Katie and Casey chatted about what clothes they were going to make the boys buy for them—Casey glancing at Adam every now and again, blushing whenever he caught her eye.

As the train pulled out of the station the group began to talk in hushed, excited tones about their planned adventure—Devon forgetting his upset with them all the moment they asked their 'leader' for more details. Entering the tunnel, the lights dimmed, and they felt the strange yet familiar pressure build in their heads. It wasn't the first time they had felt the build-up associated with a jump from their present to the past. Countless history field trips had prepared them so it didn't stop their conversation, even if they all felt a little uncomfortable.

As the pressure reached its peak and the tunnel began to glow Devon grinned. "Three, two, one—we have liftoff!"

"He has no idea where he's going, does he?" Katie sighed, glaring at Devon. They had been walking around Providence for over an hour, following the hastily written directions their 'leader' had copied onto a notepad since their holophones had no signal in this time period.

"I'd like to see *you* navigate through a town you don't know in a place where your NavCom doesn't connect," Devon muttered, sticking his tongue out at her as he squinted at the town map he'd bought from a convenience store, trying to locate the street he was looking for.

"Kat, he couldn't find his way to the toilet without his NavCom, you know there is a simpler solution," Casey added, flicking her long hair over her shoulder, pushing past her brother and marching over to a group of boys a year or two older than their own group. "Hi, my friends and I are from out of town, we've got bored with the usual sightseeing. We heard that there is an abandoned apartment block that's meant to be haunted, don't suppose you could point a girl in the right direction?" She grinned, hands clasped behind her back to push her breasts out, swaying back and forth slightly as she batted her eyelids at them—more than aware of where their eyes drifted to.

"Er yeah sure. I mean, we all know where it is, but don't think you want to go there," the tallest of the boys replied.

"Oh? And why not?" Tom shouldered Casey out of the way, the tall, muscular lad barely noticing as he caused her to yelp and stumble sideways. Casey looked up gratefully when Adam caught her elbow and steadied her. She blushed, trying not to stare at him.

"Because it's haunted?" one of the other boys said as if the question had been obvious. "As in, do not go there because you're likely to *die,* haunted. If you know about the apartment, then you know how dangerous it is."

"Oh, come off it, that's just a rumour, though, right? To scare the kids and keep them out because it's like a drug den or something?" Devon scoffed.

"You really are from out of town, if you believe that. Look, no local would go there because we're not fucking dumbasses, it's dangerous and morons like you have died before, usually when they won't listen."

"Who you calling a dumbass?!" Devon snarled.

Tom growled beside his friend; hands balled into fists.

"You Devon, not that he's wrong," Casey weighed in once more, pushing both Tom and Devon out of the way and sighing heavily, smiling apologetically to the boys. "Look, my idiot twin brother wants a good story to tell all his friends and they've all heard about this place.

Just direct us so he can get one foot in the door? He'll only run away like a screaming girl the minute a rat scurries past him, anyway. Please?"

"Sure whatever, not our fucking fault if you all die because you wouldn't listen and the thing inside eats you," the first boy muttered.

Casey thanked the boys for their instructions, herding her friends off in the direction they had been instructed to go before she turned on her twin. "Why? Why can't you just stop aggravating everyone?"

"What did I do now?! Tom started it!"

"And *you* had to make things worse, as usual, and what's this about people dying in the place Devon? You never mentioned *that* when plotting this little 'field trip' of yours."

"Didn't I? Oh, come on Case, they're nothing—probably stupid kids falling off crumbling stairwells or something, or overdosing on drugs."

"He said there was a 'thing' inside that eats you Dev," Katie protested, pouting at him. "That's why you wanted to come isn't it?"

"Alright, alright! So I read a bunch of books on myths and legends from the 21st century and there was this one about *this* haunted apartment block; people have been coming here for years and yes some people have died—*some*, not all—and they could never explain what had killed them but come on! It's all nonsense, same as all the rest of the myths and legends we ever studied in English Lit for crying out loud. It's just a scary old abandoned building, that's it, that's why we're here—and to shop for you girls of course," he grinned, sliding an arm around Katie's shoulders and winking. "Bet we could find you some pretty cute dresses here Katie-Kat, give me a little fashion show back home. Alooone."

"When you've quite finished debasing yourself *and* my best friend could we get on with this insane fiasco of a trip so that we *can* go shopping please," Casey sighed, flicking her brother in the temple as she rolled her eyes and strode past him. "How I'm related to you is beyond me."

Thankfully, the instructions were straightforward, and it only took them ten minutes to reach their destination. The minute they stepped onto Spruce Avenue they stopped.

While each house was clearly lived in, the street felt abandoned. There were no children playing outside, no adults chatting on their lawns—in fact, the lack of any noise of any kind was so oppressive it was almost deafening.

"Yeah, because this isn't remotely foreboding, is it?" Casey muttered, glaring at her twin before looking back over her shoulder, scowling at a figure on the horizon.

"Oh, knock it off Case, fuck sake. So, no one is about and there are no birds or anything—they did suffer that plague around this time remember? That we're all immune to before anyone starts fucking moaning about that as well. Maybe they're just cautious about coming outside, you know, they just like to stay in."

"Smooth Dev, smooth. Are you trying to convince the girls or yourself?" Adam whispered, patting Devon's shoulder as he moved past his friend. "Come on, might as well get this over with since we're already here."

Sarah and Katie cast a nervous glance at one another, then looked to Casey for guidance, but Casey was too busy squinting at the shadowed figure following behind them.

"Casey, what is it?" Sarah asked.

"I swear that they're following us," Casey muttered.

"Isn't that the same woman from the Time Line station?" Katie gasped.

"So, it's *not* my imagination! Come on, let's catch up to the guys, I don't like that she's following us," Casey hissed, pushing Katie and Sarah after Adam.

As the group trooped down the street they fell back into idle chatter, occasionally glancing at the quiet houses either side of the street, the girls keeping an eye on the woman in the distance.

At the far end of the road, they came to a sweeping corner lined with tall trees and high, overgrown hedges. Devon bounced excitedly to the head of the group as he spotted a narrow opening in the hedgerow—thorns and vines stretching out from either side of the gap as though straining to take hold of one another and seal the void permanently. Seemingly unperturbed by the years of plant growth, or the thorns that threatened to cut them all to shreds, Devon turned sideways and shuffled through the gap, vanishing from sight.

"Come on slowpokes! We're here!" he called excitedly.

Casey sighed heavily, motioning for the others to go through first—the woman was closer now and she needed to speak with her. "Go on ahead! I'll be right through, I've got a stone in my shoe," she called through the gap, moving away from it to confront their stalker as the woman jogged toward her. "What do you want?" Casey hissed under her breath, making sure none of the others were coming back through. "Why are you following us?"

"Casey listen to me, you can't go in there—those local boys were right it's dangerous and you'll die," the woman gasped, hands on her knees as she caught her breath.

"H-how do you know my name?! Who the hell are you?!"

"I can't tell you that, I'm sorry I wish I could because then maybe you would listen to me but I can't. I tried to catch up to you in the Station to stop you but I was too late, please I'm begging you, don't go into that building."

"Case ya coming?" Devon called from behind the bushes.

"You're crazy… just leave me alone and stop following us," Casey snapped quietly, "Coming!" She called back to her brother, turning to head through the gap.

"No!" The woman hissed, hand snapping out to grab Casey's wrist. The pair gasped, pulling their hands away swiftly.

Casey flexed her tingling fingers, holding her trembling arm to her chest as she felt it going numb, her eyes wide as she stared at the woman reflecting her movements exactly. "Who the hell are you?" She asked quietly, it was more demand than a question.

"You know, deep down you know. I'm sorry, I can't tell you, I shouldn't even *be* here. They're going to pull me back, now that I've touched you the Agents will be coming to fetch me because I've broken the rules. I am *begging* you, Casey, don't go in, don't let them get to the third floor. You will lose everything if you do just like I did,

I can't let it happen, not again," the woman looked down at her wrist as the emergency beacon began to flash and vibrate violently.

Casey used the woman's momentary distraction to dart away, ignoring her hissed plea, pulling away from the fingertips she felt a brush against the back of her shirt. She put her hand in front of her eyes to protect them from the thorns, stumbling through and into her waiting friends.

"What the fuck took you so long?" Devon barked.

"Nothing, never mind let's just get moving," Casey muttered, pushing her brother away from the hedge, glancing through the entrance and hoping the woman wasn't going to follow.

Behind them, the dilapidated apartment block loomed, like some terrible monolith from an ancient age (which for them it was). It leaned to the right, slouching upon its foundations as though it had grown tired of reaching for the sky. The right-hand corner of the roof had crumbled away to expose the hollow innards of the building. Four floors laid bare where concrete and brick had given way to the elements. Twisted, rusty steel struts that had once held the walls together seeking the concrete they had once held. It was hard to imagine the building as it had been when occupied, the outside was weathered and cracked, covered in vines that looked as though they were the only thing keeping the building from splitting in two.

Between them and the apartment lay a field full of debris. Large chunks of the building strewn across brown lawn dotted with thorn bushes. Tall weed grass throttled the flower beds that had once lined the pavement leading to the front door. The pavement itself had fractured; the plant life having reclaimed it through disuse.

"Well, isn't this joyous," Sarah snapped, glaring at Tom.

He held his up his hands to ward her off. "Come on babe, I raided Dad's card for spending money remember. Maybe we can get you some nice jewellery? You keep saying you want a necklace."

"Think big Tom, think *diamonds*," Sarah snarled, wrapping her arms about his waist as he grinned sheepishly at her. "I fucking hate you. Why can I not be angry at you, like ever?"

"Because you love me. Diamonds it is then, but first *that*." Tom grinned, pointing to their goal and winking at the boys.

"Yes, indeed!" Devon clapped his hands together, grinning fiendishly before he turned and led the way through the overgrowth, winding over the long-abandoned path toward the front door.

Just like on Spruce Avenue the area surrounding the apartment block was unnaturally quiet—while the flora had thrived with the lack of human interference it seemed that the fauna had avoided it entirely. As they waded through the grass, disturbing the weeds, the girls had waved hands in front of their faces out of instinct, to beat away swarms of mosquitoes, only to slowly lower their arms when they realised there *were* no insects at all. There was no birdsong, no rodents scurrying away in the grass there was just... nothing. Other than the crunch of dry grass, twigs, and stones beneath their feet there was no sound at all, making their racing heartbeats and their breaths seem inexplicably loud.

The closer they came to the building, the more Casey was plagued by the woman's words, haunted by the image of someone she felt she knew despite them being a stranger. She looked back at the hedgerow in the distance. She hoped to catch a glance of the woman, to make sure she *had* been real since nothing about this place felt solid to her now, she was closer to the apartments.

The building entrance stood open like the gaping maw of a monster, the door hung at an angle—clinging to its last remaining hinge, beckoning the weary into the dark depths within

"Right then! Who's going in first?" Devon grinned, standing just shy of the shadowy entrance as he looked over each of his friends, a lion picking out his prey.

"I will," Tom replied, stepping forward, hands shoved into his pockets. "Fucking bunch of pussies, it's a fucking *building*, always the same with you lot."

"Oh no, if that's how we're going to be," Casey chimed in, shaking Katie from her arm as she pushed Tom out of her way, shooting him a smug glance. She needed to do this, she had to shake off what that woman had said to her, and the only way to do that was to ignore everything she'd said. "Try this on for size, badass," she added, sticking her middle finger up at him as she ran straight inside. "Come on, slowpokes!" she called from within, her voice echoing from the empty entrance.

Tom followed without hesitation, Devon, and Adam slipping in behind him with Katie and Sarah.

The lobby mirrored the state of disrepair of the outside—the floor tiles had buckled and cracked with the shifting weight of the building. The stairs crumbled at the edges to reveal its steel skeleton, clinging to what concrete it could, desperate to keep itself together. The door to the elevator lay at a haphazard angle, revealing the bottomless shaft beyond. No elevator car to be seen, but given the steel cables snaking out from the open door, it was safe to assume it had long since crashed into the basement.

The air was stale and full of dust, the heavy scent of urine and other unspeakable rubbish caused Casey to gag, and the other girls to hold their hands over their noses. It was enough to make Casey's eyes water, blurring her vision as she looked up the stairs to the floors above.

"What died in here?!" Devon cried, retching and holding his hand over his mouth.

"Heading up?" Tom asked, his arm around Sarah's shoulder as he looked up, leaning slightly to get a better look up the stairwell where remnants of banister clung precariously to their place, twisted and threatening to crash down upon their heads at the slightest disturbance.

"Duh. Come on, should be safe if we keep to the edges, maybe it smells less high up," Devon said as he placed a tentative foot on the bottom step.

"Should be safe—comforting, thank you for that brother dear. And just how high up *are* we going?"

"Only to about the third floor, that's where the book said the spooky stuff starts."

"Brilliant, I can't see this ending in tears at all, do we *have* to go to the third floor? Really?" Casey muttered. The woman's warning echoed in her head '*don't let them get to the third floor*'.

202

"Yes. Yes, we do," Devon grinned.

Casey sighed and reached out to take Katie's hand, there was no point in arguing with her brother now. She let Adam and Devon lead the way, following behind with Katie while Sarah and Tom brought up the rear. They kept their backs to the wall, steering clear of the decaying edge. Despite the buildings dilapidated state, it appeared quite sturdy. The group was forced to dodge fallen concrete from the upper floors, kicking empty cans and bottles of alcohol out of the way.

As they reached each floor, Devon gave the cavernous entrance that led to what would have been the apartments, a cursory glance—just in case there was anything worth exploring.

"Nope, something died in here too," Devon gagged, blinking furiously as he ushered the group on.

The second floor yielded much the same, and so on they trekked to the third floor and the beginning of their goal.

Looking back as they made their way up from the second floor Casey realised the rubbish was minimal now, they weren't forced to kick it away. The graffiti that had covered the grey walls below now sparse, revealing the apartments drab grey skin. At least the smell of urine was less up here.

Casey scowled as a shiver ran down her spine, subconsciously rubbing her arm with a hand to rid herself of the goosebumps forming there. The air hung strange, heavy and sick, foreboding almost, as though warning them back. Glancing at the others, she wondered if they had felt it too; there was no use in asking Katie, she was afraid of everything, and Devon wouldn't admit it even if he had. Could she bring herself to ask Adam and look like she was afraid? Looking over her shoulder at Tom and Sarah she felt bolstered by the other girl's smile—if Sarah was still grinning then things would be fine.

"Third floor! Dun dun duuuuun," Devon sang as he bowed with a flourish, motioning for his friends to go ahead of him.

"That's right Dev, sacrifice the rest of us to the ghost why don't ya?" Tom laughed, punching his friend playfully in the shoulder. He shoved his hands into his pockets, leaning around the doorless frame before disappearing into the shadows within.

"Anything?" Devon called.

"Fuck all, don't know why everyone gets worked up. It's a fucking empty room with all the walls and most of the ceiling above on the floor, how fucking exciting are you expecting it to be?" Tom replied.

Devon's face fell and Casey sighed, rolling her eyes at her twin. "Come on, let's explore it a bit and see if there's something exciting hidden in a dark corner, hm?"

The girls walked around the edge of the room together, muttering about how stupid boys were and how ridiculous this entire trip was. Tom stood to one side smoking while Devon checked behind every nook and cranny for *something* spooky, Adam following as he usually did.

"What the hell is this?" Adam asked suddenly, his gaze turned to a place above where the ceiling had fallen away to reveal the floors above them.

The group hurried to see what had caught his attention. Collectively they gasped at the claw marks gouged deep into the concrete above them.

"What the fuck made *those*?" Tom snapped, looking to Devon for answers.

"How the hell would I know?!"

"*You* were the one reading the books, Dev; surely they said something about what the fuck is meant to be here?" Tom seethed, shaking Sarah off his shoulder and grabbing Devon by his shirt.

"Hey!" Devon yelped. "Look it said this place was haunted and people died here, it didn't say by what because the legends said no one ever survived it!"

"Oh great, no one survives and you drag us here? Really smart move Dev," Sarah yelled.

"Come off it Sarah, if no one survived there would be no story would there? It's just a story! I just thought it would be a bit spooky and we could have a cool story to tell the others!"

Tiktik.

Tiktik

"Did you not think to fucking tell us about this, Devon?" Tom continued, shaking his friend.

Tiktik.

Tiktik

"What was that?" Adam muttered.

Tiktik...

Tiktik...

"Because you wouldn't have come if I had?" Devon replied.

"Shut up," Adam demanded.

Tiktik…

Tiktik…

"You should've told us the—"

"Shut the fuck *up*!" Adam ordered angrily. "Can you hear that?!"

The group fell silent, shocked at Adam's sudden rage. That's when they heard it too.

Tiktik…

Tiktik…

"What the fuck is that?" Tom whispered.

"I don't know, but it sounds to be far away, let's get out of here while it is," Adam replied, gently pushing Casey out in front of him, motioning for the others to follow back to the door.

Hurrying for the stairwell not one of them dared utter a word, straining their ears to hear the thing and keeping as close to the wall as they could—not quite daring to look around, none of them wanting to know what had made the noise. Even Devon, who had been adamant about making this trip, kept his jaw tightly shut, grinding his teeth as he tried to calm his racing heart.

The door was within reach when the silence was pierced with a bloodcurdling scream. Casey, Adam, and Devon turned to look behind them, their eyes growing wide, colour draining from their faces at the sight of Sarah.

Her scream seemed never-ending and for a brief moment, Casey wondered how she had the breath left to continue. There stood their friend. Alone.

Entrails draped over Sarah's shoulders like some horrifying scarf.

Her blond hair now red and matted, blood covering her from head to toe. One of Tom's trainers lay on the floor beside Sarah, his foot still attached to the shoe, snapped off just below the knee. A pool of blood and some tattered strands of Katie's clothes the other side.

Casey screamed; her eyes fixed on the ragged remains of her best friend's clothes.

"*Run!*" Adam roared, darting back to Sarah, grabbing her hand and forcing her to move as the other scurried toward the door, all of them scanning about in a desperate search for the thing that had taken their friends.

Sarah continued to sob as they made it to the stairwell, throwing the entrails from her shoulders and shivering.

"Are you ok? Are you hurt?" Casey whispered, eyes checking over her friend.

"Th-they're dead," Sarah stammered, trembling as Casey breathed a sigh of relief that Sarah seemed unharmed.

Adam took the first few steps down before he was forced to throw himself back up to the third-floor landing. Something came hurtling from above them, landing with a sickening crunch and a splat as bone snapped and blood sprayed upon impact.

The group screamed in unison, the boys recoiling. A mixture of shock and fear at the sudden appearance of the thing—the realisation that the mangled, bloody mess, blonde hair covering her face, was once their friend.

"Up! Go up!" Adam commanded, scrambling to his feet, herding his friends up.

They were forced up the next two flights of stairs, the steel doors from the fourth and fifth floors were still intact and locked, leaving them with no choice but to keep going up.

Tiktik.

Tiktik.

The faint call drifted from above them as they reached the sixth floor. Adam tried the door, exhaling loudly as the handle turned.

Tiktik.

Tiktik.

Adam opened the door and stepped inside, dragging Sarah behind him. He halted, toes over the precipice of a gaping hole that led to the floor below, only just stopping himself from falling through with Sarah in tow. "Carefully," he hissed, keeping hold of Sarah's hand as he pressed his back to the wall and led her around the gap to the left, toward a more solid floor.

Tiktik.

Tiktik.

"This way Casey, we have to hurry, it's getting closer," Devon said desperately as he took hold of his sister and led her to the right while the others continued left.

TIKTIK.

TIKTIK.

The sharp sound echoed through the empty room, deafening as it bounced from wall to wall. Their hearts in their throat Devon and Casey ran to a pillar, pressing their backs to it and huddling together. Sarah and Adam managed to hide to one side of the room, the ceiling above had fallen through and created a temporary shelter where it rested against the wall. The steel webbing within the concrete was exposed just enough for Devon and Casey to see their friends watching them with fearful eyes. Sarah was visibly shaking in Adam's arms, eyes bulging, white as a sheet as she stared at Casey.

Tiktik.

Tiktik.

Tiktik.

Tiktik.

"Where the fuck is it? Can you see it?" Devon whispered, eyes wide and searching every direction for the source of the sound.

"No, now shut *up* or it will hear us," Casey replied through gritted teeth, fingers digging into her brother's arm, back pressed against the cold concrete pillar.

Tiktik.

Tiktik.

Tiktik.

Tiktik.

"Did anyone press their emergency beacon?" Adam said as quietly as he could.

"*Fuck,*" Devon hissed, "No I forgot about it because we were running."

Collectively the teens pressed their palms to the watch-like beacon on their wrists, it would take ten minutes for Agents to arrive at their location, it would take that long for the signal to bounce back to their time and sound the alert. All *they* had to do was outrun whatever this was and get back outside…

Tiktik.

Tiktik.

Tiktik…

The sound grew quieter, and the group breathed a collective sigh of relief as the thing moved further away from them.

"Right, let's move while it's gone again," Devon whispered, the others nodding their agreement as they slowly moved against the wall, shuffling toward the door.

Casey flexed her fingers, wincing at the pain in her joints from how tightly she had been gripping her brother's arm. She swallowed hard, the sound loud in her ears now that silence had fallen around them. She turned to Devon, intent on urging her brother toward the door since he had not moved… but it was not Devon who looked back at her.

Jagged fangs grew in all directions, a whip-like tongue lolling from its lipless maw. It's hot breath on her face stank of death and decay. Casey shuddered, whimpering as she clamped her jaw shut, desperate not to vomit despite the wave of nausea caused by each inhalation of its foul miasma. Its eyes were pure white, set wide on its face, two slitted nostrils just above its mouth opening and closing as it breathed in her scent—it could smell her fear and sweat… and the urine now leaking down her trousers.

The creature raised a hand towards her, long claws dripping in the blood of her friends millimetres from her face. Casey whimpered, closing her eyes to shield herself from the sallow-skinned creature, though she could still picture its skeletal frame, could still smell it with every breath she took. Her dry mouth filled with a metallic taste which was unmistakably the blood the thing was covered in.

She was next, or so she believed. A loud crash caused her to open her eyes in time to see the thing whip around to face the direction the foreign sound had come from, it glanced back at her and she gasped— its face had *changed*. Where the fang-filled mouth had been there was now a razor-sharp beak, its corpse-like skin had sprouted feathers in the same hue and the claws that had reached out to her were now *wings*. The giant bird turned away from her, raising its wings and bringing them down in one powerful swoop that drove it up and out of sight, vanishing to the floor above with the familiar 'tiktik, tiktik, tiktik' returning as it flew away.

Casey's entire body was trembling, she was frozen in place, for fear the thing might come back for her. Something touched her shoulder, and she screamed, her screech stifled by a hand and the desperate shushing of Adam who hugged her close and shuffled her backward against his taller frame.

"Come *on* Casey, we have to go," he urged, dragging her back.

Casey nodded, reaching to take his hand in hers. She saw Sarah scurrying back to the door they had come through. She turned, her foot slipping on something, and her heart stopped. There was something wrong here, something missing, more than just the creature…

She whimpered her expression shattering, vision blurred by tears as she dared to look back at the place she had been standing. The building echoed with the tell-tale '***tiktik***' of the creature, but that didn't matter anymore. Lying on the floor, torn to bloody shreds, his guts like coils of rope, were the remains of her brother, had she not been standing beside him she wouldn't have known it was him. The thing had crushed his skull.

Adam pulled her towards the stairs and the pair hurried from the room, Adam making his way around the hole and vanishing through the door while Casey navigated her way around herself. Back at the stairs, the pair bolted for the exit below.

As Casey and Adam ran down the last of the stairs, they were met with a squad of armoured Agents—rifles to their shoulders, who were already ushering Sarah out to safety.

Casey knew who the woman was now, she'd known deep down but hadn't wanted to admit it. If she had listened to herself, then maybe none of this would have happened. She'd been right—she *had* lost everything. Casey stopped as she caught a glimpse of something out of the corner of her eye.

Tears blurred her vision at the sight of it and her resolve shattered, her knees giving way beneath her. Someone caught her, their touch sent a familiar shock through her arm, sobering her from her grief as she looked into the face of her older self. "How?" She gasped.

"We failed this time, but we won't fail again. We have to go, it's not safe here," her future self whispered, glancing over at the agents, her eyes fixed on Adam.

Casey followed her line of sight as the oppressive silence hit her. Adam looked back at her, opening his mouth to 'smile', fangs protruding from his jaw in different directions, elongated tongue slithering from his maw.

Above the door was a warning, in peeling painted red letters, for all to heed:

"Tiktik, tiktik,

The louder he calls, the safer for you.

Tiktik, tiktik,

He can shift his form, his voice can too.

Tiktik, tiktik,

Listen for him and pray not for silence.

The Tiktiks behind you, and then comes the violence.

BEWARE THE SILENCE."

THE BROKEN CLOCK

Amelie shut her eyes tightly. She held her breath as the wind pulled against the Rolls-Royce, threatening to pull it from the rain-drenched road into the ditch at the edge—invisible in the darkness, waiting to snatch the wheel of a car that came too close to it. Bullet-like drops pelted the windows so hard that any conversations had long since ceased.

A sigh from Amelie's left side forced her to reluctantly open her eyes, and she immediately gave her mother an apologetic look, bowing her head under the stern gaze of the older woman.

Biting her bottom lip, Amelie stared out at the darkness, squinting as she tried to pick out the landscape through the torrent. Everything seemed bleak, rolling black hills with no real shape or substance—just a dark, empty void filled with rain where the world was supposed to be.

Leaning her forehead against the ice-cold glass, she peered forward, attempting to use the headlights to distinguish more of their surroundings, but could see no more than a foot ahead of the car.

Sitting back in her seat, Amelie clasped her hands together in her lap, steadying her breathing as the convoy continued its journey up the winding country road to what would be their new home.

A loud crack of thunder boomed above their heads, Amelie jumped, looking around frantically as though a bomb had gone off beside them, she had to force herself to remember that the war had ended the year before—there were no more German bombs to threaten them.

Lightning shattered the sky, illuminating the desolate landscape and revealing the hulking mass of their destination. The young woman pressed her face to the glass, ignoring the disapproving tut from her mother, as she tried to get a better look at what was now Marston Manor. The building had once been a monastery, before the monks abandoned it, a hundred years before. Or so Theo had told her when she'd asked about how her stepfather had come to purchase the place.

Amelie smiled as she thought of her stepfather's handsome business partner—he was eight years her elder and unlike most of the people associated with her mother and her mother's husband, Theo treated her like an adult—not the sheltered twenty-six-year-old her mother seemed to think she was, or maybe hoped she was. The thought of his slightly lopsided smile and his brown hair falling into his vibrant emerald eyes calmed her heart. The rest of the car journey did not seem so arduous, especially knowing that Theo was in the car ahead with her stepfather.

***

The car tires crunched along the gravel driveway, coming to a halt before the imposing double doors. Black varnished oak studded with metal nails loomed eight-feet-tall in the stone arch. Amelie's eyes were drawn to the sheer size of them, and she wondered how anybody could open such monstrosities on their own.

A figure jogged to the car, opening the door for her, and offering a gloved hand.

"Miss Amelie," the man said with a bow, holding an umbrella above the door.

"Thank you, Benson," she replied softly, bobbing her head gratefully as she took his hand, delicately placing elegant fingers into his palm as she had been taught, swinging her legs from the car and ensuring her skirt would not catch as she stood.

"Leave the young lady to me, Benson, I'll escort Miss Amelie inside, would you fetch her mother? Your etiquette is far better than mine, I fear Mrs. Marston will only scold me if I fetch her," Theo's dulcet tones flowed like honey as he said her name.

Amelie blushed as he took her hand from Benson's, the Steward nodded and hurried to the other side of the car to fetch Amelie's mother as instructed.

"Welcome to your new home Amelie, how did you find the journey?" he asked, moving so her hand was on his arm, his free hand held the umbrella above their heads.

"Harrowing, I hate travelling when the weather is so foul."

"Sadly, your father had no intention of waiting for the storm to clear, he wanted to be in the Manor at the earliest opportunity."

"You mean my stepfather," Amelie chided softly, a hint of sadness tingeing her tone.

"He will come to love you eventually, Amelie, and you him, I know he can be a cold man, give him time." Theo smiled, winking at her as he stepped toward the house, forcing her to follow.

The rain lashed at them despite the umbrella, forcing their progress to the house to be slower than either would have liked. The angle at which Theo held the umbrella skewed her view of the Manor, making it impossible for her to see the nature of her new home. Somehow it seemed more foreboding for that, if she could have seen the structure in all its glory maybe that apprehension clutching her heart like a vice would dissipate.

A gust of wind wrenched the umbrella from Theo's hand, whipping it past Amelie's face. She let out a gasp, the air pulled from her lungs alongside the umbrella through the sheer force of the wind. Letting go of Theo's arm she shielded her face from the heavens, daring to look up at her home just as lightning split the sky. Amelie stepped back, shocked at the face of the gargoyle who met her gaze. The shadowy stone figure with its sharp beak, dead eyes, and outstretched wings seemed to stare right back at her and she whimpered.

Theo reached out for her, throwing his jacket over her head and hurrying her under the shelter of the impressive stone archway, keeping her shielded from the elements as they slid through the open doorway, into the shelter of the entrance hall beyond.

"Well, that was brisk!" Theo laughed as he removed his jacket from Amelie's head, grinning at her as he shook the rain from it and slid it back on.

"A little rain never hurt anyone Mr. Addington, but I thank you for ensuring my stepdaughter was kept as dry as possible."

Amelie looked up, bobbing slightly in greeting to the daunting man coming to meet them. Her mother's courtship with the man known as Marston had been short. The man had handled it just as he did his business, matter-of-factly, with no-nonsense, and no smile. It had felt more like a business deal to Amelie than a marriage, but she had no say in the matter, and given the financial disarray her own father had left them in upon his death they had needed this 'contract' to stay alive.

"I trust you are alright?" he asked her, his tone as cold as the rain outside.

Amelie dared to look up at him, her reflection staring back at her from his deep brown eyes set beneath harsh greying eyebrows. "I am, thank you, stepfather," she replied, nodding to him, lowering her gaze respectfully once he nodded in acknowledgment. He marched past her and Theo to retrieve her mother.

"Laura, are you alright?" There was no compassion in his tone as he offered a hand to her mother when she entered with Benson.

"I am, now I'm inside, the weather is as foul as the drive here Anthony, could we not have waited another day for the storm to clear?" Her mother snapped.

"No, the new owners of our old house want to be by tomorrow, we had to be out of the property into this one today, I refuse to pay for unnecessary hotels and storage. I have been through this with you, Laura."

The change in her stepfather's tone and her mother's attitude was subtle, many would not have heard the octave he used drop nor see her mother look down at the floor—but Amelie lived with them both, she knew their nuances and how to recognise when her mother had pushed her stepfather to the limits of his short patience.

"Fine, but the house best be cleaned to my satisfaction and our belongings transported properly otherwise the servants will be without a job or a reference," Mrs. Marston continued, clutching at what power she had—which was very little indeed.

Thunder roared above them, echoing through the vast entrance hall which still lacked furnishings to make it feel welcoming. Amelie jumped, but Theo squeezed her arm and she felt immediately calmed by his presence. Looking up at him, she smiled, nodding to him as he winked.

"I'd better go and help take our luggage up to the rooms. Will you be alright here on your own?"

"I will be fine, thank you, Mr. Addington, I should get to know my home I suppose."

"That you should. Amelie—call me Theo when the others aren't listening, I've told you before," he smiled, nodding to her as he turned and jogged over to help Benson carry their suitcases up to the rooms.

"Amelie, I want you to wash up and get dressed for dinner once the luggage is upstairs, don't loiter girl," her mother hissed, narrowing her brown eyes at her daughter.

"I will be up presently, mother," Amelie replied, clasping her hands in front of her.

She looked nothing like her mother, her long golden ringlets, and stunning blue eyes she'd inherited from her father. In fact, Amelie was very much her father's daughter, she had none of her mother's spite nor malice—her mother told her she was as naïve and foolish as her father had been, that she was too trusting and had too big a heart. Innocents would be stepped upon, best to find a colder heart and wear it well to survive, after all, her father's niceties had left them destitute had they not?

As their party filed out of the entrance hall, Amelie allowed herself a moment to look about the cavernous foyer. Dark doorways led off in all directions along the walls, only the one to the right of the main door was lit so she assumed that the dining room or the lounge would be in that direction since her mother had mentioned dressing for dinner.

The staircase dominated the space, huge marble stairs lined with banisters so thick that two people could easily have sat next to one another and slid down them safely. A silly thought, as if she would ever do something so brave and childish, it wasn't becoming of a woman her age to have such thoughts.

Tiktik, tiktik, tiktik, tiktik, tiktik, tiktik.

The sound filled the hall, a thunderous drum beat that drowned out even the storm raging outside. An ornate grandfather clock nestled against an alcove to Amelie's left. She looked over her shoulder for her mother or stepfather, once sure neither was going to chide her for still being downstairs, she allowed her curiosity to draw her to the clock.

Delicate fingers ran across the dusty mahogany, tracing the vines and leaves carved into the edging. She flicked the dust off and smiled, standing on tiptoe so that she could look through the crystal to the clock face. The mother-of-pearl inlay was yellowed slightly with age, but it was still beautiful, the delicate golden hands pointing to the Roman numerals were out of time but the clock itself was magnificent.

Closing her eyes, Amelie enjoyed listening to the comforting *tiktik tiktik tiktik*, until she felt a hand on her shoulder and gasped. Hand clutched to her chest, Amelie spun to face the person who had touched her, fearing it would be her mother looking at her with anger or her stepfather with disgust in his eyes.

"My apologies Miss, I didn't mean to startle you!" The man bowed deeply; his hands clasped together by his clavicle. He stood upright the white-collar by his Adam's apple, stark in comparison to the rest of his black garb.

"It's alright Father, I did not realise you were there," she replied softly, bowing her head slightly as her cheeks flushed—she must have looked like such a fool jumping out of her skin like that.

"You were admiring the clock were you not? Beautiful isn't it? Neglected with time and lack of ownership sadly."

"Maybe now we can restore it to its former glory, I would hate to see it left in the shadows as it is now, it should have pride of place."

"Apologies again Miss, I realise I have not introduced myself. I am Father Curtis, I assume that you are Mr. Marston's stepdaughter, am I correct?"

"You are Father, I am Amelie. It is a pleasure to make your acquaintance. Are you here to finalise the sale of the Monastery to my stepfather?"

"You are very astute Miss Amelie, I am."

"If you're looking for my stepfather, I believe he is getting ready for dinner, would you like me to fetch him for you?"

"No, no, I was just wandering the halls while dinner was being prepared. I am staying the night myself, given the state of this storm I do not wish to brave the elements if I do not have to, and paperwork always takes some time. Your stepfather was kind enough to invite me to stay."

"Well then, I look forward to speaking to you further at dinner, Father. If you'll excuse me, I must go and get ready myself before mother comes looking for me," Amelie smiled and gave the Priest a small curtsy before she maneuvered past him, hurrying upstairs to find her room.

***

Tiktik, tiktik, tiktik, tiktik.

The grandfather clock marched out her steps as Amelie strode down the stairs, the skirt of her sequined black evening dress clutched in her hands, carefully placing each foot upon the slippery marble stairs and wishing that her stepfather had at least put a carpet upon it for their arrival. She was already late for dinner and her mother was going to be furious, she would have run down the stairs if she was not so afraid of slipping and hurting herself.

"Amelie!"

She flinched as she reached the last step, her mother's ireful tone screeching her name and stripping away the comforting ticking of the clock.

"Coming mother!" Amelie replied as she jogged across the entrance hall to the lit room beyond.

The lounge, while furnished, was as unwelcoming as the rest of the house. Cold stone walls, bookshelves devoid of books, curtainless rails. She'd heard her mother arguing with her stepfather from their room down the hallway from her own—Amelie's mother was used to a certain lifestyle, even after her father's death and their fall from grace. The lack of furnishings and home comforts in this place only fuelled the hatred in the new Mrs. Marston.

Admittedly, Amelie agreed with her mother, a rare occurrence— why her stepfather had not sent their belongings ahead of them and asked the servants to furnish the house properly was beyond her. Amelie would happily have come along with their staff to help, as much as her mother loathed her being involved in anything manual (it was not becoming of an eligible young lady) Amelie found solace in being busy.

"Apologies for my tardiness, I had trouble locating which case held my dresses," she explained, bobbing slightly, keeping her eyes on the floor.

"You see, Anthony? Had our things been sent on as I suggested,

Amelie's clothes would have been in her wardrobe and my daughter would not have been made to look irresponsible," her mother snapped and in a rare show of affection, she placed her arm around Amelie, looking defiantly at her husband.

"It's alright mother, it's my fault. I was late coming upstairs. A grandfather clock in the entrance hall caught my attention, then I met Father Curtis and spent a few minutes introducing myself. If I had not allowed myself that distraction, I would have found my dress and been on time."

Amelie glanced at her mother, forcing herself not to wince under the woman's steely gaze and thin, pursed lips. Her mother's hands dropped from her arms and she returned to stand by her husband, abandoning her daughter and any defence Amelie might have had.

"Grandfather clock? Is that what's making that infernal ticking noise I can hear from my room?" Theo cut in, his jovial tone diffusing the tense atmosphere.

Amelie looked up at him, hoping her eyes expressed how grateful she was for his intervention. She caught the slight twitch in the left side of his mouth, that tell-tale lopsided smile of his that told her he was happy to help, and she smiled in return as her cheeks flushed hot.

"Sir? Dinner is ready to be served, would you all like to come through to the dining room?"

The room's attention turned to the door opposite the one from the entrance hall where Benson stood, head bowed, arm motioning to the room beyond.

"Thank you, Benson. Laura." Amelie's stepfather offered his arm to her mother, and the pair went inside, though they shared a look between them that made Amelie shudder, cementing her theory that this marriage was little more than a contract.

Amelie smiled as Theo moved around one of the threadbare lounge chairs, his eyes fixed on hers as he made his way to accompany her to the dining room.

"Miss Amelie? Might I escort you through to dinner?" Father Curtis appeared before her holding out his hand causing Amelie to jump as she had forgotten the man was even there.

"Thank you, Father, I would be honoured," she replied with a nod of her head, placing her hand reluctantly in his. As the Priest led her through to the dining room Amelie cast a quick glance over her shoulder at Theo, her heart skipping a beat at the look of disappointment on his face.

Her stepfather was seated at the head of the long table, her mother to his left. The table was designed for large parties, able to seat at least twenty rather than the five they had tonight. The chandelier above cast a soft glow across the otherwise empty room, save for the table and chairs it—like the rest of the house so far—had no other furnishings.

Father Curtis pulled out a chair, offering it to her, Amelie smiled and took it with a nod, glancing up at Theo as he sat next to her mother, opposite her. As his eyes met hers, he smiled back at her and she breathed a sigh of relief that he was not angry at her for taking Father Curtis' offer of an escort—not that she could have even though she'd wanted to. The Priest sat down beside her, on her stepfather's right, and immediately the serving staff entered.

They had not brought many servants with them—Benson as Steward (who was serving as her stepfather's Valet for the time being) with Christopher and Thomas the Footmen, Mrs. Tremaine the Housekeeper (who was looking after her mother as her Lady's Maid, much to her mother's consternation), with Louisa the House Maid assisting her, Mrs. Letterman the Cook and Annie the Kitchen Maid. The only unknown out of the servants was the Groundskeeper Mr. Williams, who had come with the Manor itself—Amelie had yet to meet the man but Theo had said he was a rough-looking character and that the man was not well-liked by the locals.

Benson went round the room pouring wine into the crystal goblets they had brought with them while Christopher and Thomas served up the soup. Knowing Mrs. Letterman, the food would be delicious. It was the one comfort they had with them, she always looked forward to her meals from the cook, and since nothing else in this place felt like home at least this would.

They fell into idle chatter as they ate dinner, Father Curtis favouring conversations with Amelie while she braved glances in Theo's direction, wishing she could speak with him more however she knew better than to be rude to a guest. Wine flowed freely as Benson kept their glasses filled, the Footmen clearing the plates without needing to be called.

Once they finished their meals the men bowed to the ladies and went to take drinks in the lounge they had been in before dinner, while Amelie and her mother took tea in the dining room. She watched Theo shut the door, giving her one last wink before he vanished from sight.

Turning back to her mother Amelie flinched under the narrowed gaze boring into her soul.

"You can stop making eyes at Mr. Addington Amelie, there are better men out there, more eligible bachelors who will be suitors for you, not him," her mother said, fingernails tapping out a beat in time with the clock.

Tap, *tiktik*, tap, *tiktik*, tap, *tiktik*.

"I'm not making eyes, mother. Mr. Addington is kind to me, that's all," Amelie muttered, head hung low as she cradled her teacup in her hands.

"The girl thinks I'm a fool! The sooner Anthony marries you off the better, I'm sick of being burdened with you—the last reminder of your father's failures. I'm retiring for the evening; I suggest you do the same and reflect upon your place in this world my girl."

Amelie bit her bottom lip, knuckles white as she held the teacup, forcing herself not to look at her mother—it would do her no good to sob in front of the woman, she would find no sympathy nor comfort with her.

Tiktik, tiktik, tiktik, tiktik.

Slowly, steadily, Amelie used the ticking of the grandfather clock—remarkably loud even in the dining room—to slow her heartbeat, though the ache remained in her chest. Her mother would never forgive her for being her father's daughter, cruel though that was, it was who the woman had always been.

Finishing her tea, Amelie stood up and considered going to bed as her mother had instructed when Theo's deep tones caught her attention from the other room. Biting her bottom lip, she looked at the servants still lingering in the dining room—Benson spotted the look and nodded to her, motioning for the Footmen to leave without saying a word to them. He took her cup and her mother's, gave her a small smile and a nod, leaving the room to give her some privacy.

Once alone she tiptoed to the lounge door, conscious of the loud click of her kitten heels on the wooden floor as it reverberated around the empty room. Amelie held her breath, as though this would somehow lessen the noise, exhaling as she reached the door without seeming to alert anyone in the room beyond. Pressing her ear to the cold wood, she closed her eyes, listening intently to the conversations within.

"Come along Father, we have tiptoed around the subject all evening, the ladies are not here now. Tell us the real reason the Church sold this place—it's been empty for how long now?" Theo asked, making Amelie smile as he asked the question she had been dying to ask.

"It's been thirty years since the Manor was last occupied, though it was under the name of the Monastery, Mr. Marston renamed it, Marston Manor, upon its purchase." Father Curtis replied.

"And it reverted back to the Church once the last family left?" Theo pushed.

"That's correct, just as it did ten years prior with the family that owned the Monastery before them," Curtis added.

"But why, there must be a reason Father? I want to know why the Church first sold this place, and why no one seems to keep hold of it once they do buy it!" Theo urged again.

"That will change under my ownership," Amelie's stepfather said darkly, causing her to flinch even from another room—she could imagine the stern look Mr. Marston would have given Theo and she was thankful she was not able to see it.

"True, but I still want to know *why*," Theo continued, of all the people who knew her stepfather he was the only one who seemed unperturbed by the man's mannerisms.

"I'm afraid I do not know the history of the Monastery as well as Mr. Williams, he and his family have been working here since the Monks inhabited these halls. I defer to you sir, maybe you could enlighten our curious guest to the eccentricities of this place?"

There was a derisive snort, followed by silence and Amelie pressed her ear closer to the wood, wondering if the man was talking too quietly for her to hear—either way, the silence was awkward, filled with the distinctive *'tiktik, tiktik, tiktik'* of the clock nestled in the hall.

"Centuries ago, the Monks who lived here received gifts from a Monastery in the Philippines—the crates were sent over on ships that, rumour has it, suffered great losses to bring them here. Within the crates were handcrafted gargoyles, the workmanship second to none, and the Monks quickly erected them upon the roof to guard their home from evil spirits," the man's voice was gruff, almost hoarse as he recalled the tale—Amelie had not met the man personally but could guess who was speaking since Father Curtis had named the Groundskeeper.

"Several men lost their lives in settling the gargoyles onto the roof, and soon rumours began to spread of a curse associated with them.

The Monks became paranoid as more and more accidents began to happen, even after the gargoyles had been installed, and they too began to believe in the curse. Too many deaths occurred and eventually, the Monks abandoned the Monastery, refusing to return and claiming that an evil creature had been brought alongside the gargoyles to kill them all. The Church did not believe them, but they had no choice but to sell the Monastery once none of the Monks would return.

"Wealthy families have bought the place on occasion, but when they heard rumours of the curse, they too suffered injury or death and eventually they left just as the Monks did. It's all hokum—I've been in and out of this building a thousand times and suffered little more than a stubbed toe. It's paranoia and negligence that caused those deaths—people worrying about curses and not sleeping, leading to accidents and fatalities, that's all."

A shudder ran down Amelie's spine, pushing herself away from the door—she had heard enough for one evening; in fact, she had heard far too much. Exhaling heavily, she scolded herself for her curiosity—whatever nightmares she suffered would be of her own making because of her eavesdropping. She was just thankful her mother hadn't caught her; she wasn't sure she could cope with another lecture from the woman.

***

Amelie lay on her bed, staring at the canopy of the four-poster bed. Every time she closed her eyes to sleep, she was jolted awake moments later by images of gargoyles springing to life and causing her death in a variety of horribly novel ways. Every monster bore the same dead eyes as the gargoyle she had seen when she and Theo had hurried into the house out of the rain.

Tiktik, tiktik, tiktik, tiktik.

The clock was further away now, but still, she could hear the faint, comforting heartbeat of the device from her room and she let it ground her. It was exactly as Mr. Williams had said, the paranoia of the stories had caused sleepless nights and deadly mistakes, nothing more. She was being silly, worrying about gargoyles and monsters. There was no such thing.

Sighing heavily, she threw off her heavy covers, grabbed her robe and threw it on over her silken nightgown as she went to her window and watched the rain beat against the windowpane. The storm still raged on, in her preoccupation with the ticking of the clock and the terrible story Mr. William's had told she had forgotten all about it.

A loud knock on her door was echoed by a sudden clap of thunder and Amelie yelped in surprise, clutching her robe to her chest as she desperately swallowed against the lump in her throat.

"Amelie? Are you alright?" Theo's muffled voice called through the door.

"I'm fine Theo, you frightened me that's all. What are you doing calling upon a lady at this hour? It's not appropriate for you to come to my room like this," she replied, hurrying across the room, her fingertips caressing the wood as she longed to reach out and touch his face.

"I know, and normally I wouldn't but we cannot find your mother, do you know where she is?"

"She's not in her room? She had tea with me and then retired early."

"Did you come up with her? Did you see her go to her room?"

"I... no. I stayed in the dining room a little longer before coming to my room alone," biting her bottom lip Amelia unlocked the door and opened it a crack, looking into Theo's eyes with tears blurring her vision. "What's happened?"

"Hush don't worry. Your stepfather went back to their room and found the clothes she had been wearing at dinner folded on the bed, but your mother was not in their room. We've been looking for her, but the Manor is huge and we've had no luck yet, I suggested I ask you lest she came to sit with you awhile."

"I doubt my mother is wandering the halls in her nightclothes... let me help, I will just put on something more suited to running up and down the hallways. Will you wait for me?"

"Always, as if you even have to ask?" He replied, turning his back to the door to wait for her.

Amelie picked out her riding clothes, the jodhpurs and boots would be far easier to run around the halls in than her skirts and heels. She finished buttoning her shirt and grabbed her riding jacket, glad that she had thought to pack them despite their stables being currently empty—who knew she would need them to search a dusty former Monastery for her mother?!

She joined Theo in the dark hallway, shivering as thunder boomed overhead followed by a flash of lightning that lit either end of the corridor for a moment in ethereal light.

"Where do we start?" Amelie asked.

"The staff is scouring downstairs and your stepfather, Mr. Williams, and Father Curtis are on the floor above, I said we would start here and meet them. I checked the rooms down the hall on my way to your room, but no luck."

"Alright, we keep going I suppose," Amelie sighed, striding in time with Theo while trying to swallow the lump that was still in her throat. Where could her mother have gone?

They worked in silence—Theo checking rooms on the left, Amelie the right. With every empty room, the sense of dread in Amelie's heart grew, consuming her little by little. This wasn't like her mother—she could hear the staff below and the men on the floor above calling out for the woman, but no answer came. No answer, other than the ever-present '*tiktik, tiktik, tiktik*' of the grandfather clock.

"Mother, are you in here?" Amelie called hesitantly as she opened the last door on her side of the corridor, her heart heavy with the disappointment and worry she felt. Another empty bedroom, the skeleton of a four-poster bed shoved against one wall. As Amelie stepped inside the layers of dust fluttered into the air and she coughed. Gasping for breath Amelie held her hand over her nose and mouth as she entered the room fully, casting her gaze over the moth-eaten remains of a lounge chair and warped dresser under the window.

Amelie sighed heavily as she turned to leave the room, chalking it up to another loss, when a shadow caught her attention from the far corner hidden by the door. Scowling, she stepped toward the mass, placing her feet slowly to keep from disturbing the dust.

"Mother?" She called again, though she knew her mother would not lie on the floor, and how could it be her when the only footprints here were her own? A sickening feeling twisted in Amelie's gut, a niggling doubt shivering across her spine, causing her to tremble as she reached out with a shaking hand to turn over the mass of dark cloth she had found.

There was a sickening 'thunk' as the crumpled mass turned over and flopped against the floor, one clawed hand laying against the dust, wearing her father's family ring on the middle finger.

The world went still, the storm outside hushed suddenly, drowned out by the pulsing beat of Amelie's heart drumming violently in her chest. Lightning flashed through the curtainless window, casting its harsh light across the remains of her mother's face, her torso torn asunder, a large chunk of her side clawed away to expose her ribs and innards. The next clap of thunder woke Amelie from her fear and ripped a scream from her throat.

She never heard Theo enter the room, only vaguely aware of him calling her name, her ears filled with the sound of her scream. Unable to look away from what had once been her mother, barely registering the harsh tone of her stepfather as he joined her and Theo in the room, she was left breathless.

"Laura?" Her stepfather uttered beside her as Theo gathered Amelie into his arms, pressing her face into his chest and holding her tightly as her scream turned to sobs and her legs went weak.

"Oh, Heavens help us, Lord Father save us from whatever manner of demon did this," Father Curtis whispered, crossing himself and turning away from the mangled body.

"Amelie, did you see what happened? Who did this?" Her stepfather snarled, grabbing her arm and turning her to face him, harsh eyes glaring down at her.

"She's been with me Marston; we've been going room to room looking for your wife—there's no way she saw who did this. No one came or went from this room as we went down the corridor."

"She's dead. Mama is dead," Amelie whimpered, tears flowing down her cheeks.

"No *person* could do something like this," a gruff tone added, and Amelie glanced at the man kneeling to inspect her mother's wounds. Mr. Williams, his hoarse tones unmistakable. He looked up, his wizened face softening as his dull blue eyes met Amelie's.

"I'm taking Amelie down to the lounge, Benson put some tea on please, I suggest we all go downstairs and take a moment to decide how to proceed from here," Theo suggested, pulling Amelie against him and cradling her against his body.

The Steward nodded, bowing, and leaving the room in silence as the others stood still, shocked by the carnage before them. Theo led Amelie from the bedroom, holding her steady as she forced one foot in front of the other, her legs threatening to buckle with each step.

Once in the lounge Theo gently lowered her onto the sofa, pulling off his jacket and draping it over Amelie's shoulders before he sat next to her, keeping her hand in his.

"Amelie, look at me," he whispered, his fingers brushing against her chin as he forced her to meet his gaze, "Whatever happens, I will not leave your side, I swear I will keep you safe." He gave her a small, weak smile, squeezing her hand.

Any other day Amelie would have been over the moon at his words, that simple implication that he felt the same way that she did for him— but that paled in comparison to the horror she had just seen. The vision of her mother's bloody, twisted grimace, her organs exposed to the air behind her broken rib cage, that was all she could see whether her eyes were open or closed. She swallowed hard, forcing herself not to vomit.

Tiktik, tiktik...

"What could have done that? What killed my Laura?" Her stepfather demanded, rounding on Father Curtis and Mr. Williams.

"You ask us as though we should know?" Father Curtis seemed alarmed by the accusation in the man's tone. "I am at as much of a loss as you, sir!"

"You both know something; you work for the Church Curtis and you damned fools let this place go for next to nothing—your Church could not sell this property to me quick enough! You've worked here all your life, Williams; you know what this is!"

Tiktik, tiktik...

"I know the rumours of this house, that's all, the same ones I told you earlier. I'm the Groundskeeper, I watch the land, keep people out of the property, and make sure the house isn't falling into disrepair that's all. I don't know what did this!" The old man snarled in return.

Tiktik...

"Would someone stop that infernal ticking?!" Marston roared. "Benson? Benson! Stop that blasted grandfather clock immediately."

236

"Grandfather clock? That clock hasn't worked in decades…" Williams interjected, eyes growing wide as the group looked from one to the other, silence filling the room as they all listened to the steadily dimming '*tiktik… tiktik…*' until it too stopped.

"Where the hell is Benson?" Marston said suddenly, causing Amelie to jump at the sound of his voice cutting through the quiet.

"In fact, where are the rest of the staff?" Theo added, looking over at the dining-room door. "None of them came to see why Amelie screamed, not one of them has appeared since we came downstairs."

The men exchanged worried glances and Amelie sobbed, her heart filled with dread. With the ticking gone and the realisation that the sound had never come from the clock in the first place, the silence that descended upon the group weighed heavily.

"Theo, stay with Amelie. Williams, Father Curtis, come with me. I want to see where the rest of the staff is," Marston spoke, breaking the quiet and the tension.

"I-is that wise?" Father Curtis fussed, hands ringing together as he looked from Williams to Amelie's stepfather and back again. The man looked like a deer caught in the headlights.

"Now, Father."

Marston nodded to Theo who mimicked the gesture, pulling Amelie closer to him as the three men left the lounge via the dining room to search for the staff.

"I don't understand any of this," Amelie mewled, burying her face into Theo's shoulder. "Why is this happening? Why is any of this happening?"

"I don't know, Amelie I'm sorry but I have no answers for you. Just stay with me," he replied, his voice barely a whisper, his breath brushing against her cheek.

Amelie looked up at the man and nodded, brushing the tears from her face. "I promise. We'd best go after them, I hate being sat here on our own, I feel exposed."

"I know what you mean, come on let's go, they can't have got too far ahead of us. Let's see if they found the others." Smiling, Theo stood up, helping Amelie to her feet, and taking her hand in his, their fingers entwined.

The pair made their way through the empty dining room to the door opposite that logically would take them to the stairs leading to the servant's quarters below. Theo kept a step ahead of Amelie, never letting go of her hand but angling his body so that he could shield her from anything that might come up the stairs. As with the rest of the house, it was deathly quiet and dimly lit, their footsteps echoing off the stone steps and walls as they made their way down.

Amelie shuddered once they reached the bottom of the stairs, a cold wind blowing through the corridor, bringing with it the smell of something rancid. Amelie gagged, her free hand swiftly covering her nose and mouth, eyes watering as she forced herself to hold on to her dinner for the second time that evening.

"What the hell is that smell?" Theo uttered, grimacing with each breath.

"I don't know, I'm not sure I want to know," Amelie replied through gritted teeth, bile rising to the back of her scream-torn throat.

"Oh! Benson!" She gasped, pointing to the far end of the corridor to their left where the Steward stood, silhouetted by one of the dim bulbs.

"Benson! Good man! We are glad to see you." Theo called to him, smiling with relief. "Benson?" The Steward offered no answer, merely stared at Theo and Amelie in silence, and then vanished from sight around the corner. "What the hell…"

"Maybe he's too afraid to say anything? Should we follow him?"

"Might be best, come on and stay close."

Together they hurried after the man, following him around the corner to another corridor. They could see his silhouette in front of them, and then he vanished around a corner again.

"I think he's gone up here," Theo whispered, craning his neck as he looked up the stairs.

"I don't really want to follow him that way… why don't we look for my stepfather and the others and come back this way once we're all together?"

"Good idea."

"Theo? Amelie? I thought I told you to stay upstairs." Marston snapped, causing the pair to jump at the sound of their names.

"We didn't feel comfortable lingering in that room. Did you find the others?" Theo asked.

Marston looked pale as he joined them, Williams, and Father Curtis behind him looking just as gaunt and haunted. "All dead, the kitchen is a massacre." He admitted.

Amelie whimpered, her eyes drawn back to the stairs where Benson must have gone—her stepfather blocked the other way and the man clearly had not passed her and Theo.

"Well, we saw Benson, he's gone this way," Theo sighed, motioning to the stairs leading back to the main part of the house.

"Benson?" Father Curtis snapped. "You can't have! I've just seen his severed head."

Tiktik, tiktik, tiktik, tiktik.

"It can't be…" Amelie whispered as the sound of the clock drifted down the stairs. "You said that clock didn't work." She accused Mr. Williams, glaring at him.

"It's not the clock making the noise." Williams retorted. "Which way did you two come from? I suggest we head that way."

"This way, we came down the stairs from the dining room the same as you," Theo replied.

"Right, let's head back that way and get to the cars. I ain't waiting for whatever it is to take my head off." Williams added, barging past Marston and shouldering Amelie and Theo out of the way.

Theo held Amelie close, glaring at the man. Amelie squeezed his hand and looked up at him with a gentle expression, she was fine, she didn't want to stay here any longer than she had to. The group hurried back toward the dining hall stairs, none of them daring to utter a word.

Tiktik, tiktik, tiktik, tiktik.

"Turn back! The damned thing is louder this way, go back that way!" Williams hissed.

Terrified by the clicking, ticking sound now reverberating off the walls the group broke into a run, Marston following behind Father

Curtis who was sprinting ahead of them all.

Tiktik, tiktik, tiktik, tiktik.

Tiktik, tik...

Silence fell once more and Amelie exhaled heavily, the thing had vanished again, they could get past it! Rounding the corner, Father Curtis took the first few steps leading up in one bound, only to stop dead in his tracks, causing the others to crash into one another as they too came to a halt at the bottom of the stairs.

The Priest went pale, his eyes bulging from their sockets, mouth opening, and closing in a voiceless scream. Amelie watched in horror as Benson descended the stairs to meet the Priest. His skin a sickly pallor, a horrid miasma exuding from his body just like the one that had assaulted them when they came downstairs. His eyes were white like that of a corpse—lifeless and searching.

'Benson' turned his head to look at the group below and he gave them a smile that made Amelie scream. The expression was beyond anything she could comprehend, his jaw distended with fangs too large for his mouth, jutting in different directions and needle-sharp, between the front teeth a slimy pink tongue like a whip lolled from the maw of the thing.

Theo squeezed Amelie's hand, pulling on her arm. "We have to go, *now* Amelie, come on!" He snapped, forcing her to move—but not before the thing leaped forward and sank its fangs into Father Curtis' neck, biting his head clean from his body, blood spraying like a terrible fountain from the wound.

Any further hesitation was pushed from Amelie's mind and she sprinted alongside Theo, daring to look back only once, bearing witness to the death of Mr. Williams and her stepfather all at once.

'Benson' had changed completely now; the face was more rounded and far less human—the slitted nostrils high on its face and position between its dead eyes. The creature filled the corridor with its stinking, skeletal mass of sickly flesh and muscle. Long arms snapped forward. Williams was snatched from his feet. The man screamed and beat at the clawed hand, but the thing barely noticed. Pursuing her stepfather, it clawed at his legs, causing the man to fall onto his face as the limbs flopped uselessly to the floor.

This time Amelie could not stop herself from vomiting—but even hit with this wave of nausea and despair she did not stop running, she could not, her feet were moving on their own now.

Theo led Amelie back through the dining room and the lounge, stopping only to pick up the jacket that had fallen from her shoulders when they had gone in search of the others. Bounding across the entrance hall, Theo pulled open the great entrance door and hurried Amelie out into the still-raging storm.

Rain and wind buffeted them as they ran for Theo's car, Amelie throwing herself into the passenger seat as Theo turned on the ignition and began to turn the car around in the vast gravel drive. Amelie dared to look out of the window, staring up at the roof where the gargoyle no longer kept watch on the visitors to the Monastery.

Amelie could not drag her eyes from the dark form of the building, its features growing less distinct as Theo pushed the car as much as he dared in the storm; for which Amelie was grateful, the faster they left this place behind the better. As they passed through the gates to the estate, she let out a sob and she reached over to grasp Theo's leg to comfort herself and him.

They smiled weakly at one another, Theo taking Amelie's hand in his and squeezing it—her heart felt lighter, the relief of being out of that place, away from that *thing* with Theo by her side. She had lost her family, but she was alive and maybe now she could be the woman *she* wanted to be.

The house was behind them, growing smaller as they drove on. The storm quieted for a moment, and the pair shared a look at the booming sound that followed their escape.

TIKTIK, TIKTIK, TIKTIK, TIKTIK.

DEATH AT THE THEATRE

"Extra, extra! President Lincoln and General Grant to attend Ford's Theatre this evening!"

"I'll take one," the man in the black coat said, as he handed over a silver coin to the grinning boy.

He stared at Abraham Lincoln's name, the bold black lettering stark against the white of the paper.

He'd been on his way to the theatre to pick up his mail, but no one told him that Lincoln was attending the performance—it must have been a last-minute decision by the President. The makings of a plan began to form in the back of his mind as he shoved the paper under one arm.

He greeted those that recognised him, exchanging pleasantries out of instinct. All the while his mind wandered to his destination, the theatre where his life might change for the better after the bitter disappointment of the last few days.

"That's right ladies and gentlemen, you heard correctly—our beloved President is attending this evening's performance of '*Our American Cousin*'. Tickets on sale here, get them while they are still available for a glimpse of the man himself!" A rotund steward announced from atop the Theatre's steps.

Just as he hoped, there were tickets left to purchase. It was too good an opportunity to miss—a chance to be close to President Lincoln. He would have to be a madman to look this gift horse in the mouth.

Naturally, there was a line at the ticket booth when he went to satiate his own indulgent nature, but when the crowd saw him they immediately moved out of his way with hushed whispers, their eyes wide as he smiled at them.

"How many tickets would you like, sir? Would you like a box? I'm sure we could make room for you in one Mr. Wilkes-Booth," the young man said from behind the glass, stammering over his words as Booth held up a hand to stop the lad from continuing to gush at him.

"A seat amongst the circle will suffice, whatever you have, I would hate to deprive another patron of their seat just because of my name," Booth's voice was low, his tone silken as he let the words roll from his well-trained, silver tongue.

"Are you definitely attending Mr. Wilkes-Booth?" A woman hurried to ask from behind him.

Turning toward the growing crowd by the theatre he smiled. "Of course! I may not be performing, but as an actor, I can appreciate a good play all the same, and with the President attending how can I resist? A chance to see the great man himself? Honest Abe? Only a fool would miss out on tonight."

Smile still upon his face, Booth turned back to the lad in the booth and paid for his ticket. "I wonder if I might just pop in, I was on my way here to pick up my mail when I heard of the President's visit, but I'd best complete my original errand rather than just indulging in my whims!" He chuckled.

"Of course, Mr. Wilkes-Booth! Did you need an escort? I know you've been here several times before, but I'm sure Mr. Ford would be delighted to accompany you?"

"Young man, don't trouble yourself, or Mr. Ford. There are other patrons who require your attention more than I, I know where the mail is kept and I would hate to be a nuisance."

"Are you sure, sir? It's no trouble," there was an edge of disappointment in the lad's voice that made Booth's smile grow.

"I'm sure it isn't, but these lovely people here have come to buy tickets as well, it would be entirely improper of me to make them wait any longer." Nodding his head to the lad, he gave him a small salute with the edge of his newspaper, tucking his theatre ticket into his lapel as he made his way up the stairs to speak with the steward.

The steward had been only too happy to wave Booth through the doors, allowing the man to retrieve his mail without the need for a chaperone. Mail in hand, Booth returned to his apartment, sending word to Powell and Atzerodt that he was to attend the play that evening, and that there was a chance he would get to meet Lincoln.

***

His co-conspirators did not hesitate in joining him at his abode, which was as he expected.

"What do you plan to do, John? It's a perfect opportunity to get rid of the man; can you imagine the blow that would be for the Union?" Powell whispered earnestly.

"What Union Lewis? There's no Confederacy anymore, so there's no Union," Booth spat disdainfully.

Powell and Atzerodt shared a look under Booth's baleful gaze. The Confederacy's surrender five days prior hit Booth hardest out of the three of them; he'd gone from being their most ambitious conspirator to a disillusioned and lost soul. He was angry and broken—everything that he fought for and believed in had been tossed aside by the powers he once put his faith in.

General Lee *surrendered*.

Booth had been left heartbroken.

"If you kill him tonight, we could reignite the war; give our compatriots a reason to fight again," Powell pushed.

"And then what?" Booth asked as he sat at the table with the pair. "I kill Lincoln and Johnson takes his place. Everything that he stands for will still be there, and we will still have lost."

"Not if *we* lend you our aid, just as we have in the past, John. We failed to kidnap Lincoln, but we always said we would take the first opportunity we could to get rid of the man. You've *got* that chance now, right here. It landed in your lap!" Atzerodt hissed, picking up

Booth's theatre ticket and waving it in the man's face. "I'll go to the Kirkwood Hotel; we know Johnson is there. Powell can go to Seward's home and eliminate him as a threat while *you* take out Lincoln and Grant in one fell swoop. Two birds with one stone, John, just think of the blow dealt to the Union with that!"

Booth snatched the ticket from Atzerodt's hand, his fingers running across the theatre's name printed upon the paper.

"You'd be a legend, John. Just think of it. The man who brought the spark of war to life once more!" Powell added, leaning forward as he noted Atzerodt's nod toward him—not unnoticed by Booth.

A legend. There was a glimmer of hope in his heart, a spark of his own he could use to ignite and rekindle the flames of the war… but it was dampened by his sense of loss, by the quagmire of depression that settled upon him since the surrender.

Could he kill Lincoln now? He hated the man, loathed everything that the President stood for, and yet he was curious as to what kind of *man* Lincoln was. He had turned down the invitations to the White House, not because he'd been otherwise engaged, but because the thought of sitting across from his enemy made him feel nauseous. To have to *pretend* he enjoyed the man's company had been a deplorable thought, better to avoid being put into that situation entirely.

"I'll attend this evening," Booth sighed as he took the ticket and slid it into his inner jacket pocket, close to his heart.

"Good man. We will leave a horse for your escape at the side door furthest from the entrance to the theatre, the one directly off the stage, you know the one. Leave the others to us, strike a blow for the

Confederacy, John, do what needs to be done!" Atzerodt smiled, squeezing Booth's arm before he motioned to Powell and the pair left Booth's room.

He stood in silence for a moment, his eyes fixed upon the closed door. He would attend the theatre; he'd even take his gun—but he needed to get a measure of the man called Lincoln before he would consider killing him. Everything that Booth believed in had been cast aside by his own fellows, he needed to re-evaluate, and he could only do that once he shook Lincoln's hand.

***

Booth stood on the edge of the sidewalk across from the entrance to the theatre, eyes fixed on the crowds of people bustling around the door, chattering excitedly at the prospect of the play and the special guest in attendance that evening. His compatriots were right. It was tonight or not at all, but his heart still felt constrained, as though someone had taken hold of it and was squeezing tightly, he still wasn't ready to commit to doing *anything*.

He could not shake the despair that had befallen him at the Confederates' surrender, even now with his Deringer tucked into a sash around his waist, hidden beneath his shirt. The gun offered no comfort, no confidence, he'd brought it out of habit more than anything. That shadow of a doubt still loomed despite his being at the theatre, and he still questioned whether he would go on with the plan even as he handed his ticket to the steward on the door.

"Mr. Wilkes-Booth! Welcome back, sir!" The young lad from the ticket booth enthused as he wove through the crowded foyer, waving merrily at Booth who smiled in return.

"Good evening to you, young man, are you well?"

"I am sir, I am, better now I get the chance to properly say hello to you."

"What's your name, son?" Booth asked, his Southern drawl filled with charm, his tone drawing eager looks from those around them, the closest patrons whispering behind their hands as they stared at him.

"Thomas, sir."

"Well Thomas, thank you very much for your service this afternoon. I'm glad I got the chance to buy my ticket, I'd hate to have missed out on a chance to see the President face-to-face. Has he arrived yet?"

"Not yet, Mr. Wilkes-Booth, though we fervently hope he will not be too long in arriving. I have to say, the chance to see you in person is equally as exciting as catching a glimpse of President Lincoln!" A young woman gushed.

Booth smiled as he turned toward her, bowing politely, amused to see her cheeks flush at his gesture. "Then I am happy to have made your evening even a little brighter Miss...?" He offered her his hand, kissing her gloved fingers as she placed them into his palm.

"Miss Eleanor Dumont. This is my mother, Mrs. Adelaide Dumont," the girl replied, bobbing slightly in greeting, her blond ringlets bouncing against her shoulders with the movement.

"A pleasure to meet you, Miss Dumont, and you Mrs. Dumont."

"Oh, the pleasure is all mine, sir. I saw you perform at this very theatre when it first opened. You starred in *The Marble Heart*. Your performance moved me to tears Mr. Wilkes-Booth, so much so that I forgot that President Lincoln was in attendance that evening as well!" The elderly mother replied as Booth reached out to kiss her fingers just as he had her daughter's, the Deringer dug into his ribs as he bowed lower to the shorter woman, reminding him of its presence and of the conflict he'd momentarily forgotten.

"Ah, Mr. Wilkes-Booth!" A voice called and Booth looked up, grateful that Ford came to offer him another distraction from the war within his head.

"Good evening, Mr. Ford. Has he arrived yet?" Booth asked.

"Sadly not, though it may be that he arrives late, we shall see I suppose. We can but hope that President Lincoln still finds the time to visit us."

"We can indeed," Booth replied, forcing himself to sound hopeful. Was it relief he felt at knowing the man was not here? Or was it disappointment? His compatriots' words still lingered from earlier that evening—what a grand blow he could bring down upon the Union if he assassinated Lincoln here, and grand it *would* be. Yet curiosity had sprouted at the chance to meet him; the war was over now. While he could start it again, he wanted to *know* the man who had been his enemy for so long. And tonight, was that chance if Lincoln still came.

"I'm well aware you've been to our beloved theatre several times before, but have you actually had the chance to look around it?" Ford asked him.

"Not really, I have to admit. Every time I come to your beautiful establishment it is as part of a troupe, it does not exactly afford much time for exploring."

"Precisely. Come, Mr. Wilkes-Booth, let me properly introduce you to Ford's Theatre," Ford grinned.

"John, please. We're old friends now are we not?"

"I would like to think so, then you must call me John as well."

"Ha! I knew I liked you, how could I not when we are of one name?" Booth joked, chuckling as he placed an amicable hand upon Ford's shoulder. "Come, John, show me the wonders of your Theatre. My apologies ladies, but you will have to excuse me," Booth bowed to the pair, winked at Thomas, and followed after Ford. He stopped to give cursory greetings to others in the foyer who recognised him as they wound their way through the crowd.

Truthfully Booth knew the layout of the place already—his training from the Confederate Army taught him to be aware of his surroundings, to quickly learn the escape routes of any building he might find himself in. You never knew when you would need to make a quick escape, but the tour was a welcome distraction, as was Ford's constant chatter.

"And here is the Presidential Box," Ford said proudly, motioning to the golden letters embossed upon the door.

"Where the man himself shall be in attendance this very evening if he turns up of course," Booth said with the correct amount of reverence to his tone—even though the very thought of Lincoln was a dagger to his heart. Thank God for his years as an actor, no one needed to know of the true hatred he felt for the man who may sit behind this door.

"Indeed, he shall! Have you met the President before?" Ford asked.

"Sadly, no. He has invited me to the White House on several occasions for dinner, unfortunately always at a time when I was previously engaged and unable to attend. I hope to shake his hand tonight. Of course, it is why I hurried to buy a ticket."

"I'm sure with your credentials there should be no issue with that, I'll make sure you get some time with him during the interval."

"I would appreciate that, thank you, John," Booth pulled his pocket watch from his waistcoat and feigned surprise. "Ah! I must tarry no longer; the play will start shortly and I must visit the washroom before the first Act. Would you excuse me, John?"

"Of course! Use the washroom we passed just down there; it's reserved for the President and his men however I don't think he would have any arguments about you using it. It will be quieter than the ones in the foyer. I will ensure you get to speak with President Lincoln if you've been unable to accept his invitations previously. I'm sure he will be eager to meet you as well."

The two men shook hands and Booth hurried away to the washroom, the promise of meeting Lincoln alone ringing in his ears.

Tiktik, tiktik, tiktik, tiktik.

The clock in the bathroom was unusually loud. Booth cast a glance at it, set high on the wall, the minute hand counting a steady beat that seemed to match his racing heart. "You're losing your mind, John, you've got to calm down," he chastised himself quietly, running the tap and splashing water onto his face.

Tiktik, tiktik, tiktik, tiktik.

Closing his eyes, Booth let the cool water drip from his face to the basin beneath his hands, steadying himself with the use of the clock. With each '*tiktik, tiktik*' he inhaled, exhaling on the next two. After a minute his fingers released the basin rim from the deathly grip, they'd held it in, his heart rate lowered, and the pressure pulsing in his ears dissipated at last.

He knew what he needed to do. Lincoln and Grant would surely arrive soon, and he could put his plans into motion—once he met the man, he could decide to follow through with the plan Powell and Atzerodt had laid out in his apartment.

Opening his eyes Booth stared at his reflection in the mirror—he looked pale, which would work to his advantage as an excuse for leaving the stalls during the performance he supposed. Funny, he had hoped to use feeling unwell as an excuse, if he decided to go through with the assassination, but he hadn't expected to actually reflect that outwardly.

Standing tall, he took a towel and dabbed the water from his face, sweeping a stray strand of hair from his face, before straightening his waistcoat.

Tiktik, tiktik, tiktik, tiktik.

Booth looked back at the clock; eyes narrowed as the ticking seemed to be less intrusive. *'Nerves, that's all it was, old man, nerves, and doubt getting the better of you,'* He left the bathroom, thinking nothing more of the sound as he re-joined the crowds outside.

***

The patrons bustled into the theatre hall, the auditorium a cacophony of buzzing voices, each one indistinguishable against the next unless you were part of that particular conversation. Booth settled himself into his seat, eyes immediately locating the Presidential Box. He'd picked this spot because there was a perfect view of the box and its patrons. Booth scowled, eyes growing wide. Quickly he averted his gaze, fixated upon the stage in front instead.

The box was empty.

He hoped that Lincoln and Grant would have arrived by now, Ford had said that the party was late but now it seemed that none of them were coming at all. His heart sank, their plans were in ruins. The play was due to start at any moment. There were mutterings of disappointment throughout the crowd, each patron had been looking forward to catching a glimpse of Lincoln and now he hadn't come.

Tiktik, tiktik, tiktik, tiktik.

Booth scowled at the ticking sound, looking around as though expecting to find the washroom clock lingering nearby—it was the *exact* same tone, but how could it be? Did someone possess a particularly loud pocket watch? Or was he going mad?

He shook his head, trying to rid himself of the incessant sound— though he should have been grateful to it for that moment of distraction from the failure the evening would now become.

The ticking vanished as suddenly as it started and Booth settled into his seat, ready to watch the play.

There was a flicker of movement in the President's Box from out the corner of his eye, Booth's head whipped around, eager eyes searching for what caused it, his heart in his throat as he dared not hope it was his quarry. His eyebrows furrowed, there was nothing there—but he had definitely seen *something* moving amongst the shadows of the box, a clear figure of someone.

Booth sighed heavily and shook his head, dragging his attention back to the stage so that no one could question why he was staring at the empty seats above. Was it paranoia or disappointment that created the vision? Rubbing his face Booth forced himself to concentrate on the actors before him; to little avail.

A shiver ran down his spine and Booth found his eyes drawn back to the President's empty chair—he was more cautious this time, turning his head ever so slightly and straining his eyes to search without making it obvious. The box was dark and empty, devoid of any life whatsoever... so why did he feel as though he were being watched?

"Sir? Are you well?" The wizened old woman beside him asked in a hushed whisper, arthritic claw reaching out to touch his hand tentatively.

He jumped a little at her touch, his heart beating hard in his chest as she drew his attention away from the shadows to her age-worn face. He gave her a weak smile and placed his hand upon hers. "Apologies dear lady, I am not feeling at my best and clearly disturbing your enjoyment. Maybe it would be best for me to get out of the way," he whispered in reply.

"Not at all," she hurried to add, waving her free hand dismissively, her wrinkles shifting upward as best they could to allow her thin lips to smile. "It was my son that dragged me from the comfort of my home this evening, all to see the President, and what disappointment we found in that!" She let out a small chuckle that eased Booth's racing heart and distracted his mind from the eyes he had felt boring into him from the darkness. "You sit with me Sir, I will see you right, not to worry," the old woman patted his hand and settled back into her seat, eyes on the stage once more.

How little she knew of him, though he was glad of the comfort she offered. That niggling feeling remained; that instinct to look back at the box clawing at his mind, desperately trying to tell him that something was there—but Booth chose to ignore it, dismissing it as his hope that the President would be there.

Movement again caught Booth's eye, and he looked cautiously to the box, his heart leaping in his chest as he hoped to see Lincoln taking his seat. This time something looked back. A figure loomed in the shadows; its hulking mass too big to be human. Its wide, corpse-like eyes sunk into its spectral face. Its pallid skin bleak against the unlit hollow of the box. Booth's heart stopped, his body silenced as it looked directly at him, smiling its horrific smile, spittle covered fangs glistening in the faded lamplight of the auditorium. That was *not* Lincoln.

Booth's entire being screamed at him to run, to cry out and warn the theatre-goers of the thing amongst them—but all at once, the theatre was alive with drama of its own. The door to the Presidential box opened, flooding it with light and casting out the spectre Booth had been staring at. The play was interrupted as the orchestra enthusiastically broke into a rendition of 'Hail to the Chief'.

Booth shot to his feet, his attention no longer on the prey he'd been waiting for, but for the thing, he had seen moments before. Where had it gone? Where in God's name had it gone?! The entire theatre was on its feet, applauding the late arrival of their Country's Leader. The clapping died away, Lincoln waving to his people as they all began to sit down—Booth collapsed into his seat, staring at the box, eyes still searching for a sign of the thing.

Booth's fingers dug into the arms of his seat, knuckles white, his entire body trembling as he forced himself to watch the play now that it started up again. Sweat beaded on his skin, trickling its way down his spine—chasing the shiver that ran from his head to his toes.

What Demon had he just seen? That creature was not of this Earth, it could only be one of the Devil's army, for he'd never seen nor heard of such an ungodly beast before.

The old woman put her hand upon his, concern written on her ancient face. What a state he must have looked, clammy and sweaty, trembling with an uncontrollable fear of something he could barely comprehend. He waved her off gently, not wishing to upset her, given her kindness. She gave a small smile, nodded, and turned her attention away from him, for which he was eternally grateful.

Booth pulled his handkerchief from his pocket, dabbing at the sweat upon his brow, his eyes drifting back to where the President now sat. There was the man who had taken his entire life from him—yet his hatred of Lincoln paled to nothing in the face of the thing he'd seen there moments ago. Something in the back of his mind observed that Grant had not attended, but no matter, he had bigger things to think of now. Such as where that nameless horror had gone?

Closing his eyes, Booth swallowed hard, desperate to rid himself of the bile rising in his throat, concentrating on holding back the wave of nausea that threatened to overwhelm him. Unfortunately, with his eyes closed the vision of that monstrosity seemed clearer than before—its own dead gaze fixated upon his, within his memories.

Tiktik, tiktik...

Tiktik, tiktik...

Booth looked around at the crowd, desperately searching for another patron in the same state, alas it seemed he was alone in this revelation. *'Calm yourself John, your mind is racing, and your heart cannot keep up with the pace, think logically man. The thing was just a trick of the light, that's all, what in God's name has got into you this evening?'* he chastised himself internally, forcing himself to take slow, deep breaths.

Booth kept his head still as he forced himself to watch the actors on the stage, their play was utterly lost to him, to the booming beat of his pulse in his ears. Even now he could not help but feel his attention drawn to the Presidential Box—although his gaze lingered only momentarily on Lincoln. He could still *feel* that thing's presence, felt it looking into his soul like before. It was no figment of imagination, he'd *seen* it.

A shadow flickered to the left of his vision and slowly Booth turned his head toward it—he couldn't quite make out the shape, not in any way that would identify it, but there was *something* clinging to the back corner of the auditorium by the ceiling. Pressed against the wall in the darkness where the light could not reveal it.

Booth's eyes widened as he saw the shadow shift, the light of the lamps glinting off the needle-sharp fangs jutting from the creatures distended maw. He shot to his feet and turned toward the creature, intent on alerting the rest of the theatre to its presence, but it had gone and the other patrons joined him a split second after he had risen.

It was the interval. Now was his chance to meet with the President as he'd planned. As Booth swallowed, he winced, his mouth devoid of saliva, the action like someone had jabbed a dagger into his throat.

He moved with the crowd, making his way through the row of seats and into the larger aisle, winding his way through the bustling theatre-goers into the foyer, hurrying to the washroom he'd been to previously.

He leaned over the sink, fingers gripping the basin as his legs threatened to give way beneath him.

"I will only be a moment Mary, go on ahead. I'll meet you at the box."

Booth spun toward the voice at the door; it couldn't be, of all the chance encounters he could not afford to be distracted by right now, *Lincoln* was the one man he did not wish to see.

"Ah! What luck I have to run into you here, sir! Mr. Ford said you'd come to the theatre this evening, Mr. Wilkes-Booth, but he could not find you to introduce us. Are you alright? You look unwell," the President continued, striding toward Booth, gripping Booth's shoulder and arm to support him, concern written upon his face.

"Apologies Mr. President—I felt fine this morning but have felt ill since I came to the theatre this evening. I would have stayed at home, however, Mr. Ford promised to introduce me to you and I could not pass up the opportunity."

"If you accepted my previous invitations, you would not have had to struggle so much Mr. Wilkes-Booth," Lincoln chuckled, smiling at Booth as their eyes met.

Booth chuckled and gave the President a weak smile. "I cannot apologise enough, sir. I was honoured to receive them, sadly I had prior engagements that I could not get out of. It has been my greatest regret, not being able to sit at your table and enjoy your company."

"Well, let's see if we can rectify that shall we? I'd best take care of business and get back to my wife before she sends out an army to find me, but I will send another dinner invitation—I expect you to accept it this time," Lincoln chuckled. "Will you be alright if I leave you? Should I send someone to look after you?"

"Thank you for the concern Mr. President, but I will be fine. I think I just need another moment or two to gather myself together."

"As you wish, one minute and I will be out of your hair," Lincoln smiled, disappearing into a stall.

Booth took little notice, though he heard Powell and Atzerodt's voices in his head, urging him to shoot the man while he was in the toilet—a prime opportunity to rid themselves of the Confederacy's largest enemy. Lincoln didn't take long, washing his hands and nodding to Booth before exiting the washroom, leaving Booth alone once more.

Alone with that incessant ticking.

Tiktik, tiktik, tiktik, tiktik.

Slamming open a stall door, Booth's trembling hand struggled to bolt the lock in place as the sound reverberated through his aching head.

Tiktik, tiktik, tiktik, tiktik.

The cacophonous ticking of the clock drowned out Booth's laboured breathing as he braced himself against the walls of the toilet stall, head hanging upon his neck as he fought against his own mind. That thing wasn't real, it *couldn't* be! Surely someone else would have seen the creature if it was! No, no, his mind had begun to play tricks on him, he'd worked himself into a stupor in regard to Lincoln, that was all it was.

Wasn't it?

Tiktik, tiktik, tiktik, tiktik.

Tiktik, tiktik, tiktik, tiktik.

Tiktik, tiktik...

Tiktik...

Tik...

The door to the washroom opened and Booth wretched at the stench that washed over him like a tidal wave. Scowling, he cast his eyes to the white tiles of the washroom floor, watching the growing shadow of whoever entered as they moved in his direction. By God, what *was* that smell?!

Covering his mouth and nose with his hands, Booth winced, his vision blurring as his eyes began to stream. It evoked a sense of death and decay, and Booth was reminded of meat that had turned sour, flesh a sickly grey-green, infested with maggots and all manner of other horrors.

He scowled, concentrating on the shadow that came to a halt right outside his stall. The smell was acute now that whoever it was stopped there. They made no sound. There had been no footsteps, Booth could not even hear their breathing… in fact, the entire washroom had fallen silent, even the clock seemed to have ceased in its machinations.

Fear gripped his throat with its hand, snatching the air from his lungs and leaving his eyes bulging in their sockets as his body began to tremble. Whoever, no, *whatever* stood outside the door was the same thing he'd seen in the Presidential Box. He did not dare bend down to face the thing from beneath the door, and he had absolutely *no* intention of unlocking the stall to confront it. He knew what awaited him, could feel that same dead-eyed stare boring into him through the flimsy wooden barrier that separated them.

Taptaptaptaptap, taptaptaptaptap, taptaptaptaptap, taptaptaptaptap.

The steady clicking reminded Booth of his childhood when his mother would rap her fingernails across the table waiting for him to confess to whatever childhood crimes he'd committed. As suddenly as the tapping started, it stopped, the shadow retreated and vanished back into the crowds beyond the washroom.

The thing was taunting him, toying with him. Sweat dripped down Booth's face and he finally let out the breath he'd been holding, his lungs burning from the pressure. He had to find the thing, he had to kill it before it killed him—before it killed Lincoln.

Booth unlocked the door slowly, ears straining for any sign of the thing—but all he could hear was the theatre staff calling for the end of the Intermission, urging the crowd back to their seats.

Tiktik, tiktik, tiktik, tiktik.

That wretched sound again! Booth turned on the clock, ripping it from the wall and smashing it against the side of the basin—cogs, and screws clinking against the porcelain.

Tiktik, tiktik, tiktik, tiktik.

It wasn't the clock…

Tiktik, tiktik, tiktik, tikik.

Booth stared at his reflection, barely recognising the horror-stricken man looking back at him—his skin devoid of colour, clammy and sweaty, he almost believed it was the creature standing before him, wearing *his* clothes. No, the face had been less than human, nothing he'd encountered before had eyes as dead as that creature.

He had to find it. Hurrying from the washroom, he was grateful that the patrons had returned to the auditorium to watch the remainder of the play. Cautiously, he investigated the foyer, ignoring the odd looks from the staff who remained there.

"Sir? Are you well? Can we help at all?"

Booth rounded on the young man who spoke to him, barely recognising Thomas as he grasped him by the shoulders and towered over him. "Did you see it? Did you see the thing?"

"S-sir? I, I don't know what you're talking about. What thing?" Thomas asked eyes wide as he looked at his colleagues for aid.

"The thing! The thing that came into the washroom, the thing that smells like death!" Booth hissed.

Tiktik, tiktik, tiktik, tiktik.

"There! The thing making that infernal ticking sound. I thought it was the washroom clock, but I've smashed that and *still* that incessant ticking persists. It gets quieter you know, the closer the thing is the quieter the sound gets. I've figured it out now, I understand how its foul sounds work."

"Sir please, you are not well, why don't you come and sit down. We can get you a glass of water and a doctor."

"No! I have to find it before it harms someone, don't you understand?! It was in the President's Box, that's where I first saw it, it might be after the President! Useless, all of you!" Booth snarled. Pushing the lad away and sprinting up the stairs that led towards where the boxes were located, he heard Thomas call to one of the other staff, urging them to fetch Mr. Ford *'Mr. Wilkes-Booth is not well!'* the lad had said. No matter, there was no time to worry about those ignorant fools.

Tiktik... tiktik...

Tiktik... tiktik...

Tiktik...

Tiktik...

Tik...

With his back against the theatre wall Booth's eyes never stopped searching, darting here, there, and everywhere in search of the thing— following the steadily quieting *'tiktik'* sound. He knew he was going in the right direction as the voices of the actors became clearer, the creature's voice growing quieter as he drew ever closer. He had it now,

265

he'd figured the bloody thing out.

Booth came to a halt by the door to the President's Box—the ornate gold lettering identifying it as such catching his eye. He dared to reach out and run his fingers along the letters. He'd met the man now. Lincoln had been kind; he'd been funny and despite how much Booth *hated* him for beating the Confederacy the man was worth getting to know better. With a Demon such as this on the loose the entire country was at risk—whether Lincoln was alive or dead meant nothing if that creature was allowed to live, Powell and Atzerodt would have to understand that when he told them of his change of heart. Of his betrayal to their cause. For now, he had to protect the President from the monster stalking these halls.

Shaking his head, Booth hurried down the corridor, he had to find the thing he had to…

Tiktik…

Tiktik…

The sound had returned…

Booth whipped around, eyes trained upon the gold lettering, his heart gripped by the hand of fear. There had been silence while he'd been at the door, not even the faintest trace of that creature's voice— had it returned to the place he'd first seen it? It stood to reason that it might, did it not?

'Reason with yourself all you like John, you no more understand the thinking of that beast than you do the Union. If you're going to do something about it, do it now,' he chastised himself silently, hand slipping under his shirt to retrieve his Deringer. As he walked back to

the Box it struck Booth as odd that it was not guarded, had the thing made off with the President's bodyguards? Was that why no one watched the door?

He reached out with a trembling hand, fingers tentatively touching the cold metal of the handle. He wrapped his hand around it, grounding himself with the feel of something real. He attempted to wet his parched lips with a tongue that held no moisture itself, it felt thick and foreign in his mouth as he swallowed hard. Slowly he turned the handle and opened the door.

Light from the hallway flooded into the inner entrance of the box. Gun at the ready Booth searched the shadows, his lungs bursting as he instinctively held his breath so that he could hear the slightest sound from the room. Thankfully, it seemed the creature did not lurk within, which meant it was in the box where the President sat with his wife and guests.

Booth entered the room, moving swiftly to the second door that led directly into the President's Box. This time he could not hesitate for he knew he would not have long—he would have to look for the creature and dispose of it in a matter of seconds. Exhaling, he took another deep breath before he made his move.

He turned the handle slowly, the rancid smell of the thing causing his eyes to water—any thought of the nausea he'd felt before cast aside due to the urgency of what he needed to do. He made as little noise as he could, peering through the crack he made. The occupants of the box were fully focussed on the play, their eyes fixed on the stage and not on the nameless horror looming above the President from the ceiling.

Booth's eyes grew wide as he watched the skeletal frame of the thing unfold from the darkness, its pallid skin stark in contrast. It reached out an arm toward Lincoln, claw adorned fingers inches from the back of his head—it's corpse-like gaze fixed on Booth.

Booth made his move, throwing open the door as the creature opened its jaw wide to snap Lincoln's head from his shoulders, Booth took his shot. The sound of his gunshot was drowned out by the laughter of the crowd, but his ears rang nonetheless.

"Freedom!" He shouted triumphantly, believing he'd killed the beast... but all was not well.

Horror struck him as he saw Mary Lincoln slump in her chair and fall backward, the President leaping to his feet to gather his dead wife into his arms, screaming her name. Booth did not have time to reflect on his actions. To mourn the loss of the innocent woman, or to regret the look of betrayal now etched to Lincoln's face in place of the friendliness that had been there only minutes before.

"No!" Booth roared, his eyes fixed on the beast as it slithered away around the edge of the Box, out into the auditorium, sticking to the shadows as it had before. Booth turned and made for the door when Major Henry Rathbone, who had attended in Grant's stead, leapt from his seat, grabbing Booth's arm.

The pair tussled, but Booth's eyes were not on the man—he was searching for the creature that had escaped him. Booth dropped his pistol and pulled a knife from his jacket, stabbing Rathbone in the arm to force the man off him. He rushed to the edge of the box, leaning over as far as he could, his eyes searching for his quarry.

Finally, he spotted it on the opposite side of the stage, taunting him as it clung to the curtains just out of sight of the audience—not that anyone was looking for the beast other than Booth. A hand grasped his shoulder painfully, whipping him around until he came face-to-face with Lincoln's fury. Booth's heart ached unexpectedly at that expression, but his face ached more as the President pulled back his arm and hit Booth full force in the nose, propelling him over the side of the box.

Booth grunted as his riding spur caught in the flag attached to the edge of the box, preventing him from dropping to the stage, swinging him into the wall and dangling him by his leg instead.

"Grab him!" Rathbone roared, hanging over the edge and reaching to grab Booth's leg.

"No! I have to stop it!" Booth yelled in reply, kicking Rathbone's hand away and dislodging himself at the same time. He fell, landing awkwardly on his left foot onto the stage twelve feet below. Wincing Booth pulled himself upright and began to limp across towards the beast, slashing his knife at anyone who dared come close to him.

"Stop that man!" Lincoln's enraged shout boomed through the auditorium, following Booth as he tried to sprint across the stage, dragging his left foot as he made for the side door that was his intended escape route.

The creature lingered by the exit, drawing him onward, mocking his failures so far. He watched it open the stage door, slipping through into the night, but he would not let it go, he could not!

Stumbling into the night, he looked around, hoping to catch another glimpse of the creature—but it was nowhere to be seen. His heart dropped through his stomach, he had failed to kill it, he never stood a chance!

He'd killed the President's wife, killed an innocent woman, and he'd let that monstrosity escape. There was a ruckus behind him, and Booth looked over his shoulder, the voices of the patrons bringing him back to the reality of the situation.

He had no choice; he could not linger—he needed to get to the rendezvous point, he would explain himself to his compatriots later.

Booth moved as quickly as he was able, every step on his left foot sending shooting pains throughout his body. He pulled himself onto the horse that had been left outside for his escape. Cutting the lead rein holding the beast in place, he kicked it with his right foot and sent it galloping away, moments before the side door swung open. The cries of the angry patrons followed him into the night—Lincoln's mournful wails haunting him as he spurred his steed on.

***

The pace of the horse was brutal on his left foot, each jolt sent another stabbing pain up his leg into his hip, the sole of his foot prickling as though on fire, but he knew better than to slow the beast— he had to put as much distance between himself and his pursuers as he could.

Booth breathed slowly and deeply through the pain, forcing himself to endure it. As he inhaled, he was struck by the reek of rotting flesh that his panic had caused him to ignore. The stench caused him to heave, his stomach doing somersaults as he bent double.

The smell assaulted him alongside the crushing recollection of where he had last smelled something so foul. Slowing his horse's gait, Booth put a hand to his face to shield himself from the odour.

Sitting upright Booth's eye grew wide, his jaw dropping as his heart fell through the floor at the sight of what was looking back at him. As his horse came to a halt it turned its head to look at him—but it was not the long, soft face of the bay he had mounted.

No; soulless eyes met his, and he knew them all too well. Booth screamed, falling backwards from the saddle, landing hard on the ground. He scrambled backwards on his hands as the horse's body twisted grotesquely into the thing's true form.

It loomed over him, wiry muscle beneath sallow skin, its limbs long and skeletal. It sat back on its haunches, tilting its head to one side as though assessing him. Never looking away, never blinking. The needle-like fangs that protruded from its terrible, blood-stained maw forced its jaw to remain constantly open, unable to close let alone hold the terrible long tongue that hung between its teeth.

"No… No," Booth whimpered as the creature stood and stretched out its clawed hands toward him. Booth closed his eyes against the grotesque vision inches from his face, its vulgar breath filling his lungs. Pain shot through his body as he felt the creature's fangs sink into his flesh slowly, piercing his neck, his blood hot as it spurted from the wounds, and then Booth felt nothing at all.

THE MONSTERS WITHIN

"Illia, take point with the brothers. I want your eyes, ears, and noses on this one. Get us inside."

"Yes, sir."

Crouching low, ready to spring into action if they were attacked, Illia made his way along the line of soldiers, stopping to gather the brothers as he passed them. They made their way to the locked main door, flanking their Corporal.

Once they reached the door Illia motioned to the brothers, giving them a hand signal. The pair gripped the glass front doors, wiggling their fingers into the crack. Pulling with all their might until they slid back on their rollers to expose the massive steel shutter behind.

Illia nodded to them and they moved out of the way as he stepped forward. Raising his hands, he placed his palms against the cold, metal surface. Closing his eyes, he took a deep breath and centred himself. Concentrating on the solid steel beneath his fingers, the sound of the breeze as it whipped through the leaves of the trees around them. Illia channelled the area's magic through his body the life of the forest coursed through his veins, filling him with its immensity.

He released his breath along with the magic, which jolted from his fingers into the steel door. It buckled inwards before ricocheting off the wall beyond with an almighty 'CLANG'. The sound echoing through the silent forest.

The siblings moved past him as soon as the entrance was open. Illia shook the residual magic from his hands, flexing his fingers and concentrating on ridding himself of the tingling sensation. Opening his eyes, he stepped through the threshold to join the brothers.

Delan and Samme moved to opposite ends of the lobby, crouched low just as Illia had, two coiled springs ready to release at the slightest threat.

Illia adjusted to the darkness, acclimatising to the red glow of the emergency lighting that blinked on and off, casting strange shadows over everything. His sharp, storm-grey eyes looked over the huge steel shutters that had locked down every door and window of the facility, flickering with makeshift warding magic that was sub-par compared to what he and the rest of the Magus' could conjure.

"All clear Corporal! The internal security doors have come down and dead bolted further in and the window bars and shutters have been triggered, as expected, the lobby is safe and secure for the moment,"

Delan reported as he and his brother re-joined Illia at the empty reception desk.

"Until we breach the doors, as we have this one," Illia sighed, motioning to the huge, twisted metal lying discarded on the floor.

"Yeah, but you can put the door back in place Corporal, we've seen you do it before!" Delan said cheerfully.

"That's not what he meant," Samme snarled at his sibling, elbowing Delan in the ribs.

Illia gave the younger man a smile and a grateful nod. "No, it wasn't, but thank you for the vote of confidence nonetheless Delan. Go inform the Sergeant that we're secure, might as well get this over with."

While Delan informed the Sergeant of the status of the entrance, Illia and Samme attempted to log into the facility's computer via the reception. As Illia suspected the power was completely dead, which meant they would need to find the breakers if they were going to retrieve any research materials—the Company's number one priority, of course.

"Corporal, I've just had another, somewhat horrifying thought," Samme uttered under his breath, keen amber eyes watching their colleagues file through the entrance, taking up their positions without further instruction. "If the power is down here and throughout the facility, that means any electrical deterrents or detainments are down doesn't it?"

"Yep."

"So, all that's keeping those nasty nightmares inside is...?"

"Some steel doors, some old warding that will likely give out before long since the maintenance on it leaves much to be desired. And us."

"I was afraid you were going to say that... Do we even know what's housed here?"

"No, but I'm sure we're about to find out." Illia placed a gentle hand on Samme's shoulder and raised his delicate eyebrows slightly. The man sighed and gave the Corporal a small nod. "Do you ever regret staying behind?" Samme asked suddenly.

"You're referring to when the rest of my kin chose to leave before the Barrier was put in place," Illia replied.

"Yeah. I mean, how many of you remained behind when the Council decided to separate the Magical realm from the Human one? I was born here but you, you weren't, you remember what the world was like before."

Illia smiled slightly. "I do, I remember the Elder Council debating how best to handle the humans since they were growing dangerous. I also remember thinking that maybe, if we stayed, we could help humans to be better, to evolve as a species, and I wanted to do my part for that."

"So, regretting that decision yet?" Samme snorted.

"Right this minute? Maybe a little," Illia chuckled.

"How we looking Corporal?" Baryon asked as the rest of the squad searched the area for anything that might be of use to them once they breached the next set of security doors.

"Power is out, can't access any of the systems, and the security doors might be the reason we've been unable to get in touch with anyone here since the Scouts pushed the second level lockdown."

"Making it hard for anything to get out, let alone in," Baryon sighed.

"The scout teams know the drill— no contact from them in more than eight hours immediately triggers our involvement. Shutting the entire building kept the 'acquisitions' secured and meant we would be sent to deal with the situation."

"Is that sarcasm I hear there Illia?" Baryon snorted, his right eyebrow-raising in surprise at the Corporal's tone as he said the word 'acquisitions'. Baryon's scarred face pulled into a difficult smile, the burns on the left side pulling the skin taut.

"Not sure I have that capacity, Sarge. Merely a statement of fact. Do we have a list of what they're keeping here?"

"Trust you to ask the important questions Illia, you insufferable Elf," Baryon chuckled. "Alright listen up all of you, you're going to need to know what you're potentially facing down there. I was given the list once we left the truck, the higher-ups didn't like the idea of us finding out what's here and deciding not to carry out the mission."

"Well, that's fucking comforting," Marcus said under his breath. Illia moved to the newest Magus' side, placing an elegant hand upon the man's shoulder to stifle any further comment, as well as to save him from a rebuke from Baryon as the man's attention rounded on the Private.

"Sorry Sarge," Marcus uttered softly, hanging his head.

"You're not wrong Marcus, it isn't fucking comforting, but it's part of our job and we all know it. We're expendable, always have been, it's why they send us into the shitty jobs—we're good at what we do and no one gives two shits if we die," Baryon added. "This facility houses some of the most dangerous creatures in existence, primarily those on the verge of extinction or those with particular talents deemed useful to Medeis Corp."

Silence filled the room for a moment as the Sergeant's words filtered through the squad of forty men and women. The possibilities ran through all their minds, though no one other than Illia himself would truly understand what the Sergeant meant.

"Dare I ask what the worst of them is?" Illia asked, long arms crossed over his muscular chest, delicate blonde eyebrows furrowed above his enchanting grey eyes. He didn't look like a soldier, far from it, but the men and women in the room had seen him in action and knew better than to question his strength.

Baryon's good eye met Illia's gaze, the glazed left one staring through the Elf. The rest of the room shuffled uncomfortably beneath the expression shared between these two giants of men.

"Depends on what you call the worst," Baryon sighed, breaking the stare and running a hand over his mangled features as he looked down the list he'd been given. "Dragons are a dead cert for strength and, literal, firepower."

"But?" Illia interjected as he heard the hesitation in his Sergeant's tone.

"But, ya damned Elf, there are things like the one Tiktik they have to consider."

Illia's eyebrows raised, his hands falling to his sides as he stepped toward Baryon with a look of disbelief upon his elegant features—his pale, flawless skin seemed to have turned grey and the other soldiers shared a worried glance. They'd never seen the Elf look this way.

"A Tiktik," he repeated, now an inch from Baryon's face, his head tilted down to look at the man, Illia's long platinum locks falling into the Sergeant's face. "Of all the creatures to lock up and study… how in the name of the All-Mother did they capture one?"

"Not info I'm privy to Illia, but that's why they've called us in, there's no one else that can handle it."

"Handle it?! If that creature is loose, we should be looking to burn this entire building where it stands and call it a loss!" Illia snapped. "None of you have ever dealt with one, have you? If you think the beast that nearly cost you your face was bad it's nothing compared to what that monstrosity can do."

"What is a Tiktik, Corporal?" Elena asked cautiously, the Private flinching as the Corporal's attention turned her way.

"Best you tell them Illia, you know it better than me," Baryon growled, pushing the Corporal away from himself, and scowling at the man.

"The Tiktik is originally from the Philippines, they're cousins of the Wakwak and the Aswang. All I can say is be grateful they only have one of these listed in their collection. Tiktik's are named for the sound they make; their call is distinctive because the louder it is the further away the creature is."

"So, if it's absolutely deafening it's miles away?" Marcus asked.

"Correct, that's why it's so dangerous. Tiktik's are rare. Very few people know about them, so when they are unfortunate enough to stumble into its lair they believe, as you would expect, that the louder it is the closer it is. In reality, it's when they're quiet you have to worry."

"But wouldn't that mean we should hear them all the time if they get louder the further away, they are?" Elena asked, looking from Illia to Regina who stood beside her, the usually cheerful Private had lost her infectious smile.

"A good theory, sadly distance still plays a part in hearing them— if there isn't one in your vicinity you won't hear it."

"But just because you don't hear it doesn't mean there isn't one right behind you either…" Elena added quietly, biting her bottom lip.

"Hence they are one of the most dangerous creatures anyone has ever encountered; how they captured one is beyond me, as I don't know of anyone who has got close to one and come away from it unscathed. Hunting them is damn near impossible. Not only are they silent when close to you, but they're also shapeshifters. We have no knowledge of what, if any, limitations they have with their shapeshifting ability."

"So, it could change into any creature it likes? Or one of us, or maybe even the furniture?" Marcus added scathingly.

"I don't know Marcus, legend states its preferred form, other than its original, is that of a giant bird, but there have been tales of people being eaten by their horse after discovering it was a Tiktik. They are truly masterful in staying hidden and staying alive. They're vicious, bloodthirsty creatures with no qualms about tearing their prey apart,"

Illia shivered, trying to keep his composure. "I know of two people who survived this monster, they lost everything to it and barely managed to escape the same fate as their loved ones. It does not have mercy; it does not have reason... but it is known for toying with its prey."

"Fucking brilliant... as if Dragons, Banshees, Gorgons, and fucking Faerie Folk weren't bad enough to deal with, now we have this?!"

"Marcus, that's enough," Baryon snarled. "It's shit, but it's our job. If we're lucky the Tiktik is still in its cage, either way, keep your eyes open, protect each other's backs and make sure your detection spells and barriers are maintained while we're inside. We might not be able to hear it coming, but we can detect it's movements in the air at the very least."

"That and the smell. It's not always apparent until it's on top of you, from what records state at least, but the Tiktik is unable to hide the stench of death and decay that follows it, so keep your noses open. Delan, Samme, we'll be relying on your keen senses for that one, you might sniff it out long before the rest of us do," Illia said as he secured his helmet to his head, clicking the chin strap in place.

They still should have set fire to the building... safer than facing off against his worst nightmare, but they didn't need to know that, none of them needed to know that he was one of the two that had survived it. Him and his Aunt who raised him.

It had been centuries since he'd thought of the thing. Years since he'd slept without its dead-eyed gaze waking him from his dreams in a cold sweat. Only a glimpse, that's all he had been afforded,—one blink and the Tiktik that had killed everyone in his family was gone... His stomach twisted painfully, a wave of nausea rippling through him at the memory of its foul stench.

"You've all studied the blueprints of the building, once we get through this door, we will split into two groups and search the facility on both sides. Delan, Samme, going to need the pair of you to split up, one on each team. Since the facility basically folds in on itself, we will cover one floor at a time, meet in the middle, and clear that before heading down a floor and doing the same again. Understood?" Baryon's orders cut through Illia's thoughts, dragging the Corporal back to the job at hand.

"Understood Sarge. Do you want the door back in place or a Barrier instead?" Illia asked.

"Our combined warding will be stronger than that door ever was, get a Barrier up and let's get this done."

Illia motioned to four of their team, pointing at the now exposed doorway. The five of them formed a semi-circle, with Illia at the centre of the line. Palms turned to the ceiling, they closed their eyes and lowered their heads in unison. Raising their hands, palm-to-palm, synchronising their breathing as they concentrated on their magic.

The air surrounding the group wavered, a soft yellow glow enveloped their connected hands. A deep, throbbing hum filled the foyer as the magic built up within them. As the vibration reached its crescendo, they broke their connection, clapping their own hands together with a deafening 'CRACK'. The air whipped around the entire squad, whooshing past them as it filled the void the door had left.

The group opened their eyes and smiled at the sight of the shimmering glow that stood between them and the world outside.

"Barrier in place Sarge," Illia called, nodding to the group that aided him, motioning for them to return to their positions. He lingered a moment, glancing at their handy work—their incantation was perfect, which meant they were trapped in the facility with that thing.

"Alright, let's get this internal door open and get on with this," Baryon snorted.

Illia stood to one side while their Sergeant split the squad into two groups of twenty, he smiled when Samme was assigned to his team. Of the two werewolves, Illia found the younger, more level headed of the pair easier to get along with.

The two teams were ready, the room thick with the metallic taste of magic as the Magus' all summoned forth their signature spells, ready to be used at a moment's notice. The delicate silver hairs on Illia's arms stood on end with the buzzing, electrical charge the magical residue created in the air, and he allowed himself a small smile of satisfaction at the tingling excitement now coursing through his veins. It was difficult not to lose yourself to the sheer power you inhaled with every breath, it reminded Illia that he wasn't a child anymore, he had a job to do and this was his chance to get revenge.

Baryon took a deep breath, Illia spared his Sergeant a glance as the scarred man balled his hands into fists, slamming his knuckles together with a thunderous boom before he pulled back his right arm.

Another breath and Baryon threw his body forward, hand connecting with the door, sending it flying in a similar fashion to the one Illia eliminated.

The metal crumpled in on itself, bending and twisting unnaturally. The door shattered from its hinges, flying from the frame and landing in a heap against the wall opposite. The clatter created reverberated through the empty corridors filled with the same eerie, steadily flickering red glow as the foyer.

Silence befell the squad as Samme and Delan immediately bolted through the door, crouching low, their noses twitching as they scented the stale air beyond.

**

"All clear," Delan called softly.

"The air's stagnant, ventilation must have gone down with the power," Samme added.

"Does that mean that anyone inside could have suffocated?" Marcus asked softly, large brown eyes staring up at Illia.

"No, just means that fresh air isn't being pulled in, so whatever foul stench lies beyond is lingering," Illia replied gently, placing a reassuring hand upon Marcus's shoulder. "Some of the creatures listed give off a foul stench, with the ventilation down it just means the putrid aroma has pooled. We will be able to breathe just fine."

"You may vomit, however," Delan added.

"Just breathe through your mouth and try not to think about it too much," Samme offered gently, rolling his eyes in Illia's direction as a way of an apology for his brother—Illia had seen that look a thousand times before, and always after Delan said something he probably shouldn't have.

"Ant, next time you say you're going to take me on a date, can you pick somewhere better than this?" Elena snorted, turning her eyes to the man beside her.

"Sure sugar, though I don't know what's so wrong with this, the lightings... romantic?"

"Alright enough, you all know what to do. Illia take your team right, check the offices on that side, and meet us in the main stairwell once you've cleared your side of the building," Baryon snapped.

"Yes Sir," Illia replied, motioning for his team to get a move on.

The first floor was blissfully uneventful, the red glow of the strip lights turning desks into monsters in the darkness—thankfully Illia and Samme were able to distinguish what they were looking at swiftly, allowing the team to continue to move from room to room efficiently.

The two teams converged at the stairwell as planned, silently descending into the darkness, splitting up to search their respective floors once more.

Illia and Samme led the way as they searched the first few rooms before opening a door into a larger office. The pair stopped, Illia's eyes narrowing at pitch-black void beyond them.

"Lights are out, I can't see a damned thing," Samme said in a hushed tone.

"We take it slow; we have to clear it. Ant, light it up," Illia called over his shoulder toward the man standing behind him.

"You got it, Boss."

Stepping around Illia, the slight man removed his gloves and wiggled his fingers. Illia watched him carefully, always conscious of his team members, and how they performed. The Elf's eyes fixed on Ant's back, watching the steady rise and fall of his shoulders as he breathed in, and out. Suddenly there was a bright glow illuminating the doorway and with a flick of his hands, Ant sent eight orbs of light flickering into the air. They floated over the room, chasing away the darkness and revealing a cluster of strange stone objects at the far end.

"What the hell is that?" Ant asked, turning to Illia and scowling, his face bathed in red from the corridor.

"They look like statues," Samme replied, glancing at Illia himself. "But what the hell would they be-"

"Gorgon," Illia cut off Samme's question. "Ant cut the lights, we're going to have to go by instinct, if we can see her eyes then we're all screwed."

"Thermal goggles?" Samme asked.

"She doesn't give off a heat signature, remember? Ant, lights."

Ant nodded, stepping into the room and raising his hands to disperse his magic—but he was too late. low, slithering hiss shot across the room. Illia pulled Samme back but—Ant was a step too far away. There was a gasp and something that resembled rocks grinding against one another.

"Ant!" Samme shouted beside Illia, though it surprised the Elf that Elena hadn't uttered a word.

"Keep your eyes down, don't look at her. Marcus, Shane, we need your mirror skills," Illia called, dismissing Elena's silence as shock at the loss of her lover, concentrating on the two men as they hurried forward.

Marcus and Shane turned to face one another, raising their right hands and clasping them together. The air stirred around them; their left arms bathed in soft blue light. After a moment the pair shook their left arms and with a sound like shattering glass, their left hands shrouded by a large, moving mirror seemingly made of a mosaic of broken pieces. Nodding to one another they relinquished their grip, stepping back to allow Illia to stand between them.

"Slow and steady," he whispered, closing his eyes as he drew the sword at his hip, entrusting himself to his soldiers as they placed their hands upon his shoulders to lead him.

Shane and Marcus looked into the other's mirror, using the shards to guide them into the room—the Gorgon had left her victim where he stood before vanishing once more. Stepping around the statue that had once been their friend, they would mourn Ant's loss later, they had to deal with the thing that killed him.

The trio moved one step at a time, Illia cocking his head from one side to the other as his exceptional hearing picked out every sound in the room—searching for the slither of their opponent, the others searching with their mirrors.

The room filled with a rattling sound and they stopped, Illia's hand tightening upon his hilt—she was close. There was an angry hiss as the Gorgon lunged forwards.

"Fill the room!" Illia barked, ducking low as Shane and Marcus swung their left arms—throwing the shards of mirror from themselves.

They turned the room into one giant, reflective surface.

Illia's eyes opened, and he caught sight of the Gorgon as she flung herself at Shane. The trio moved, their eyes darting from shard to shard—never looking at the Gorgon directly. Hours of training paid off as they danced out of the creature's way, the cursed thing screaming angrily as Shane ducked under her attack, slicing across her belly with his sword before dodging backward to allow Illia to rush forward, deftly removing her head with a flick of his wrist.

Panting, the three stood up, Marcus and Shane dispersing their spell and grinning at the lifeless corpse at their feet.

"Good work, both of you. Let's clear this level."

The rest of the floor was uneventful—it seemed only the Gorgon ventured up this far, there was no sign of any other creature at all.

"This isn't right is it?" Samme asked under his breath, glancing at Illia as they stood at the stairwell, waiting for the second team to join them.

"No, it isn't."

"Ok so it's not just me that's disturbed by the lack of... well... disturbance then?"

"No, it isn't."

"Well, thanks for that Illia, that's reassuring," Samme sighed, rolling his eyes at the Elf.

"Sorry... nothing about this situation is sitting well with me."

"What's bothering you the most? The fact that we've cleared three floors, and only encountered one creature?"

"That. But mostly the fact that this facility is silent."

Illia let his words sink in, nodding as Samme flinched at the realisation of what that meant, his nose working overtime as his eyes began to search their immediate area.

"You think it's following us?"

"We haven't heard it at all, but we should have been able to hear it the minute we opened that inner door," Illia replied, looking around himself and shuddering; its slimy tongue, hanging between needle-like fangs fresh in his mind.

"Let's just hope the damned thing is already dead then," Samme muttered, looking around desperately, his eyes widening suddenly. "WHAT THE FUCK IS THAT?!" He grabbed Illia's shoulders and spun the Corporal around, pointing amidst their own team with a quaking hand.

Marcus and Elena seemed to be gripped in an epic battle, Marcus gasping for air while Elena held his throat in her hands so tightly that his skin had split with the pressure. Elena looked human until she turned her head and met Illia and Samme's gaze with eyes that looked to have been plucked from a corpse. A long, slimy tongue lolled from the open jaw of the 'Magus' who opened her mouth, jaw dislocating with a sickening crack. Needle-like teeth glistened with spit as the transforming creature snapped its mouth around Marcus' head, severing it from his neck in one bite.

How? How had the foul creature got past them? How had Samme not smelt it?!

That was when it hit Illia, how the Tiktik managed to slip in amongst them from the beginning of their ill-fated mission. The air was stale, it already stank of decay and rot—no one would question the fact that the stench grew stronger, because of course, it would with the ventilation off!

"Run! All of you run!" Illia shouted, reaching for his sword, the metal singing as he drew the blade and held it out before him, forcing himself to stay strong and control the quaking in his hand.

Without hesitation the team bolted for the stairs, not one of them daring to explain to Baryon's group, rather encouraging them to make their way down while they still had the chance.

"Corporal?!" Baryon called, trying to push against the tide of the fleeing squad.

"Tiktik Sergeant! We can't stop it here; we need an open area where it can't hide. Gotta head down, find a better place to corner it!"

"Head for floor seven Corporal, there's an arena down there that should do the job."

"Samme and I will hold it back, we'll meet you there," Illia replied, eyes fixed on the fully transformed Tiktik.

It was just as horrifying as he remembered. It's skeletal face and limbs, with their pallid, sickly skin pulled taut across its muscles. A stark contrast to the swollen torso of the beast. In another life, it might have been human. Stood upright on legs that looked ready to buckle under the weight of its body, its torso tilted forward to balance, long arms hanging low so that its clawed hands almost scraped along the floor.

If Illia hadn't seen it before, he would have assumed the creature to be ungainly and slow—but he knew better, Tiktik's moved with a speed and grace even the Elves would envy.

The Tiktik cocked its head to one side; slitted pupils, positioned closely between its dead eyes, its skin pulled across its smooth skull so that its features were more pronounced. Now that it was here its stench was more obvious to him, and Illia cursed himself inwardly for not immediately recognising it. The acrid stench of rotting meat haunted him as a child, leaving him a gibbering wreck in a cold sweat whenever he'd caught the slightest whiff of anything similar.

"Samme, we need to slow this thing down," Illia whispered as they both took a step toward the stairwell, eyes never leaving their opponent.

"What do you suggest?" Samme replied sceptically.

"We set fire to this floor and bring down the ceiling on top of the stairwell, I have no doubt it will find a way down eventually but it might give us a chance to deal with the rest of the creatures in here."

"And blocks our way out Illia," Samme hissed, glancing at his Corporal.

"Not quite, there's an underground tunnel for emergencies but the only way to open it is to blow the two upper floors. It was built to ensure there was a way out, but only if it was the last option left."

"That's fucking comforting."

"It's this or nothing."

"Shit. So, you're handling the fire while I bring the ceiling down?"

"Glad we're on the same page," Illia said with a weak smile, his hands already glowing with the magic pent up in his body, flames flickering down the blade of his sword. "Now!"

With a flick of his wrist, Illia aimed the flames at the Tiktik. It leaped backward, claws digging into the concrete wall as it hung above them, head tilting the other way as it snapped its jaws together in irritation at the attack. Tiktik's weren't used to being on the defensive, they usually didn't give their prey the chance, that or their prey wasn't dumb enough to anger them.

Whirling the sword above his head, Illia created a firestorm. Samme crouched, one hand protecting his face from the heat of the flames above them as Illia poured his very being into the tornado.

"Now Samme!" Two hands upon his hilt, Illia slashed at the air, throwing the flaming tornado at their foe. Beside him, Samme raised his fists above his head, bringing them down with all the strength he could muster—muscles flexed beneath his leather armour. The tiled floor cracked under the blow, ricocheting up the wall to the ceiling.

Illia and Samme dashed for the stairwell as the upper floors began to tremble, their supportive struts shattered by the strike. Samme took the stairs three at a time ahead of Illia, who stopped briefly to look for the Tiktik as the ceiling came crashing down. Nothing, the only sign the Tiktik had been there was the bloody headless body of Marcus and the claw holes in the crumbling wall.

Illia hurried after his colleague, throwing himself down the last few steps as the ceiling collided with the stairwell. Rolling gracefully out of the way of the debris, he hurried to his feet, joining Samme at the top of the next set of stairs.

"Straight down?" Samme asked.

"Sergeant said we could trap it on floor seven, that's where the others will have gone."

"And what about the other things we were meant to be worrying about?"

"No chance to clear each floor with that above us."

Tiktik, tiktik, tiktik, tiktik.

Samme and Illia looked at one another.

Tiktik, tiktik, tiktik, tiktik.

The pair grinned, visibly relaxing at the sound now filling the stairwell. All at once, they burst into laughter, genuine and clearly relieved, if a little hysterical.

"Well, at least we know we trapped it for a minute," Samme sighed as he composed himself, wiping tears from his eyes.

"I never thought I'd be happy to hear that sound again," Illia exhaled slowly.

"Again? Illia... you've seen one of those things before?" Samme asked.

Illia flinched, cursing himself for his carelessness. "A story for another time maybe, let's catch up with the others."

Samme's eyes narrowed, but he nodded nonetheless, choosing not to press the matter further. Together they made light work of the fourth-floor stairwell, followed by the growing sound of the Tiktik.

Tiktik, tiktik, tiktik, tiktik.

Tiktik, tiktik, tiktik, tiktik.

Samme threw an arm out, catching Illia in the chest as the man stopped the Elf mid-stride as they were about to reach the fifth floor.

"Something's wrong," Samme kept his voice low, lips twitching as he bared his elongated canines, inhaling deeply. "I can smell blood and ash."

"Dragon?"

"Hard to tell, the fire could have been one of us, there are too many scents in this sodding building to be able to tell, it's overwhelming."

"So, either the others have taken something big out."

"Or something big took a load of us out," Samme growled.

"Proceed with caution, let's assess the situation and go from there. When we get out of this, we need to seriously look at getting radios organised that can work in Magic heavy atmospheres."

TIKTIK, TIKTIK, TIKTIK, TIKTIK.

With the Tiktiks' call booming in their ears, the pair proceeded slowly around the corner until they were met with a horrific sight. The walls were scorched black, still smoking where the residual heat remained from the intense blast of fire—Dragon fire, it was unique in its effects and the smell it gave off at closer quarters, no elemental fire could compete with such ferocity.

The tiles beneath their feet were sticky and slippery with blood and gore, mutilated bodies piled high against the wall opposite the next staircase all in a range of states. Some were burnt beyond recognition, their twisted skeletons blackened, skeletal jaws frozen mid-scream. Others were nothing more than a bloodied mess, masses of torn flesh with their insides spread across the floor like a grotesque carpet.

Samme's nose wrinkled and Illia's brow furrowed as their eyes swiftly scanned the onslaught for their companions. "This wasn't us," Samme muttered. "The blood is in varying stages of coagulation," he added, lifting his boot and shuddering at the sickening sound of it peeling from the floor, half glued down by the congealed mess.

"No. This looks like the staff to me."

"They never stood a chance with the power out. You think the creatures will be killing each other?" Samme asked.

"We can hope… would save us some trouble at least. Best keep moving."

"At least our friend is still some distance away," Samme snorted, motioning with his thumb to the steady 'TIKTIK, TIKTIK, TIKTIK, TIKTIK'.

"Probably not for long, let's find the others quickly."

They carefully picked their way through the bloodbath, the Tiktiks' voice following them, echoing through the empty corridors. TIKTIK tik, TIKTIK tik, TIKTIK tik, TIKTIK tik.

The pair followed the bloody footprints of their squad, Samme breathing heavily beside Illia, struggling to distinguish the scents mingled in the air. The copper tinge of blood and the iron scent of magic were heavy in the air, stifling their senses.

Tiktik, tiktik, tiktik, tiktik.

Stepping down onto the sixth floor, Illia strained his ears for a sign of their comrades, or any of the beasts they were meant to be watching out for. Everything was too quiet.

Tiktik, tiktik, tiktik, tiktik.

And now it seemed the Tiktik was creeping closer again…

Illia glanced over his shoulder into the darkness above, half expecting the dead-eyed monster to be looking back at him.

A scream from the floor below pierced the silence, and both men were unable to keep themselves from flinching. They shared a glance before breaking into a run. Illia pushed his fear deep within, swallowing the hard lump forming in his throat as his sword hummed with the magic, he infused into it.

Tik…, tik…, tik…, tik…

Tik…, tik…

Tik…

"Regina! It's behind you!" Baryon's bark echoed through the corridor as Samme and Illia followed the shouts of their comrades.

Skidding around a corner, they came face-to-face with the decapitated head of a Dragon, its limp tongue flopping from its jaws, eyes rolled back in their sockets. It took Illia a moment to recover from his shock at being faced with fangs the size of his body—not to mention the fact that the Dragon's head had been ripped from its lifeless body on the opposite side of the massive, enclosed, arena. That hadn't been done by any of their group, not even Baryon's magical strength could have pulled a Dragon's head straight off its spine.

"Illia! I thought you were slowing this fucking thing down?!" Baryon barked, grabbing Regina by the back of her collar, dragging her out of harm's way seconds before the Tiktik clawed the air where she'd been.

"But we trapped it upstairs. There's only one fucking stairwell!" Samme snarled as he leaped forward to join their team.

Illia could not move, his entire body frozen to the spot, blood running cold as his eyes remained fixed upon the Tiktik. He'd been able to control his fear when he'd had the stairwell at his back and a plan to escape—but faced with the monster, and their team in disrepair... all the Elf's composure was lost.

The barricade failed. The distance they'd 'heard' from it was the damned thing finding a way around and ambushing their team from below. He and Samme left it and walked right back to it.

Illia swallowed hard, dragging his eyes away from the blood-drenched monster to the remainder of their comrades, scattered around the arena amongst the deceased creatures that had been on the list. Something huge had killed the Dragon, the Tiktik was big but not that big, yet nothing on the list could have done it.

"Illia you lanky sack of shit we need you!" Baryon's voice cut through his thoughts, but still, he could not move, his arms like lead, his legs moored in place.

They'd lost at least half of their group, whether to the Tiktik or to some of the other monsters that managed to gather in the arena, Illia did not know. His sharp, shallow breathing roared in his ears, pulse pounding like the beat of a war drum. He watched the Tiktik reach down and grasp Delan in one of its massive, bony hands.

The ice in Illia's veins melted as fire coursed through them. Flames fuelled by anger as he watched Samme leap at the Tiktik. The man's form twisted in the air, skin becoming sleek black fur, face contorting as he spread his jaws wide. He sank his fangs into the creature's arm attempting to free his brother from its grasp, now fully transformed into a colossal wolf.

Closing his eyes, Illia took one long, deep breath... and the world grew still. He'd lost enough to this fiend; he would lose no more. As if a switch had flicked in his body, he was no longer crippled by fear, the terror giving way to rage.

The steel of his sword burned bright as flames flickered from tip to hilt, up Illia's arms, encompassing his body. The inferno reflected in his storm grey eyes as he opened them, setting them alight.

He moved with grace, feet barely touching the floor as he all but flew across the arena, dodging the remnants of friend and foe strewn across the ground. Eyes fixed on the creature crawling along the walls by the ceiling, Illia threw himself forward.

Baryon spotted him and knelt down, turning his back to face the charging Elf. Illia leaped the last few feet, nimbly landing on his Sergeant's shoulder as Baryon used his magic to thrust them upwards. Baryon drove Illia into the air at the exact moment the Elf jumped away—boosting him through the air at their adversary so that Illia could focus on maintaining his flames.

The Tiktik turned its lifeless eyes to the flame-covered Elf and gave a sickening smile, saliva dripping from its needle-like teeth. There was a repulsive crunch as the creature closed its fist around Delan's body, shattering his bones, Samme's mournful howl filled the arena as the Tiktik threw the Werewolf from its arm, casting aside Delan's limp form as well.

Illia roared with rage, the inferno surrounding him matching it. His comrades shielded themselves from its ferocity. Two hands wrapped around the hilt, Illia swung with all his might as the Tiktik launched itself at him.

He winced, feeling the cold sting of its claws as it tore through his warding, and armour, slicing across his stomach. Tucking his shoulder under him, Illia rolled as he fell back to the ground, hurrying to his feet, stumbling slightly as the pain in his belly. There was a dull thud behind him, followed by a collective cheer from the remainder of their squad.

Pressing his hand to his stomach, Illia grimaced at the sting of his wound and the hot, viscous liquid steadily pouring from it. Looking over his shoulder, his eyes met the gaze of the Tiktik's—it's head now severed cleanly from its swollen torso, cauterised by the flames.

Limping toward the dead beast, he stared into its glazed eyes; it always looked like a walking corpse, its eyes never held any life to them, but now that it was dead it seemed somehow unreal.

Illia spat on its corpse, turning his back on it—Samme needed help, they'd lost Delan... they'd lost half of their squad to this insane mission, they had to... to...

Tiktik, tiktik, tiktik, tiktik.

Tiktik, tik...

Tik...

Illia's sword fell to the floor with a clatter, his eyes wide as he stared just above the arena entrance. The auxiliary lighting flashed on and off, illuminating a twelve-foot hulking nightmare in blood-red.

Illia was reminded of a spider covered in her own offspring, tiny, newly hatched arachnids writhing all over her as she protected them from any would-be predators. "There was only meant to be one..." He whispered, stepping backward, his foot slipping on the gore, taking his leg out from under him. Pain coursed through his wounded stomach and his knee from the impact, but his eyes never left the flickering, monstrous image of the Tiktik crawling in her own children. "There was only meant to be one!"

A soft, whispering 'shhhhhh' filled the arena. The baby Tiktiks scattered from their mother's colossal body, scuttling across the walls until the concrete was one huge, squirming mass of bloodthirsty creatures.

Illia came to his senses as Samme let out a howl of pain, the Elf's eyes drawn to his companion as he was overcome by at least five of the offspring, their needle-sharp teeth tearing fur and flesh from bone with ease. Illia didn't hesitate, despite his pain, and the fear gripping his heart he knew he had to get out—three floors below was the emergency access tunnel, he could blow the top two floors and be free.

Illia bolted for the open doorway, he couldn't save the others—they couldn't match his speed or agility. Keeping his eye on the swaying mother, she watched her children, leaving them to their first hunt. The Elf dared to look over his shoulder, catching a glimpse of Baryon punching the rapidly transforming youngsters away from him, but there were too many. The arena was a sea of monsters and blood. These things were designed to be the perfect hunter, and they were proving to be just that.

Whimpering, Illia ducked around the decapitated head of the Dragon, realising that the female Tiktik was more than capable of such a feat. Breathing deeply, he forced himself to ignore the cries for help, the screams of pain, the gurgling gasps of his dying comrades—the

Magus were done for, they were no match for this monster, they never had been… They were all fools.

Glancing up at the Tiktik, Illia took his chance as she shifted away from the door, making a beeline for her fallen mate. He caught a glimpse of her poking the severed head with a claw, as though intrigued at how such a thing came to pass, but she was soon out of sight as he dashed for the stairwell.

Tiktik, tiktik, tiktik, tiktik, tiktik, tiktik, tiktik, tiktik.

The air was filled with the chattering of hundreds of voices as Illia took the stairs five at a time, swinging around the railing with little to no thought for his own safety, adrenaline coursing through his veins numbing the ache in his body.

Tiktik, tiktik, tiktik, tiktik, tiktik, tiktik, tiktik, tiktik.

Tears blurred his vision as Illia made short work of the stairs, reaching the tenth level in no time, his entire body moving out of pure instinct.

He was glad he'd memorised the blueprints to the building, he didn't need to search for the tunnel—it was the last right turn down the corridor. Skidding along the tiled floor, Illia slammed his hand into the glass panel that kept the emergency failsafe lever protected. He wrapped his bloody fingers around the handle and pulled it downward sharply. The building shuddered above, casting dust and bits of plaster onto his head as the top floors exploded, releasing the mechanism that locked the door to the tunnel.

The click of the lock was the most wonderful sound Illia had heard in all his centuries. Grasping the wheel on the door, he spun it quickly, undoing the remaining locks before pulling with what little strength he had left, the thick steel door swinging open.

Illia jogged down the long tunnel, hand pressed against his wound to stem the flow of blood, his breath ragged as he forced his feet to move one in front of the other. The steady, sloping ascent was exhausting but he continued, rewarded with the promise of freedom.

Sunlight shone ahead.

How long had they been down here? All concepts of time became meaningless in the face of his worst nightmare. Sprinting the last few metres, Illia let out a sob of joy as he hit the exit button, pushed open the door, and felt fresh air on his face. He was free…

His jaw trembled, relief washing over him, threatening to steal his remaining strength. Stumbling forward he cried out in surprise and pain as he banged into something solid and unmoving. Collapsing backwards, Illia grasped at his wound as a sharp pain shot through his stomach at the impact.

Blinking rapidly, Illia caught sight of the slight haze in the air, his heart sinking as he realised what he was looking at. "No," he whimpered, struggling to his feet, reaching out to touch the magical Barrier keeping him from being finally free.

"Corporal Illia? You survived."

Illia turned toward the voice, immediately recognising the Medeis Corp. logo on the armoured uniform of the man speaking with him.

"I'm sorry Corporal, when your team didn't contact HQ after twelve hours, we were sent to secure the facility. We have to ensure the Tiktik remains here, she's a valuable asset that the Corporation cannot afford to lose. You understand."

"No, no, you have to kill it, you have to kill it and all her offspring. You have to, you have to!" Illia cried, banging his fists upon the Barrier as the man turned and walked away.

They were expendable, Baryon had said it, their team meant nothing to the Corporation. He had betrayed his friends; abandoned them in the end, their screams echoing in his mind, fuelling his despair.

His back against the Barrier, he stared at the door he had escaped through as it was pushed open by a large, clawed hand. The grotesque face stared at him from the shadows of the tunnel, tongue dangling from its foul maw.

They were expendable…

A DREAM OF DRAGONS

Throughout history, many cultures both embraced and abhorred dragons and the dangers that accompanied them. There are hundreds of stories of heroes who rose up to conquer dragons, as well as tales of dragons that helped humanity in their time of need. These four stories are such tales.

VONNIE WINSLOW CRIST

VEIL

On June twenty-first, a dragon appeared behind Dylan Goodwin's grave marker.

Vision limited by the dark veil she wore, Leanna didn't notice the creature until it tapped the top of Dylan's tombstone with a wickedly-curved claw and said, "It's a shame he was executed. He was, as you know, innocent of murder."

Too shocked to respond, Leanna stood, took several steps away from the dragon, tripped over an urn, and landed with a *whompf* on the soft cemetery grass.

"Sorry to startle you," apologized the beast. "I've witnessed you visiting this spot for a year, and decided to offer you a chance to right this wrong." The dragon tilted his head. "You can stop Dylan

Goodwin's hanging." He scratched an eye ridge, then continued, "but only if you have the courage to cross time and tell the truth."

"If I do so, my husband will likely kill me." She drew the fabric of her veil through her fingers. "Still, I'd give up this last year for a chance to save Dylan," answered Leanna "Though it seems, no one but you knows what I did, or what I failed to do on the day of his hanging."

"What of your husband?" inquired the dragon as he rested a front paw on the next tombstone over.

"What of him?" Leanna stood, brushed the dirt off her skirt, and even though her heart threatened to burst from her chest with its pounding, looked the dragon in the eye. "I thought Dylan and Garret Goodwin to be much the same until I married Garret. Only then, did his true nature became apparent."

"I think Garret wore his nature on his sleeve, but you were blinded by his charm," said the beast as it traced Garret Goodwin's birth and death dates with a claw. "Then, only two days after Dylan's hanging, Garret was knifed. So, when Garret's widow wanders these hills in her black veil and lingers in the graveyard, no one questions why she's here. Or which Goodwin brother she mourns."

"You're right," responded Leanna before putting her palms to her face and moaning softly. Even after removing her hands, her head hung down. "The people of Old Fort think I'm a dutiful widow. In truth, I'm grieving for a man I only held in my arms one evening."

"But a most eventful evening," the dragon reminded Leanna

"It's all my fault, isn't it?" She looked at the reptile, hoping he could somehow offer her absolution.

"Not all of it," replied the dragon, "even though a portion of the blame rests on your shoulders. But that's not the question you need to answer tonight."

She frowned. "What do you mean?"

"I offer you a chance to go back to whatever moment in the past you'd like to change. Perhaps, we can alter the course of this tragedy." Cocking his head at an angle like a curious hound, the beast continued, "Will you cross time to right a wrong?"

"Yes," whispered Leanna as she dropped her veil to the ground. "Yes."

The dragon smiled. "Very well, but there's a price to be paid."

"Name it. I'll pay," answered Leanna

"Don't be too quick to agree to a fee which I've yet to set," warned the dragon as he studied her. The creature narrowed his eyes, licked his lips, then said, "The cost of traveling to the past is the hearing in your right ear."

Leanna remained silent for a few seconds. After pressing her fingertips lightly to her ears, she said, "I agree."

Quick as lightning, the dragon reached forward with his left paw, brushed aside her fingers, cupped her right ear, and with a sharp pain that felt like it pierced her brain, he took her hearing.

For a few moments, Leanna felt off-kilter. She turned her head, and realized she could no longer hear the tree frogs' songs with her right ear. Suppressing her desire to weep, she said, "An instant of discomfort and less noise is a small price to pay for a man's life."

"True. But before I send you off, you'll need to know my name." The reptile touched a paw to his chest then swung it to the side while lowering his head in strange dragonish bow.

"I am Tionil the Ageless. I can travel to Before, Now, Yet-to-be, Never-was, and Never-will-be. Remember my name, repeat my name, and tonight, you'll return to yesteryear."

"Tionil the Ageless," repeated Leanna. At first, she said it quietly to herself to commit the name to memory. Soon, she spoke the dragon's name louder.

"Very good," said Tionil. "Next, you must continue to repeat my name while spinning around and thinking of the exact moment to which you want to return."

Leanna nodded, then resumed chanting, "Tionil the Ageless. Tionil the Ageless." She pictured the hanging platform as Old Fort's executioner, sheriff, judge, and priest escorted Dylan to the noose. Then, she spun around as fast as she could. She'd closed her eyes to avoid becoming dizzy, so the last thing Leanna remembered about the dragon was his warm, smoky breath surrounding her like a cloud and his voice wishing her good luck.

***

"What's wrong with you, Leanna?" asked Garret as he grabbed her shoulder. "You're twisting around like a top."

"Nothing," she answered. "I was just trying to see better."

"Not much to see." Garret yawned. "They don't even have the rope around Dylan's neck yet."

"He's your brother—aren't you upset he's to hang?"

"Better him than me," answered Garret Goodwin.

As her husband spoke these words, even though she only heard them with her left ear, Leanna realized Garret's voice sounded much like Dylan's voice. She glanced at Garret's face, and noticed how similar the brothers looked.

"Then, I'm not too late."

Leanna pushed through the crowd toward the gallows. Even deaf in one ear, her head rang with the cries of people gathered in the square. They smelled death coming and wanted to watch the murderer, Dylan Goodwin, dance on air. Except, she knew he wasn't the man who'd shot Perce Dundee outside the Old Fort Town Hall—because he'd been with Leanna that evening.

Finally, she shoved her way to the edge of the hanging platform. Leanna waved her arms and hollered at the judge, executioner, sheriff, and priest, "He's innocent. He was with me that night. He couldn't have shot Perce. He was with me."

But no one heard her above the screams of the people cheering on the hanging. No one but the man standing beside Leanna—her husband, Garret Goodwin.

Just like the first time, Dylan was hung by the neck until dead. And just like the first time, Garret Goodwin was stabbed to death outside The Dapple Pony two days later—but not before he beat Leanna for admitting she'd been with his brother on the night Perce Dundee was shot.

***

As she'd done on each full moon for the last year since Dylan and

Garret Goodwin's deaths, Leanna stood at the foot of Dylan's grave quietly repeating, "Tionil the Ageless, take pity on me again."

But tonight, like so many before, only the calls of owls and the flickering of lightning bugs answered her. She wiped her tears on her veil, dropped a daisy on Dylan's grave, and turned to leave Old Fort Cemetery.

"If I give you another chance to change the past, what will you do differently?" asked a deep voice.

Leanna whirled around. "Tionil!" She ran towards the towering reptile. Paused, then took the last few steps slowly. Tionil hadn't shown any ill-intent on their first meeting, but that had been a year earlier. Perhaps, the dragon's disposition toward her had changed.

As if he could read her thoughts, Tionil said, "There's nothing to fear, child. I gave up eating women and children eons ago."

"Of that, I'm glad," replied Leanna with a smile. She tucked several wayward strands of her dark hair beneath her veil. She took a deep breath, exhaled slowly, then took a step forward and gazed intently into the dragon's sapphire eyes. "Will you help me?"

"Yes, but again, there's a price to be paid."

"Name it. I'll pay," answered Leanna

"Caution, child. The price is steeper this time," warned Tionil. The dragon reached out a paw, tilted her chin up with one claw and stared into her amber-colored eyes. "The cost of traveling to the past a second time is the sight in your right eye," he said.

Leanna felt tears slide down her cheeks. She looked beyond Tionil at the treetops twinkling with fireflies, the summer moon, and the ocean of stars covering the heavens. Despite the fact the night wind seemed to whisper, "No," Leanna said, "I agree."

Swift as rattlesnake's strike, Tionil reached forward with his left paw, covered her right eye, and with pain like a hundred bee stings, the dragon took her sight.

For several seconds, Leanna shook with fear. She turned her head from side to side trying to see everything that surrounded her. With only one functioning eye, she knew a bear or cougar could easily attack her from the right. Digging her fingernails into the palms of her hands to stop herself from crying, Leanna said, "A moment of discomfort and seeing less ugliness in this world is a tiny price to pay for a man's life."

"True."

The dragon continued to observe her, and had she not been taught otherwise, Leanna would've sworn Tionil cared for her. Lest she let her guard down, she reminded herself that dragons are cold-blooded creatures who only do what pleases them.

If Tionil read her thoughts, the dragon didn't acknowledge them. Instead, the creature warned, "This time, choose more carefully when to arrive in the past. A hanging is a bit late to proclaim someone's innocence."

"Agreed." Leanna took a deep breath and smoothed her skirt before asking, "Is the process the same?"

"It is," replied Tionil. "You may start to chant as soon as you've focused your thoughts on the exact moment to which you'd like to return."

"Dylan's trial," she said. "Surely, my voice will be heard there."

"Perhaps," said Tionil the Ageless before exhaling a cloud of smoke. Leanna coughed, then began to repeat his name and spin.

***

The courtroom was filled to capacity. As the defendant's brother and sister-in-law, Garret and Leanna were given seats near the front. When he was brought in, Leanna saw Dylan brush aside his shaggy hair and scan the room until his eyes found hers. With her one good eye, she spotted no fear on his smooth, clean-shave face—just resignation.

"All rise," proclaimed the clerk as Judge Dittimus entered.

Leanna stood. As she did so, she glanced at her husband. Garret's hair was clipped so short, people might think he was in the military. After she sat down, Leanna continued to think about Garret's appearance. The day after the shooting outside Old Fort Town Hall, Garret had visited the barber for a buzz-cut and he'd stopped shaving his beard. Whereas before the shooting, Dylan and Garret had looked alike, now it was difficult to tell they were brothers.

During the opening statements, Leanna stared at the back of Dylan's head. How had she been so blind? If Dylan hadn't murder Perce Dundee, the person who looked like his doppelganger must have. She turned her head, gazed at her husband, and knew sure as rain that Garret killed Perce and intended to let his brother hang rather than tell the truth.

Farnel Tifton was the first witness. He swore when he exited The Dapple Pony on that fateful night, he saw a man who looked like

Dylan Goodwin shoot Perce Dundee. Dylan's lawyer got Farnel to admit he'd been drinking, the lighting was poor, and he was a fair distance from the site of the murder. Nonetheless, his testimony was compelling.

Farnel's half-brother, Butchie Tifton, testified next. His story seemed to corroborate Farnel's account of the murder. Though the defense attorney did his best to challenge the accuracy of Butchie's version of events, again the testimony was damning.

The final eyewitness was Janie Sue Whitsun. Janie Sue had worked as a waitress at The Dapple Pony since she was eighteen. Most everyone in Old Fort knew who she was, because she also picked up day shift hours at the Battlecry Diner, Mondays through Fridays. One of Leanna's few friends, she knew Janie Sue would tell the truth.

"Miss Whitsun, what did you see and hear the night Perce Dundee was killed," said the prosecutor.

"I come out for a smoke," explained Janie Sue, "saw them Tifton boys staggering down the steps, and just about the time they hollered a goodbye to me, I heard a pop sound."

"Did you see where the sound came from?" asked the prosecutor.

"I did," answered the waitress. "I looked over to the town hall and saw a man standing over Perce Dundee."

"Is that man in the courtroom?" inquired the prosecutor.

"He is," replied Janie Sue as she pointed toward Dylan Goodwin. "The man who shot Perce is sitting right over there."

She's right, thought Leanna. Because sitting directly behind Dylan, right where the waitress's finger pointed, was her husband, Garret

Goodwin.

At the end of the first day of the trial, the sheriff took Dylan back to jail, but not before Leanna caught his eye and smiled at her brother-in-law. He managed to respond with a half-hearted smile before being led away.

Next morning, Leanna got up early and dressed for court. As she watched the minutes tick by, she thought about what she had to do today. First, she needed to tell the defense lawyer she was Dylan's alibi. Second, she had to get on the stand in front of her husband, the minister, and the rest of the town and reveal she'd been with her husband's brother at the time of Perce's murder. She knew they'd all be leaning forward focused on her every word. Next, the prosecuting lawyer would try to punch holes in her story. Lastly, once she was finished testifying, she'd have to face an angry husband and admit she didn't love him.

I married the wrong brother. And after I testify, Garret will kill me, she thought. *But I need to set things right by telling the truth.* Of course, that'd mean the sheriff would be looking for another suspect. Even though he'd done everything possible to change his appearance, it wouldn't be long before someone figured out who looked a lot like Dylan. Someone who was known to always be in a bit of trouble. Someone Leanna couldn't be made to testify against, because he was her spouse.

So deep was she in thought, Leanna didn't notice her husband stroll into the living room.

"What are sitting here for?" asked Garret as he grabbed her upper arm. "I've decided we're not going to the courthouse today."

"We've got to go."

"We don't *have* to do anything," replied her husband, shaking her by her arm. "I didn't like the way people were looking at us like we were guilty, too."

"Are you?" asked Leanna. "Are you guilty?"

If Garret answered her question, she never heard his response. He hit her on the jaw, she saw stars, then she crumpled to the linoleum.

That evening, Janie Sue stopped by on her way home from work, told Leanna that Dylan was convicted of murder and Judge Dittimus sentenced him to hang on Friday. "Shame he's to die," said the waitress. "Dylan seemed to be a nice fellow."

"He didn't do it," whispered Leanna

"That's not what the court says." Janie Sue patted the back of Leanna's hand, then gently touched her bruised upper arm. "Honey, what happened to your arm and face?

"She fell," said Garret from behind Janie Sue. "And she needs her rest, so kindly leave."

"She no more fell than I did," snapped Leanna's friend as she got up, walked to the door, and turned around. "And I better not see evidence of any more falls, or I'm talking to the sheriff."

"Leave," growled Garret before switching on the charm and adding in a pleasant tone, "Please."

"Later," said Janie Sue as she waved to Leanna then slammed out the screen door.

Garret wouldn't let Leanna out of the house until Friday. Then, just like the first and second times, Dylan was hung by the neck until dead. And just like the times before, her husband was stabbed to death outside The Dapple Pony a couple days later for his womanizing ways.

She'd given up half of her hearing and sight and failed to change a thing.

***

On the twelfth full moon since Dylan and Garret Goodwin's deaths, Leanna knelt at the foot of Dylan's grave repeating, "Tionil the Ageless, take pity on me once more."

The whirl of cicadas was the only response.

"I now know the moment to which I need to return," said Leanna as pulled back her long, black veil. "Isn't three the magic number? The third time *will* be the charm, if only you'll give me that chance."

"Three *is* a magic number," agreed the dragon as he stepped from the shadows of the white pines which edged Old Fort Cemetery.

"Tionil!" She ran to the dragon, spread her arms wide, and did her best to hug the beast. "It's so good to see you—to know you still watch over me."

"Child," said the dragon, "I'm no guardian angel. We've bartered for time. Nothing more."

Leanna stared up at the huge, scaly muzzle above her. Maybe her dealings with Tionil *were* nothing but business. Still, she was certain the creature felt more toward her than he let on.

"Then, let us make one more deal," she said. "I want to return to the moment when I walked into the Old Fort Mercantile and saw two brothers stacking sacks of feed."

The dragon nodded. "So, you want to return to the beginning?"

"Yes."

"Do you think you'll be able to resist Garret's teasing, grins, and devil-may-care charm? Instead, choose the quiet, shy brother this time?" asked Tionil the Ageless.

"Yes. Please, let me go back in time once more and change the past."

"The price this time is higher," warned Tionil.

"Name it."

"I claim bone," replied the dragon.

"Bone!" Leanna bit her lip. Maybe the price *was* too high this time.

"I claim half an inch of your leg bone," said Tionil. "You will still be able to walk, but you'll have a limp."

"The partial loss of hearing and sight were explained by a serious fall I suffered as a child. Will the limp be the result of that same fall which I cannot remember?"

"It will," answered the dragon, "and though you can't recollect the fall from your neighbor's tree fort, others will remember it."

"How are you able to accomplish this?" asked Leanna as she crushed her veil between her hands.

"Did you forget I'm able to travel to Before, Now, Yet-to-be, Never-was, and Never-will-be? I went back to Never-was and changed it to Before," explained Tionil the Ageless. "I'll do it again to explain your limp, if you agree to pay me in bone for your third attempt at changing the past."

Leanna relished her long walks beneath the towering trees, along stream banks, across wildflower-filled meadows, and through snowy drifts—but a man's life was worth more than a few hikes.

"I agree," she said, then steeled herself for the expected pain.

This time, her leg felt as if it was being torn asunder. With a sob, Leanna fell to the ground.

"You must stand, repeat my name, and spin around whilst thinking of the moment in the past where you want to arrive," said the dragon in a solemn voice. "And this, child, is the last chance I will give you."

Unable to stand on her own, Leanna reached for the dragon. Tionil allowed her to grasp his black-scaled leg and pull herself upright. "I'm not sure I can spin," she gasped.

"Focus," urged the beast. "Once you begin, I will exhale and surround you with dragon's breath. It will help ease the pain as it floats you back through time."

Leanna nodded and began to chant, "Tionil the Ageless," as she thought about her first encounter with the Goodwin brothers. Lastly, pushing through the pain, she began to spin.

***

Old Fort Mercantile looked exactly as Leanna remembered it on the crisp October Tuesday, she'd arrived in town the first time. With her father away at sea most of the year, when Momma passed away, Leanna had been sent to live with Beatrix, her mother's first cousin. An unclaimed blessing, Momma's term for a spinster, Beatrix was a seamstress who lived alone in a stone house just off Main Street.

"Leanna!" exclaimed a short, gray-haired woman with wire-rimmed spectacles perched on her nose as she hurried toward Leanna.

Resisting the urge to say, "Nice to see you again," Leanna reminded herself that in the past reality, she'd never met Beatrix prior to today. She'd relied on a photo Momma had kept on her bureau to identify her mother's cousin.

"Cousin Beatrix?" Leanna raised her eyebrows in a quizzical expression.

"You look like your mother," said Cousin Beatrix as she swooped in and gave Leanna a hug. "Let's head home and get you settled in."

"That sounds wonderful." Leanna enjoyed seeing Beatrix once more. With information from the future, she knew Beatrix would have a heart attack in three months' time. She'd linger for a day, then die holding Leanna's hand. Leanna would inherit her stone cottage, its contents, and a tidy sum in her bank account. Thus, making her a *catch* for whichever local man she married.

"Dylan. Garret. Would you boys please carry Leanna's suitcases and other belongings to my house?" said Beatrix as she held Leanna's hand and headed toward the Mercantile's front door.

That's when Leanna spotted the Goodwin brothers stacking bags of feed. Just like the first time she'd met them, Dylan smiled, gazed at her briefly, nodded, and said, "Yes, Miss Beatrix. I'd be happy to carry Leanna's things."

Whereas Garret stepped forward, bowed grandly, grinned, winked at Leanna, then announced, "I'm Garret Goodwin. Welcome to Old Fort, pretty lady."

This time, Leanna didn't blush and lower her eyelashes. Instead, she looked directly into Garret's eyes and replied, "Thank you for the welcome. I'm glad to be here."

While leaving the Mercantile and on the short stroll to Beatrix's home, her cousin chatted about the town of Old Fort and its history. Pretending to listen to information she was already familiar with, Leanne instead studied the Goodwin brothers.

As they exited the store, Garret pocketed some penny candy and winked at a young woman standing near the cash register. She knew he'd never drop a few cents into the register to cover the candy he'd stolen, and single or married, he'd probably try to court the woman.

Meanwhile, Dylan set down the suitcases he was carrying, opened the door for Beatrix and her, then called over his shoulder to the store owner, "I'll be back shortly, sir."

They'd only gone a short distance when Dylan said, "I noticed you're limping. Are you okay or do you need a doctor?"

"I'm fine. It's an injury from childhood," she replied, suddenly aware of his honest concern.

"Why don't you let me carry that, too," offered Dylan as he reached for a small parcel she held.

As Leanna started to hand it to him, Garret grabbed the package from her.

"Let me carry that for you, little lady," said Garret as he leaned close to her. "And is that enticing scent filling the air rosewater or lavender?"

Not a wide-eyed innocent this time, Leanna caught the practiced nature of his flirting. As she relinquished the parcel to Garret, she answered, "Neither. It's Lily-of-the-Valley."

"Makes sense," he replied. "A beautiful flower for a beautiful woman." Then, Garret smiled in his most charming manner and brushed his long hair out of his eyes.

"Is May your birth month?" asked Dylan as they reached Beatrix's house.

"Actually, it is." Leanna tried to remember if he'd asked her this question the first time she arrived at Beatrix's home. *He did ask me,* she recalled, *but I was so busy flirting with Garret I don't believe I even answered Dylan.*

"There's a dance tonight in the Mercantile's warehouse if you're interested," said Dylan. "Unless you're too tired from traveling."

"Are you asking me to go *with* you?"

"Why should she go with you when she can go on the arm of the most eligible bachelor in Old Fort?" Garret stepped in front of his brother, took Leanna's right hand and kissed the back of it.

"I'd like to go with you, Dylan," said Leanna as she firmly removed her hand from Garret's grasp. "I'd like to go with you very much."

***

The first full moon after Garret Goodwin's hanging for the murder of Perce Dundee, Dylan and Leanna stood at the foot of his grave.

"I wish there was something I could've done to save him," said Dylan as he wiped his eyes with the back of his hand.

"He was fun loving, but flawed," Leanna reminded her husband. "There wasn't anything anyone could have done."

"I know he wasn't perfect, but I loved him." Dylan reached for her hand, squeezed it.

"We'll get through this," replied Leanna. "Now, you go on back to the house. I want to visit Beatrix's grave for a few minutes."

"I can come with you."

"No. I'm fine," she assured her husband. "But a hot cup of tea when I get home would be nice."

"Done," he replied before kissing her forehead and striding toward the cemetery's gate.

"Tionil the Ageless," called Leanna as she pulled her black veil away from her face. "Are you here? Tionil?"

"I am here, child." The dragon rose up from the shadows until he loomed above her.

"Thank you for letting me save a decent man—the man I love—from a wrongful hanging." Voice quavering, she continued, "What I couldn't have guessed, is that in saving him, I saved myself."

Tionil was silent. His stare seemed to penetrate flesh and bone and see directly into Leanna's heart. "You don't regret the loss of hearing, sight, and mobility?"

"No," Leanna assured him. "They're nothing compared to what I've gained. And though you claim our relationship is nothing but bartering, I'll always be grateful to you."

"In that case, I will tell you a secret," said the dragon. "I've offered countless people the chance to go back to the past to right a wrong. Most decline when they hear the price. A few have crossed time once to attempt to change things. Several have crossed time twice. But you, Leanna, are the only one who's been willing to endure the pain and pay the price three times."

"I didn't know that."

"How could you know?" Tionil the Ageless's sapphire eyes glinted as moonlight struck them. "But I never said price was non refundable."

Leanna frowned. "I don't understand."

The dragon exhaled. As the cloud of dragon breath surrounded her, she felt her right eye burning, heard a ringing in her right ear, and felt a pinch in her right leg.

When the mist cleared, Leanna gasped. "I'm healed. How is this possible?"

"I am Tionil the Ageless. I can travel to Before, Now, Yet-to-be, Never-was, and Never-will-be. I've been to Before, changed a thing or two, and returned to Now before you knew I was gone."

"The fall..."

"Never happened," finished the dragon. "As to this veil," Tionil snagged the length of lace with a dangerously-curved claw, "it should be white." He closed his eyes and drew the veil though his paw. "Then, it can serve as a christening wrap for your children." He handed the now white-as-bone veil back to Leanna.

Before she could ask, "What children?" Tionil the Ageless melted into the shadows.

***

The snowdrops had just begun to bloom when Dylan and Leanna Goodwin welcomed their first born and named her Beatrix. When Dylan and the doctor left the room for a few minutes, Leanna held her daughter close and breathed in her sweet scent. Happier than she'd ever been, she adjusted little Bea's receiving blanket and noticed a small birthmark on her daughter's right arm.

"Tionil," whispered Leanna, "Thank you."

For the birthmark was shaped like a dragon.

BAYOU

There are things living in the bayou which nobody wants to know about. At least that's what Latrell's grandfather said.

Pappy had told him stories about were-gators who walked like men, snapping turtles big as tables who'd bite your leg off, and bobcats roaming the marshlands searching for a person walking alone. But Pappy's tales weren't needed to make a boy mindful when he lived beside the bayou—Mother Nature did that.

Just this afternoon, Latrell had found a copperhead curled among the sweet potato vines. Using a shovel, stick, and a great deal of care, he'd scooped up the serpent, carried it to the bayou, and tossed it into the water. It wasn't the first poisonous snake he'd discovered on the grounds of Swamp Oak Manor this summer—and it wasn't the first time he'd felt someone watching.

"Shake it off," Latrell told himself. He was allowing the superstitions of the heavily vegetated swamp lands to spook him. Nobody spied on him this afternoon or tonight, but bayou critters.

"I wish you were still alive," said Latrell as he studied the moonlight reflected by the eyes of dozens of alligators floating in the brackish water on either side of Swamp Oak Manor's wooden wharf. The reptiles poked their snouts just far enough above the surface of the murky bayou to spot a careless muskrat or marsh rabbit. "The buildings are falling into worse disrepair without your know-how," he added. The gators continued studying him with hungry intent.

Pappy had died of a heart attack on June sixth. Seven days later, when school closed for summer vacation, Latrell had moved in with Nana. With Pappy gone, Nana and Latrell did what work they could around the manor, but they didn't have the time or skills to do most of the much-needed maintenance.

Laden with the odor of decomposing plants, a slight breeze from the bayou caused Latrell's shirt to press against his chest. "Swamp Oak Manor gives me the creeps," he told his grandfather's spirit—wherever it floated. "But Nana won't leave Miss Coralee. She says she can't abandon her to Mr. Judson's cruel ways." Latrell tossed a pebble into the center of the moon's reflection. "And I won't leave Nana to do all the cooking, cleaning, and waiting on the Beauregards by herself."

A part of him hoped Pappy would appear as a misty figure drifting above the duckweed and cypress knees to offer Latrell some sage advice. No such luck. An increase in the intensity of the bullfrogs' croaking and the cicadas' song was the only response.

Latrell sighed, turned around, and strode back to the decaying manor house. He glanced up at the once opulent three-story structure. More than a hundred-years-old, the main house and both wings were slowly crumbling away. The covered veranda where, according to Nana, dozens of guests would in the past sit, sip lemonade, and discuss the news of the day was moss-covered and in disrepair. The latticework below the veranda was broken, entwined with kudzu, and infested with vermin of all sorts. The window shutters, needed when a bad storm blew in from the swamp, were missing some slats and shutter-dogs. No longer secure, they'd be of little help if a hurricane arrived.

His musings on the shabby condition of the once grand estate were cut short by a hair-raising wail.

Latrell's eyes searched the back of Swamp Oak Manor for the source. Gaze finally stopping on a slender figure dressed in a long gown of pale fabric staring into the bayou with arms outstretched, he whispered, "Miss Coralee, don't you go jumping."

As if she'd heard him, though he spoke no louder than a cottonmouth's hiss, Coralee Beauregard grasped the third-floor balcony's railing and looked down at Latrell.

He froze. The strangeness of the Lady of Swamp Oak Manor was not lost on him. Since moving in with Nana three weeks ago, Latrell had only seen Miss Coralee at meal times and tonight on her balcony calling to the swamp. And there was no doubt in his mind that's exactly what she was doing—calling to the bayou.

Miss Coralee didn't smile or wave, instead she straightened her back, spread her arms, and for a second time, wailed an inscrutable message that sounded more like a wounded animal's cry than something uttered by a human. The pain in her cry rang in his ears as Latrell hurried to the door to the east wing where he and Nana had their rooms. A split second before entering the structure, the Lady of Swamp Oak Manor wailed a third time.

Before he could say anything to Nana, she looked up from her mending and noted, "It's almost a full moon. Miss Coralee calls to the swamp sometimes on waxing moons."

"The sound makes my skin crawl."

His grandmother nodded. "Mr. Judson will make her stop. He doesn't tolerate her keening."

"Keening?" There was a familiar sound to the word, but Latrell didn't remember hearing it in conversation before.

"It's a pitiful lament," explained Nana, "for things lost or taken away. Though I don't know what Miss Coralee is mourning after."

"Probably her freedom," said Latrell as he grabbed a handful of molasses cookies from a large, covered, glass jar on the sideboard.

"Could be true," agreed his grandmother as she set down her darning egg and several newly-mended socks. "Mr. Judson keeps her hidden away, even from you and me. Sad life for a woman to be caged."

"You don't really mean *caged*?"

Nana smiled, though her eyes weren't happy. "I clean the private rooms. There are no iron bars or padlocks, but something keeps that woman chained to this place and Mr. Judson."

"I'd free her if I knew how," replied Latrell. "The noise she made tonight was filled with more suffering than I've ever heard in another person's voice."

"As would I," said Nana. She pushed up from her rocking chair. "I don't understand their relationship—despite Mr. Judson's meanness, she stays. I swear, I never saw love between the two of them. Ever."

"She's so much younger than him, too," said Latrell, thinking of the pale-as-starlight woman whose footfalls barely made a sound when she came to the dining room for some of her meals.

"It's not our problem," Nana reminded him. "Lights out," she added as she turned their living room lights off. "Tomorrow will arrive before we know it."

"Yes, ma'am." Latrell headed to his bedroom on the left side of the wide hall which led to the kitchen, laundry room, and eventually, the rest of the east wing of Swamp Oak Manor as Nana closed her bedroom's door on the right side.

Sleep didn't come for Latrell for what seemed like hours. As the night sounds of the bayou poured through his bedroom window's screen, his mind churned with thoughts of Miss Coralee and what hold her husband had over the woman to keep her in this rotting mansion. If it wasn't love, what could it be? Threats of violence? A family money debt? A promise made by their parents? The possibilities seemed endless. The last thought Latrell had before finally falling asleep was of a terrible secret that Mr. Judson knew and threatened to reveal.

When he woke in the morning to the sounds of Nana getting pans out to cook breakfast, Latrell was soaked with sweat. The night had been balmy, so though he couldn't remember dreaming—his sleep must have been filled with nightmares. He dressed quickly, then hurried to the kitchen where Nana was almost finished plating scrambled eggs, fried ham, and grits for Mr. Judson and Miss Coralee.

"Please take these plates into the dining room. I'll carry in the coffee, tea, sugar, and creamer," said his grandmother as she handed the plates heaped with a steaming hot breakfast to him.

He could hear the concern in Nana's voice. Mr. Judson demanded mealtime punctuality. If they served any meal a minute late, he'd be sitting at the table looking at his watch with a scowl on his face. Though a scowl was Mr. Judson's most common expression.

In the nick of time, Nana and he carried breakfast into the dining room. Mr. Judson sat straight-backed at one end of the long, mahogany table, while Miss Coralee sat at the other end. Though it was summer, the dining room was dim. The huge windows on one end of the room, like all the windows in the manor house, were covered with drapes to keep the sun from fading the upholstery fabric. Upholstery fabric which, according to his grandmother, hadn't been replaced in all the years Pappy and Nana worked for the Beauregards.

Two silver candelabras on the table, plus four wall-mounted candle holders provided limited lighting. Enough, supposed Latrell that the silent couple could see what was on the plates he was placing before them, but unlikely enough for them to clearly discern each other's facial expressions.

"Ma'am," he said as he put Miss Coralee's plate before her.

"Thank you, Latrell," she said, then fell quiet as the statues on either side of the brick walk leading to the mansion's front door.

He walked to the other end of the table, set Mr. Judson's plate before him, and said, "Sir," before taking two steps back, then turning and exiting the dining room.

Nana did the same with the bone china tea and coffee pots, sugar bowl, and cream pitcher. Then, they ate their breakfast in the kitchen and waited for the owner of Swamp Oak Manor to ring a bell for them to clear the table.

"That poor woman," said Nana as she cut two slices of pecan pie, then placed them onto dessert plates. "Pale as mashed potatoes."

Latrell smiled. Nana always thought of everything through the lens of a cook.

"Well, she never goes outside in the sunlight." At least she hadn't since he'd moved in three weeks ago.

"That's because *he* won't let her." There was an edge to his grandmother's voice. "He brought her here before you were born. Back then, she had hope and a sparkle in her eye. She'd jabber with Pappy, me, and your mom."

"Where'd she come from?" Latrell tried to picture the sad woman garbed in filmy dresses who spent most of her day in her room on the swamp side corner of the house laughing. He couldn't.

"Don't know," replied Nana. "I suppose it's far away, because none of her kin has ever come to visit."

"Does she get letters from anyone? Or a phone call?"

"No." There was a finality to the tone of his grandmother's response,

330

which squelched any further questions. "You take these pieces of pie out to the Beauregards," she ordered. "See if they need anything else, while I start to do the dishes."

Latrell did as he was told. Miss Coralee declined the pie. Mr. Judson took both pieces.

Before he could leave the dining room, Mr. Judson said, "You tell your grandmother I've got business in town today. I won't be back for lunch or dinner—so my wife will be eating those meals in her room."

"Yes, sir." Latrell glanced at Miss Coralee to see if she was happy about sitting in her room for the rest of the day, but her expression was hidden by the dimness of the dining room.

***

Focused on vacuuming the first two floors of the main section of Swamp Oak Manor—including the drapes—Latrell was surprised at the time when Nana called him to the kitchen for lunch.

"There must be rain coming, because my knees are aching bad," said his grandmother as she handed him a tray. "So, I need you to carry Miss Coralee's lunch up to her rooms." Before he exited the kitchen, Nana touched his upper arm, and said, "And be careful when you're climbing the stairs not to spill the iced tea."

"No worries," he answered.

This was the first time Latrell had gotten to take Miss Coralee a meal or view her rooms on the third floor. Now, he could see for himself if she was chained. As he climbed the stairs to her rooms, he sensed a change in the air. Instead of the expected dryness, the third-floor air felt moister and had a slight swamp vegetation smell. He breathed deeply. The word, *bayou,* popped into his mind.

"Miss Coralee," called Latrell as he walked past a living room furnished with heavy wooden furniture. Upon the walls, he noticed tapestries featuring forests, streams, fair maidens, and mythical creatures.

The Lady of Swamp Oak Manor didn't answer him, so he went down the hall to the first door on the right. He stuck his head in, saw the walls of the room were lined with bookshelves filled with old, leather bound books. "Miss Coralee?" he said.

No response.

Mindful of the tall glass filled with iced tea balanced on the lunch tray, Latrell proceeded to the next doorway. "Ma'am?" he said before taking one step into the room.

"In here, Latrell," called a woman's voice.

He took a couple more steps into what appeared to be a sitting room with a small dining table. He saw Miss Coralee seated by a pair of open French doors. She was painting.

Those must lead to the balcony I saw her on last night, he mused.

"Come, have a look," said Coralee Beauregard. She stood, gestured toward the canvas she was working on.

Hesitating for a moment, Latrell thought, *What's the harm?* before moving closer to the easel and studying Miss Coralee's painting: The image was so realistic, it appeared to be a photo of the bayou. A full moon hung like ball lightning from the clouds and willow-the-wisps flickered from between loblolly pines, black willows, and river birches. Wads of Spanish moss draped over some of the tree branches, and hidden among the undergrowth were snakes, lizards, and alligators. The most curious part of the image was a pair of golden eyes peering from the depths of the bayou.

"Wow," gasped Latrell as he placed the lunch tray on the eating table. "That's amazing."

"Thank you." The corners of Miss Coralee's mouth curled up. "I love painting my home."

"Maybe you should paint Swamp Oak Manor?" suggested Latrell as he waited for her to dismiss him or tell him to fetch something else for lunch.

She laughed—not a fun laugh, but a bitter one. "The manor house isn't my home." The woman pointed at the canvas. "*That* is my home."

"You mean the bayou?" Latrell frowned. Maybe that's why no family visited Miss Coralee. If her people were poor folk who lived deep in the bayou, they might be uncomfortable visiting a mansion— even if it was a dilapidated one.

She nodded. "The bayou is where I was born and raised. Where I lived happily with my sisters until Judson Beauregard decided to wreak his revenge on me."

"Revenge? For what?"

Miss Coralee tilted her head and looked at him from beneath her partially lowered eyelids, "I felt your compassion yesterday with the copperhead, then again last night. Therefore, I'll share with you what binds me to Swamp Oak Manor and its owner. But if I tell you, you cannot speak about it to my husband. To do so would mean punishment for me, and dismissal for you and your grandmother."

"I won't say anything," whispered Latrell. He knew there was a secret about to be shared. One which might answer the questions in his mind concerning the Beauregards and their relationship.

"Judson's grandfather, Homer Beauregard, bought this ground and brought his new wife, Sarah Ann, here. They welcomed a son, Willis, shortly thereafter. Homer had barely finished the main house when the first Lady of Swamp Oak Manor was snatched by an alligator, because she wandered too close to the swamp. So, Willis was raised by a bitter father angry at the bayou and its inhabitants."

"Did they ever get her body back?" asked Latrell. He didn't want to think about how the gator probably drowned Sarah Ann, then stashed her under the roots of a cypress to ripen before eating her flesh.

"No," answered Miss Coralee. She sighed, then continued, "Willis married late. Then, he and his wife, Nettie Mae, moved into Swamp Oak Manor with Homer. It looked like good times had returned to the mansion after they had a little boy whom they named, Judson. Even though both Homer and Willis loved little Judson, they weren't affectionate men, so Nettie Mae gave the child most of the hugs, kisses, and kindness he received. It would've been enough; had she not been bitten by a coral snake when Judson was five. Nettie Mae died a few hours later. Which meant Judson was raised by a strict, unfeeling father and bitter grandfather. Both of whom were angry at the bayou and her reptiles."

"I can't blame them," said Latrell. He thought how he'd feel if a gator killed Nana. "I'd be mad, too, if the bayou took someone I loved."

"But I don't think you'd be cruel," observed Miss Coralee.

"No," he agreed.

"Sadly, Homer Beauregard died a year later of swamp fever. Which left Judson working and living with Willis until eighteen years ago when his father died and he married me." She patted down a few of her hairs, which were frizzing due to high humidity. "But it could never have been a normal marriage. You see, Judson blames his unhappy childhood, the decline of this manor house, even his nasty temperament on reptiles. To satisfy his need for vengeance, he kills snakes, alligators, even turtles whenever he gets a chance to do so."

Confused, Latrell continued to stare at the Lady of Swamp Oak Manor. There had to be more to the story. She was leaving something out.

Miss Coralee remained silent. She stared at the open space between the French doors and out at the bayou, then turned her golden-brown eyes on Latrell. "Eighteen years ago, Judson spotted me sitting on a log by the edge of the swamp. He saw me remove my scaly skin and assume womanly form. But rather than be enamored with a shape-changer, he was filled with hate and stole my skin. Thereafter, I was under his control, and will remain that way until I can regain my skin."

If she wasn't so serious, Latrell would've laughed. "So, you're a..." He searched for the correct word. *Mermaid* was a half-fish woman who could take human form. *Werewolves* were humans who could take wolf-shape. "...a were-snake?"

She shook her head. "No, Latrell. Though that's a good guess." Miss Coralee smoothed the front of her dress with her palms, then studied him with golden eyes. "I'm a very rare bayou creature—a swamp dragon."

"Seriously?" The question slipped out before Latrell could stop it. He knew he'd said it in a mocking tone. *Way to lose both Nana's job and yours,* he thought.

"Deadly serious," responded Miss Coralee. "The only way I can leave Judson Beauregard is to find my skin, put it on, and return to dragon shape."

"Find your skin?"

"Yes," said the Lady of Swamp Oak Manor. "Judson took my skin and hid it. I fear time is running out. For years, my sisters returned every full moon to this part of the bayou in the hope I could join them. They'd call from the bayou, and I'd answer. Now, only one sister comes looking for me. You heard me calling to her last night."

"She didn't answer?"

"No. But I have hope she might answer tonight." Miss Coralee lifted her chin, glanced once more at the bayou before continuing. "Unfortunately, if I don't return to the swamp soon, I'll never see my family again. Or worse, Judson will burn my skin, and I'll die screaming in agony in this woman-shape. Which is why I need your help."

"My help!" He should walk—no *run* away from the woman. But the image of her screeching with pain and crumbling to the floor in agony was more powerful than his fear of Mr. Judson.

"I beg you, please find my skin and return it to me before tonight's full moon." Coralee fell to her knees and clasped her hands in front of her.

"Get up Miss Coralee," urged Latrell as he helped the woman to her feet. "I'll help you, just eat your lunch before Nana has *my* hide."

The reed-thin woman smiled, sat on ladder-backed chair pulled up to the table, and picked up the chicken salad sandwich Nana had prepared. "I knew you were the one to save me when I observed that you've spared three poisonous snakes since you arrived. Then, last night I felt your compassion for me. Which was why I spoke to you..."

"in my dreams," finished Latrell. Suddenly, he could remember bits and pieces of his dreams. Dreams of sliding through the bayou, smelling waterlilies floating on the swamp's surface, feeling tiny fishes swim by, seeing egrets standing on stilt legs, and watching alligators bow their wide heads in reverence.

"What does this skin look like?" he asked.

"Much like a very large snakeskin," replied Miss Coralee. "Not the thin, colorless skin shed by snakes, but the thicker, patterned skin removed from a living snake after it's killed. Mine will be mottled green with flecks of gold, yellow, and turquoise."

"I suppose you've hunted for it before?" Latrell wanted to eliminate the places which had already been scoured.

"Many times," said the Lady of Swamp Oaks Manor. "The third floor has been thoroughly checked from floor to ceiling. As to the second floor, Judson's bedroom, office, and bathroom have been meticulously scrutinized. The other second floor rooms have also been examined—though with less intensity. The wing to the west of the main house was used for parties and balls. I've gone over that area with a fine-toothed comb as well as the second-floor storage area in the east wing."

"So, parts of the second floor, the manor house's first floor, and the first floor of the east wing needed to be searched?"

"Yes," said Miss Coralee, "and today."

Latrell scratched his head. This was going to be tricky. If he told Nana what he was doing, she'd likely put a stop to his quest to free Miss Coralee. If he didn't tell Nana, she'd wonder what on earth had gotten into him.

"Cleaning!" he exclaimed. "I'll tell Nana since we don't have to serve dinner in the dining room tonight, I'll do some extra cleaning for her."

"Thank you for lunch," said Miss Coralee as she pushed the tray towards him. "Tell your grandmother it was delicious." She reached out, placed her hand on top of his, "And thank you, Latrell, for trying to rescue a trapped swamp dragon."

He nodded, picked up the tray, clamored down two flights of stairs, and took the dirty dishes to the kitchen.

***

After drinking a glass of sweet tea and eating two chicken sandwiches, Latrell began his quest for a large snakeskin secreted somewhere on the first floor of the main house. Disguised as additional cleaning, dust cloth and furniture polish in hand, he went from room to room feeling under love seats, sofas, and chairs. With a keen eye he scanned drapes and sheers and looked in drawers and cupboards. Not deterred by the enormity of his task, Latrell reached behind highboys, book shelves, and china cabinets. Dust was his only reward.

It was late afternoon when he began his search of the lower level of the east wing where Nana and he lived. First, he checked the laundry room, then the kitchen. Both rooms were his grandmother's domain, and had been so since she began working for the Beauregard family. So, as he'd expected, he found no snakeskin. Before he rummaged through his bedroom then Nana's, Latrell went into the spare bedroom which had belonged to his mother when she was younger.

The room still smelled like his mom. The closet had some of her old clothes hanging from pegs. A pair of her shoes rested beneath the bed as if she were going to climb out from under its quilt and slip them on in the morning. Her books lined the bookshelf. Her brush and comb lay before the dresser mirror. Of course, the curtains in the window weren't the cheerful gingham the rest of the room seemed to demand. They were the same heavy drapes which hung below painted wooden cornices that served as fancy, yet practical window dressings throughout the mansion.

As he had done with every window checked this afternoon, Latrell climbed up on a small ladder he'd lugged from room to room, and ran his hand across the top of the cornice. But this time, instead of dust, he touched something leathery.

"Snakeskin!" he exclaimed as he pulled a carefully folded bundled of shimmering emerald skin down from its hiding place. "Or more correctly, dragon skin."

"Latrell."

He climbed down the ladder nearly dropping the precious skin.

"Latrell, where are you?" hollered Nana. "I need you to carry Miss Coralee's supper up to her."

"Coming," he shouted. He slipped the folded reptile skin inside his shirt. It felt like chilly, textured silk. Where it touched him, his flesh tingled.

When he hurried into the kitchen, Nana pursed her lips, put her hands on her hips, and asked. "What's gotten into you, Latrell? You've been cleaning like a crazy man."

"I wanted to get ahead of things, so maybe we can take a break this weekend." He smiled at Nana.

"You don't fool me," said his grandmother as she handed Latrell Miss Coralee's supper tray. "You're up to no good. I just haven't figured out what it has to do with yet."

"Relax, I haven't done anything you wouldn't do."

Nana replied with a shake of her head and a loud, "Harrumph!"

***

When Latrell entered Miss Coralee's sitting room where she'd been painting earlier, she looked at him with lips parted, ready to ask about the skin Mr. Judson stole from her eighteen years earlier.

"I've got it," said Latrell as he pulled the reptile skin from beneath his shirt.

Fingers trembling, the Lady of Swamp Oak Manor reached for her skin. Once she clutched the bundle to her chest, a tear trickled down her bone-white cheek. "Thank you, Latrell. Now, you must go. And tonight, no matter what you hear, you and your grandmother must stay in your rooms."

He nodded, then said, "After Nana takes out her hearing aide, she doesn't hear anything. As for me, I'll stay in my room, though I might take a peek out the window."

"Look if you must, but don't come near," warned Miss Coralee. "I hope to retain all my human memories when I return to dragon shape, but I can't be certain I won't harm you. Because I assure you, I *will* repay Judson Beauregard for eighteen years of imprisonment. Eighteen years of proudly showing me every reptile he killed. Eighteen years of snarling nasty words at me. Eighteen years of slaps and shoves."

She gently rubbed the dragon skin given to her by Latrell, then regarded him with a gaze more piercing than a water moccasin's fang. "Dragons *always* settle their debts. Tonight, I plan to settle mine."

Heart beating like a woodpecker hammering an insect infested hickory, Latrell backed out of the room, fled downstairs, and hurried into the east wing of the mansion.

***

A full moon had risen and flooded the bayou with silver light by the time Mr. Judson returned from town. When they saw his car's headlights swing into the driveway, Nana suggested it was time for bed as tomorrow would be a long day. Eager to be safely in his room, Latrell offered no argument.

Rather than go to bed, Latrell sat in a chair by his window and listened to the rhythm of the bayou. The swamp's peacefulness was disrupted as through the open third floor French doors, he heard shouts and curses from Mr. Judson directed at Miss Coralee.

"Look what I killed on the front walkway," bragged Mr. Judson in a harsh voice. "One of your belly-crawling relatives."

"Judson, don't." He heard Miss Coralee say.

Then, the sound of a loud slap.

"I'm warning you, Judson," said Miss Coralee in a tone darker than the muddy waters of the swamp.

"Warning me of what?" snarled Mr. Judson. "You're mine to do with as I will. And one of these nights, I *will* toss your skin into a lit fireplace. Then, as you shriek in agony, I'll feel in some small degree the bayou and I are even."

What Latrell heard and saw next was bound to haunt his dreams for the rest of his life:

First, the sound of furniture being knocked over. *She must be transforming into a dragon,* thought Latrell.

Second, a terrible scream from Mr. Judson, then the word *no* shouted again and again. Latrell's imagination conjured images of the owner of Swamp Oak Manor being torn to shreds and eaten.

Finally, the sound of Miss Coralee keening from her balcony—but tonight, the timbre of her voice was different. He ventured a peek out his window. He couldn't see what was going on, so he removed the screen, then leaned as far out of the window as possible.

Scene illumined by the moon, he witnessed a beautiful serpentine dragon crawl from Coralee's balcony, down the side of the crumbling mansion to the veranda's roof, and onto the grassy lawn. The beast which was the former Lady of Swamp Oak Manor swiveled its fierce head and gaped at Latrell with gleaming gold eyes.

"Latrell," he heard whispered on the wind. "Fear not, I remember you."

Truth be told, if the lady dragon had *not* assured him of his safety, Latrell wasn't certain he'd have had the wherewithal to get back inside and close the window. He was dumbstruck by the creature's size, power, and terrifying face. He'd thought Miss Coralee's reptile head would be more serpent-like—but with a lizard's snout, frilled crest, and wide mouth brimming with teeth, there was no doubt she was a dragon.

"Miss Coralee, is Mr. Judson dead?" It was a silly question he knew, but Latrell wanted to hear of the man's fate before he found what was left of his body in the morning.

"Not yet," she replied with a flick of her tail, "but he's suffered a fatal reptile bite." The dragon smiled. "It will appear the rattlesnake he flung at me this evening bit him prior to its death."

"But it was you, wasn't it, Miss Coralee."

The dragon nodded.

Latrell watched as her forked tongue slid out and appeared to moisten her lips. Then, the swamp dragon tilted back her fearsome head, opened her mouth, and called to the bayou with so much bottled-up pain and longing that Latrell felt his throat tighten and tears fall unbidden from his eyes.

"My name is not Coralee. It's Coranth, Lady of the Bayou," said the dragon as she studied him with such intensity, he began to chew on his fingernail. "I cannot reward you with possessions, Latrell."

"I wasn't expecting a reward," he managed to say.

"But good luck will be yours, and you never need fear any reptile," promised the swamp dragon.

Before he could respond, the creature exhaled a cloud of greenish smoke which surrounded Latrell. In the blink of an eye, he felt the fumes pouring into his ears, nose, and mouth. Even the pores on his exposed skin felt like they opened and absorbed the dragon's breath.

Suddenly, a keening came from the depths of the bayou.

"My sister!" cried the dragon. Latrell would've sworn the creature's intricately patterned skin shimmered with joy. She didn't acknowledge Latrell again. Instead, she slithered toward the wharf.

"Good bye, Coranth, Lady of the Bayou," whispered Latrell as the swamp dragon disappeared into a thicket of scrub trees beside the bayou's edge. He heard a splash as she entered its shallow waters. Then, in a haunting duet, the sisters wailed a farewell to Swamp Oak Manor, and the doomed Judson Beauregard.

Latrell stepped back, locked the screen in place, and sat on his bed staring into the bayou. With Mr. Judson dead, Nana and he'd pack up their things, find a nice bungalow, and move back into town.

As for Swamp Oak Manor, it wouldn't take long before the bayou swallowed the buildings, reclaimed the land, and erased any memory of the cursed Beauregard family and the strangely beautiful Miss Coralee.

DRAGON RAIN

Safety, thought Voruntil, Beloved of Nyzenth, as she spotted a cave opening at the base of a rocky outcrop. She scanned the horizon. The stars had already faded and the pale apricot of sunrise tinted the edge of the sky. Her wyrmlings and she needed to find shelter before daylight revealed their presence to humankind.

"You've had a drink, now it's time for sleep," she told her brood as she corralled them into the cavern which would serve as today's sleeping quarters.

"Supper?" asked several wyrmlings.

"Not this morning." Voruntil stroked the necks of her offspring. "But tonight, after sunset, I'll find breakfast."

This seemed to satisfy her brood. With scraping of belly plates, scratching of claws, and rustling of wings, the ten juveniles settled into a scaly heap around Voruntil.

"Tell us a bedtime story," asked Nukai, the runt of the clutch. "One about the Long Ago."

"I will tell a story, if *everyone* promises to go to sleep when I'm done," said Voruntil.

A chorus of "Yes, we promise," erupted from her wyrmlings.

Voruntil reviewed the distance they'd covered last night. Even on fresh mounts, the men who'd slayed her beloved Nyzenth wouldn't catch up with them until late tonight. Voruntil smiled, there was amble time for sleep and story. Leaning her muzzle down, she started retelling the history of dragonkind.

"In the Long Ago, dragons ruled the world," began Voruntil. "Our reign began two-hundred-and-forty million years ago. Maybe more."

Her wyrmlings snuggled close, lifted their scaly chins, and with eyes fixed on Voruntil's face, listened to their mother's storytelling.

"The Earth was wetter in the Long Ago, with shallow oceans where deserts and plains are today. The world was newer, less spoiled, as warm as summer sun on your belly, and filled with dragons."

"Tell us about the different kinds," urged Ombin. He pushed closer to Voruntil. *He's the spitting image of his father,* she mused. She sighed. Even a passing thought of Nyzenth brought back the pain of his recent death.

"As you wish, son." Voruntil patted Ombin's crested head with her paw. "There were dragons who rode the air currents on great leathery wings. They filled the skies with their lovely shrieks and dove to the ground faster than the wind to catch their prey. Dinner in foot, they'd flap to their nests far up on the cliff tops where they surveyed the dragon empire spreading out to the horizon. There, they'd thank Gralba, the Great Mother, for this blessed planet, and the prey creatures for their gift of life."

She studied each wyrmling face before adding. "The wings of the flying dragons were wider than the wings of any of today's birds. When the dragons moved them up and down to soar from one place to another, it sounded like thunder. In the Long Ago, lesser creatures would scurry to their hiding places and peek out once in a while to admire the kings and queens of the heavens."

"Tell about the water dragons," said Nukai. Not one to be outdone by her clutch-mates, she stretched her neck above the rest of the wyrmlings and fluttered her undersized wings.

"Patience, Nukai," said Voruntil. She itched her daughter's forehead between her ears with an obsidian claw. Smallest of the clutch, Nukai often demanded notice.

But she's strong for her size, mused Voruntil before continuing.

"In the Long Ago, the oceans were brimming with shellfish, a wonderful assortment of fishes, and other good things to eat. With food so plentiful, the oceans were also filled with dragons. The sea dragons were enormous. Even so, their huge, muscular bodies floated easily in the oceans of two-hundred million years ago. Wingless, the water dragons propelled themselves through the waters with strong tails and mighty feet. And in today's world, there still exist miniature versions of those long ago water dragons."

"But there are no flying dragons anymore," said Ombin sadly.

"No, son, not like the sky dragons of the Long Ago," agreed Voruntil. "But little ones, once your wings have grown, you *will* be able to fly short distances."

Her statement was met with growls and snorts of excitement.

"Lastly, there were land dragons," said Voruntil.

"Like us," added Ombin.

"Like us," agreed Voruntil.

The wyrmlings gleefully yelped and flapped their tiny wings.

"In the Long Ago, there were plant-eating dragons with necks long enough to reach the leaves on the tree tops," Voruntil told her clutch.

"They never ate prey?" said Nukai.

"Never," replied Voruntil.

She let the strangeness of plant-eating dragons sink in. The brows of her children were furrowed like wind-blown sand. She knew they craved fresh meat, not vegetation.

"Alas, their dependence on plants would lead to their demise," stated Voruntil. "But I'm getting ahead of myself. Where was I?"

"You were telling us about the land dragons," said Ombin.

"So I was." Again, Voruntil scratched each wyrmling's neck.

"Dragons with armored collars walked the lands as well as dragons with bony heads hard as rock." She rapped a stalactite hanging down from the cave's ceiling for emphasis.

Her children grinned.

"There were dragons with one, two, or three horns sprouting from their heads who wandered the great plains and sweltering swamps of the Long Ago." Voruntil noticed several wyrmling's eyelids were partially lowered. She smiled.

"There were dragons covered in armor and dragons with spikes marching down their spines like great, wide teeth." She pulled her lips back to reveal her teeth.

Two of her children didn't see her toothy storytelling antics. They were already asleep.

She continued, "Some of the land dragons walked on two feet and some on four. Some laid eggs in nests, while other dragons gave birth to live wyrmlings. And all of them honored Gralba, the Great Mother, and the prey creatures."

"Just like we do every day and when we take life," said Nukai.

All of her clutch-mates still awake nodded their muzzles in agreement.

"Yes. It is important to honor Gralba, as well as those whose lives we must end in order to live." Voruntil scratched the eye ridges of each of her ten offspring, even the three who were sleeping, before continuing.

"Thus, as rulers of Earth, the blessed children of Gralba thrived for eons until The Darkness arrived."

The wyrmlings who were still awake pressed closer. She could see fear in their bright, sun-illumined eyes as they listened to the details of the turning point in the history of dragonkind.

"Heavy with evil, sixty-six million years ago The Darkness rushed between stars. It raced past the moon and crashed into Earth sending dust, dirt, and tiny rocks into the atmosphere. The strength of its impact wounded the planet, so Earth's scorching blood burst from her skin with loud rumbles and explosions beyond imagining."

The six wyrmlings still awake gasped.

Voruntil lowered her voice. "The steam and ash from those explosions added to The Darkness until most of the planet's life succumbed to foul air, sunless days, food-less nights, and bitter temperatures. Without enough sunshine and warmth, the plants soon withered and died. The first dragons to perish were those who survived on plant life. Then, the dragons who consumed plant-eaters could find no food, and they died. The dragons who remained consumed one another rather than starve, but there was still insufficient food."

She opened her wings and spread them like a leathery blanket over her brood. "It was then the dragons died—except for a few who took refuge in the oceans and deep caves in the still tepid parts of the world. But all was not lost, our smaller cousins lucky enough to live in those warmer climes survived as well. In this way, the reign of dragonkind ended. The Age of Dragons lasted more than one-hundred-and-eighty million years. And though we are Gralba, the Great Mother's chosen ones, even she couldn't save us from The Darkness."

Only Nukai and Ombin weren't asleep. They gazed at her from beneath half-lowered eyelids.

"Now, humankind gathers the bones of dragons from where they were buried beneath the ash, mud, and pebbles of the Long Ago. They gather the dragon bones, raise them up in awe, store them in sacred places, and tell stories of the fantastic dragons of the Long Ago."

"Then why do they hunt and kill us?" asked Ombin.

"Because humans, who've only been here for three-hundred thousand years, fear that which they don't understand. It is a flaw in their nature," observed Voruntil as first Nukai, then Ombin finally closed their eyes.

Silence filled the grotto where Voruntil and her children hid. As she gazed down on her wyrmlings, her heart ached. With her mate murdered, Voruntil would produce no more eggs unless she found a new partner. Her throat tightened. She realized this was likely her final clutch. And there was no doubting her mate, Nyzenth's death. She'd seen his wounded body decapitated.

Beheaded so a human king can hang a trophy in his throne room, she thought bitterly.

As for Nyzenth, like all the dragons before him, at his death he'd risen as a vaporous spirit. Before fleeing from the soldiers with her children, Voruntil had witnessed Nyzenth's misty essence depart his corpse like smoke rising from a dying fire.

It gave her some comfort to know at this moment above the crawl-way in which her children and she sheltered; her beloved mate hovered over his family in the day sky. Like his forefathers and fore-mothers, when Voruntil and her children's mouths were parched, Nyzenth would shed tears. Then, dragon rain would save them from thirst.

But lack of water was the least of Voruntil's problems.

The familiar history of dragonkind told in Voruntil's soothing voice had sent her wyrmlings into dreamland. While her brood slept, she needed to carefully plot the remainder of their land journey. It was her duty to get her children to the safety of the waterways, then to the seas and oceans beyond.

On day one, she'd fled the Tantali Mountains with their clutch while Nyzenth fought the dozens of Roman soldiers who came to slay a dragon. For the past four days, Voruntil had managed to locate various caves and hidey-holes in which to take haven during the sunlit hours. According to her calculations, tonight would be their final night to travel by land. She prayed to Gralba they'd reach the shores of the Seihan River by moon-down. Then, they'd begin the long swim to the Mediterranean Sea.

But she knew soldiers didn't quickly give up a prize as desirable as a dragon. After slaying Nyzenth and searching their Tantali cave, the men would soon locate footprints left by Voruntil and her children. There was little doubt, the soldiers would follow Voruntil's family's trail with murder in their hearts.

Though it was not dragonkind's way, fame and fortune among humans seemed a goal many of them deemed worthy of pursuing. Therefore, Voruntil believed she and her clutch were in imminent danger of losing their heads.

***

Voruntil managed to grab a few hours of sleep before moonrise. The stirrings of her wyrmlings woke her as twilight dimmed the patch of sky visible through the grotto's entrance. She was certain her children would soon be asking for food.

"Wake up, my babies. Time to find breakfast," said Voruntil. She stood, stretched her wings, refolded them against her back, and walked out of the cave into the night with her wyrmlings following. She was grateful the usually noisy youngsters were silent. Even at their age, they knew sound warned prey of a hunt.

Voruntil's ears twitched as she scanned the surrounding terrain with her night vision. Her shoulders relaxed when she spotted a flock of goats to the east of their location.

A food source found in the direction of the Seihan—what could be better? Perhaps we will successfully make our escape, she thought.

"Stay here," she told her children. "I'll fly to that field," she pointed to the east with a black claw, "and kill eleven goats. You may begin walking in that direction after counting to three hundred."

"What if there are men watching over the herd?" asked Nukai in a quavering voice.

"Let's hope the herders know it's safer to run from a hungry dragon than to confront one."

The wyrmlings' heads bobbed up and down in agreement.

Sure, her children would comply with her instructions, Voruntil leaped into the air and winged her way to the goats. She'd already killed six of the animals when the bleating of the frightened herd woke the man assigned the task of watching for predators. He rushed to the field where the terrified goats were racing around, saw Voruntil standing over a fresh kill, and backed away.

Wise man, thought Voruntil. *He decided no prey animal was worth dying for. Thus, he will live to see another sunrise.*

As her clutch arrived, Voruntil grabbed the eleventh goat with her front claws and quickly broke its neck. She saw no reason to prolong the suffering of panicked prey. She embraced the rule of Instant Death taught to her by her mother when Voruntil was a wyrmling. She hoped her brood would follow this compassionate practice as well.

"Thank the prey for their sacrifice, then eat, children," said Voruntil. "We cannot linger. I'm sure soon the goat herder will return with friends."

"Will we reach the river tonight?" asked Ombin between bites.

"Yes, but only if we hurry." What she did not add, though it was in her thoughts, was they were likely being pursued by glory-seeking soldiers eager to slaughter more dragons. Frightening her wyrmlings seemed counterproductive. Their focus must be stealthiness and speed.

***

After traveling for six hours, the wyrmlings begged to take a break in the shelter of a cluster of heavily-leafed trees. Voruntil decided the oasis was suitable for a rest stop. In addition to cover, it had a pool of water in its center, so the young dragons could quench their thirst.

She surveyed the landscape and listened for approaching humans. She neither saw nor heard anything worrisome.

"We will rest here briefly," Voruntil told her children. "Then, we push to the Seihan. Think how wonderful its chilly water will feel on your feet."

"Will we swim all day before sleeping?" asked Ombin before laying his head on his front legs.

"No." Voruntil studied her exhausted wyrmlings. "We'll swim until I spot a suitable hollow or hideaway to spend the sun-bright hours. There, we'll rest until dusk."

"We will never see Father again—will we?" Nukai gave voice to the question Voruntil knew all her children wanted to ask.

"No, we won't see him again in this life." Voruntil lowered her head slightly. "But we'll feel his love for us every time it rains. He'll shed tears to wash away the dirt and dust of our journeys. He'll shed tears to fill the watering holes and cool our heated brows. He'll shed tears to swell the Seihan, so we can escape to the Mediterranean Sea."

"Just like all the dragons from the Long Ago until today," added Ombin. "They all watch over us."

"Yes." Voruntil was pleased with Ombin's understanding of the ways of dragonkind. She hoped it was an indicator of the thoughts of his clutch-mates.

Suddenly, she swung her head in a westerly direction. She smelled horses and humans.

"Soldiers are near," Voruntil told her wyrmlings. "We must race with the speed of the dragons of the Long Ago to the river."

Her children got to their feet. Silenced by fear, they awaited her instructions.

"I will lead the way," she told them with as much calm as she could muster, "but you must keep up. If you notice anyone falling behind, let me know." Voruntil studied each of her children's precious faces. "I will try to protect you from harm, but the soldiers are determined— and they might be riding fresh horses."

Her brood nodded.

"We're going to make it," said Ombin with certainty. "Gralba will protect us."

His clutch-mates chimed in with words of agreement.

"Let us hope so." Voruntil pointed her head in the direction of the river. "Off we go," she said, and trotted eastward at a speed she felt her clutch could match.

The wyrmlings ran behind her. She heard them calling words of encouragement whenever one of their siblings fell behind.

Voruntil smelled the scent of river water at about the same time she heard a man shout, "There they are!"

She ventured a glance at the flatlands behind her wyrmlings.

Mounted on a white horse was the man she'd heard called *George* when the soldiers were attacking Nyzenth. He wore armor and carried a spear. She'd witnessed his heartlessness, so there was no doubt in her mind he'd gleefully impale all her children if he was given a chance.

"Faster," she urged her ten offspring. "Look deep in your minds. Feel the strength of the long ago ancestors. Though we be few, we are still dragonkind."

Inspired by her speech, her clutch moved more rapidly.

Voruntil looked back at the soldiers once more. They were closer.

She recognized a second soldier. The other dragon-killers had called him *Theodore Tiro*. He rode a horse as black as his soul must be to murder a dragon guilty of nothing more than protecting his family. Beneath his helmet, Voruntil saw his hate filled eyes staring at her. She knew Theodore Tiro longed to behead her and her wyrmlings with the metal sword strapped to his side.

"The Seihan isn't far, my children," she shouted as she swung her head forward once more.

"I see the river," yelled several clutch-mates. "We're going to make it!"

A sense of relief washed over Voruntil. She was going to fulfill the promise made to her beloved Nyzenth before he sacrificed himself to guarantee his family's escape from the Tantali Mountains.

"I've done it, Nyzenth. Our clutch will live, grow, find mates, and keep alive dragonkind," whispered Voruntil as she, too, spotted the green waters of the Seihan River flowing between several low-rising hills.

She peered behind her wyrmlings one last time. The soldiers had drawn even nearer. She recognized a third man. His battle mates had called him Demetrius of Thessaloniki. Mounted on a red horse, Demetrius was in the lead. He yelped a blood curdling scream before kicking his horse. Voruntil noted the stallion jumped forward—his hooves a blur.

Her eyes moved to the location of her two slowest children.

Nukai had dropped behind her clutch-mates. Legs shorter than her siblings, she was having trouble maintaining the pace set by Voruntil. By choice, it appeared Ombin had slowed his pace to run beside his sister.

Voruntil's heart told her to swing around and face George, Theodore Tiro, Demetrius of Thessaloniki, and the rest of the soldiers. Such an action on her part would give all of her children a chance to reach the river. But if she made that choice, ten wyrmlings wouldn't know where to go or how to survive the arduous journey to the sea— much less how and where to locate more dragons. Because she realized if Nyzenth, with his greater fighting skill, hadn't been able to defeat these men, she'd surely be killed by them and her orphaned wyrmlings would soon die.

As much as it pained her, Voruntil knew she must listen to her brain. The sacrifice of Nukai so nine of her children could survive was the only choice. She studied her daughter's face one last time. Nukai's skin was the green of juniper trees with orange flecks specking her muzzle. Her eyes were the color of garnets and full of curiosity. Even racing for her life, Nukai's mouth curved pleasantly upward.

Voruntil would grieve for her daughter for the rest of her life. But a wise mother chooses the action, no matter how painful, which results in the greatest good.

Ombin, she mind spoke.

Mother? he replied.

Nukai cannot keep up. She won't reach the river before the soldiers overtake her.

I know, responded Ombin.

You must leave her, said Voruntil in her son's mind, *and join the rest of the clutch.*

No, replied Ombin. *I am Ombin, son of Nyzenth, and like my father before me, I will sacrifice myself to save my family.*

Before Voruntil could argue with her son, Ombin slowed his pace.

In her mind, Voruntil heard Ombin speak to his sister. *Nukai, run like your life depends on it. I will drop behind and face the men.*

No, Ombin, answered Nukai. *Let them have me.*

No, Nukai. You can raise many clutches of wyrmlings. I am male, and therefore, more expendable.

Then, Ombin spoke with a force which sent his voice into the minds of Voruntil and all of his siblings. *I will face the men. The rest of you must get to the river, swim to the sea, find other dragons, and raise another generation of dragonkind. Please, remember me.*

Ignoring the protests of his clutch-mates and Voruntil's wail, Ombin stopped running and turned to face the humans and their weapons.

Instantaneously, the moon was swallowed by clouds and the sky changed from star-strewn to solid black as generation upon generation of dragons gathered above the soldiers: George, Theodore Tiro, Demetrius of Thessaloniki, and their comrades.

As one by one, her children splashed into the Seihan, Voruntil stood on the riverbank and watched Ombin.

Mimicking his father's stand of a few days before, Ombin flailed his tail, swung his neck, snapped his teeth, and slashed at the soldiers with his claws. But his small size and inexperience made his efforts less effective than Nyzenth's had been. Ombin had only managed to kill one of the soldiers, before George charged forward on his white stallion and impaled the wyrmling.

Dragon tears poured from the sky as Theodore Tiro and Demetrius of Thessaloniki rushed forward and slashed Ombin. Soon, the rest of the men crowded around Voruntil's child and stabbed his lifeless body with their knives and spears.

When the cruel George raised a blade to decapitate Ombin, the thousands of dragon spirits who'd gathered above the self-sacrificing wyrmling roared. Their roar echoed across the land. Voruntil witnessed the murderers fall to their knees with their bloody hands pressed to their ears.

Then, midst the torrent of tears falling from the heavens, she saw Ombin's spirit lift from his headless carcass. Next, with their spirits glowing soft as moonlight, she observed Nyzenth and hundreds of long-gone kin embraced Ombin.

Voruntil tried to push the carnage she'd just witnessed to the back of her mind, and instead focus on the wonder of the dragon spirits welcoming her child.

Tears of his own slid down her snout as a misty Nyzenth, arm still wrapped around their son stared at her. She felt his love cross the barrier between them.

Leave before they notice you, she heard in her mind as clearly as if Nyzenth stood beside her. *Nine wyrmlings paddle southward. You must catch up with them, protect them, guide them to the sea and beyond.*

Yes, Beloved, Voruntil answered Nyzenth's spirit. *As long as I live, I will watch over our children.* Then, in the torrential rain, she slipped into the Seihan River and swam away from the wyrmling Ombin's dying place.

***

Voruntil and her children traveled down the Seihan and into the Mediterranean Sea without further incident. They searched the Mediterranean's inlets, islands, and sea caves until they found other dragons. When her brood matured and they were able to fly, Voruntil and her last clutch traveled to the Atlantic.

360

As decades turned to centuries, one by one, her children found mates and began their own families, but not before they discovered accounts written and artwork created by humans of the dragon encounters in the Tantali Mountains and on the shores of the Seihan.

Always, Nyzenth and Ombin were wrongly described as vicious beasts who consumed human flesh and wreaked destruction. The settings of their slayings as well as the year of their killings were changed. The physical appearance of father and son were altered. Voruntil's family members were even cast as servants of a creature more evil than The Darkness, which had ended the Age of Dragons.

Worse still, George, Theodore Tiro, and Demetrius of Thessaloniki were treated as heroes and given sainthood. Countries and towns placed the images of the dragon slayers slaughtering Nyzenth and Ombin on their shields, crests, and logos. Sometimes, they showed one dragon. Sometimes, two. And sometimes, though Voruntil never quite understood why, the dragon portrayed had two heads.

Perhaps the most heart wrenching image was the one carved in red stone on the facade of Basel Cathedral in Basel, Switzerland. The statues of George and Ombin had been designed to show the true difference in size between man and wyrmling. One twilight, as Voruntil perched on the cathedral's roof watching the people who'd come to see the carvings, she listened to what members of the crowd said.

"That dragon looks like a baby," observed a fair-haired woman holding her child. "What sort of man was Saint George to kill a little dragon?'

What sort of man indeed, thought Voruntil as she took to the night sky vowing never again to visit the cities of humankind.

***

"I cannot leave you alone," Nukai said one morning as Voruntil and she sunned on a rock jutting into the North Sea.

Voruntil studied her daughter. Nukai had turned down many opportunities to begin her own family, choosing instead to keep her company.

"But I grow lonely for a mate and children of my own," said her daughter wistfully.

Voruntil placed her paw on top of Nukai's. "But I am never alone," she said. "When I close my eyes, I see your father, Ombin, and my parents waiting for me in the clouds."

"Really?" Nukai's brows ridges were raised.

"Yes," said Voruntil. "Gralba, the Great Mother, blessed me with a life-mate who valued me above all others, and clutch after clutch of wyrmlings. I have contributed to the survival of dragonkind, and now, I wish to join those who bring dragon rain to their children and grandchildren and great-grandchildren to the millionth generation."

As she gave voice to her wish, a sudden, fast moving storm rolled in from the sea. Voruntil spotted the spirits of hundreds, perhaps thousands of dragons riding the clouds. The towering cumuli nimbus formations opened and dragon rain poured down. As the deluge of dragon tears pelted her face, Voruntil saw a misty Nyzenth sailing toward her.

"Beloved," he said in a voice like thunder.

"Go find your future," Voruntil shouted to her daughter. "Gralba calls me. It's my time to join the dragons above."

Before Nukai could speak, a lightning bolt shot from the clouds and struck Voruntil. Then, Voruntil felt herself grow thin as dreams as the wind swept her heavenward and into the arms of her beloved.

MAGIC

Trees had spirits. As did waterfalls, fjords, and even the land itself.

Which was why Oddvar was told to be careful when selecting wood for carving the dragon heads and tails to be mounted on the stems and sterns of his village's longboats. One *had* to be careful. Humans weren't the only beings living in the forests, waterways, and caverns.

Tomorrow, he'd be going into the wilds alone to find the wood for the next dragon head to be carved. His thoughts jumped from one otherworld creature to the next, wondering if he'd encounter any of them on his wanderings.

"Where are you, Oddvar?" asked Farfar Tor as he nudged his grandson with his elbow.

"I'm here," answered Oddvar with a smile. He paused a second to clear the cobwebs from his mind before continuing. "I was thinking about the soul of the ship we're working on. Wondering where the gnome who guards this longboat hides when we're onboard."

"One doesn't need to see the otherworld folk to know they're here," replied his grandfather. "When the tree used for the keel was cut, the ship-spirit emerged from the tree. Then, he came with the timber to the shipyard. Now, he's somewhere on the boat, keeping the timbers clear of rot and woodworms. But if we should fail to properly construct and attach the figurehead, I dare say he'll make an angry appearance."

Farfar Tor raised his bushy brows, pulled his lips down, and glanced sideways at Oddvar.

Oddvar laughed at his grandfather's grimace before rubbing the last of the oil into the carving of a fearsome drake which graced the bow of the boat. When whittled from a blessed tree and well-shaped, the carving would scare away enemies and ward off evil spirits on both land and sea.

No other local woodcarvers could guarantee this protection. Only Oddvar's family, because Farfar Tor, like his father and grandfather before him, knew how to imbue timber with the magic of dragons. The trick, which their family kept secret, was to boil a dragon scale in the oil used for polishing figureheads.

"I think the iron curls we inserted into the wood add a regalness to the drake," said Farfar Tor as he caressed the arched neck of the dragon.

"And they provide protection for ship and crew from sea serpents, merrow, and kraken when they journey across the waters," added Oddvar. "Just like our trollkors," he touched the iron troll cross hanging from a leather cord around his neck.

"Iron works most of the time," agreed his grandfather, "but be cautious nevertheless when wandering in the forest. Some creatures of the otherworld won't be dettered by a trollkor alone."

"You don't have to worry, Farfar Tor," he boasted as they climbed off the longboat, "I'm always careful."

His grandfather answered him with a shake of his head as they hiked back to their house.

***

After feeding and watering the livestock, Oddvar and Farfar Tor locked the barn, then entered their stone, wood, and wattle-and-daub home. The fire crackling in the central hearth took the bite off the evening air. Though the days were still bright, the night time chill indicated autumn's first frost was near.

Oddvar sighed. It was always comforting to return home at the end of the day. He felt the tension in his shoulders vanish when he saw his grandmother's loomwork hanging at one end of the room and her preparing a meal at the other.

I'm lucky to live with Farfar Tor and Farmor Britt, he thought as the aromas of one of his grandmother's savory stews bubbling in a pot and fresh bread made his mouth water. When his mother died in childbirth and his father was killed in a raid across the sea a year later, Oddvar could've been given to another family, sold into servitude, or even left out for trolls to find. Instead, he was cherished by his grandparents.

"Another boat outfitted with a dragon head and tail," announced his grandfather as he stretched his arms above his head, yawned, then sat on one of the wooden beds running the length of each side of their home.

"I'm sure it looks fearsome indeed," said Farmor Britt before handing her husband a bowl of stew and a hunk of bread.

Oddvar's grandmother smiled at him. "Are you ready to whittle and mount the carvings by yourself yet?" she asked as she gave him his supper.

"I think so," he answered. "I'm going out tomorrow morning to look for a piece of wood from which to carve the next dreki.

"But not alone!" exclaimed Farmor Britt.

"Yes, alone. If Oddvar is to someday run the business, he must do more on his own," insisted Farfar Tor. "Now, sit, woman. You need to eat, too."

***

The sun had not yet risen when Oddvar woke. His grandmother was already up preparing porridge, while his grandfather was carefully placing items into Oddvar's travel bag.

"I can do that," he said as he pulled on his boots.

"I know," replied his grandfather. "But now that packing is done except for the ax, you'll have time to help me with the animals before you depart."

Oddvar grinned, slipped on his outerwear, and followed Farfar Tor to the barn. They filled the hay bins, milked the goats, collected a few eggs, then turned the livestock out in their pen—except for their horse, Stig. They left Stig in his stall with extra feed. Then, they attached the harness to the cart. By the time they returned to the house, Farmor Britt had sliced what remained of last night's bread and ladled steaming porridge into three bowls.

"You're wearing your trollkor and caring a knife?" his grandmother asked after breakfast when Oddvar slipped his leather travel bag over his shoulder.

"Yes, Farmor Britt." He kissed his grandmother on the cheek. "We even tied a small trollkor onto Stig's halter and nailed one to the cart.

"Remember, mark your path as you hike so you can easily find your way home," said his grandfather. "And once you locate your tree, thank the guardian spirit before chopping it down and loading it onto the cart."

"I will."

"Stig won't wander, so free him from the harness and let him graze while you chop." His grandfather scratched his chin, then cleared his throat. "And make sure you're back before dusk. There's no sense tempting the otherworld folk."

"Tor," snapped his grandmother. "Don't frighten the boy."

"There're gasts, ghosts, and dark elves of all sorts out by dark. I'm just reminding him to be mindful of the time," replied his grandfather.

"I'll be back long before sundown," Oddvar assured his grandparents as he exited the door.

Stig raised his head and whinnied when Oddvar entered the barn. An even tempered work horse, the gelding stood still while Oddvar secured him in the harness and attached a lead to his halter. After placing the ax and his travel bag in the cart, he gave a slight tug on the lead and Stig began walking beside him. They hiked north along the fjord's edge into more densely forested land.

To keep his spirits up and settle his racing pulse, Oddvar talked to Stig.

In response, the work horse twitched his ears, snorted, and occasionally nickered.

As they walked, the flat lands near the water, Oddvar marked trees with his knife. The notches he cut were big enough he'd be able to see them on their return journey, but not large enough to damage the trunks. There was no sense in angering the Huldra.

Even thinking about the Wood Wife caused him to stare into the thickets on either side of the path. The Huldra could take the shape of a woman, tree, animal, moss-covered rock—even an old troll woman.

While scanning the forest, he spotted a stump about fifteen steps into the tangled vegetation.

"Whoa," said Oddvar. He went back to the sledge, rummaged around in his sack, and tore a piece of bread and a bite of cheese from his lunch. After again scanning the wildwood pressing close to the trail, he left the relative safety of horse and cart, and headed for the remnants of a felled tree.

"A small offering to the Huldra," he said as he placed the food upon the stump. "Thank you for allowing us to pass through your domain."

Rather than wait beside the stump, Oddvar back away, grabbed Stig's lead, and resumed hiking. He'd only gone a few steps when he heard a branch snap behind them. Oddvar stopped and looked back at the stump. The food was gone. He swallowed the fear which rose up in his throat and resumed treading the forest path.

A half an hour later, as if the Huldra had read his mind and knew his purpose, Oddvar saw a sunbeam slice through the forest canopy and spotlight an oak tree. The oak had storm damage to its upper branches, but a perfect, undamaged, disease-free trunk of the circumference and length Oddvar was searching for.

"Perfect!" he exclaimed. "It's already been gifted by the Wood Wife and blessed by Thor—even before we carve protection runes into the oakwood."

As if agreeing with him, Stig nodded his head and stomped his right front hoof.

Oddvar released Stig from his harness. Thus, allowing the gelding to nibble on the underbrush. Next, he retrieved the ax, went to the spotlighted oak, and thanked its spirit. After chopping a deep notch on one side of the trunk, he began to chop vigorously on the other side of the oak. When the tree was ready to fall, he checked to make sure Stig was out of the way, then pushed against the trunk. With a series of snaps and groans, the oak fell.

"Whew!" Oddvar wiped his brow with the back of his sleeve. Then, noticing Stig was wandering farther down the path, he carried the ax to the cart, grabbed his leather sack, and ran after the work horse.

Stig picked up his pace.

By the time Oddvar was able to catch up with the work horse, Stig had reached a small pond fed by a spring bubbling from between a pile of boulders. The gelding had lowered his head, and was drinking from the pool.

Suddenly wary, Oddvar held onto his trollkar with his left hand, pulled his knife from his belt with his right, and plunged the blade into the soil at the edge of the water to bind the Neck should he be near. He doubted the Neck would be looking to drown the careless in such a small body of water, but one could never be sure until they were dragged to the bottom. Rather, Oddvar thought this was just the sort of place inhabited by a spring guardian.

As if to confirm his guess, he spotted a large frog half-submerged in the middle of the pool.

"Thank you for allowing us to drink of your water," he told the frog before breaking off a bit of cheese and bread and placing them on a mossy spot by the edge of the water.

"A kind and wise gesture," said a voice from the shadows on the far side of the pool. "Do you have anything in your bag for me?"

Oddvar retrieved his dagger, then stepped back until he was pressed against Stig. He felt the horse quivering behind him.

"Who are you?" he called. He squinted his eyes. "I can't see you."

"Is this better?" said the voice as an enormous snake-like beast crawled out from the shaded roots of an oak tree.

Oddvar gasped. The lindwyrm, who must have been watching since Stig arrived, was now clearly visible as it slithered its huge body over stone, grass, and fallen trees. The beast's crown-like mane of white spines sprouted from its head, then ran down the length of its sinuous body. As Oddvar's eyes traced the path of the wyrm's pale, spiky mane, he noted it slowly grayed to nearly black by the time it reached the creature's tail. Having no wings and only two front legs, wyrms were thought of as lesser cousins of drakes and sea serpents. But now, standing before it, the lindwyrm was quite impressive.

"Yes," he managed to say to the wyrm, "I see you now."

"And what do you think, boy?" asked the reptile.

Oddvar chose his words carefully. "I think you're amazing. The green-gray pattern on your upper scales is more intricate than the finest dragon carvings my grandfather whittles. Your diamond-shaped scales shine like polished silver. Your eyes are redder than the sun as it slips below the horizon at dusk. I am honored to meet you."

The wyrm clacked its dangerously sharp claws upon the boulder on which its belly rested and seemed to consider Oddvar's response.

"I could swallow you both whole," stated the lindwyrm.

"I'd rather you didn't."

There must be a way out of this, thought Oddvar. *What can I offer the beast to save our lives? Or is there a way to kill it before the wyrm consumes Stig and me?*

"Unfortunately for you, boy," began the lindwyrm, "I haven't had a meal in days. So as much as I've enjoyed our conversation, I must eat you and your horse."

"Wait!"

The wyrm lowered its snakish head and gazed at Oddvar and Stig with burning eyes.

"We would both be more tender and taste better if we're smoked."

"Smoked?"

"Yes," responded Oddvar, trying to retrieve the details of killing a wyrm from his long ago memories. He'd heard Farfar Tor tell the men working on a longboat with them when he was a child that there was a way to kill a lindwyrm. Of course when questioned, his grandfather admitted no one he knew had ever tried, much less succeeded in, such a feat.

"Tell me about this smoking," said the wyrm leaning his bearded chin upon a paw.

"It's quite simple," explained Oddvar. "I'll build three bonfires beside the pond. Then, my horse and I will dash through them. By the time we've run through the third bonfire, we'll be smoked, flavorful, and tender."

"I suspect you'll try to run away." The lindwyrm ran its forked tongue around the rim of its mouth.

"Which is why you must follow directly behind us," he explained. "Then, it will be impossible for this boy and his work horse to escape your jaws."

The lindwyrm yawned, then scratched its belly. "I've never had smoked meat before, so I'm willing to give it a try." It yawned again. "But hurry, my stomach is grumbling."

Oddvar nodded. Certain the horse would bolt the first chance he got, he tied Stig to a tree. Next, he gathered three piles of wood being careful to pile sufficient kindling and tinder for lighting in the center of each pile.

"How much longer," asked the wyrm as poisonous drool dribbled out of its mouth and splattered the nearby vegetation.

373

Oddvar cringed as the affected plant life wilted, then shriveled to a pile of brownish mush.

"Not long," he answered as he took a piece of flint from his belt and knelt by the first heap of wood. He struck the flint with his knife until a spark caught. Then, he babied the flame. Soon, the bonfire was crackling. Once the first wood pile was burning brightly, he took a flaming stick from the fire and used it to light the two remaining heaps of wood.

He glanced at the lindwyrm. Its head still rested on a paw. It appeared to be mesmerized by the flames.

This just might work, Oddvar thought as he untied Stig, tossed the lead over his neck and knotted it to the other side of the horse's halter. Makeshift reins in place, he used a nearby rock to climb onto the gelding's back.

"Ready?" he asked the wyrm.

"Yes," it hissed—once again dribbling poison onto the ground.

"Come on, Stig," Oddvar urged the work horse as he gave Stig a nudge in the ribs. "I know you can do it."

The horse tossed his head back and forth, backed away from the first fire, and seemed to dance in place. Suddenly, perhaps because he saw the lindwyrm winding its way closer, Stig snorted and lunged forward. Unwilling to run through the bonfire, the gelding gathered his legs beneath him and jumped over the blaze.

"Run!" hollered Oddvar. He gave Stig another nudge in his ribs, but it was unnecessary. The work horse hadn't slowed his cantor. Rather, he'd increased his pace. Without further encouragement, Stig raced toward the remaining bonfires. Then, he leapt over them.

Oddvar tugged the reins, slowed Stig, and turned him around to face the oncoming lindwyrm. He was careful to keep his horse well back from the final fire.

Eyes blazing and jaws hanging open ready to consume Stig and him, the beast crept through the first two fires. Protected by thick scales, Oddvar doubted the wyrm felt the heat. Then, staring at its smoked dinner, the lindwyrm squirmed into the final bonfire. When the creature had crawled halfway through, it stopped—caught in the magic of which Farfar Tor had spoken.

Clear as the dragonish wail pouring from the lindwyrm's throat as it turned to ash, in his mind Oddvar heard his grandfather's words, "To kill a lindwyrm, you must trick it into crawling through three bonfires. But stay back—or the wyrm will drag you into the third fire as it dies."

Hungry and exhausted, Oddvar slipped from Stig's back. He patted the work horse on his neck.

"I need what's left of my lunch, and I expect you need more water and to graze," he told the gelding.

Stig leaned down and pushed gently against him before trotting over to the pond. Oddvar followed, sat on a rock, and unwrapped bread, cheese, and a pouch full of dried berries. As he ate, he studied the surface of the pool. The frog was nowhere to be found, and the food offering he'd left before the lindwyrm showed up was gone.

Maybe a wood mouse took it, he mused. But in his heart, he knew the spring's guardian had taken the bread and cheese.

When he was finished eating, Oddvar walked to the first bonfire, took a piece of blazing kindling, and went in search of the wyrm's home. Not twenty steps from the pond, there was a burrow beneath the roots of a gigantic oak. Knife in his right hand and torch in his left, he climbed into the lindwyrm's lair.

"Thank the gods," he whispered as the torchlight revealed a heap of gold. Coins, goblets, wrist cuffs, necklaces, and other items gleamed like sunlight on water. But even more valuable than the precious metal items were the piles of shed skin.

Long had Farfar Tor's family boiled dragon scales in oil, then used that oil to imbue the figureheads they whittled for dragon ships with magic. But his grandfather had warned Oddvar there were only three scales remaining from the hundreds his great-great-grandfather had collected when he'd stumbled on a treasure hoard near the edge of a fjord. Ignoring the gold, he'd gathered as many scales as he could before the drake returned to its nest. For magic is worth more than gold.

With magic a priority, Oddvar cut three huge swatches of lindwyrm skin with his knife, folded them up as compactly as possible, and stuffed them in his satchel. Only then, did he grab handfuls of coins and drop them into the bag. When the bag was near overflowing, he picked out a beautiful necklace for Farmor Britt and slipped in the top. After tying the satchel closed, he filled his pickets with additional gold coins and stepped out of the burrow.

Stig waited for him a short distance away. The gelding, who'd been munching on grass and swishing his tail, lifted his head and took several steps toward him when he spotted Oddvar. But the sky behind the horse was already darkening.

"We're never going to make it home before nightfall," he told the work horse.

Stig seemed unconcerned.

"I'm going to need to ride you again," he said. Using a rock for added height, he climbed onto Stig's back. He made a clucking sound, and the horse trotted back to the site where the cart and cut oak waited.

In the dimming light, Oddvar used his ax to chop off branches and shorten the length of the oak trunk until it was perfect for carving a figurehead. The only thing left to do was to load the oak onto the cart and secure it. He re-harnessed Stig, making sure the gelding's trollkor was still attached to his halter. Next, he had the horse pull the cart into position beside the oak log. Then, he contemplated the best way to maneuver the log onto the cart. So focused was he on the task at hand, Oddvar didn't hear the trolls until one of them spoke.

"We could lift that for you," offered someone behind Oddvar.

He spun around and found himself face to face with three trolls. Two were males. Both of them were bald with low foreheads, tiny eyes, and over-sized mouths, ears, and noses. The third was an ancient troll woman. Slightly hump backed, she had stringy hair and carried a walking stick.

"My sons could lift that log for you onto the cart," said the troll woman.

As she spoke, Oddvar recognized her voice. He realized she'd been the one to offer assistance initially.

"I'd be grateful for your help," he responded. "I can offer you payment, or if it is more acceptable, gift you with valuables for your help."

Her sons standing like two hulking bears on either side of her, the troll woman wrapped all eight of her thick fingers around her walking stick, and took a few steps forward. She studied him with her all-black eyes. Moments later, a gap-toothed smile spread across her face.

"What can a youngling like you offer us?' she asked.

"The location of a lindwyrm's nest filled with gold and shed skin," he replied.

"We've no intention of tangling with a wyrm. Their poison is deadly."

"You don't have to," responded Oddvar. "I killed the wyrm. Its treasure trove is there for the taking."

"What proof do you have that you killed a lindwyrm?" asked the troll woman.

Again, he thought before responding. *If I show them what's in my bag, they'll likely take it all. If I empty a pocket, they'll believe me, but I'll still have something to take home.*

"I grabbed what I could, but I was afraid to linger in the forest any longer," said Oddvar, pulling a handful of coins from his pocket.

The trolls leaned forward.

"He's telling the truth," mumbled one of the troll brothers.

"Mm-hmm," agreed his sibling.

"We're not hoarders of gold, but it would be useful for trading," said the troll woman. "As for the lindwyrm skin, that *does* have value in trolldom."

When she'd finished speaking, she pointed at the oak log, then snapped her fingers. Obedient as hounds, her sons each grasped an end of the log and placed it on the cart.

"It's nearly dusk. Night creatures will be out soon. You'll never make it home in one piece," warned the troll woman. She tilted her head, then added, "But for the gold you have in your pockets, we'll escort you home."

"I'd be grateful for you company," responded Oddvar with a bow. "I'll give you the coins in my pockets when we're in front of my grandparents' house."

"While we walk," said the troll woman, "you must tell me how you killed the lindwyrm. It seems a task too great for a youngling."

Knowing better than to argue with a troll, Oddvar didn't challenge her classifying him as a *youngling*. Instead, he told her in great detail, with embellishments here and there, about his defeat of the wyrm as they followed the tree notches, he'd made earlier in the day southward.

Her sons soon tired of the slow pace.

"Can't we unhitch the beast and pull the cart ourselves?" asked one brother.

"We'll be back at the human settlement three times faster," said his sibling.

"As you wish." Their mother waved her large trollish hand. Then, she stopped walking and stared at Oddvar. "Get on your pony, so you can keep up."

"If you think that's best," he replied.

Before he could find a rock or stump to help him climb onto Stig, the troll woman picked Oddvar up and placed him on the work horse's back.

"Now, I can look you in the eye while we're speaking without bending down, youngling," she said. All three trolls laughed.

Again, rather than argue with her about his age or lack of trollish height, Oddvar forced a pleasant expression and tolerated the trolls' humor. When the trio stopped their laughter, he asked, "Would you tell me about trolls?"

The troll woman pushed her hair behind her pointed ears, nodded, then began, "Trolls have been here longer than humans...

Though he heard occasional moans and growls on either side of the trail on the rest of the hike home, Oddvar felt no fear. Instead, he listened to the troll woman tell of trolls, giants, elves, and otherworld creatures. When she finally stopped speaking, he glanced around and found he was home.

"Slip down from the pony and hitch him to the cart," said the troll woman. "We're not going any closer to your house and grandparents."

After doing as she asked, Oddvar emptied his pockets of coins by giving them, a handful at a time, to the troll brothers.

"Go back to the lindwyrm's lair. Gather the treasure and wyrm skins," the troll woman directed her sons. "I'll join you shortly."

Once the brothers had lumbered away, she turned to Oddvar.

"Before you leave," she began, "you should know your troll cross only stops us from stealing you or any of your possessions which also bear trollkors. We can still harm you."

"But I thought..."

She held up a four-fingered hand to stop his objections, then continued, "The iron from which your trollkors are made will protect you from some magical folk and creatures, but not all."

"Like the lindwyrm," said Oddvar. He shivered, recalling how close he'd come to being the dragonish creature's dinner.

The troll woman nodded. "Dragons and their kin aren't held at bay by iron. But used correctly, the wyrm skin hidden in your bag will prove quite useful in protection."

He gaped at her. Suddenly afraid she'd take the lindwyrm's skin and remaining treasure from him, he stepped away from her.

"Not to worry, youngling," the troll woman assured him. "Your honesty and good nature have served you well. We were watching you before you'd even killed the wyrm, and witnessed your efforts to honor the nature spirits. You'll be allowed to keep your part of the plunder."

"Thank you." He felt his heartbeats return to a more normal pace.

"But do not share the details of our encounter with anyone— including your grandparents," the troll woman warned. "Most magical folk prefer to keep interactions with humans private, and become quite annoyed if their privacy is not honored."

"No one shall know of our meeting," promised Oddvar. He'd share the rest of the day's experiences with Farfar Tor and Farmor Britt, but leave out the trolls.

"As to the magic of the wyrm skin..." The troll stared into his eyes with such intensity, he felt like she was looking into his soul. "Before you do anything else, cut a small piece from the skin, then boil it in water. Next, drink the water. Once it's gone, do your best to consume the now softened lindwyrm skin. You'll be blessed with future-seeing skills, good health, long life, and most importantly, no dragon or any other creature of magic will harm you."

"Will it work for my grandfather and grandmother as well?"

She shook her head. "This magic is yours to claim, not theirs, for they didn't kill the beast."

Then, the troll glanced at the nearly forgotten oak log. "Whittle a marvelous dragon head, use the wyrm skin to give it magic, and mount the figurehead upon the bow of one of your village's longboats." She reached out, touched Oddvar's brow with her forefinger, then continued, "But I've seen your future. You're not destined to carve dragon heads for the rest of your life, or sail on a dragon ship. Instead, you're destined to sail with dragons."

Before he could question the troll woman about her prediction, she turned and strode away.

With thoughts of dragon wings thrumming in his head, Oddvar took Stig's lead and walked beside the tired horse up the path toward his grandparent's barn.

"You hear that? I'm going to meet a dragon," he whispered.

The work horse stopped, turned his head, and gazed down at Oddvar. As if the gelding understood the implications of every action taken and word uttered today, Stig winked, then nudged Oddvar with his velvety nose.

"I should give you a sip of lindwyrm water and a bite of its flesh," said Oddvar as he laid the palm of his hand on the horse's shoulder. "You've earned a swallow of magic, too."

The work horse whinnied and nodded his head.

As Oddvar, Stig, and the cart carrying the wood for the next dragon head neared the barn, Farfar Tor and Farmor Britt ran out of the house.

All of a sudden, a cold gust whistled through the evergreens scattering leaves, whipping Stig's mane, and tugging at Oddvar's hair.

"Magic," the wind seemed to whisper. "Embrace magic."

ABOUT THE AUTHORS

DAVID GREEN

David Green is a writer based in Co Galway, Ireland. Growing up between there and Manchester, UK meant David rarely saw sunlight in his childhood, which has no doubt had an effect on his dark writings. Published with Black Ink Fiction, Red Cape Publishing and Eerie River Publishing, David has been nominated for the Pushcart Prize 2020 and his dark fantasy series Empire of Ruin launches in June 2021 with "In Solitude's Shadow."

Website: www.davidgreenwriter.com

Newsletter: https://tinyurl.com/y6ah8brp

Twitter: @davidgreenwrite

DIANA BROWN

Di Brown couldn't decide what to do when she grows up, so she's put off growing up until she has a plan. In the interim, she's been a Cold War spy, learned to knit (badly) and programmed computers (well). Her fiction is included in anthologies from the UK to Australia, and her nonfiction appears in Magazines in the USA, but she's most proud of her Pushcart-nominated essay "Tatort" in Dark House Books' Descansos Anthology. More stories (and links to her published work) can be found on her web site, at www.DianaBrown.net

https://www.goodreads.com/author/show/15675585.Diana_Brown

https://www.imdb.com/name/nm7037326/

Facebook: AuthorDiBrown

Twitter: @1nixie

LYNDSEY ELLIS-HOLLOWAY

Lyndsey Ellis-Holloway is a writer from Knaresborough, UK, where she spends her time in the dark recesses of her mind. Specialising in fantasy, sci-fi, horror, and dystopian stories, she focusses on compelling characters and layering in myth and legend at every opportunity. Her mind is somewhat dark and twisted, and she lives in perpetual hope of owning her own Dragon someday, but for now, she writes about them to fill the void… and to stop her from murdering people who annoy her. When she's not writing she spends time with her husband, her dogs, and her friends enjoying activities such as walking, movies, conventions, and of course writing for fun as well!

Website: https://theprose.com/LyndseyEH

Twitter: @LEllisHolloway

https://www.facebook.com/groups/199284024728104

VONNIE WINSLOW CRIST

Born in the Year of the Dragon, Vonnie Winslow Crist is author of "The Enchanted Dagger," "Beneath Raven's Wing," "Owl Light," "The Greener Forest," "Murder on Marawa Prime," and other books. Her fantasy, horror, and science fiction appear in publications in Japan, Australia, India, Pakistan, Spain, Italy, Germany, Finland, Canada, the UK and USA. Believing the world is still filled with mystery, miracles, and magic, Vonnie strives to celebrate the power of myth in her writing.

Website: https://vonniewinslowcrist.com

Goodreads:

https://www.goodreads.com/.../620828.Vonnie_Winslow_Crist

Blog: https://vonniewinslowcrist.wordpress.com

Twitter: https://twitter.com/VonnieWCrist

Facebook: https://www.facebook.com/WriterVonnieWinslowCrist

ABOUT THE PUBLISHER

IRON FAERIE PUBLISHING is a small, independent publishing company based in Perth, Western Australia.

Founded in 2018, Iron Faerie Publishing was created with the desire to help authors with all aspects of their publishing journey and brings to life anthologies steeped in myth.

WEBSITE: www.ironfaeriepublishing.com

Made in the USA
Middletown, DE
21 May 2021